D1098980

Harry and the Treasure of Eddie Carver

The draught sucked smoke up the stairs. Harry raced up to shut the roof door and ran back down again. Then, clutching the metal rail, he began to descend. The smoke grew thicker. Though the staircase lights were on, he could hardly see. He began to cough. Before him the smoke glowed red. He felt heat, and as he swung round the last bend he saw flames. The outer door, ten centimetres thick, was ablaze. A wall of fire blocked his path. There was no way out.

Also by Alan Temperley:

Harry and the Wrinklies

Ragboy

Huntress of the Sea

The Brave Whale

The Simple Giant

Harry and the Treasure of Eddie Carver

ALAN TEMPERLEY

SCHOLASTIC

For Jean
for her friendship, kindness
and sense of fun.

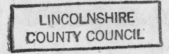
Scholastic Children's Books,
Commonwealth House, 1–19 New Oxford Street,
London, WC1A 1NU, UK
a division of Scholastic Ltd
London ~ New York ~ Toronto ~ Sydney ~ Auckland
Mexico City ~ New Delhi ~ Hong Kong

First published in the UK by Scholastic Ltd, 2004
This edition published in the UK by Scholastic Ltd, 2005

ISBN 0 439 96400 8

Typeset by M Rules
Printed and bound by AIT Nørhaven Paperback A/S, Denmark

10 9 8 7 6 5 4 3 2

Contents

1 Flames in the Night 1

2 The Fuzz 11

3 The Lagg Hall Gang 25

4 Shots in an Empty House 37

5 Mad Ruby and Her Son 47

6 A Bed in the Attic 61

7 The Bicycle 68

8 The Car with Black Windows 78

9 Eddie Carver 86

10 Scares, Schemes and Saturday 99

11 Okky in the Gulag 113

12 Wreckers Crag 124

13 The Gunpowder Plot 137

14 The Ambulance and Whortleberry Yawkins 149

15 *Fisherman's Tryst* 166

16 Killer Dogs 180

17 The Lock-Up 193

18 Whitewater Hall 203

19 The Gazebo 215

20 The Swimming Party 227

21 Summer Fair 233

22 Scrumpy Bottom 249

23 Baba Triumphant 264

24 The Cosh and the Smile 274

25 The Raid on Felon Grange 281

26 Ruby Meets Her Match 294

27 Caisteal an Uisge Ghil 307

28 Gunther Draws a Map 319

29 Hooligans 332

30 A Fishy Story 343

31 The Swimmer 357

32 The Stove and the Speedboat 371

33 Night on Lady Island 386

34 Full Moon 401

35 *Red Sky* at Night 418

36 The Oak Wood 432

37 The Bean is Mightier Than the Bullet 441

Chapter 1

Flames in the Night

It was a hot Saturday in June and Harry was busy. In the morning he played rugby and got a long scrape on his leg from an opposing player's boot. The boy said it was an accident but he'd done it before, so accidentally Harry gave him a punch on the head in the scrum. It wasn't the sort of thing he normally did but he felt pretty good about it. In the afternoon he went to the pasture and gave Chalky and Socrates a curry comb and hard brush which made him sneeze. Then he took Tangle rabbiting in the Lagg Hall woods. Finally he helped Nutty to change the number plates on the old Merc and spray it a different colour.

By the time he had finished all this dinner was on the table, so the evening was well advanced before he had the chance to heave an old mattress up the spiral stairs and lay it out on the flat roof of the tower. His bedroom, the only room in the ancient tower, was directly beneath, away from his aunts and their criminal friends who slept in the main house. Not that he didn't like them, they were great and Lagg Hall was enormous, but he'd been given this room and it was brilliant: twisted beams, metre-thick stone walls and a view for miles across the surrounding countryside. Harry shared it with Tangle, his mongrel terrier, and Morgan, an African green parrot which flew free and bit chunks out of people's fingers.

This night, however, Harry planned to sleep on the roof. As the light faded he carried up pillows and a sleeping bag, an old canvas to keep off the dew, a paraffin lamp, his book and half a packet of chocolate digestives.

Normally bedtime was a ritual:

"Come on, Harry, off you go."

"Oh, Aunt Bridget, have I got to? There's this brilliant new series I—"

"If you go this second we might video it for you. Now up the stairs and brush your teeth. Goodnight."

From the others: "Night-night, laddie ... sweet dreams ... kiss for Auntie Florrie? Mmm-mm!"

Then Harry circled the front of the house and made his way up the forty-seven worn steps of the tower to his room.

That night he was early. Mrs Good, the housekeeper, gave him a thermos of hot chocolate and within five minutes of bolting the studded door against whatever might be lurking in the bushes, he was changed into pyjamas and jersey, the lamp was lit and he was snuggled into his sleeping bag.

It was strange up there on the roof, and a bit scary. A trillion stars filled the sky, right down to the battlements that surrounded him. Owls hooted in the woods. Bats flitted overhead, hunting moths attracted by the light. An occasional car drove along some distant lane.

For a while, munching biscuits and drinking chocolate, Harry read *Playgrounds of Blood*. But he could not concentrate. A breeze stirred his hair. The next day his best friends, Akku and Charlie, were coming round. They planned to put up a tent on the lawn and play in the woods. Maybe go fishing on the lake. He had got things ready, stacked the old tent and groundsheet, camping stove and the rest at the foot of the spiral stairs. It would be great.

His eyes kept closing. Harry set the book aside. "Night, Tangle." He reached across to the bed he had made beside his own and rubbed Tangle's scruffy ears. Then, noting where his torch lay, he blew out the lamp. Instantly all turned black. He pulled his pillows close and, hoping the child-eating teacher from the story had not got inside his tower and was at that moment mounting the steps towards him, he disappeared inside his sleeping bag.

Tangle did not like the idea of spending a night on the roof. As soon as Harry's breathing announced that he was asleep and there was definitely no chance of a biscuit, he trotted downstairs to his regular sleeping spot on the foot of Harry's bed.

Morgan regarded him with a wrinkled eye.

Tangle muttered briefly, turning round and round until the duvet was to his satisfaction, then flopped to his belly.

A minute later all three, boy, dog and parrot, were dead to the world.

It was Tangle who raised the alarm.

"Wow! Wow! . . . Wowooo!"

The sounds became part of Harry's dream.

"Wow! . . . Wow!"

He struggled back to consciousness. A three-quarter moon had risen. Tangle stood on his hind legs, looking down through the battlements.

"Tangle, shut up. What is it?" Harry pushed back his sleeping bag.

"Wow! Wow!"

There was another noise, a piercing electronic screech beneath him.

His eyes stung with sleep and would hardly focus. He rose in confusion. The slabs beneath his feet were damp and cold.

"What is it?" He put a hand on Tangle's head and peered down at the garden.

At once he saw. Lagg Hall was on fire. Orange flames leaped at the curtains of the french windows. Two figures moved in the moonlight. Strangers.

"Hey!"

They turned towards him, faces pale splodges above dark clothes.

"Hey! Get out of there!"

A voice came back, a woman's voice he did not recognize: "Get out of there'a yourself. If you can."

"Aunt Bridget! Auntie Florrie!" Harry shouted at the top of his voice. "Fire! Huggy! Fire!"

Barefoot, he ran across the roof and started down the twisting stairs. Smoke rose to meet him. Thirty-four steps led to a small landing. On one side lay his bedroom. He switched on the light. It was full of smoke. The noise of the alarm was deafening. Morgan battered his green wings against a window that was just ajar. Harry threw it wide and he flew off into the night.

He pulled the window shut to stop the draught. The screaming alarm stopped him from thinking. He switched it off. Tangle stood at his side, shivering with fear. Harry had been taught about fire by his aunts; officers from the fire brigade had visited his school. Smoke was dangerous. The place to find any clear air was right down on the floor. That's why the tips of firemen's noses were dirty. But the wasn't that thick yet and he had to get out. He ran acro landing to his small bathroom. A blue-striped towel hun; the rail. He soaked it in the basin and wrapped it across nose and mouth.

The draught sucked smoke up the stairs. He raced up to shut the roof door and ran back down again. Then, clutching the metal rail, he began to descend. The smoke grew thicker. Though the staircase lights were on, he could hardly see. He began to cough. Before him the smoke glowed red. He felt heat, and as he swung round the last bend he saw flames. The outer door, ten centimetres thick, was ablaze. So were the tent and ground sheet. A wall of fire blocked his path. There was no way out.

The ancient stone walls rose on every side. Was there any way the fire could spread? He looked round. Where was Tangle?

"Tangle! Tangle!" The smoke entered his lungs. He coughed convulsively. "Tangle!"

Now he saw that the camping stove with its pressurized can of methane lay in the heart of the fire. He felt a bit dizzy. Turning, he began to grope back up the staircase.

At the halfway point there was a tiny window. Whatever it did to the fire, he had to have air. Harry flung it wide and leaned out, gasping like a fish. Smoke billowed into the moonlight. Sweet air struggled into his lungs. The dizziness began to recede.

At that moment, with a loud bang, the can of methane exploded. A sheet of flame and blast of heat flashed up the staircase, enough to shrivel the little hairs on the back of his hands. A split second later it was gone.

As soon as he felt it was safe to continue, he banged the window shut, clamped the towel across his face and ran on.

He reached his room and shut the door. Tangle stood by the window, whining and looking up for Harry to do something. He opened it to let out the smoke and took more deep breaths.

The intruders had gone. The alarm in the main house sent its shrill note into the night. Figures came tumbling from the door. A woman in a chiffon dressing gown ran towards him across the lawn. "Harry!" she was calling. "Harry!"

"Auntie Florrie!" He gave a big wave.

"Darling, are you all right?"

"Yes, I've got the ladder."

"Oh, Harry! Take care."

"Of course. Don't worry."

He turned back into the room. "There! There!" He crouched beside Tangle. "All right." He pressed the trembling dog to his side. "Who's my best boy? It's going to be OK. Ssshhh!"

The room had been inspected for safety. A fire ladder lay coiled up in a cupboard. Harry dragged it out and tied the ropes to his bed. He hoisted the heavy bundle to the window sill and pushed it out into the darkness. "Look out below," he shouted belatedly. With a rattle the ladder tumbled down the face of the tower.

Tangle screamed, "Yi-yi-yi-yi-yi!" and raced round the room. Harry was frightened he would jump out of the window.

"Tangle!" He pretended to be angry. "Come here. Come here!"

Tail between his legs, the terrified dog crept to his side.

Harry looked about him, hunting for a way to save his much-loved companion. "Stay there! Lie down. Lie down!"

Reluctantly Tangle did as he was ordered.

Were the flames licking up the stairs? In a fever, Harry tugged his duvet from its Superman cover and threw it aside. Holding the cover open, he closed in.

With wary eyes Tangle watched him. His eyebrows twitched. Something was about to happen.

"Stay there!" Harry's voice was furious.

Tangle cowered to the floor.

Before he could escape Harry grabbed him with one arm and forced him into the big cotton bag. Tangle fought and struggled. Blind with fear, he bit Harry on the hand. The next second he was a prisoner, a leaping, yelling shape in the bottom of the cover. Harry tied it in a fat knot and slung the bundle to the window sill.

His pyjama trousers had come loose. He tightened the cord and looked out at Lagg Hall. A small crowd of old people had gathered near the flaming window. A few wore dressing gowns, most were in their pyjamas and nightdresses. Aunt Bridget, legs astride and clutching a fire extinguisher, directed a jet into the blazing interior. Nutty dragged a long hose from the kitchen garden. Beneath Harry's window, Auntie Florrie had been joined by Fingers in his vest and baggy underpants.

"Take care, darling," she called.

"Course he'll take care, what d'you expect?" Fingers said. "Think he's going to jump?"

Harry clambered to the sill. Suddenly it looked a long way down. He clung to the window frame and stretched a leg down the ladder, feeling for the rungs with bare toes.

The moon shone on the smoking tower and silver lawns. The breeze felt chill against his sweating skin.

"That's the way, 'Arry, boy," called Fingers, who had climbed through more windows than he cared to remember. "Past the worst bit. You're doin' fine."

He descended two rungs. Grasping the ladder with one hand, he lugged the struggling Tangle through the window and gripped the duvet cover with strong teeth.

"Whatcha got there?"

As if in answer, Tangle gave a scream of protest.

A trickle of blood crossed Harry's wrist. He did not feel it. Steadily he groped for the wooden rungs. The nail of his big toe raked the stone. For a second it hurt. He climbed on.

Shrubs by the tower door were reddened by the leaping flames of the fire.

Auntie Florrie dug her embroidered slippers into the lawn and pulled out the bottom of the ladder. Three metres to go . . . one metre. . . He stepped down on to the grass.

Instantly he was clutched to his auntie's emotional bosom. "Oh, Harry! You're safe now. It's all over. Auntie Florrie's got you." She planted a lipsticky kiss on his forehead.

"Dear, oh dear!" Fingers said. "Leave the poor boy alone, Florrie. Give 'im a bit of air. 'Asn't 'e been through enough?"

In a way it was quite nice but Harry escaped. "I'm fine," he said. Then looking at Auntie Florrie, lit by the moon and the blazing door, he saw her wrecked mascara and the black tears on her cheeks. "Really I am." He gave her a big hug.

"I'm sure you are, darling." She smiled bravely. "We're not called the battling Bartons for nothing."

"I didn't know we were called that."

"We're not, really. I just made it up."

"The battling Bartons," Harry said. "I like it." He bent to the bundle on the ground. "Come on, Tangle. Who's a good boy?" He tussled with the knot. "Who's my *best* boy?"

Tangle struggled free. Finding himself in the open air, he ran in mad circles.

Harry realized his hand was stinging and saw the smear of blood. He licked it clean and discovered the punctures and little cut where Tangle had bitten him. He glanced down.

Tangle interpreted it. A dim memory remained. Filled with remorse, he crept to Harry's side.

"It's all right." Harry crouched and hugged him tight. "Lovely boy, it's not your fault, is it."

Tangle looked up anxiously and tried to lick Harry's face.

"All right," Harry whispered. "All over now." He stroked the rough coat and pressed his mouth against Tangle's ragged ear. "Come on. Come on then."

He stood and Tangle, knowing himself forgiven, trotted around him in the dewed grass.

Fingers led the way to the blazing door. He was a weedy man, five foot three with hair that needed cutting and legs like twigs. "Not much we can do there, boy. Not without an 'ose or 'alf a dozen fire extinguishers." He scratched his skinny chest.

The heat scorched Harry's face.

Whoever started the fire had piled brushwood against the door and soaked it with paraffin or petrol. A five-litre oil can lay in the heart of the blaze.

"Will it spread?" Harry asked. "Will the whole tower go up?"

"Nah," said Fingers, a notorious burglar and safecracker

whose exploits were the stuff of legend. "Nothin' to set fire to." He felt for cigarettes and discovered his underpants.

"No beams?" said Auntie Florrie.

"Solid stone till it gets to 'Arry's room. Make an 'ell of a mess, mind, the smoke an' that. Still, the insurance'll take care of—"

"Sshh!" Harry swung round.

A moment later they all heard it. Beyond the house a car drew away down the long drive that led through woods to the road.

"It's not showing any lights," he said.

Auntie Florrie, who had once been a racing driver and knew about engines, ran from the fire and listened intently.

"What d'you think it is?" Fingers said. "Can you—"

"Shhh!" She held up a hand for silence.

The car reached the road and revved away.

"Range Rover." She listened a moment longer. "That's right: 2.5 TDI."

"Who's got a Range Rover round here?" Harry said.

Auntie Florrie adjusted her frills. "Well, we'll just have to find out, won't we," she said.

Chapter 2

The Fuzz

The reason for the Range Rover's departure was soon apparent. Three fire engines with lights flashing and bells ringing came racing along the country lanes. They swung into the bushy entrance to Lagg Hall and roared up the winding drive through the trees.

Although they came quickly, by the time they reached the house the fire had been extinguished. The beautiful Georgian drawing room where Harry, his aunts and their friends spent their evenings and watched TV had been reduced to a smelly, smouldering, saturated mess. The rest of the house was saved. Only a stink of smoke in the broad corridors bore witness to the fire that had raged within.

The bonfire at the door of the tower, meanwhile, continued to burn brightly. The first fire engine was dispatched to deal with it, leaving deep tracks across the lawn, and soon the flames on the outside were extinguished. The ancient, creosote-impregnated door had burned well and continued to burn on the inside, fed by the remains of the tent and groundsheet.

"How did it get through the wood?" Harry asked.

"Prob'ly poured petrol," said a helmeted fireman. "Look,

you can see bits of paper. Soaked it an' pushed it underneath, piled up the brushwood, lit a match – whoosh!"

The studded door was locked and bolted. He looked up at Harry's window. "Have to get at it from the inside."

The ladder was raised. Dragging the hose behind them, two firemen vanished into Harry's bedroom.

They waited. Some insect in the grass bit Harry's foot. Sounds came from the far side of the door and moments later water erupted from the gap beneath. Harry's pyjamas were splashed. There was a noise of hammering, metal on metal.

"Lock's jammed," called a voice.

The hammering was resumed and the door cracked open. "Give it a push."

The outer firemen sprayed the wood and tried to force it.

"Hinges have buckled." More hammering. "Try again."

They were strong. Backs and arms strained. Centimetre at a time the charred door yielded to force and suddenly swung half open. There it stuck.

The two firemen emerged and pulled off smoke masks. Their faces shone with sweat in the floodlights. "That's about it," one said. "Solid old place. Not much damage apart from the door."

Harry saw the blackened walls. "Is my room all right?"

"Bit smoky, that's all. Can't sleep there tonight, son, needs a chance to air."

The centuries-old studs that covered the door stood proud of the wood. A thread of fire shone round a flake of charcoal.

"Stand back, please."

They chopped off the charred wood and sprayed the door again.

At last they were satisfied. Carrying the burned-out can, a fireman accompanied Harry to the house. "What's the story, son?"

Harry told him.

"You're a lucky lad. Wet towel's right for putting out a chip pan; doesn't keep out carbon monoxide though."

"I know," Harry said. "I just wanted to get out."

"Well, if you're in that position again, shut the door, face to the floor, right? Whoever done this wasn't just playing some dirty game. He could have killed you."

"It wasn't a man," Harry said. "Least one of them wasn't. It was a woman."

"That right?" The fireman seemed surprised. "Useful bit of information that."

The police had arrived, two white fuzzmobiles, as Auntie Florrie called them, drawn up on the gravel.

The fire engines departed. So did Harry's elderly friends, vanishing into shadows at the first glimpse of the flashing blue lights. Though believed to be retired, they were well known to the police, not just locally, but at Scotland Yard and Interpol.

"Oh, 'elp!" Fingers ducked instinctively. "'Ere's the pork chops."

"Ma new Rembrandt!" squeaked Angel. "The paint's no' even dry yet." The artist's eyes swam like blue fish behind his pebble-lensed spectacles.

"I not done nothing wrong," said Huggy, her voice an octave deeper. "I just not vant meeting the cops at three in the morning. Too many memories."

"What you mean, nothin' wrong?" Fingers stared at her. "It's only four days since we done that whisky ware'ouse."

13

"Oh, ja." She nodded. "You right, I am forgetting. I mean nothing *wrong* wrong."

"Makes no difference to the fuzz, does it," Fingers said. "I'm out of 'ere anyroad."

Like snow in a south wind they melted into the night, leaving Aunt Bridget and Auntie Florrie to answer the questions.

Harry headed for the kitchen where it was warmer. The gravel forecourt hurt his bare feet.

"Harry." Aunt Bridget called him back. "We want you here. Goody will give you a cup of tea when the police have finished their questions." Tall and straight, she wore a pair of man's pyjamas. Her iron-grey hair was cropped short. Intelligent blue eyes regarded the world through a bright pair of granny glasses.

The midges were maddening. Harry rubbed the back of his ears and scratched in his hair. Gingerly he returned to the lawn.

"Don't see we need keep the lad out here," said a friendly young constable. "Why don't we all go into the kitchen?"

"Oh, no!" said Auntie Florrie. "Everyone will—"

"Good idea," said Aunt Bridget. "Harry, run and tell Goody we'll be there in a couple of minutes. Meanwhile," she steered the constable, his sergeant and a female officer in the opposite direction, "come and see what happened to the tower. It's a lovely old place. My nephew has his room up there." She pointed to the hanging ladder.

Harry followed Auntie Florrie into the house. The smell of burning was strong. Water had flooded under the drawing room door but otherwise the hall with its splendid staircase was untouched.

Together they entered the kitchen. As Auntie Florrie had predicted, the other members of the gang had gravitated there. Most sat at the big scrubbed table though Max, the actor and con man, leaned elegantly against the sink while Dot, aged seventy-three, practised her back-flips by the pantry door. Also present were Mrs Good and Nutty Slack, the handyman. Everyone had a cup of tea or soothing mug of cocoa. Most, after the double whammy of fire *and* the arrival of the fuzz, had a glass of whisky as well. Crumbs from a large cherry cake and a batch of millionaire's shortbread scattered the table.

All turned to the new arrivals.

"That them away then?" Mr Tolly was a large, bald man, a famous stage magician. He was also a pickpocket. "Can we relax now?"

"'Fraid not." Auntie Florrie mixed a Bosun Blinder. It was her favourite cocktail, the alcoholic equivalent of a neutron bomb. "I think you'd better take your drinkies upstairs – unless you want to stay, of course. Bridget's bringing them in here. They want to speak to Harry."

"Ah, give me a break!"

"No rest for the wicked."

"I wouldn't mind but we give it all away!"

Grumbling, panicking, they piled plates, refreshed glasses and tumbled from the room. Nutty, his hands streaked with car spray, went with them. In thirty seconds only Harry, Mrs Good and Auntie Florrie remained.

"Give me a hand, Harry." Mrs Good opened the window to let out the fumes. "Don't want the police to think they've done a flit. Might think we've got something to hide." She wiped the table and straightened the chairs.

Harry stacked the dirty plates in the dishwasher and looked

in the corridor for something to put on his feet. He selected a pair of Huggy's old slippers, size thirteen.

Tangle, recovered from his doggy trauma, retreated to his basket with a biscuit bone.

Auntie Florrie took a reviving sip of Bosun Blinder. "I look such a mess!" She tossed the pink ruffles of her dressing gown and examined her face in the mirror. "Oh, my goodness! Give the cat a heart attack." She stared round the kitchen for inspiration. "I don't suppose you've got any make-up removers, Goody? Skin fresheners?"

"Soap and water's what I use," said Mrs Good.

"All right, all right. You're such a Puritan. Dear me," said Auntie Florrie. "Well give us a bit of kitchen towel anyway. Can't face the old Bill looking like this. A girl needs a *bit* of warpaint."

She folded the paper into a pad and dipped a corner in her cocktail. Standing at the mirror, she wiped away the tracks of mascara and did what was possible to repair the ravages of the night. There was a lipstick in her pocket: Auntie Florrie had a lipstick in every pocket. She examined the colour, a startling red, not ideal for three in the morning. "Ah, well!" She applied it liberally and combed her yellow curls. "There, how's that?"

"Baby Jane come to life," said Mrs Good.

A door shut and there were voices. Seconds later the constable and his sergeant were in the kitchen. The policewoman had departed.

"Do sit down." Aunt Bridget shot Harry a warning glance.

"Cup of tea?" said Mrs Good.

"Or something stronger?" Auntie Florrie indicated the whisky bottle, remembering too late that it came from a crate they had taken during the job on the warehouse. "You can't both be driving."

The sergeant was a fattish man with a bristly moustache and greasy eyes. He did not like the public, especially those of the criminal sort. "You know better than to offer alcohol to a police officer on duty." He tried to avoid his constable's eye.

"My sister was just being hospitable," said Aunt Bridget. "A cup of tea it is then."

"You know the score," he said. "Enough records in this house to stock a music shop. Trying to get one over us, I wouldn't be surprised." He raked in an ear and examined the tip of his finger. "Think we don't know about you lot? Reckon us country coppers are a load of PC Plods got heads that zip up the back?"

"After that business last New Year," said Aunt Bridget, "I'd be more surprised if you *didn't* know about us."

"Tcha!" He threw his cap on the table.

"If you don't mind." Mrs Good set it aside and clattered plates. "This is *my* kitchen and I don't want any trouble. Not this time of night. And certainly not with the boy here. Harry, pass round the cake."

"Thank you very much." Harry saw the constable wore a bright new wedding ring.

"Where's the rest of them anyway?" The sergeant examined the plate and took a thick slice from the back. "Whole place was swarming when we drove up."

"They've gone back to their beds, naturally." Aunt Bridget bit back her anger. "Where would you expect them to be this time of night?"

"Knocking off a bank." The aggressive sergeant dropped crumbs. "Some millionaire's pad."

"Oh, dear!" Aunt Bridget sighed. "Give a dog a bad name. Let me tell you that every person in this house has paid her dues, we are free men and women. We're in our seventies, for goodness sake. We've all got pensions. Do you really think we're interested in wandering round half the night carrying out scams for a few measly quid? Risking the Queen's hospitality again? Pull yourself together."

"Once a bad 'un, always a bad 'un," said the sergeant. "That's what I reckon. Leopards don't change their spots. I've seen enough in my time."

"I've never heard such nonsense!" declared Aunt Bridget.

"What about Sniffy Mick, Eddie Carver, Benny the Teeth?"

"Exceptions that prove the rule."

"Back inside's more to the point. Should never have been let out. Rory the Glory, there's another. Says he's been saved. TV evangelist. Next thing he's knocking off church silver the length of the country."

"For every one of those you've mentioned I could name—"

"Well I'd rather you didn't, Bridget," said Mrs Good firmly. "The night's been quite bad enough without you two going at it hammer and tongs."

Though there was not a nicer, kinder, more loving woman than Mrs Good in the whole wide world, she had the makings of a fine sergeant major.

Instantly the antagonists fell silent.

"That's better." She passed the tea. "Now, who takes sugar?"

"Thank you." The young constable took out his notebook. "Perhaps we should get down to business. We're here because of the fire, Miss Barton, nothing else. Now, what was the first indication you had that something was wrong?"

"It was our nephew," said Auntie Florrie. "He was shouting. He woke us up."

All eyes turned upon Harry. Suddenly his chest felt tight. Was it the effect of the smoke? Or being the centre of attention? Or what he knew about his aunts' criminal activities? He cleared his throat. "It was Tangle really. He was barking. I've got a room up in the tower and it was a nice night so I was sleeping on the roof."

Slowly and precisely his story was written down in the black police notebook.

"Do you always lock the door at night?" the constable asked.

Harry glanced at Auntie Florrie.

"Of course he does," she said. "Don't you?"

"I was just wondering if there was any particular reason — beyond the obvious."

"If this is another reference to the trouble we had last year with our neighbour, Colonel Priestly, and his vile fiancée, Lavinia McScrew," said Aunt Bridget, "yes he has a particular reason. Thanks to the old boy network, the judge let *that* pig of a man off with five years. Fence for some of the nastiest gangs in Britain, corruption, kidnapping — and he gets five years! Out in three. One wonders how much the pay-off was for that particular piece of English justice. And Lavinia McScrew — Gestapo Lil, we call her — she gets off with a caution. She's an *appalling* woman. A thief, accessory before, during and after the fact, threatens a whole houseful of people with a machine gun, and she's let off with a caution. A caution! What's she got to use, heavy artillery? An Exocet?"

Her eyes flashed. "And she's got this mad hatred of Harry. Yes he locks the door, wouldn't you? And where is she now? Tell me that. You're the police. When's she going to come after him again?"

The sergeant helped himself to a second slice of cake. "Seems to me you're the one with an attitude problem."

The constable was more thoughtful. "The people you saw," he said to Harry, "the arsonists. You say one of them was a woman. Could that have been Miss McScrew?"

Harry shook his head. "I'd know her voice anywhere."

"How's that?"

"She used to look after me when I lived in London."

"She was his nanny, poor lamb," said Auntie Florrie.

"His parents were away a lot," Aunt Bridget explained.

"A lot? All the time from what I can make out," Auntie Florrie said indignantly. "And left him with that nasty, vicious piece of work for a companion. Used to beat him. Robbed them all blind."

The sergeant slopped his tea and sucked the spill from his saucer.

The constable said to Harry, "What about the other one?"

"I don't know." He pulled his pyjama trousers together. "It was dark and they were setting fire to the house. I had to wake everybody up."

"But you got no impression? Tall? Short? Old?"

"Well, maybe not very tall." He tried to remember. "And I don't think old. Not sort of creaky anyway."

The constable wrote it down. "And apart from Miss McScrew," he looked from one to the other, "is there anybody else you can think of might have a grudge against you, might want to burn the place down?"

"No one at all," said Aunt Bridget. "I'm sure you're well aware, as the sergeant said, that some of us here have – let's say colourful pasts. But that was—"

"Colourful, is that what you call it! Some of you!" The sergeant exploded. "Every last one of you from what I can make out. The house is neck-deep in *crooks*. Enough convictions here to paper the walls."

Aunt Bridget counted to ten. "Be that as it may, I was about to say that it was a long time ago. As far as I'm aware – in fact I know – none of our past associates retains the slightest animosity towards us. The very opposite, I should say. We had a big reunion just last month. Took over a seaside hotel for the weekend and it was a very happy occasion."

She was being mischievous. There had been no such reunion. Harry held his breath.

Steam gushed from the sergeant's nostrils. "Took over a hotel for the weekend!"

"Mm." Aunt Bridget sipped her tea. "Good wasn't it, Florrie."

"All our old chums." Auntie Florrie smiled reminiscently. "George the Greek, Bearded Bella, Molly Three-arms, hadn't seen her for ever so—"

"I give up!" The sergeant threw his arms in the air and reached for the whisky bottle. "Here, pass us a glass."

The constable put his notebook away. "If anything else occurs to you, you'll let us know."

"Of course," said Aunt Bridget.

"And you, Mrs Fox," he said to Auntie Florrie, whose husband had walked out when she won the Isle of Man TT for the second year in a row and he only came twelfth. "How are things going in your retirement?"

"Fine, thank you." She blinked, wondering where this was leading. Unfortunately the alcohol she had used to repair her make-up had turned the mascara gluey and her eyelashes stuck together so that it appeared she was winking.

The young man was taken aback. "You haven't been, er, practising recently?"

"Practising?"

"Yes, practising." The sergeant butted in. "You know what practising is. One of my men saw a motorcycle streaking along that deserted stretch between here and Bulford. A blur, he said. Small figure on what he thought was an old Norton *Commando*."

"Well, I do have a *Commando*," Auntie Florrie admitted. "But all I ever use it for these days is a bit of shopping."

"Said the driver was wearing studded leathers, an old-style helmet and goggles. Registration BL something."

Auntie Florrie brightened. The plates had been changed. "Oh, it couldn't have been me then. My registration's nothing like that."

"What is it, just for the record?"

Her brain raced. Which, of the half-dozen plates she used, was the legal one? She giggled and flapped a hand. "Old age, forget my own name next. Anyway, I'm sure it's nothing like what you said."

Mrs Good came to her rescue with the teapot. "How about a top-up?"

"Millionaire's shortbread?" Harry went round with the tin.

It smelled irresistible. But Mrs Good had been interrupted in the middle of making it. The caramel was thicker than usual, almost toffee.

"Thank you." The sergeant pushed aside a small piece in

favour of the one underneath. "Tell me, Miss Barton. This load of old cons you got living here, where did you—"

"I beg your pardon?" He had gone too far. Aunt Bridget's eyes were blue as glaciers. "What kind of language is that from an officer of the law? Old cons? Are you referring to the kind-hearted men and women who have pooled their life's savings to live in this house in peace? To our family of friends?"

"Yeah, if you like. You could say."

"Well, if that's the way you speak it's a comment on you, not us. You won't find *me* using any of the derogatory terms that are applied to members of *your* profession. And while you're in our house I'd appreciate it if you'd pay us the same courtesy."

The sergeant tried to appear cool. He pushed back his cup, stretched out his legs and took a bite of the shortbread. It was a gesture calculated to annoy. Everyone in the room, even his own constable, longed to slap him across the ear.

Luck was with them. For the sergeant had a full set of false teeth, upper and lower, and as he bit into the caramel slice they became hopelessly stuck. He tried to open his mouth but the grip of the toffee was too strong. His teeth became dislodged. They were everywhere. They filled his mouth and stuck out past his lips. It was like a shot from a horror movie.

Harry stared.

The sergeant covered his mouth with a hand. "Oh, by Gog! 'Ere's de batroob?" His voice was distorted.

Mrs Good pretended she did not understand. "I beg your pardon?"

"Kick! Huhee! I deed de batroob. By teet a tuck. Peas!"

"I'm sorry." She shook her head. "I can't make out—"

"Oh, debber bide!" Still hiding his mouth, he rushed from the kitchen.

Mrs Good relented. "Third on the left, after the Van Gogh."

The sergeant spat the mouthful of teeth and toffee into his handkerchief. His lips caved in like an old man.

Shouts of laughter rang through the smoky house.

Chapter 3

The Lagg Hall Gang

Harry's teeth, unlike those of the police sergeant, were solid as rocks. He had no difficulty whatever in disposing of three pieces of toffee shortbread in quick succession. In fact he could have eaten three more *and* a third slice of cake if Mrs Good had let him.

But where was he going to sleep for the rest of the night? Nobody wanted him.

"Kid's all right," Max said. "Love him like my own flesh and blood, but I can't stand snoring."

"I don't snore!" Harry said.

"Rubbish, all kids snore," Max said. "Had a room next to my niece once. Twelve years old, you should have heard her! All the pictures rattling on the walls. Ornaments falling off the mantelpiece. Didn't get a wink all night – and I had a matinée the next day."

Angel said, "I'm gey fond o' the laddie mysel', but I wake in the night, ye ken. Canna settle till I played a wee pibroch an' mebbe practised a twa-three steps o' Hielan' dancin'. I sleep in ma sark, ye ken, it wouldna be fittin'."

Mr Tolly gave Harry a hug. "Dear boy, I'd have your camp bed in my room in a minute but I talk, you know. In my sleep. There's things I wouldn't . . . things in my past. . ."

"You come into my room, 'Arry," Fingers said. "Smoke in bed, mind. Few fags wiv a cup o' tea, couple o' chocs, good thriller. Don't mind that, do you?"

Harry was all for it. "I could practise a bit of lock-picking," he said. "I keep going wrong on—"

"You are *not* sleeping with a smoker." Aunt Bridget intervened. "You'll have to practise your lock-picking tomorrow."

Harry looked at the clock. It was three a.m. "It's tomorrow now," he said. "Where *am* I going to sleep?"

Huggy came to the rescue. "Ach, you men. Harry sleep in my room, ja? Come on, Harry, you need your beauty sleep. Ve both do, specially me."

"No you don't," Harry said gallantly. "You're great."

"Oh, you silver-tongued charmer. Vhat chance the girls have vhen you a few years older?" She clapped a hand the size of a Yorkshire ham on his shoulder. "Come on, up ve go."

Mrs Good said, "I left the camp bed and everything on the landing."

For the second time that night a chorus of 'happy dreams . . . sleep tight' followed Harry from the room.

Huggy led the way upstairs and along the broad corridor to her big bedroom. A woman the size of Huggy needed a lot of space. The camp bed was soon made up and Harry ran to the bathroom to wash his feet and change into dry pyjamas. Returning, he knocked on the door.

"Von minute." Huggy's voice boomed from within. "Right, now you come. I respectable."

Harry knew Huggy well. She had taught him to wrestle out on the lawns, wearing her old professional leotards with *Bonecrusher* and *Bête Humaine* across the back in blood-red lettering. For months they had tussled as he learned to fall and throw and got trapped in Huggy's agonizing arm locks. He had not, however, seen her climbing into bed in a pink frilly nightgown. Nor had he seen her stupendous bra and pants laid out on a chair for the morning.

Huggy laughed, her big Russian face and rug of brown hair on the pillow. "Svitch out the light. I not vanting they give you nightmares."

Harry did so and climbed on to his wobbly camp bed.

"Comfortable?"

He shifted around. "Yeah, great."

"Good. Now go to sleep. I remember vhen I in old Vladivostok, my little brother, he. . ."

Harry let the words wash over him. It had been an eventful night, the fire and the police and— The moon shone through a chink in the curtain. He tucked a hand beneath his face and closed his eyes. Max saying he snored – cheek!

Huggy finished her story and laughed. "Harry? . . . Harry, you hear me?"

There was no reply.

"Oh, my vord. You only get into bed thirty second. Harry?"

Total silence.

"Oh, you make me feel so *old*." Huggy turned and gave a sigh. "I vish I eleven again."

An hour passed. The moonbeam crossed the carpet and faded as the curtains brightened.

Often, in his tower room with the window ajar, Harry had been wakened by the dawn chorus of blackbirds, rooks, thrushes and many other birds which inhabited the Lagg Hall gardens and surrounding woods. This was a different sound, a deep rumble like thunder or an avalanche. It came again, and again, penetrating Harry's dream, becoming part of it. Finally he woke.

It was Huggy. The snoring which made china rattle and plaster crumble did *not* emanate from Harry. For a minute he listened then pulled his head beneath the bedclothes, stuck his fingers in his ears, jammed the pillows over his head until he nearly suffocated. Nothing kept out the terrible noise.

"Huggy," he hissed. "Huggy!" Trying to wake her just enough to turn over.

"Knhknhrrrr! . . . Knhknhrrrr! . . . Knhknhrrrr! . . ."

For fifteen minutes he tried to ignore it. Sleep was impossible and at length he rose.

"Vatch it, you big gorilla!"

Harry jumped out of his skin.

"You vant I tear off your legs? T'row you out the vindow?" Huggy was dreaming. "Sit down! I tell you vhat ve do. . ." The words trailed away.

Harry stared at the dim figure in the bed. He loved her like a favourite aunt. She was kind and funny and affectionate. But in the past Huggy had been a heavy for Black Morrie's Bunch and the Chicago Mob. What scary dreams was she having now? Quietly he gathered the duvet and blankets in his arms and let himself from the room.

Tangle, half forgotten in the confusion of the night, had been lying at Huggy's door. He rose, wagging his tail with pleasure, and pressed round Harry's legs. Harry dropped his bedding on the carpet and made a fuss of him.

He snorted away the smell of cold smoke and went to the landing. The grandfather clock showed four-thirty. Daylight was growing. His eyes felt full of sand. Where could he and Tangle go for the rest of the night? Somewhere quiet, somewhere they wouldn't be disturbed again.

A cupboard below the stairs was full of old coats, an umbrella stand, the Hoover and various bits of junk. Harry turfed them out and spread his blankets in the dark. It was a nice place. He pulled the door nearly shut. Cosy beneath the duvet, Tangle at his side, he settled down for the third time that night.

After ten minutes Tangle began to emit little wuffs of excitement; his paws twitched as he chased rabbits through the woods of his doggy dreams. Harry did not hear him, for by this time he was lost in dreams of his own.

It was nearly a year since Harry's parents, the Honourable Augustus and Lady Barton, had died in an accident far from home. They were bankrupt. Every last penny of the family fortune had been wasted in extravagance. They had loved Harry when they thought of him, and sent expensive presents from all over the world. The house in Hampstead, however, where they had abandoned him to the tender mercies of Lavinia McScrew, was a place they seldom visited. When they died it was sold to pay off debts and Harry, having no other relatives, was packed off to live with his great aunts in the country. He was dreading it, but far from being terrible old bores, Aunt Bridget, Auntie Florrie and their crowd of elderly friends had turned out to be lively as crickets, full of fun and a sense of adventure.

He had been taken aback, it is true, to discover that the residents of Lagg Hall, with the exception of Mrs Good and Nutty Slack, were distinguished crooks. All had spent periods of their lives in jail. But unlike other crooks, the Wrinklies, as Harry called them, now used their naughty skills for the benefit of people in need. After a lifetime of crime they wanted to do good. But a swimming pool for handicapped children and hot meals for the homeless cost money. So a bank was robbed and children in calipers learned to swim; a cigarette manufacturer found his safe blown wide and the citizens of cardboard city had steak pie and potatoes beside a radiator.

So many people needed help. The Wrinklies did what they could. The fifth wife of a billionaire found her jewellery gone – and a donkey sanctuary on the brink of closure was enabled to buy a whole farm and build stables for the winter. Art dealers were fooled by a forged Cézanne – and a bus full of surgeons travelled Africa, healing the blind.

There were eight in the gang, all good friends, average age seventy-two. Aunt Bridget was the brains of the operation; Auntie Florrie the getaway driver; Dot the cat-burglar; Huggy the muscle; Fingers the burglar and explosives expert; Max the con man; Angel the forger; Mr Tolly the pickpocket.

They operated as a team, every job planned to the finest detail. But somehow, although every member of the gang was a star, things rarely worked out as intended. So much went wrong that, as Aunt Bridget crossly remarked, it was a wonder they weren't all back behind bars. Yet somehow, so far, they had got away with it.

"Perhaps," Auntie Florrie once said, looking up at the starry sky, "somebody up there likes us."

"Perhaps," her sister agreed. "But I'm not sure that would cut much ice with a judge."

Occasionally they acted alone, such as the night when Dot, climbing the outside of the Stilton-Roquefort Hotel, looked through a window on the eighteenth floor and saw the necklace of that bitchy actress just lying on her dressing-table. And the day when that mafioso on the train asked Fingers to keep an eye on his briefcase while he went to the toilet.

"Well, what did he expect, horrible man," Auntie Florrie said on that occasion as Fingers unloaded bundles of twenty-pound notes from inside his underwear. "We're only human."

"Absolutely," agreed Aunt Bridget. "*Carpe diem, utere copia*: seize the day, grasp the opportunity."

They had tried, and failed, to hide their activities from Harry. On the very night of his arrival he had overheard them discussing a bank job. Now, eleven months later, he knew as much about lock-picking and forgery as he did about maths and geography. He could wrestle and did card tricks. His knowledge of the European underworld was greater than his knowledge of the ancient Roman Empire – which, as he pointed out at dinner one evening, had been even wickeder.

"But nobler and more brilliant," Aunt Bridget said.

"Yes," he admitted.

"Bit like us," said Mr Tolly, making the potatoes vanish and reappear on a different part of the table.

"Quite right," said Auntie Florrie.

"Spot on, Mr Tolly." Fingers raised his wine glass. "'Ere's to the Lagg 'All gang."

Aunt Bridget caught Harry's glance. Behind the granny glasses her eyes were clever and bright blue. She winked. "Harry and the Wrinklies."

He smiled and took a drink of juice.

And now he lay sleeping in a cupboard.

Tangle rose at eight, pushed open the door, scratched and trotted through to the kitchen for breakfast.

Mrs Good let Harry lie.

He surfaced at ten.

"I've been thinking," she said as he sat at the kitchen table. "You can't go back to the tower till the door's been fixed, so we'll make up a bed for you in the attic. You'll like it up there. Plenty of room, a light for reading. Nutty'll rig up a curtain over the skylight. It'll only be for a few days. All right?"

"Yeah," Harry said through a mouthful of grapefruit. "That'll be great."

"Don't say *yeah*," she corrected him. "The word's *yes*. You're not some hobbledehoy."

He shovelled in more grapefruit. "Sorry."

"And don't talk with your mouth full."

Mrs Good was the mother, or gran, Harry had never had. She scattered a lump of dough with flour and pummelled it into submission.

"Oh, there was a phone call for you. Akku's mother, such a nice woman. He was sick during the night and he's got a temperature so she's keeping him in the house. He's furious with her so could he come next weekend instead?"

Harry was disappointed.

She rumpled his hair with a wrist. "I'm sorry, love, but

with the fire and everything it's for the best. There's a lot to do: all the sofas and easy chairs have gone for a start. I didn't want to wake you up so I rang Charlie before he set off. He says next week's fine. I hope I did the right thing." She collected two slices of toast. "If you want you can phone back. Your friends are welcome here any time, you know that."

"No, that's OK." He spread thick butter and slipped a corner to Tangle. "The tent's burned anyway. I'll give Nutty a hand then go out on the bike."

"You do that, love." She sliced the dough into lumps and pressed them into bread tins. "Really, when I look at what they've done to that lovely sitting room I could cry. I really could. It's wicked, that's what, just wicked."

"It could have been worse."

"Indeed it could. We could all have been burned in our beds!"

"When will we start clearing up?" Harry munched. "When they come back from church?"

"No, we've got to leave everything just the way it is for the insurance people."

"Tomorrow? I could stay off school to help."

She smiled. "So you could, love. And I'll be an astronaut."

He reached for the marmalade. "D'you think it *was* Gestapo Lil?"

"Who else do we know's mad enough to try a trick like that? Who else hates us that much?"

"But Felon Grange is empty. They took all the furniture when Priestly went to jail."

"And she disappeared, I know. Maybe she's come back. Maybe he escaped. Who knows?"

"I think I'll cycle over and have a look."

"You'll do no such thing!" Mrs Good stared at him. "Someone who'd do that, who knows *what* they're capable of. You stay well away from that house. You hear?"

"Yes, I hear." Harry crammed his mouth with the last of the toast and carried his dishes to the sink.

By daylight the sitting room looked worse than ever. After a sad inspection, Harry climbed the tower stairs to look for Morgan. He found the parrot on his favourite beam. "Hello, Morgan," he said. "Where'd you spend last night?"

Morgan considered him. "Aark, piss off," he said and waggled his tail. A big dropping rattled to the paper below.

"Thanks very much," Harry said. "That's the last time I save your life."

"Get lost." Morgan had been reared by a sailor. Harry was teaching him polite phrases but he preferred the riper words of his chickhood.

"Say thank you! Thank you!" Harry stood on a chair and gave him a millet spray.

Morgan took it in his hooked beak and transferred it to a claw. "Fatface!" he said distinctly. "Aark! Show us your knickers."

Harry continued to the roof and draped his bedding over the battlements to air. Afterwards, munching a digestive, he went to look for Nutty Slack.

He found the handyman caring for his menagerie. In his work about the woods and gardens, in fact everywhere he went, Nutty came upon a surprising number of injured and helpless animals. He had a way with the wild creatures and carried them back to hospital cages he had built in the stables where he had his workshop. At that moment he was nursing a kestrel with a broken wing, a poisoned fox cub, a feral cat with an ulcerated eye, a nest of baby weasels whose mother had been killed by a car, and three or four others.

Tangle sniffed the cages curiously. Harry stroked the sick fox and dangled shreds of red meat above the weasels to make them jump.

"Some excitement last night, eh?" Nutty pushed back his cap to scratch his bald dome. "Get me 'ands on them that done it an' they'd be sorry, I can tell yer."

Harry glanced across. "I reckon it was Gestapo Lil and – Ow!" One of the weasels had grabbed him. He jerked back his hand. The little creature came with it, needle-like teeth sunk through the ball of his finger.

Nutty laughed.

Harry didn't. "Ow! Ow!" He caught the baby weasel behind the forelegs and pulled. It wouldn't let go. He held out his hand and it dangled in space. He shook it and the determined animal flapped like a rag in a gale.

"Here, divvent hurt the wee thing." Nutty led Harry to his work bench. Tenderly he caught the weasel in a cloth, dipped his finger in paraffin and dabbed its nose. The little creature got the fright of its life. It writhed back, twisting its head and biting at the air. Harry snatched his hand away and scrubbed the finger against his jersey. Deep punctures oozed blood. He sucked them and smelled the stink of weasel. Running to the door, he spat his mouth clean.

"Poor wee thing." Nutty soaked a corner of the cloth in water and wiped the weasel's nose. "Divvent want the paraffin to burn it."

"Poor wee thing?" Harry said. "I'm probably going to die of rabies or something." He shook red drips to the floor.

"Divvent be so soft!" Nutty returned the weasel to its cage and took out his watch. "Here, man, it's time for wor elevenses."

"I've just had breakfast."

"Am I hearin' right? What sort o' lad canna eat a couple o' currant buns or summat straight after his breakfast?"

Harry agreed and they started round the kitchen garden. "Hey, Nutty," he said. "How can you tell a weasel from a stoat?"

"A weasel from a stoat?" Nutty felt for his old tobacco tin. "Why, a stoat's bigger an' it's—"

"Shall I tell you?" Harry said. "You weaselly know, 'stoatally different."

"Why, you young –" Nutty slapped him with his cap and they walked on together.

Chapter 4

Shots in an Empty House

After lunch Harry got his bike from the stables and set off down the bumpy drive. It was an old black sit-up-and-beg with a crossbar and Sturmey-Archer three-speed. It was too big for him; even with the broad leather seat right down, his bottom slid from side to side. Years earlier, when Aunt Bridget was a university professor, she had ridden it about the streets of Oxford. Harry loved it, though sometimes when he was standing on the pedals to climb a hill, the gears slipped and he crashed down on to the crossbar in a way that was very painful.

It was about three miles to Felon Grange, one and a half as the crow flies. Harry had seen no reason to tell everyone he was going, especially when Mrs Good made such a fuss about it.

He had not been near the Grange for six months. The last occasion had been New Year's Eve when the Wrinklies made a snowy raid. That had ended in the capture of the owner, Colonel Priestly, and his vile fiancée, Gestapo Lil. He was now in jail, but where was she? After the events of the night Harry wanted to know if she was back or if the house, which had been stripped of its furniture, still stood empty.

The sky was blue, the lanes white with hawthorn and cow parsley. He turned up a long hill. The fields gave way to woods that met overhead and formed a misty green tunnel. Harry stood on his pedals and waited for the gears to slip. They did not and soon he reached the entrance to the Felon Grange estate. In the past there had been a magnificent arch with wrought-iron gates, but since Fingers blew it up all that remained was a tumble of stones, bulldozed aside to give access.

Harry cycled through and started up the long, beech-lined drive. Beyond an iron railing, where once there had been a famous herd of longhorn cattle, the pasture grew rank with weeds. On the other side, where in the past there had been racehorses, a border of shrubs gave way to ploughed fields. Beneath his wheels the pink tarmac was covered with beech mast and creeping moss.

After nearly a mile the huge white mansion appeared round a bend. Harry dismounted and searched for signs of life. There were none. The ornate fountain was scattered with leaves, the windows uncurtained, the car park empty. He waited, lurking behind a grey trunk, then cycled across the courtyard.

A towering portico with seven steps and Corinthian pillars rose before him. Alert for danger, he left his bicycle and mounted between them. A few metres of flagstones led to the heavy door. It was locked. He peered through a window and saw an empty lobby. The stained-glass inner door stood half open, revealing the noble hallway beyond. It, too, was deserted.

Harry stood back. Common sense told him to get on his bike and cycle away as fast as his wheels would carry him. No one knew he was here. Mrs Good had told him not to come.

What if Gestapo Lil or one of the intruders was watching him all the time? He looked all round. A confident squirrel crossed the red courtyard. A chaffinch landed on the fountain and dipped its beak to drink. Harry tightened his lips. He had not cycled three miles to turn tail the second he arrived. Leaving his bike at the foot of the steps, he started round the house.

Window after window revealed nothing but empty rooms. He began testing them to see if any was unlocked. The seventh yielded beneath his fingers. It was bad luck. If it, like the rest, had been fastened and he had turned the corner twenty metres further on, he would have reached the coach houses. There he would have discovered a bright red Aston Martin and a black Range Rover, a Vogue 2.5 with dark tinted glass, registration RIP 1.

But Harry did not reach the corner. Greatly frightened, he pushed up the small-paned window. The sill was nearly head high. He gripped the window frame and scrabbled with his trainers against the wall. Next moment he was through and found himself standing in a sort of pantry. He shivered, it was chill in the house, much colder than outside. The room smelled. Long-dead pheasants had rotted from the hooks and lay desiccated on the floor. Loaves of bread, hard as bricks, stood among pasta, herbs and cans of soup on the shelves. Mice had nibbled into bags of flour.

Harry had raked the soft skin of his forearm. He pulled up his sleeve and licked it to take away the sting, then listened at the pantry door. All was silent. Softly he eased it open and found himself in a long corridor. People, a lot of people, had been there recently, for a track was trodden through the dust. A back door led to the outside. He tried the handle. It was locked. In the other direction the corridor led to the grand hallway. Harry left the pantry door wide in case he needed to make a quick getaway then started towards it.

Other rooms opened off the corridor: the kitchen, the gun-room, a cloakroom. The sun shone through dirty windows. All were bare, though a toaster, kettle and scatter of unwashed dishes stood on a worktop in the kitchen. A workman's overall lay on the floor. A clean, sharp smell made his nostrils tingle and as Harry entered the hall he saw that joiners and plasterers had been busy. The banisters and panelling were being repaired. Swathes of wall were spread with plaster. Harry stood in the dusty shavings and looked all round. He was relieved, workmen were no danger. Besides, on a Sunday afternoon they would all be at home.

He went through the stained-glass door to the lobby. A big iron key stood in the front door. He turned it and stepped outside. Before him were the giant pillars and courtyard. There lay his bicycle. The trees were full of birdsong. He returned into the silent house and locked the door behind him.

Harry had drunk a lot of juice at lunch. He visited the cloakroom and flushed the noisy toilet, then ran water into the washbasin until it turned icy cold and drank several handfuls. Feeling much refreshed, he explored the remainder of the ground floor. There was nothing to see but empty rooms and naked windows. Gaping shutters gave them an abandoned look. He walked back to the hall and looked up the grand staircase. Silently he mounted.

People had been up here also. He wandered into a couple of bedrooms, bare to the floorboards. Standing at a window, he unwrapped a stick of chewing gum. It seemed there was nothing to be learned at Felon Grange. Rolling the wrapper between his fingers, he strolled back into the corridor.

But seconds later, as he approached the bedrooms in the west wing, Harry got a fright that stopped him dead in his tracks. A breath of warm air hit him in the face. A whiff of perfume, faint and fresh, reached his nostrils. And as if that were not enough, a babble of voices, a man arguing with a woman, exploded in the empty house.

Harry darted into a nearby room and swung the door to. It was a bathroom. Towels hung on a chrome rail, bottles stood beside the bath, toothpaste lay on the window ledge. Instantly his courage became panic. Why had he not listened to Mrs Good? He was so stupid!

The argument grew louder. It was backed by music. A fusillade of shots rang out. Somebody was watching TV.

He looked through the gap in the door. The corridor remained empty. Only the programme disturbed the silence of Felon Grange. He recognized the soundtrack. It was *Raiders of the Lost Ark*, his favourite film. Harry had wanted to watch it the night before but it did not start until after midnight. At that time he was sleeping on the roof, waking to flames and the smell of smoke.

He waited then stooped to remove his trainers. Carrying them in one hand, he emerged into the corridor. The sensible thing was to beat an immediate retreat but the TV was coming from a room only a few paces away. It was a chance he would never get again. He tiptoed to the door and peeped through the crack at the hinges.

In the deserted house this was a furnished bedroom: fluffy carpet, pretty curtains, wardrobe and dressing table, television, rose-patterned duvet on a tumbled king-size bed.

An electric fire glowed red. Harry recognized the perfume.

Gestapo Lil wore a floating housecoat above champagne silk pyjamas and was painting her nails. Her honey-coloured hair hung loose. She sat in an easy chair, feet up, watching a video of last night's film. He was surprised, it wasn't the sort of film she liked at all. Indiana Jones uncoiled his whip. Carefully she dipped the blood-red brush and painted round a cuticle.

Harry watched for a full minute then crept away. Intent on silence, he had taken several steps before he looked up and stifled a cry of fright. A fierce little woman stood at the head of the stairs. She looked Spanish or Italian. Everything about her was black: black hair, black eyes, black dress, black cardigan, black shoes. A blue scar ran down her shrivelled cheek.

"Who are you?" She spat the words. "What do you want'a?"

"I . . . I . . ." Was this the woman who had shouted in the night?

"Burglar! Trespasser!" She took a step towards him.

Harry looked behind. More shots came from the television.

"Come here! Lavinia!" she screamed. "Lavinia!"

Harry ran for the stairs, hoping to dodge or fight his way past her.

"Oh, no you don't!" Clawed hands fastened on the sleeve of his jersey. He wrenched his arm free. She grabbed him by the chest. Though she was fifty or sixty years old and thin as a stick, she was strong. Harry tried to tear his clothes from her grip. She would not let go. He swung his trainers and hit her across the side of the head. She shrieked. He swung them again. She staggered. Her grip weakened. He dragged himself free and stumbled to the floor. "Lavinia!" She grasped him by the belt. Harry scrabbled on hands and knees. He struck out behind him, leaped and twisted and fought like a wild cat.

Her grip was broken. He reached the staircase.

"Stop! Stop!"

But Harry didn't stop. Three at a time he raced down the broad stairs.

A second voice was above him. "Ruby? What is it?"

"A boy! A trespasser! He hit me in the face'a."

"A boy! What boy?"

"There! See!"

Harry looked back. The old woman was gone. Gestapo Lil stood in her place.

"Harry Barton!" Housecoat flying, she started after him. "Come back here! When I get my hands on you I'll. . ."

Harry reached the foot of the stairs and skidded across the hall on the slippery shavings. He regained his balance and raced along the corridor to the pantry with the open window. In moments he was there and slammed the door behind him. Headfirst he tumbled from the window to the untended grass. He picked himself up and sprinted for his bicycle.

Gestapo Lil reached the hall. Briefly she hesitated then ran to the front door, out between the pillars and down the steps to the courtyard.

Harry pulled up sharply. She had cut him off. To reach his bicycle and the drive he had to get past her. Five metres apart, they stood facing each other.

"Nosy little beast!" She pulled back the sleeves of her dressing gown. "You'll not get away this time."

Harry feinted to the left, the right, the left again, and sprinted round her to the right. Her painted nails caught his flying jersey. He swung his trainers and kicked her legs. Her grip was broken. Socks trailing, he raced for his bicycle, grabbed it up and ran on, leaping to the saddle as he went.

"Stop!" The little woman in black had returned. "Stop!"

Harry glanced behind and saw something in her hands.

Bang! The noise of a shotgun sent rooks whirling into the air. *Bang!* Pellets pinged off the metal of his bike.

She was crazy.

Gestapo Lil was shouting.

Harry put his head down and trod hard on the pedals. The gears slipped and he crashed down on to the crossbar. The bike wobbled. He freewheeled for a moment then pedalled on. A baby rabbit hopped out of the long grass. He swerved to avoid it and dropped his trainers.

A minute later there was the sound of a car starting up behind him. It revved hard. He was a good half mile from the road. Even if he reached it, there was no house nearby.

The red Aston Martin appeared behind him, accelerating down the avenue of beech trees. Harry knew it from the past. It belonged to Gestapo Lil. Desperately he looked to left and right. One way lay the open pasture, the other lay thickets of rhododendron with waxy leaves and huge pink blossoms. He swung between the beech trunks, crashed through bushes until he could go no further and flung his bike to the ground.

A few steps took him to a tiny clearing. Nettles were sprouting. Thistles and brambles barred his way. He struggled through and ducked past a holly bush. To his dismay the undergrowth was only a narrow strip. Beyond lay a barbed wire fence and steep ploughed field. In trailing socks he looked for a way across.

The sports car skidded to a halt. There was crashing in the bushes.

Trying to avoid the savage spikes, Harry set his foot on the wire and leaped across. One of his socks was pulled right off. He left it hanging and started up the ploughed hillside.

His pursuers were slower. They had not been shot at. He heard Gestapo Lil's shout: "Here's his bicycle."

"He'll not get far."

"What's that on the fence?"

By the time they spotted him, Harry was eighty metres away. He was running, gasping. The second sock had gone. His feet were balls of clay.

"There he is!" shouted the little woman in black.

"Snooping rat!"

Harry stopped to look back. Ruby, as Gestapo Lil had called her, carried a sawn-off shotgun. She had replaced the cartridges.

Bang! Bang! Harry covered his face. A couple of pellets hit him on the legs. A third stung the back of his hand. He was too far off for them to penetrate.

"We'll get you, don't fear." Gestapo Lil picked twigs from her hair. A nail was broken. "You and all those geriatrics you live with. Putting my Percy in jail!"

"Our Percy!"

"He'll not be there for long, you can count on that."

"*Then* you'd better watch out."

They put their heads together.

"Gahhh!" With a shake of the fist they turned from the wire.

Harry stood on the hillside and heard the Aston Martin start up. It headed for the road, appearing and vanishing behind the banks of bushes. They could hardly, with Gestapo Lil in pyjamas and a frothy housecoat, be going shopping. Instead, they would lie in wait in some secluded spot, hoping to ambush him on the way home.

He thought about it and changed direction. Though a detour was twice the distance, it was safer. As he crossed fields, climbed gates and picked his way through woodland, his feet began to bleed. But that afternoon, at least, Harry did not see his pursuers again.

Chapter 5

Mad Ruby and Her Son

"It has to be," Max said. "Mad Ruby Palazzo."

"Ouch!"

Aunt Bridget said, "Tell us again. We need to be sure. A little woman, you said. Smaller than any of us here?"

"Except Dot," Harry said. "Ow!"

"And dressed in black."

"Like an Italian," he said. "With snappy eyes and all this terrible black hair."

"Dyed," Auntie Florrie said. "How did she wear it?"

"Piled up and sort of falling down."

"Trying to make herself look taller. She always did that."

"What sort of figure?" Aunt Bridget said. "Fat? Skinny?"

"Sort of shrivelled up, like a walnut. And all this energy, like she was wired up."

"And a voice like a tin scraping along a wall. And carries a sawn-off. In Priestly's place," Max said. "Mad Ruby, who else can it be?"

"Ow!" Harry said again.

They sat in the big conservatory. He had arrived while the family – his aunts and their friends – were finishing four o'clock tea. They had frozen in mid-chew, teacups halfway to their lips, as he burst in from the garden, barefoot and frightened. Then several ran forward.

"Oh, Harry!" Auntie Florrie hugged him tight. "Darling, where have you been? What's happened? Never mind, you're safe now."

That was then.

Now, half an hour later, having heard the bare bones of his adventure, most had left to play croquet or watch TV in the dining room, which had been turned into a temporary lounge. While Harry was endangering his life at Felon Grange, a crowd had driven out to a secondhand furniture barn a few miles away to buy easy chairs and sofas. They had been chosen for comfort and looked horrible, red plush and green corduroy and ginger moquette. Angel had stared around, wild-haired, blue eyes swimming behind his thick spectacles. "I think mebbe I'll mak' a paintin' o' them. I'll call it *Hell*."

It was pleasantly warm in the conservatory. The writhing stems of grapes cast shadows on the tiled floor. Tea and cherry scones stood on a cane table. Harry's heels rested on a towel on a chair while Mrs Good pulled out thorns and dressed the cuts on his feet.

"It's no good complaining now," she said crossly. "Did I tell you not to go to that house? Did I warn you? I might have saved my breath. You're as bad as your aunties and all the rest of them."

Aunt Bridget was placating. "You're quite right, Goody, of course. But what boy worth his salt always does what he's told?"

"Hmph!" Mrs Good examined Harry's toes with a magnifying glass and pulled out thistle spines with a pair of tweezers. "What boy with an ounce of brains goes wandering round a house full of crazy people who try to burn us all to death? What boy dumps his bicycle and loses a brand new pair of trainers?" She scrubbed him fiercely with a wad of cottonwool soaked in TCP.

"Ahh! Hey!" Harry grimaced and looked up. "Who is she, anyway? Mad Ruby what-you-said."

"Palazzo." Max was elegant as ever, slim, cream shirt, cravat. He stroked a thin moustache. "She's a Mafia queen."

"From Naples," Auntie Florrie said.

Harry stared.

"Priestly's mother."

"His mother?" he exclaimed.

"Scary."

"Nasty piece of work."

"How's she his mother?" Harry said. "She's Italian. Priestly's like a – like a ginger pig."

Auntie Florrie finished her tea. "His father was English."

"But you said she's – ow! – she's called Palazzo. I don't understand."

"How could you?" she said. "You've got to go back forty years, before Priestly was born."

"Tell me."

"Oh, you don't want to know about all that."

"Yes I do," he said. "She's just been shooting at me and I've never even heard of her."

"Wouldn't you rather play croquet?"

"No."

"All right, if that's what you want." She dabbed her lips. "Well, going back all those years, like I said, Priestly's father was a young bookie."

"Gerald Rowland Priestly," said Aunt Bridget.

"That's right, everyone called him Jellyroll."

"A handsome man."

"So they say, before he got fat anyway. Liked the good life. Made a bit of money, spent it like water: booze, girls, hotels."

"Sounds good to me," Max said.

Auntie Florrie laughed. "Except when it came time to pay the bill he did a flit. Nothing nasty about him, mind, nothing vicious. Just couldn't be trusted. Ended up in clink."

"How did he meet Ruby?" Mrs Good loved a story.

"I'm just coming to that. So one time he goes over to Naples for some big race. Makes a few bob and that night he goes to the casino. In his twenties, nice smile, couple of drinks. And he meets this girl, Ruby Innocente."

"Not very innocent if you ask me," Aunt Bridget said.

"I couldn't agree more. She was a hostess. Never be a film star but a nice figure, little black dress. More classy than the girls he usually went out with. So Jellyroll shoots her the line: tells her how he's over for the racing, got a string of betting shops, big place near Epsom, breeds racehorses, that sort of thing. It's his favourite fantasy. Puts the money about a bit, turns on the charm. And to cut a long story short, he stays on a few weeks and they get married. Big Italian wedding. Can't bring his parents over, of course, they'd give the game away, so he tells Ruby his dad's just been bitten by a mad dog and his mum's run off with the woman next door."

"She believed him?" Mrs Good laughed.

Auntie Florrie hitched her chair into a patch of shade. "Hook, line and stinker. Never had much of a sense of humour. Mind you, her English wasn't that hot, maybe she didn't understand. A few of his pals came over, though, and

Jellyroll tipped them the wink so all was fine. Until they got to England."

Mrs Good did not allow smoking in the conservatory. Avoiding her eye, Max reached for a cigarette and flicked a heavy gold lighter. It was inscribed:

Maxim Beauguss
our immortal *Prospero*
from the RSC
with love

He dropped it on the table and blew smoke at a trouble-some fly.

Mrs Good pretended not to notice and pushed Harry's feet off the chair. "There you go. You'll live."

"Thanks." He pulled on the giant slippers he had worn the night before. "What happened when they got to England?"

"Well, Ruby found out she'd been conned, didn't she," Aunt Florrie went on. "Discovers her rich husband's nothing but a champ dancer."

"A what?"

"Oh, sorry, love. A damned chancer, a liar. Instead of this big country house near Epsom, he lives in tatty lodgings above a paper shop in the high street. Hasn't got enough in the bank to buy a pound of carrots, never mind a racehorse. Well, the spaghetti hits the fan. Three of her brothers come over and knock the stuffing out of him. Terrible mess, can't open his eyes for a fortnight. Threaten him with a pair of concrete boots, one-way jaunt to the seaside. Jellyroll's still shaking a month later."

"What about Ruby?" Mrs Good said.

"Well, they're married, aren't they. Catholic, see, can't get out of it. And a couple of weeks later she discovers she's expecting."

"A baby?"

"Well, not an ostrich, love."

"Priestly?"

"Right first time. Their one and only. Percival Bonaparte, our favourite jailbird."

"Not an ostrich maybe," Aunt Bridget smiled. "Bit of a cuckoo though. The baby wasn't like either of them."

"That's right, bright ginger. They were both very surprised. Jellyroll wants to know where *he* came from. Ruby asks what he's implying, and did Jellyroll maybe have an orang-utan for a father? It didn't help the marriage much and Ruby can't stand the baby anyway."

"Jellyroll was soft as clarts," Aunt Bridget said, "but Ruby was a tough one. That right, Florrie? Got a will like iron. Family like hers and working in the casino she knew her way round a bit. Rooms over a paper shop weren't for her. So she pushed him here, pushed him there, demanded receipts, handled all the money, set up a few scams, got to know the Newmarket trainers. And soon they're upwardly mobile, as people say. By the time young Percy's ten they've moved into that big house in Epsom and Jellyroll's running half a dozen betting shops."

"He *was* a jellyroll by this time too," said Auntie Florrie. "Big belly, double chins. And he kept getting fatter."

"I know he was a sleazeball," Aunt Bridget polished her glasses, "but I can't help feeling a bit sorry for him. There he was, achieved his ambition, living in that big house, and not a shred of love. Except from Percy, maybe. I think *he* liked his dad well enough."

"As long as he kept buying him presents and didn't interfere in his games," Auntie Florrie said. "You know what he enjoyed: shooting cats with his air rifle, and torturing younger boys, and frying insects with a magnifying glass."

"You're quite right, Florrie. He was a little beast right from the start, wasn't he. Anyway, he got sent away to boarding school in the end. Ruby was glad to see the back of him, and his dad wanted him to meet *the right sort of people*. After that, she and Jellyroll were the only ones left in the house, both hating each other by this time. So, of course, the inevitable happened."

"What do you mean?"

"What do you think, Harry, you're not a baby."

"Did she kill him?"

"Of course not, though I'm sure she'd have liked to sometimes. No, he had an affair. Poor man needed a bit of love somewhere."

He thought about it. "Who with?"

Auntie Florrie widened her baby-blue eyes. "Well, darling, an ambitious man like Jellyroll wasn't going to be satisfied with hard-up Hannah or spotty Sue the social worker was he? All this racing brought him into contact with the tweed-and-Daimler brigade. He met her at Lord Thingummy's or the Earl of Wotsit's place. Arabella Ffarquhar-Twitch her name was. Coming from a paper shop, of course, Jellyroll quite fancied having a bit of a ding-dong with one of the aristocracy. Suited him fine: useful connections, bit of money tucked away in her stocking-top. Only it turned out she hadn't. Arabella was an even bigger con-merchant than he was. Oh, she had the Roedean lingo, knew the Chelsea nightspots, talked about the yacht in Monte. But the only way *she* could afford the right clothes was to go out on shoplifting expeditions to Harvey Nick's. And it turned out she wasn't one of the Devonshire Ffarquhar-Twitches at all. Far from it. Her father was a man called Snaith, a workshy layabout who spent his life propping up a bar in Hartlepool. Jellyroll was the one caught out this time." She reached for the teapot. "Well, when news of it reached Ruby she went – what's the word, Harry?"

"Mental," he said. "Ballistic. Ker-boom."

"That's it, *ker-boom*, like one of dear Fingers' specials. It was the last straw. After ten years, dragging the family up by its bootlaces, she finds out he's taken up with another woman. I can tell you, she didn't need her brothers' help this time, she laid into him with a frying pan. And he was a big man, twice the size of her. Put him into the hospital. Broken jaw, arm in plaster—"

Max startled everyone by breaking into a calypso, beating the edge of the table like a steel drum:

"... hit 'im on the 'ead with a frying pan,
I done kill nobody but me husband. . ."

"I love it!" Aunt Bridget joined in:

"Stone-cold dead in de market,
Stone-cold dead in de market. . ."

Auntie Florrie laughed. "But it wasn't funny really," she said. "He was hurt! Anyway, a lady friend was too much to take, Ruby'd had enough. So she draws every last penny out of the bank, loads up the Jag and takes off back to Naples."

"What about Percy?" Harry said.

"Dumps him in the hospital with his dad. Tells Jellyroll he and his fancy woman can do what they like with him, chuck him out a tenth-floor window for all she cared." Auntie Florrie touched up her lipstick. It was several shades lighter than the one she was wearing but the two-tone effect was pleasing.

"Poor him," Harry said.

"In one way, I suppose. But don't break your heart. He was a horrible child, a vicious, no-neck monster. Deserved everything he got."

"What happened then?"

"They didn't have much choice. Arabella took Percy home to the big house and when Jellyroll got out of hospital he joined them."

"Back to square one," Mrs Good said. "Stony broke."

"Not really. The house was worth a packet and he still had the betting shops."

"Didn't Ruby sell them?"

"All she wanted right then was to be rid of him," Auntie Florrie said. "Kick the dust of England off her shoes. And when she gets back to Italy she finds her brothers have got involved with the Mafia – Nico Georgio and the Palazzos and Twelve-Toes Notrianni, that crowd. Compared with them Jellyroll's a choirboy. Ruby loves it, suits her down to the ground. Before you can say knife she's running with the big boys. Can't marry again, like I said, but she sets up with Tony Palazzo anyway. Liked to go *visiting* with the men in dark suits. Designed that Velcro holster   remember, Bridget? – so she could carry a sawn-off on her thigh. Wore a split skirt to get it out fast."

"Sawn-off Ruby," Aunt Bridget said. "Got herself a reputation."

Max sat up. "I played in a Mafia *Macbeth* once at the National. Lady Macbeth carried one." He ripped an imaginary shotgun from his leg. "Pow! Pow! Terrific!"

"Not if you're on the receiving end," Aunt Bridget said drily. "I hate guns."

Dot wandered in, a tiny figure, walking on her hands. No one took particular notice, she often moved about the house that way. Blouse hanging, skirt tucked into her knickers, she stood at the table.

"This Ruby and Tony you're talking about?" she said. "I met them once, when I was touring with the Cirque de Paris. She had him right under her thumb."

Using her toes, she cut and buttered a scone, spread it with jam and passed it down to her hand. Such miracles were not uncommon at Lagg Hall but Harry applauded.

"Don't encourage her," Max said. "She's such a show-off."

Dot flicked a currant and hit him on the ear.

Max ignored her. "You knew them as well, didn't you?" he said to Auntie Florrie.

"When I was racing?" she said. "No, that was the Milan outfit up at Monza. I was friendly with Arabella for a couple of years though. Couldn't stand Jellyroll, he was so fat: big check waistcoats, podgy fingers, eyes like slits. He had these shiny red lips, as if he spent all day guzzling oysters. But I liked her, she had style. She was funny, had a bit of go about her."

"Come on, they were two of a kind," Aunt Bridget said. "Seedy adventurers."

"I suppose." Auntie Florrie shrugged. "She was nice anyway."

"What happened then?" Harry said. "After Jellyroll got out of hospital?"

"Well, Ruby going off like that, it was the best break he'd had in years. Couldn't believe his luck. He and Arabella got on like a house on fire."

"Like a what?"

"Whoops! Sorry, Goody. But you know what I mean. Took over where Ruby left off. Opened more betting shops, organized a scam here and there, bought a couple of no-hope racehorses and one won the St Leger. In two or three years they were rolling in it. Happy as pigs in muck."

"What about Percy?" Harry said.

"Spoiled him rotten. Leastways his dad did. Thought the sun shone out of his belly-button. The most marvellous boy in the world – two-faced little toad. Arabella was different, tried to teach him a bit of discipline, take some exercise, stop stuffing his face with chocolate. He didn't like that. Told her to get lost, go drown herself, jump in front of a bus. *She* wasn't his mother. And of course he never wanted to go back to boarding school where he had to do what he was told and there were rules he—"

"What school?"

"I don't know, Winchester, Rugby, some posh place. He hated it. But as things worked out he wasn't there very long anyway. When he was about thirteen he got expelled for thieving. In the blood, I suppose."

"What a horror!" Mrs Good said.

"He certainly was," Auntie Florrie agreed. "And he hasn't changed, as you know. Anyway, Jellyroll knew a governor of some other school, so he was sent there instead. Six months later he was thrown out of that place, too, for cheating and lying. No one else would have him so he had to stay at home and go to the local comp."

"What's wrong with that?"

"Nothing at all, Harry," Aunt Bridget said.

"Except everyone laughed at him," said her sister, "because he acted like he was a cut above the rest and he was thick as a pair of workboots. But somehow he scraped together a couple of A levels—"

"Prob'ly another fix, knowing him." Dot descended to her feet and twitched the skirt from her knickers.

"I wouldn't be surprised. So there's Percy, eighteen years old studying law at – well, he says it was Oxford, but some little place – when suddenly the world crashes about his ears. Jellyroll was arrested for fraud and heaven knows what else. Nothing new in that, but this time he took a heart attack in the witness box. Fell headfirst over the rail. Stone dead on the floor. Wonder he didn't go *pop*. Took six paramedics to carry him out of the courtroom."

Tangle trotted in. Head on one side, he looked up at the table. Saliva dripped to the floor. Harry rubbed his ears.

"Well, poor Arabella," Auntie Florrie went on. "It turns out Jellyroll has been so busy making money, so busy drinking champagne and enjoying the good things of life, that he'd never got round to changing his will. Heart attack came out of the blue: shouting at the barrister one minute, belly-up the next. So everything – money, house, betting shops, the lot – went to his beloved wife over in Italy. Nothing, not a bent penny, went to Arabella. Seven years of her life and all she's got to show for it's a few grey hairs.

"The moment Ruby hears, of course, she flies in from Naples, Tony Palazzo trailing in her wake. He thinks he's a tiger – spaniel more like. Stretch limo brings them from the airport. Ruby's hardly reached the door when she's telling

Arabella to get out. You know how she talks: 'Go on'a, sling'a your hook, you ugly great'a horse!'"

Max collapsed. "Thank you, darling, we'll let you know."

"We can't all be stars of stage and the silver screen," Auntie Florrie said tartly. "Anyway, she gives Arabella an hour, one hour, to get herself and all her personal possessions out of the house. Obviously it's impossible, so Ruby starts tossing them out the window: CD player, clothes, souvenirs, all scattered on the ground. And it's sleeting. Arabella standing there with her hair hanging in rats' tails. Percy laughing himself silly at the front door, pulling the heads off her collection of teddies and throwing them at her."

"That's sick!"

"I'm telling you! But Arabella's one of life's survivors. She's not going to start gathering that lot up. Walks up to Percy and socks him right in the eye. 'I've been wanting to do that for seven years,' she says, and gives them an earful of abuse would have made a soldier blush. Then she walks straight out the gate and catches a taxi."

"Good for her," Mrs Good said.

"Never went back. Never wrote. Never argued any rights she might have to stay on in the house. Went to live with a girlfriend from the old days. Shared a flat in Chelsea."

"All the same, she must have been furious."

"You bet. But she wasn't there long. Remember her background. A couple of expeditions to Harvey Nick's and Harrods and she went back on the social roundabout. Found herself a sugar daddy, lovely old man. Rich as Croesus. Doted on her. So they got married and she went to live in the old family pile up in Shropshire. Had a couple of beautiful children. Happy as Larry."

"She came out of it well," Mrs Good said.

"So she did, I'm really pleased for her." Auntie Florrie looked at her watch. "Goodness, look at the time." She rose. "What are you thinking about, Max? Time for a snifter."

"Lead me to it. All this talk about Italy's given me a thirst. How about a nice Chianti?" He sucked his teeth like Hannibal Lector.

Mrs Good saw Harry's hand drop towards Tangle. Three scones had remained on the plate. Now there were two. Tangle was less subtle than his young master. The noisy slop and chomp of his jaws filled a momentary silence.

"Come on then." She laughed. "Better make a start on the dinner. Game pie and strawberries. Harry, you can clear up here then into the bath with you. Nutty's fixed up a bed in the attic. I think you'll find everything you need."

"And after dinner, if there's time," said Aunt Bridget, "we'll drive over to Felon Grange and pick up your bike – *my* bike. I want to have a word with those two women."

Chapter 6

A Bed in the Attic

Dinner was delayed by a nail-biting conclusion to the croquet match. They lingered over wine and chocolates and by the time dinner was finished it was too late to drive to Felon Grange.

"We'll pick you up and go straight after school tomorrow," Aunt Bridget told Harry. "Goodness knows what lies they'll be telling, so I want you there."

"I come also." Huggy's shoulders bunched beneath her blouse. "I vant see those vomen vhat they do Harry. Guns, ja? Oh, my vord!"

So Harry, keeping a sharp lookout for intruders, took Tangle a walk round the woods and returned for a cut-throat game of Racing Demon.

At ten o'clock, schoolbag packed and teeth brushed, he climbed the stairs from the upper landing and opened the door of the brown attic.

A naked bulb hung on a long flex. As he entered a draught set it swinging, casting shadows across the wilderness of boxes, trunks, discarded furniture and junk that lay on all sides. A score of demons and hideous beasts could be lurking not six paces away, ready to leap out at him with claws and dripping fangs.

"Rubbish!" he muttered and bent to pat Tangle, glad of his company.

A space had been cleared for the mattress he had asked for instead of the wobbly camp bed. It lay like an island surrounded by stormy seas. On one side stood a coffee table with a bedside lamp; on the other lay a suitcase containing his clean school clothes for Monday morning, a torch, *Playgrounds of Blood* and a few other odds and ends.

Harry threw his pyjamas on the duvet and pulled off his jersey, then paused. It was a long time since he had explored up here. Taking the torch, he picked through the riot of junk: old tennis rackets, cushions, antique dolls, cricket pads, a full-length mirror with the silver peeling, a wooden radio, a rack of moth-eaten dresses, a stack of old 78s, a tailor's dummy, chipped skis with boots attached, and more. He opened a trunk and discovered Mr Tolly's props from his career as a stage magician. Another was full of Aunt Bridget's books of mathematics and philosophy. A third contained wigs and a battered box of greasepaints.

Harry had an idea. He sat back on his heels and smiled.

Ten minutes later the ghostly figure of a lady was to be seen crossing the landing of Lagg Hall. She wore a sage-green dress which trailed on the floor and accentuated her slimness – except, that is, for a pair of enormous cushion-like breasts. Her hair, too, was remarkable, heavy blonde ringlets which hung upon the fox-fur draped round her shoulders. Her face was chalk-white, her eyeshadow green, her lips the same blood-red as the Bride of Dracula. At every step, scarlet slingbacks with eight-centimetre stiletto heels winked beneath her dress. She steadied herself against the wall. Was she a sick ghost or was she drunk?

Reaching the staircase which led to the hall, she hitched up her dress in a most unladylike way, revealing a pair of sturdy legs. With a practical hand she gripped the banister and began to descend. To begin with all went well but at the sixth tread her ankle turned, the shoe fell off and bounced down to the bottom. The lady gave a cry and would have followed had she not, with surprising agility, managed to grasp the banister with both hands.

At length she achieved her objective. Bosom restored to its proper position, hair and clothes straightened, she stood at the door of the new lounge. A moonbeam pierced the darkness.

"Oohhhh!" she wailed. "Ooohhhhhh!" and giggled. The handle turned beneath her grasp. "Ooohhhhh!" With a green arm she reached into the lounge and switched off the lights.

A chorus of shrieks and terrified cries came from within: "It's the ghost! . . . Aahhh! . . . The green lady! . . . There's been a death! . . . Go away!"

Harry giggled again. That's why he loved the Wrinklies – they understood.

"Oohhhhhh!" Slowly he pushed the door wide and advanced into the room.

All was chaos. On every side people were screaming and climbing over chairs to get away from him. "No! No! . . . Is it you, Ermintrude? . . . Keep away! Keep away! . . . I never meant to kill you! . . . Have you got a message for me? . . . Aarrgghh!"

It was altogether a great success.

Fingers switched the lights back on. "Better than telly any day."

"Oh, Harry! That vas brilliant." Huggy's face was red with laughing.

Dot tickled him through a moth-hole.

"I bought that dress when I was a student," Aunt Bridget said, "for the Commem Ball."

"Look up, laddie. This way." Angel seized a biro and made a slashing sketch.

"Love the boobs!" said Mr Tolly.

Harry shook them at him then pulled out the cushion.

"I don't know about the rest of you," Mrs Good said, "and I know it's school tomorrow, but *I* think that deserves cocoa and shortbread all round. Come on, Marilyn Monroe, you can give me a hand. See if we can get that stuff off your face."

"Cold cream," Max said. "There's a tub on my dressing table."

Fingers looked at him.

"When you get to our age," Max told him, "nature needs a little hand."

"A *little* hand," Huggy said. "Vhen you get to my age, vhat nature need is a transplant."

"Tell me about it," Fingers said gloomily. He examined his hands from which several of the digits were missing. They had gone one at a time. When he blew safes his explosions were thrilling but they came at a price. "Never mind," he brightened. "I can still scratch me bum."

Half an hour later Mrs Good saw Harry into bed. "Night-night, love. It'll be a bit strange at first but you'll soon get used to it. And you've got Tangle for company. I'll give you a call in the morning." A kiss on the brow and she was gone. Harry listened to her footsteps on the attic stairs.

He looked around, from the curtained skylight to the orange-shaded lamp and Tangle curled up in his kitchen bed alongside. He put out a hand. Tangle twitched his eyebrows and closed his eyes. The bedside light was controlled by a button in the flex. He switched it off. Little sounds reached him in the darkness: owls in the wood, creaks of the cooling house. He turned on his side and tucked a hand under his head.

How long he had been asleep and what he had been dreaming about, Harry didn't know. All he did know was that chaos had descended. The attic was full of a frantic barking and crashing. Something shot across his face. Tangle followed, paws thudding into his stomach. The duvet was pulled off. The lamp fell to the floor. "Tangle!" he shouted. "Tangle, what is it?" Dazed with sleep and panic, he groped for the lamp button. It clicked. The bulb was broken. He fumbled for the torch. It wasn't where he had left it. "Tangle!" Moonlight filtered through the curtain. He stumbled to the light switch at the door. His little toe struck a hard corner. It was agony. *Click!* The attic was flooded with light. Momentarily he was blinded.

Tangle was in a corner, his head buried, paws raking furiously. A mouse shot out behind him, streaked across the floorboards and vanished beneath the junk opposite. Tangle did not see it but he heard something. He raised his head, listening intently. At that moment a second mouse, timing it badly, scuttled straight towards him. With a yelp of excitement Tangle launched himself at it. In a second he would have snapped it up but the box he took off from was unstable. In a jumble of paws he crashed to his belly. The mouse fled back the way it had come.

"Tangle!" Harry shouted again. "Tangle!"

A drop of blood had appeared at the nail of his little toe. He limped to his mattress. Reluctantly Tangle left his game and trotted to Harry's side.

"Good boy!" Tangle's collar had been taken off for the night. Harry pulled him close. "You were just doing your job, weren't you."

Tangle panted happily. Sweet doggy breath hit Harry in the face. Tangle turned his head, eager to resume the hunt.

Meanwhile there were voices below. "Harry? Are you all right?" This was Aunt Bridget. "What's going on up there?"

"Nothing." He fell back on the bed and started to laugh. "Everything's fine."

At four o'clock on Monday afternoon the old Merc, with Aunt Bridget driving and Huggy in the passenger seat, was waiting at the school gates. Children came streaming down the drive. Among them was Harry. He waved cheerio to Charlie and some other friends, told the bus driver his aunt was picking him up, and jogged to the car.

"How'd it go today?"

"Fine." He threw his schoolbag across the back seat.

"Here." Aunt Bridget passed back a chocolate brazil.

"Thanks." He popped it in and reached for the seatbelt.

Ten minutes brought them to Felon Grange. The Mercedes, currently the metallic red that Nutty had sprayed it on Saturday afternoon, drove through the fallen gateway and started up the long drive.

"Where was it you left the bike?" Aunt Bridget said.

"About halfway." Harry released his seatbelt and pointed between their heads. "See those pinky-blue rhododendrons? Just past there."

They drew up at the verge. Harry was first out and ran ahead through the bushes. His bicycle was gone.

"Are you sure this is the right place?"

"I think so." He pushed on further. "Yes, I remember that holly bush. And that's where I crossed the fence. You can see footprints." He pointed to the ploughed field.

"Tvigs broken also." Two shoots hung on ribbons of bark. Something in the grass caught Huggy's eye. She picked it up. A waxy red cartridge case. "Ve have the right place, sure."

The cartridge was clean and spotted with moisture. Harry took it and sniffed. The sharp smell of gunpowder, like spent fireworks, tickled his nose. Mad Ruby had *shot* at him with this. He looked up the field and shivered.

Aunt Bridget held out a hand. He passed the cartridge over. She sniffed in turn and dropped it into her anorak pocket. "You tell a story well, Harry. It's just the way you described it."

"The sock's gone," he said. "We might find the other one."

Aunt Bridget shook her head. "Leave it."

"Now ve go the house." Huggy turned back. "I vant hear vhat lies they are telling. I t'ink I crack their heads like coconuts."

"Good for you, Huggy."

"What do you think they've done with the bike?" Harry said.

"Don't you vorry about the bike. Ve get you another bike; ve get you ten bike. First things first."

She trod on a branch with her size-twelve shoe. It broke with a crack like a pistol shot.

Harry jumped. His heart was thudding.

Chapter 7

The Bicycle

Felon Grange was exactly as Harry had last seen it, except that a gardener had dumped a heap of grass and branches at the foot of the portico. They started up the seven broad steps but had only got halfway when Gestapo Lil and Mad Ruby Palazzo appeared between the pillars above them.

"Well, well," Gestapo Lil sneered. "If it isn't the geriatrics from over at Lagg Hall."

They stood on the top step to have the advantage. Ruby wore the black cardigan and skirt Harry had seen before. Her walnut face was ferocious, her matt-black hair piled high and held with a gold comb. Gestapo Lil was nearly a head taller. She wore, in stark contrast, a suit of white leather with green accessories: green snakeskin boots to her knee, emerald drops at her ears and throat, an emerald dress ring on her right hand to balance the flashing engagement ring on her left. Her long nails, too, were green, and a black Russian cigarette trailed smoke from a green holder. Her eyeshadow was silver-green, her lips blood-red and her golden hair immaculately coiled in a chignon.

"Got lost, have you, dear?" she said loudly as if they were senile. "Want to know the way home? You don't live here, you know." She turned to her companion. "I don't think you've met them, Ruby. This little oik's Harry Barton. I used to be his nanny. He's the one responsible for putting our Percipops away for five years, treacherous little weasel. That one there, looks like a camel, that's Bridget Barton, a right old bat. Reckoned to be the brains of the outfit. And this sub-human article – looks like Baba Yaga – she goes by the name of Huggy something. No one knows what her real name is, probably forgotten it herself."

"You vant know my name?" Huggy stepped up to face her. "Then vhy not nicely you ask? It is Karsavina, Tamara Platonovna Karsavina, after the great ballerina."

"Ballerina!" Gestapo Lil snorted. "That's a good one. I should think the only dance you're capable of doing's the elephant polka. What do you think, Ruby?"

Judging Huggy to be a victim, Mad Ruby joined the game: "The rhinoceros'a rumba."

"The hippo hornpipe."

They should have been more cautious. In a flash Huggy seized Gestapo Lil by the wrist and jerked her forward. Her big body turned, her knees bent, a little grunt issued from her nose. And before Gestapo Lil could even register astonishment, she was flying through the air in a spectacular curve, arms and legs flailing. With a thump that knocked the breath from her lungs and rearranged her internal organs, she landed on the pile of garden rubbish at the foot of the steps.

"That voman!" Huggy looked down. "I never could stand her."

Ruby's hand flew to her thigh.

Harry leaped down the steps and took to his heels across the forecourt.

The sawn-off wasn't there.

"Left your smoke-pole in the house?" Aunt Bridget said. "What a vicious little stoat you are, Ruby Palazzo." She looked after Harry. "All right, you can come back now. It's quite safe."

Already at the drive, Harry turned. Huggy was beckoning. He looked from the women by the pillars to the great white house and the rain-filled fountain. Slowly he retraced his steps.

"My, you some sprinter." Huggy put her heavy arm around his shoulders. "I t'ink ve enter you in the Olympics, ja?"

Gestapo Lil, meanwhile, was scrambling from the pile of branches. Her golden hair had come uncoiled, her tights were shredded, the leather skirt rode high up her legs. She reached the ground and pulled her clothes straight. The white suit was streaked with earth. Tufts of grass had caught in her collar and the top of her boots. Venomously she hooked them out and checked her jewellery. An earring was missing. She gave a cry and turned back to the green mound. Somewhere among that vegetation was an emerald worth more than the gardener's wages for a whole year. On hands and knees she crawled back to where she had landed. Briefly she searched, patting the grass, tugging branches, turning clods with her carefully-manicured nails. It was hopeless. She retreated to the pink forecourt.

"You'll pay for this!" With narrowed eyes she stared at Harry. "You will pay for this."

"Yes, well." Unlike her nephew, Aunt Bridget was completely unafraid. "You can't say you didn't ask for it. But that's not the reason we're here."

She climbed the last three steps and pushed Ruby aside. Huggy and Harry followed.

"The reason we are here, or rather the *two* reasons we're here," Aunt Bridget continued, "are first to tell you that if you ever – if you *ever* – point a gun in my nephew's direction again, I will personally ensure that you end up in jail for so long that your bones will have turned to dust before they sweep you out."

Ruby gave a twisted smile. "And second?"

"Much more simple, we've come for his bicycle."

"Well, that all'a very interesting." Ruby looked at Gestapo Lil who had joined them. "Can you tell me what they're talking about, Lavinia?"

"I've got no idea." She was attempting to pin up her hair. "They're losing their marbles, I told you."

"Then let me explain," Aunt Bridget said. "Harry had no right to be here, I admit that, but he thought the house was empty. When he was discovered he was attacked by both of you, pursued and shot at. I'm assuming – at least, I hope – that you only intended to frighten him, that he was too far away for a sawn-off to do much damage. Anyway, he had to leave his bike behind to escape across a field – and now it's gone."

Ruby expressed bewilderment but Gestapo Lil said, "Oh, it's *that* boy. You remember, Ruby. That boy broke in yesterday. Swearing, shouting, black balaclava. Tried to push you down the stairs. We told him to behave himself. Said he'd go if we gave him twenty quid. We thought he was some drug addict from the wrong end of town, needed the money to feed his habit. So that was you, Harry? Gone from glue to drugs now. Or was it just a bit of extra pocket money? Either way, I can't say I'm surprised. Maybe this is a side of your character your aunts haven't found out about yet."

"That's not true," Harry said.

"Of course it's not," said Aunt Bridget. "What a ridiculous woman you are, Lavinia McScrew. But I can see we're not going to get any further here. It's Harry's word against two of you and we've got no proof – although there is a *lot* of evidence. Such as this," she produced the cartridge case. "I'm sure I don't need to tell you what a four-course dinner forensic could make out of a jolly little item like this."

Ruby glanced at her companion.

"But we don't want to bother the fuzz, do we? Not again. Not at this stage."

"Again?"

"Oh, yes. Haven't you heard? Two intruders tried to torch Lagg Hall on Saturday night."

"No one told us anything—"

"Drove a Range Rover, a 2.5 diesel. You have a car like that – at least, so the garage tells us. Is that right?"

"Yes'a, but we weren't anywhere near—"

"So the fuzz came round naturally. Must have been there for, oooh, close on two hours. Harry had to make a statement because he saw the two that did it. One called out to him, a little woman with a foreign accent. Course it couldn't be you, you'd be in your beds that hour of the night. Doesn't give you much of an alibi though."

"Saturday night?" Gestapo Lil thought. "We weren't, as a matter of fact. Stayed up to watch a late-night film. Had a couple of glasses of wine."

"Oh, yes? What film, just as a matter of interest?"

"*Raiders of the* – what is it – *the Lost Ark*? It was very good."

"You stayed up past two o'clock to see Indiana—"

"I bet they didn't!" Harry shouted. "She was watching it when I was here yesterday. In her bedroom. A video. I saw her."

"What?" Gestapo Lil was flustered. "You certainly did not."

"Yes I did. You were painting your nails and Indiana Jones was on the telly. He was using his bull-whip."

"Oh, I see." Aunt Bridget nodded. "You videoed it on Saturday night and watched it later so you'd know what it was about. So that could be your alibi."

"He's lying. Look upstairs if you like. You'll not find a video of *Raiders of the Lost Ark* in this house."

"I'm sure we won't. You'll have wiped it."

"Oh, I sick of this. Go on, sling your hook. Get off'a my porch." Mad Ruby turned away. "Get out'a my grounds."

"*Your* porch?"

"What you mean'a? Whose house you think this is?"

"I thought it was your son's house."

"No, it'a my house. So get out." She waved a skinny arm.

Aunt Bridget hesitated. "What about the bicycle?"

"You find the bicycle, you take it. I know nothing about it."

"All right, we'll have a look."

Harry whispered, "What about my trainers?"

"They could be anywhere," said his aunt. "I will *not* go hunting through Gestapo Lil's dustbin."

"And the gun."

She nodded. "My nephew's asking about the sawn-off. Don't bother coming out with it, you're not going to shoot us. So you go off and have a nice cappucino and we'll look for the bike."

For a second it seemed as if Ruby might fling herself at Aunt Bridget, which in view of Aunt Bridget's boxing prowess would have been unwise. Instead she screwed up her face and spat on the ground.

"I warn you," she said venomously. "Do not come here again."

Gestapo Lil treated Harry to a basilisk stare and followed her into the house. The door slammed behind them.

"Well, that's interesting," Aunt Bridget said. "Priestly must have put the house in her name in case the law caught up with him."

"What does that mean?" Harry followed her down the steps.

"It means the courts can seize all his possessions and all his money, except what he's got salted away in Swiss bank accounts, but they can't touch the house."

"Because it isn't his."

"Exactly."

"So that's why it's been lying empty," Harry said.

They wandered towards the old stables and coach houses.

"And now his mad mother's come over from Italy," said Aunt Bridget, "and met up with his fiancée."

"A pretty pair," Huggy said. "They are vell suited."

"So they are. The horrible Percy too."

"Beastly Priestly," Harry said. He tightened a shoelace and trotted to catch up. "D'you think they're planning to stay on?"

"Seems like it from what you say. Nice bedrooms, getting the place repaired."

"I see furniture t'rough the door," Huggy said. "Big dining table."

"Chairs too," Aunt Bridget said.

Huggy sighed. "Ve have so charming neighbours again, Mad Ruby and Gestapo Lil. Oh, my vord! Vhy not Dracula and Genghis Khan also? They make a four at bridge."

Aunt Bridget laughed. "You're a tonic, Huggy. Now —" A small door was set into the double doors of the first coach house. She pulled it open. "Where would they hide a bike?"

The search began. Apart from a new lawn tractor, all they found in the outbuildings were the little red Aston Martin, the black Range Rover with privacy windows, and an assortment of tools.

"Perhaps it's in the house," Harry said.

"If they were planning to give it back maybe," said Aunt Bridget. "I can't see that, can you?"

"Or they might have dumped it miles away."

"Who knows."

For half an hour they searched the thickets and bushes, a gamekeeper's hut and an abandoned quarry.

"Let's just leave it," Aunt Bridget said as they returned to the Grange. "We could be here till midnight and never find it."

"Time for tea, ja? Goody make valnut cake specially. Ve not go now it dinner time."

Harry was reluctant. A narrow track ran alongside an overgrown hedge. It ended in a thicket of willowherb. "We haven't been down there," he said and jogged towards it. "You wait here and I'll just take a look."

He pushed past branches. Hawthorn petals covered his shoulders. Dead willowherb, head-high, barred his passage. Harry's heart jumped: new growth had been broken off. Someone had passed this way recently. He pressed on and found himself on the brink of a tangled bank. At the bottom a stream, trickling from the wood, ran into a muddy, weedy swamp. He peered down. Something caught his eye, a regular shape. It was the arc of a wheel, half hidden by coils of bramble. Close by, a silver object protruded from the ooze. It was the end of a handlebar and part of a bell.

"Aunt Bridget!" He turned. "I've found it. Over here."

It took another half-hour, avoiding the brambles, descending the long bank and splashing downstream, for Harry to reach the bicycle and haul it from the swamp.

"We don't need Nutty," he had insisted. "I can do it. Please!"

So his aunt had let him and after a hard struggle Harry and his bike stood on the red road a hundred metres from Felon Grange. From handlebars to tail-light the bike was clotted with mud. From fair hair to school shoes, so was the boy. He gave a brilliant smile, white in his dirty face.

"Good for you, Harry!" Uncaring that she got her own face and clothes messy, Aunt Bridget gave him a hard, bony hug and a kiss on his muddy hair. "I've said it before, you're made of the right stuff!"

He was pleased and surprised. Aunt Bridget did not often give way to emotion. He looked up and saw tears in her bright blue eyes.

"Take no notice." She blinked them away. "I'm just a silly old woman."

They started towards the car. The bike wheels grated with mud. How would they get it home, Harry wondered, without making the car filthy? He had an idea. In the middle of the forecourt the fountain was full to the brim with rainwater, the ducts choked with leaves.

He ran ahead. King Neptune and his dolphins were bone dry. The pool beneath them was half a metre deep. Angry faces watched from an upstairs window as Harry stepped over the rim and hauled the bicycle after him. The mud fell off into the water. With cold hands he rinsed the mudguards, spun the wheels, turned the pedals. The chain had come off. He replaced it and adjusted the little gear chain that ran into the back hub. In minutes the bike was restored, almost, to its previous state. Huggy lifted it out while Harry rinsed his face and trouser bottoms and tipped the water from his shoes.

"You two go in the car," he said. "I'll follow. We'll be home in fifteen minutes."

And that is what they did, fifty metres apart. Harry loved it. The wind blew his hair into crusty spikes, his eyes watered. He stood on the pedals, straining to catch up on the Mercedes. Aunt Bridget let him get close then trod on the accelerator. It was brilliant.

Chapter 8
The Car with
Black Windows

"I left your rugby kit on the stairs."

"Thanks, Goody." Harry shovelled in a spoonful of muesli and washed it down with orange.

"Don't bolt your food like that, it's only five past. How many rounds of toast?"

"On." Harry's mouth was full again. "No, hoo."

It was Thursday morning. Two others sat at the kitchen table, sipping coffee and gradually coming to terms with the day. Auntie Florrie was one. She was reading the *Telegraph*. Her make-up was never at its best in the morning. She wore a Baby Doll housecoat of cornflower blue.

"Oh, my goodness!" She rustled the pages and looked over the top at Mr Tolly. "Listen to this:

Gangland Killing
*D'Artagnan Jones, brother of jailed gangland boss, Eddie
'Carver' Jones, was last night slain by an unknown assailant.
He was returning to his car after a night out at Chicks-a-Go-
Go, the well-known Kensington gaming club of which he and
his brother were co-owners. According to eye-witnesses, his killer
stepped out of the shadows, said 'Mr Jones' in an educated*

voice, and when he turned, fired three shots into his chest from close range."

She lowered the paper. "Well, that's Dart gone. Can't say I'm surprised, he's been asking for it for years. But that'll put the cat among the pigeons."

Mr Tolly, a big man, wore a cosy brown dressing-gown over striped pyjamas. He stroked his bald head. "I wonder where that leaves Eddie now?"

Harry would have liked to know more but at that moment two rounds of granary toast arrived on his plate. Simultaneously he remembered he had a geography test that morning. His jotter and textbook were retrieved from the hall. Although his teacher, Mr Weldon, was popular with the pupils, he had a short fuse. Ten minutes' revision could make the difference between life and death. Crumbs and a blob of marmalade fell on Harry's jotter as he swotted up which country was Norway and which was Sweden, which city was Warsaw and which was Berlin.

All too soon it was time to go. "Pick you up at five, love." Auntie Florrie blew a kiss.

"Yes, thanks, bye!" Jacket flapping and schoolbag bouncing, he ran off down the drive to wait at the roadside for the school bus.

Mrs Good watched him go. "With all that's been happening recently, I'm not at all happy about him standing down there by himself. Starting tomorrow, one of us is going with him."

She spoke wisely, for after school that day an event occurred which gave Harry a nasty scare.

The day had gone well. Much to his surprise he came top in the geography test. The maths was easy; he wrote a story; and they watched a video about the Vikings:

"From *Norway*," Mr Weldon told them. "And you all know where Norway is – I wish!"

Their teacher was a sturdy young man with crinkly fair hair. He had joined Barleymow Junior School at New Year after their previous teacher, Gestapo Lil, had been arrested and charged with many serious crimes. Mr Weldon played fullback for the county rugby first team, and had reintroduced the game to the school.

At three-thirty on a Thursday they had practice. Akku, the fastest runner in the school, was a wing three-quarter. Charlie played stand-off. Harry was a second row forward. For forty minutes an enthusiastic bunch of seventeen boys and two tough girls passed and scrummed and practised line-outs. Afterwards they had a fifteen minutes each way game. Everyone loved it. Panting, happy, arguing, they returned to the changing rooms for showers – boys one way, girls the other. Mr Weldon saw them out safely and they trooped down the drive to walk home or be picked up by parents. Cars were waiting. Children climbed in and were whisked off home to tea.

Harry looked up and down the road. Where was the Merc?

Soon Akku and he were the only ones left. They joked, messed around, swapped tales about school and telly and football teams.

Ten minutes passed.

"Where's Mum?" Akku stepped from the pavement.

Behind them a car crept out from a side road. It was a Range Rover, gleaming black, with a 2.5 litre diesel engine.

The privacy windows, black as the body, made it impossible to see who was inside. With the softest of growls, it drew in to the kerb fifty metres away. The engine was switched off.

Akku looked back and was surprised. Where had the Range Rover come from?

Harry was frightened and retreated through the school gate.

"What's up?"

"It's those people who started the fire and took my bike."

"Come on, man, you're imagining things."

"No I'm not."

"Hey, look at the number plate."

"I know." Harry was white. "It's them."

His fear was infectious. Akku fetched their bags from the roadside.

Harry looked back at the school. The cleaners were still there. If he had to run for it, which door would be unlocked?

A noisy car sped down the road and crunched to a halt at the gates. It was Akku's mother in her old white Fiesta. His dad was a consultant at the infirmary and they had a BMW. His mum, who worked part time at the library, used the Fiesta as a runabout.

She wound down the window. "Sorry I'm late, love, Auntie Doe's not well again. How'd the practice go?"

"Good." Akku started towards the car.

"Hello, Harry." She gave her big smile. "Akku's still mad with me I kept him in last Sunday."

Harry liked Mrs Apiliga. She was nice and she was beautiful.

She liked Harry, too, and saw that something was wrong. "What's up, darlin'?" She opened the door and got out.

"It's that Range Rover." Akku took his mother's arm. "Harry reckons it's the same people set fire to the house an' took his bike."

"That nasty Miss McScrew?"

"No, it's the other woman's car." Harry joined them. "And Auntie Florrie's not come."

Mrs Apiliga pursed her lips. "First things first. Let's see who's in it. Frightening boys like that. You two stay here."

She wore a smart linen jacket and multicoloured trousers. With brisk steps she clip-clopped across the road. Before she was halfway there the engine coughed into life and the Range Rover pulled out from the kerb. She stepped aside to let it pass.

Harry stared at the windows but could see nothing beyond the shiny black glass.

Mrs Apiliga returned and they watched it draw away up the road. "What a horrible car," she said. "Makes me think of a hearse."

"Did you see the number plate, Mum?" Akku said. "RIP, like on a gravestone."

"It's her initials," Harry explained. "Ruby Innocente Palazzo. She's Italian."

"Is that right?" She put an arm round his shoulders and Harry smelled her spring-like perfume. "Well, if I had a name like that, I know I wouldn't be putting my initials on the car, would you?"

He shook his head. "Have you got a mobile?"

"Not with me, darlin'. But don't you worry, we'll stay until your auntie arrives. Or come on home with Akku and we'll phone from there. Stay for your dinner."

"Thanks very much, Mrs Apiliga. Would it be—"

The throaty roar of a motorbike distracted him. Hidden by hedges, it came speeding down the road towards them. Harry recognized the engine note and ran to the kerb. A few seconds later Auntie Florrie on her blue Norton *Commando* pulled in beside the Fiesta.

"You're all right! Thank goodness! What a time we've had." She switched off, pulled off the helmet and goggles and shook her curls free. "Somebody slashed the Merc's tyres. Mr Tolly was going to pick you up because I was getting my roots done. What do you think?" She turned her head to catch the sun. "I got her to give me a honey rinse."

"Your hair looks very nice." Mrs Apiliga's own hair, not unlike her son's, was a neat West Indian frizz.

"I think she's made a good job. Mind you, what it looks like after being stuck under this helmet I've no idea. Anyway, there they all were, no car. Nothing anyone could do till the bus dropped me off. We reckon those witches up there at Felon Grange are behind it. Getting their own back."

Mrs Apiliga told her about the Range Rover.

"It was just sitting there," Harry said. "Waiting."

"Until you were alone," said Auntie Florrie. "Oh, my goodness! That's why they nobbled the Merc. So you'd be left standing after everybody else had gone home."

"They must have been watching," Harry said. "Planning it. How'd they know we've got rugby on a Thursday?"

"We don't think it was Ruby and Lil did the job on the car," Auntie Florrie said. "No one saw them, anyway, but Nutty spotted a man at the bottom of the drive. Said it looked like that GBH. You remember, that Neanderthal used to work for Priestly. Called after him but he vanished into the trees."

They were scary thoughts: spying on them; hanging around in the Lagg Hall woods. Was the Priestly‾ gang coming together again?

"You should go to the police," said Mrs Apiliga, who had visited Lagg Hall and liked Harry's extended family.

"Yes, well, we have spoken to them." Auntie Florrie limited herself to the half truth. "They were out at the house after the fire. What we need to do now, I think, is take extra care and get another car. It's ridiculous, just the one old Merc for eleven of us."

The Apiligas drove off.

Harry donned the spare helmet, clipped his schoolbag to the carrier, and sat pillion behind Auntie Florrie. She kicked the starter. The gorgeous 750cc Norton throbbed into life.

"I told Goody we might go to *Da Vinci's* over at Cherryford for an ice cream." She shouted over her shoulder. "Or do you want to go straight home?"

"What a silly question." Harry shuffled himself comfortable and rested his hands on her waist.

"Let's go the back road through the hills. Blow some cobwebs away."

"Great!" The helmets were old-fashioned. Harry's was black with a stencilled gold wing above each ear. The goggles made him look like an early aviator.

Forty years earlier, when Auntie Florrie's face had adorned the cover of *Time*, *Paris Match* and a hundred other magazines, they had dubbed her the Flying Fox. Her glamour and daring had made her the darling of the racing circuits. With Harry on the back she took no risks. All the same, the woods and fields flashed past, bends rushed to meet them, the engine roared, the road bucked, a bee hit his lip so hard that if his mouth had been open – sometimes Harry had rude thoughts – it would have shot straight through and out the other end.

The sinister car was forgotten, and by the time they drew up at *Da Vinci's*, twelve minutes and ten miles of twisting roads later, his cheeks were aflame with the rush of the wind.

Chapter 9

Eddie Carver

The cafe stood in a cobbled yard at the edge of the village. It had once been a smithy. Three sides were old stone buildings, the fourth opened on to a lake with swans and ducks which nested in the reeds and came looking for scraps. It was a popular spot. Tables stood beneath parasols and overhanging branches. Passers-by knew better than to incur Mr da Vinci's wrath by dropping litter; chaffinches twitched their tails and didn't care.

With a final VROOM-VROOM Auntie Florrie switched off the ignition. She swung her leg across, flipped down the stand and pulled off her helmet. A group of teenagers, drawn like magnets to the *Commando* and expecting a tough biker with four days' stubble, stared in astonishment. Auntie Florrie wore her customary make-up: blusher, mascara, baby-blue eyeshadow and an abundance of cheerful lipstick. She would have felt naked visiting *Da Vinci's* without it. Her honey-yellow curls were crushed again. She drew a hairbrush and attacked them vigorously. The local youths stood watching. They were an alarming-looking group with studs and tattoos. Auntie Florrie gave a cheery wave:

"Hello, boys. Don't bother to ask. Yes it is. Yes I am. No you can't. If you touch it I'll kill you."

She turned to Harry. "They do the most fabulous ice creams you ever tasted."

"I know."

"Of course you do. My favourite's a 'Die Happy': fresh strawberries, three kinds of ice cream, maple syrup, roast pistachios, butterscotch topping, double flake and an umbrella. Give it a try?"

"Great! Thanks!"

"Then we'll do a bank job to pay for it." She went inside to place the order. Harry pulled off his anorak and flopped on a bench.

The teenagers gathered round the *Commando*, whispering and pointing.

"Fabulous bike, Gran," one called amiably as she emerged from the cafe in flapping leathers.

"Gran! I'll gran you," she shouted back cheerily. "Cheeky young ha'porth."

Soon, with spoons half as long as their arms, Harry and Auntie Florrie were tucking into the biggest ice creams he had seen in his life.

"Good, aren't they."

Harry was concentrating. "Fantastic," he agreed a few spoonfuls later.

She burrowed for a strawberry. "I think we've *got* to get another car. What do you fancy?"

"A Lotus."

"Good for getaways but too flashy. We need something that merges in."

"With a souped-up engine."

"Not too important. Nutty'll take care of that."

"Or what about a minibus? Keep the Merc for jobs."

"A minibus! And look like some old-folks' outing? I'd rather die! Why not a fleet of wheelchairs and be done with it. We'll move to Eastbourne."

Harry laughed.

"Some help you are: a Lotus or a minibus!"

Too soon the glasses were three-quarters empty. Harry sighed happily. "I was thinking," he said. "You know that bit you were reading from the *Telegraph* this morning?"

She shook her head.

"About D'Artagnan somebody. A gangster. Got shot."

"Oh, Dart Jones. Yes. Why?"

"Seemed like it was a big deal. I just wondered why."

"Well it is, darling, of course. He's – or he was – Eddie Jones's brother."

Harry was lost.

"Eddie 'Carver' Jones. We must have told you about Eddie Carver."

"No."

"But he was the one murdered Tony Palazzo, Ruby's second husband."

"I've never heard of him."

"We told you about it the other afternoon."

"Not Eddie Carver."

"Are you sure?"

"The last I heard, Priestly's father had died in the witness box. Ruby came back from Italy and threw his girlfriend out the house."

"And we never told you what happened after that?"

"Nope." The dregs of the ice cream were unbearably delicious.

"Oh, well, better bring you up to date. This was years ago remember. So here's Ruby in that big house in Epsom with her lapdog husband and the horrible ginger eighteen-year-old son she hasn't seen since he was younger than you. Doesn't fancy staying in cold, wet Britain, she's got her Mafia life back in Italy. So she sells up – house, betting shops, racehorses, the lot – and goes back to Naples, taking Percy with her. And that's the last we heard of him for ages. Nobody knows about that part of his life except he grew up the way you'd expect, nasty, dishonest and really quite dangerous. Bits about the others appeared in the papers from time to time, and of course we got news from pals: Ruby and Tony got married; one of the Notriannis ended up in the river; protection rackets; shoot-out in a casino; race fixing; usual Mafia stuff. But Percy dropped out of sight completely. Everyone forgot about him until suddenly, in his mid-thirties, up he popped again, calling himself *Colonel* Priestly now and setting himself up as an English gent."

"He's not a colonel though?"

"Course not. Pompous little pouter-pigeon like that? Private in the Catering Corps is about his level. Not a gentleman either. But he certainly had plenty of money. Bought a nice house in St John's Wood, got to know a few businessmen, became a patron of the arts, gave donations to popular charities, went to all the big race meetings. Oh, a regular good egg was Percy Priestly. Everybody loved him – except a few people like us who knew what the rest didn't."

"That he was really a *bad* egg."

"Exactly, Harry. Not even like the curate's egg, good in parts. And it didn't take him long, with *his* genes and criminal background, to get in touch with the London low-life. Not just London either: Liverpool, Glasgow, Newcastle. He wasn't a thug, of course, he hadn't the build for it, didn't carry a shooter. No, what he was good at was shady deals: backhanders for contracts, funny money, bad cement, that sort of thing. If a tower block fell down it wasn't Percy Priestly's fault.

"Then people like Eddie Carver realized what a godsend he could be in a magistrate's chair; sort out a few little problems when they came to the attention of the police. With Priestly's connections it didn't take long to organize. So there he sat, Mr High and Mighty, Rotten to the Core, letting villains off with a caution and sending poor kids that knocked off a Mars bar to the gulag for two years."

Harry's glass was as clean as his tongue could make it.

"I fancy a coffee." Auntie Florrie passed over a five-pound note. "You get it, would you, love? And whatever you want for yourself."

He chose a blackcurrant slush.

"So is that what Beastly Priestly was doing when he came to Felon Grange?"

"Well, he was a magistrate, as you know. Sent you off to that nasty Hobnail character at Grimthrash Jail, didn't he? But we've not reached that point yet. At the start he worked with a lot of gangs. I don't suppose you'll know their names: the Stepney Steelfitters, Ice Pick Charlie, Nancy the Tooth, the Bristol Butchers?"

The slush made Harry's teeth ache. He shook his head.

"Well you wouldn't. But the one he worked with most was Eddie Carver's Mob. They ruled west London, out past Richmond to Windsor and Henley. Rich pickings. Millionaire's alley. And they were ruthless, he wasn't called

Carver for nothing. After a while Priestly found himself working for them and nobody else. Eddie ran the mob and Percy oiled the wheels. Suited them both fine. Eddie wasn't going to be invited into the homes of the rich and famous, not with his manners and background. So Percy went instead and passed on the inside knowledge: where the safe was, where the wife kept her jewellery, what paintings were worth taking, details of the security system. If one of the gang came to the attention of Scotland Yard, he knew what palms to grease. And when Eddie had turned over some rich guy's pad and needed a fence to sell on the proceeds, who more natural than his old pal Percy. He had the know-how, the contacts, the Italian connection. And for a long time it worked like a charm. Who was going to question such a pillar of the community and friend of the famous as Percival Bonaparte Priestly, OBE? It's rumoured they even wanted him for *This Is Your Life* but somebody put the mockers on it."

"It would have been quite funny," Harry said. "All these gangsters coming on." He put on a hoodlum voice: "Yuh, remember that time we machine-gunned the Antonio mob? Splattered 'em all over the garage wall? Right giggle, weren't it, Perce? You're a great guy, been a privilege knowin' ya."

Auntie Florrie laughed. "But the good times couldn't last for ever. Word went round. Percy blabbed to his mother, Mad Ruby. She's Mrs Tony Palazzo now, of course, and the Palazzos are up to their oily eyebrows in Mafia business, cocks of all that southern part of Italy. So Tony thinks, why not spread their wings a little? Here's his stepson doing well in England, mingling with the big boys round London. Shouldn't be too big a problem for the family to move in and nudge Eddie and his cronies aside.

"That's what he thought anyway. Ruby and the others tried to talk some sense into him but Tony's set on it. Never been quite up there at the family's top table so maybe he wants to use this to prove himself." Auntie Florrie sipped her coffee. "He didn't last five minutes."

"Five minutes?"

"Don't be so literal. He didn't last a month anyway. Eddie's ten times the villain Tony Palazzo ever was. Pretty soon he hears about this little bantam strutting around in his patch, talking big, meeting people he'd got no business to meet. So Eddie calls to see him, have a chat. Gives Tony the big smile. Tells him, 'Sure, good to see you. Maybe we can do each other a favour. Come over for dinner Tuesday. Bring your wife.'

"Ruby's not there, of course, she stayed home in Italy. And Tony's so wrapped up in his own plans, so used to the family's protection, so confident in the piece tucked into the back of his belt, so completely taken in by Eddie's charm, so stupid, he doesn't see the danger. So he drives over to Eddie's house and Eddie takes him on to ye olde English *Duke of Clarence* tavern which he owns. Only they never got there. Instead he takes Tony to a chicken farm in which he also has an interest. And it turns out they've been making preparations for Tony's arrival.

"Eddie wastes no time, he's got a proper dinner engagement that night. So there he is all dressed up in his thousand-dollar suit and all his gold and everything—"

"His gold?"

"Oh, yes, famous for their gold, Eddie and Dart: rings, earrings, neck chains, bracelets, you name it. Even had a couple of gold teeth. Anyway, soon's they get out the car one of his sidekicks relieves Tony of his snubby. 'You're a fool!' Eddie tells him. 'Cosa Nostra – don't make me laugh! Do you seriously think, in your wildest dreams, I'd share my patch with a witless article like you? Just because the Palazzos are some brain-dead Mafia outfit down there in the Italian sticks, do you think you can muscle in here? You must be off your head. Anyway, this is what happens to people who get up *my* nose. I hope you like eggs!' And he picks him up and jams him headfirst into a barrel full of them."

"Eggs!" Harry was horrified. "Did he die?"

"Course he died. It was Eddie's little trademark – one of them anyway. That's why some people called him *Eggy* 'stead of Eddie."

"Eggy Jones," Harry said.

"Or Carver. That was his signature, if you like. Cut a big E into his victim's chest before he dumped the body. Always did that. Cops didn't know who it was but we did. A warning to anyone else who might start sniffing around."

"Eddie Carver," Harry said.

"A bit grim."

"But how do you know all this? It couldn't have been in the papers. The murder, maybe, but not what he said and everything."

"Uncle Aziz told us. He was there."

"Who's Uncle Aziz?"

"Oh, a friend from the old days. Used to be Eddie's accountant. Fiddled the books. He's nice. Lives in a sort of fortress now, very modern. Maybe you'll meet him sometime."

Harry sucked out the last of his flavour. The slush turned white, his mouth was purple.

"It was one murder too many." Auntie Florrie regarded a chaffinch that had landed on the table. "This time Eddie didn't get away with it. Word leaked out – maybe Ruby and the Palazzos had something to do with it. And the fuzz found Tony's body."

"Where?" Harry said.

"In a freezer lorry heading for the continent if you must know."

"A freezer lorry!"

"In there with the mutton and sides of beef. Heading for some canning factory Eddie had an interest in."

"Gosh! Tinned Tony! Tony bolognese!"

"What a gruesome child you are!"

"Did it lead to a vendetta?"

"No, Eddie was arrested. Huge court case. Front pages for a fortnight. Then the jury got nobbled and he had to be tried all over again."

"What was the verdict?"

"What do you think? Premeditated murder, had to be life. Packed him off to Cony Hill."

"That's where Priestly is!" Harry's stomach gurgled. "It doesn't sound like a prison, does it? More like some place you'd go for a picnic."

"No picnic there, I can tell you. Used to be out in the country, mind. Victorians thought the clean air and moors would have a healing effect, make villains into better men. Didn't, of course. The prisoners had their own name for it – Stony Hell. Just about right, too. And now the city's grown around it. Place is a nightmare. Black walls and iron bars." She shivered.

"Have you been there?" Harry said.

"I beg your pardon?" A sip of coffee went the wrong way. "The answer's no, it's a men's prison. Angel has, though, and Fingers. I've visited."

"So that's the end of Eddie Carver."

"I never said that."

"But if he's in Cony Hill Prison for life. . ."

Auntie Florrie took out a mirror. After the ice cream and coffee her lipstick needed refreshing. "Life doesn't mean till you pop your clogs. Not usually anyway. It means fourteen years or so with time off for good behaviour. Besides, Eddie might have ended up in the gulag but the rest of the gang hadn't. So he ran things from the inside. Slipped the guards a few quid, got privileges, nice telly, big cell with south-facing windows. Set up a whole network."

"D'you mean the robberies and that went on?"

"Certainly they did. Listen, when we got Priestly put away last New Year, that loot we found hidden in Felon Grange, where did it come from?"

"Marsh House," Harry said.

"And who do you think did the Marsh House job?"

"Eddie Carver?"

"Well, not him personally but the gang, yes. He organized it."

Harry thought about it.

"And Percy might have been his fence," Auntie Florrie went on, "but he didn't look after the money after the loot had been sold on. Absolutely not. Would you trust him? No, Eddie's brother took charge of the dosh. Stashed it away somewhere safe, somewhere no one can get their grubby little hands on it."

"Where?" Harry said.

"Ah, the million-dollar question. Where?"

"Don't you know?"

"If only! Nobody knows, Harry."

"But couldn't somebody follow him?"

"Lots of people have tried it. Guess where they ended up."

"The chicken farm?"

"Right in one. I wouldn't risk it, would you?"

"Drowning in eggs!" He made a face. "I don't think so. But if Eddie's brother keeps going back to – wherever it is – there must be some way of—"

"But his brother won't be going back, will he? Everything's changed."

"How do you mean?"

"Oh, Harry, do pay attention. It's what you were asking about. He's dead. Somebody just shot him."

"Dart Jones!"

"Give the boy a coconut."

A fly bit Harry's neck. He slapped it sharply. "But Eddie knows where it is."

"Of course, but Eddie's in Cony Hill, isn't he. He can't just nip out and get it. And who's he going to trust with that juicy little bit of information? And what I haven't told you, he's a sick man."

"What do you mean, how sick?"

"Not long to go by the sound of it. All those years of forty a day catching up with him."

"But *somebody* must know where the money is."

"Who?"

"I don't know."

"Nor does anybody else. Only Eddie – and Eddie's on the way out. Interesting, don't you think? There'll be a lot of criminal minds exercising themselves about that today. Not least two ladies who live not a thousand miles away from Felon Grange."

"Mad Ruby and Gestapo Lil," Harry said.

"Especially Ruby, I should think, given the circumstances."

"Will it be much? I mean, is it a fortune?"

"You'd have to ask him that. How much might a gang boss like Eddie Jones salt away in the course of his wicked life? We were talking about it today. Five million? Ten million?"

"Ten million!"

"Maybe more, who knows. And only Eddie knows where it's stashed."

"Stashed! D'you mean it's just lying somewhere?"

"Well I shouldn't think it's just lying, no. But hidden, yes. Very well hidden, I should think. He never trusted banks: banks mean questions, banks mean taxes, banks can be broken into. So what Eddie and Dart did, they just packed the car and melted away out of sight. When they came back – the bread was gone."

"What will it be like? Suitcases full of hundred-pound notes?"

"Some, maybe, but mostly jewellery, gold, sparklers, that sort of thing. Some very nice pieces from what they say. Which brings us back to today. Dart's been bumped off and Eddie's dying in jail. So what's he going to do with it all? Let it moulder away, just fall back into the earth? His whole life nothing but a violent waste of time? Or tell somebody? And who's he got to talk to from the old days? Who's there in Cony Hill with the famous Carver?"

Harry gasped. "Percy Priestly!"

Auntie Florrie dropped the lipstick into her pocket. "Don't want him, or Gestapo Lil and Mad Ruby, to get their nasty little hands on it, do we."

"No."

"So maybe we've got just a little idea of our own." Her blue eyes sparkled. "Come on, let's go home."

Chapter 10
Scares, Schemes and Saturday

On Saturday Barleymow Juniors played rugby in their gold and scarlet strips and won 33–17. Charlie and Akku both scored tries and Harry converted so it was a happy morning, especially with Dot and Fingers leaping up and down on the sidelines. "Garn, ref," they screamed as any decision was given against Barleymow. "Get yersel' to the eye hospital!" And then, "Foul! Foul! Did you see that! Send 'im off!" When Mr Foggarty, the headmaster, tried to restrain Dot from running on to the pitch, she knocked him down with her handbag.

"Brilliant!" she said as the boys emerged from the school, wet-haired after a shower.

"Well done, lads!" Fingers nipped out the stub of his cigarette. "I couldn't have done better meself. Here," he rooted in the pocket of his saggy brown trousers and extracted three pound coins. "Get yersel's some sweeties."

So they did and piled into the back of the old Merc. Akku and Charlie were spending the day at Lagg Hall. Charlie had perfected a trick with sherbet and blew yellow bubbles down his nose.

Fingers was a careful driver, rarely exceeding forty. Dot

seldom drove, she had difficulty seeing through the steering wheel. The hedges and fields of sturdy lambs slid past and in twenty minutes they turned into the potholed drive.

Fingers stopped the car. "Right, out you get."

Harry was surprised. "What for?"

"You'll see."

They did as they were told and the Mercedes drove on.

The boys looked around. Nothing seemed to have changed. The drive corkscrewed through the Lagg Hall woods. Akku and Charlie turned to Harry. He shrugged and they walked on together.

A commotion disturbed the familiar twittering and cawing in the trees. Tangle was barking and there was a jabbering, honking sound. People were laughing. They broke into a run.

The trees gave way to lawns and a gravel forecourt. Beyond lay the splendid yellow sandstone house with a red roof that was Lagg Hall. At one end stood Harry's tower, at the other the Victorian conservatory.

At that moment, however, the boys had no eyes for the house. Tangle stood on the lawn, his forepaws planted, barking and barking at five geese which had invaded his territory. Two were farmyard geese, pure white with button eyes and orange bills; three were speckled greylags. Completely unafraid, they confronted him, cackling and honking. A greylag decided to see him off. Neck outstretched and wings beating furiously, it charged. It was an alarming sight. Tangle waited as long as he dared then turned tail and fled to the gravel.

"Tangle! Tangle!" Harry ran to give his pet support. "You see 'em off. Good boy."

Emboldened by his presence, Tangle ran forward a few

paces, bristling and barking his challenge. The goose was unimpressed and walked up and down the edge of the lawn regarding him sideways as if marking out its territory. Another joined it. The rest stood watching. Then one lowered its head and pecked at a few blades of grass.

"What are they doing here?" Harry turned to a small group by the house.

Nutty detached himself. "Watchdogs," he said. "Give 'em a few days to settle down, get to know us, like. No stranger'll get near the place without them kicking up an 'ell of a racket." He crouched to Tangle who adored him. "I know, hinny. They've got no right to be here, have they? This is your patch. Never mind, ye'll soon get used to them."

"Won't they fly away?" Harry said.

"The speckly ones if they want – but they'll not. We'll feed 'em, they've got plenty o' grass, lake in the woods, what more could they want?" He looked up. "Ah, see who's comin' to join us."

Unnoticed by Harry, Morgan had been watching the action from a nearby branch. In a vivid flash of green and scarlet he sailed down and settled on his young master's shoulder.

"Hello, Morgan." Harry looked sideways and brushed his cheek against the soft feathers.

"Rat-face." The parrot nibbled his ear affectionately.

"What d'you make of all this then?" Nutty stroked Morgan's chest with the back of his forefinger. Apart from Harry, he was the only one Morgan allowed this intimacy. He turned his attention to Nutty's horny fingernail.

"'Allo, sweetheart," he croaked. "Aak! Give us a kiss."

Nutty laughed and wandered off.

Charlie and Akku were throwing bread to the geese. They loved their visits to Lagg Hall. Everyone was sparky, there was always lots going on. Charlie joined Harry and looked the parrot in the face.

"Hello, there."

Morgan regarded him with a beady eye.

"Who's a pretty boy?" Charlie examined the bright feathers.

"Be careful," Harry said.

"I know. Can I get some peanuts?"

"You know where."

Charlie ran to Nutty's workshop and was soon back.

"What's this then?" He held out a peanut shell. Morgan stretched forward, so far he almost toppled. Charlie teased him and twitched it back. "Come on." He held it close again. "Ooh, lovely peanut." A second time Morgan reached out; a second time Charlie pulled it away. Voices on the lawn distracted his attention. For a second his hand strayed too close. It was enough. Morgan struck like lightning and bit a piece out of his thumb.

"Aah! Aah!" Charlie snatched back his hand and examined the damage. Blood welled out, vivid as Morgan's red patch, and dripped to the pebbles.

Morgan trod from claw to claw on Harry's shoulder. "Piss-pot," he croaked happily. "Aak! Hello sailor."

Charlie was patched up and then it was lunchtime. They ate in the kitchen. Goody gave them fried egg, sausages and chips, home-made raspberry cheesecake with cream, and a KitKat to take from the table. After that they were free to roam.

"Back at four, mind," she told them. "Tea in the conservatory. And keep your eyes open, just in case. Stay together."

They ran off and for three hours had a brilliant time. The acres of Lagg Hall were made for games. The geese chased them on the lawn. They climbed trees and rowed on the lake. Akku took off his clothes and swam from the shore. After long hesitation, shouting at the cold, Harry and Charlie joined him. They visited the pasture and rode Chalky, the friendly white stallion, and his inseparable friend Socrates, the thoughtful donkey.

"Who's that?" Charlie pointed as they sat on the pasture gate.

A man had appeared at the edge of the wood.

"I don't know."

Harry collected a stick from the hedge. Akku and Charlie did likewise. The armed boys emerged from the trees.

"Can I help you?" Harry said.

"I am not sure, perhaps you can." He was an elderly man, brown-skinned and clean-shaven except for a thin grey beard. From head to foot he was dressed in black. A long coat trailed to his ankles, a broad-brimmed hat sat low on his brow. Grey hair, wispy as the beard, hung to his collar. "Is this house called *The Hermitage*?"

"It was a long time ago," Harry said.

"Ah! You see, I'm looking for a lady I corresponded with – oh, before you boys were born." He had a throaty, mid-European accent.

"What's her name?"

"Bridget Barton."

"Yes, she lives here. She's my aunt."

"I wonder," he stared at Harry with intense, black eyes. "Could you direct me to her – or tell her that I am here?"

Harry gripped his stick tightly. "Who shall I say it is?"

"My name is Cula. Doctor Anatole Cula from Hungary. She will know who I am."

"We'll go and look for her."

"Tell her," Doctor Cula gripped his arm, "I would be pleased to stay for dinner."

"Right, I'll just—"

"A little beef would be delicious. Lightly cooked, you understand. Very lightly cooked. Better still, not cooked at all. Nice and bloody."

The boys stared.

"And give her this." He produced something from his pocket and pressed it into Harry's hand. "In my country it means long life."

Harry looked down. It was a dead bat.

Doctor Cula's eyes gleamed. "Three such lovely boysss!" His lips – for the first time Harry saw how red they were – parted in a smile. His teeth also were red – white and red. In fact, they were not human teeth at all, they were vampire fangs.

With shrieks of fright Harry, Akku and Charlie fled to the house and slammed the door behind them.

"I'm sorry," Max said as they sat in the conservatory. "But when I found the dead bat I couldn't resist it. I hope you weren't too frightened."

"Course not," Akku said. "I knew it was you all the time."

Charlie slurped his tea. "Oh, no you didn't. You were shaking worse than any of us."

"Just so long as none of you have nightmares," Mrs Good said. "You should have more sense, Max. They're only eleven."

"Oh, I know. But I've said I'm sorry and they're tough guys. What about all those horror films and grisly computer games they play?"

They had pulled off their jerseys. Sunshine streamed through the foliage. Max's wig and Dracula fangs lay on the table beside his tea-plate.

"Anyway, I'm an actor, I have to keep my hand in." He removed black contact lenses with the tip of a finger. "Did you really recognize me, Akku?"

Akku bit into a jam doughnut and shook his head.

"Harry?"

"Nope. It was a Max Beauguss special."

"That's a relief." Comically he raised his eyebrows.

"Doctor Anatole Cula!" Mrs Good said. "Honestly, Max, you're impossible!"

Since the formation of the Wrinklies, Max had adopted many disguises. He was brilliant and it was fun, but when he was working Max lived on the edge. His impersonation of Count Dracula had been more than a game. A big job was coming up, a job where he would be under scrutiny for twenty-four hours a day. He needed to be on top of his form.

Harry knew better than to ask and was saved from speculation by the arrival of a gleaming, powder-blue Rover on the forecourt. Beyond the tomatoes and grape stems he saw Auntie Florrie at the wheel and Nutty climbing from the passenger seat.

"The new car!" He ran to the door.

"It's not going to vanish." Mrs Good called him back. "You can go out and see it when you've finished your tea."

"I've finished," he said.

"No you haven't, you're still eating and your cup's half full. Besides, Charlie's in the middle of his cake. He doesn't bolt his food like certain people. You can't leave the table till your guests have finished. So come back and sit down."

"Doesn't bolt his food!" Harry did as he was told. "That's his third slice. *And* he's had two millionaire's shortbreads and two—"

"Harry Barton, how dare you! Counting what other people have eaten! Sorry, Charlie, darling. You're welcome to everything on this table. Stick in till ye stick oot, as my granny used to say. Really, Harry, I never heard the like! And Max, would you take those teeth off the table, they're putting me off my food."

Charlie's face was red; so was Harry's; so was Mrs Good's. Max, like Harry, did as he was told.

It was soon forgotten. Charlie's cake was bolted, Harry's tea gulped, Akku's fingers sucked clean.

"Thanks very much, Mrs Good," Akku and Charlie said.

"Thanks, Goody." Harry smiled guiltily.

"Off you go," she said affectionately and they tumbled out to examine the Rover.

It was very smart, pale-blue leather upholstery to match the exterior, a walnut dashboard, vehicle guiding system. Nutty took them a run round the lanes.

"Aye, a good strong body," he said. "Canny engine. Nice handlin'. Just what the doctor ordered."

Harry loved it and hoped Nutty would leave it the way it was, at least for a while. Later, undoubtedly, he would go to work on it, reducing the body and seats to a forgettable dusty grey, boosting the engine until it had the acceleration of a Formula One, which Auntie Florrie needed for fast getaways.

It was a pity, but the Wrinklies required more of a new car than beautiful bodywork.

Afterwards they visited the animals in Nutty's hospital and went to Harry's bedroom in the attic to play. Dinner was at seven – fresh fish in breadcrumbs followed by trifle with enough sherry in it to make your hair stand on end – and at eight Akku's and Charlie's parents came for drinks.

At ten the two families departed. For the first time the geese performed their duty as watchdogs, honking loudly enough to wake Doctor Cula in his cobwebby gloom.

Aunt Bridget rested her hand on Harry's shoulder as the lights vanished down the drive. "Did you have a good day?"

"Brilliant."

"They're nice boys. Nice parents too. Mr Donkin's so funny. Must be all that red hair."

"He's a crane driver."

"I know. That story of how he demolished a police station by mistake!"

"He supports Man United."

"Well, nobody's perfect. Let's hope it's not catching." She gazed at the setting moon. "I love this house."

"Lucky the fire didn't take hold."

"I can't bear to think about it." A cement mixer, scaffolding and other builders' materials stood on the gravel. "Another couple of days and we'll be able to move back into the lounge."

"What about the tower?"

"Oh, I meant to tell you. Can't do the door for another five weeks. I've insisted on seasoned oak and hand-made nails. Sorry."

"That's OK. I like it in the attic."

Aunt Bridget was tall. She looked down and rumpled his hair. "Come on into the living room, we've got to have a powwow."

Harry collapsed into a velvet armchair and amused himself by drawing patterns in the nap until the rest arrived.

Aunt Bridget did a head count. "I think we're all here." She stood by the sideboard. "Won't keep you long, darlings. Just this business of Dart Jones getting himself bumped off. And Priestly in jail with the fragrant Eddie."

"Who, as ve all know, may not be long for this vorld."

"Precisely, Huggy."

"Who knows what the pair o' them might be talkin' about," Fingers said.

"And I think you'll all agree," Aunt Bridget went on, "that if *we* can get our hands on Eddie's treasure, it would be much better than a couple of sleazeballs like Percy P and his nasty fiancée."

"Gestapo Lil," Harry said.

"Not forgetting Mad Ruby," Dot contributed. "*And* GBH. The whole rotten lot."

"That's right. Now, I'm sure you all know the situation," Aunt Bridget said, "but what some of you may *not* know is that Max, quite heroically in my view, has volunteered to go back inside. We need to know what's happening."

"Back into Cony Hill?" Angel was appalled. "Are ye out o' yer mind? It's a hellhole."

"We've all done it before." Max had rid himself of Dracula's make-up and was elegant in a cashmere jersey and navy trousers. Every inch the actor, he brushed a fleck from his knee. "I don't intend to be there for more than a few days. I'll survive. You can stand me a champagne supper when I come out."

"*If* ye come out, more like," Angel said. "But will it no' bring us to the attention o' the fuzz? After yon visit the other night, yon sergeant. One o' us back to his auld tricks."

"Oh, I'm not going back as *me*," Max said. "No, no, that *would* be a bit reckless. At the minute I'm planning to go as Okky Daintry. After that little run-through as the Count this afternoon, I think I can get away with it."

"Who's Okky Daintry?" Harry asked.

"A tramp," said Aunt Bridget.

"You never met him?" Auntie Florrie was surprised.

"No."

"Must have been before you came." She explained. "He's quite a famous character really. Old clothes and bits of string. Enough hair to stuff a mattress. Turns up here from time to time, camps in the wood."

"Got form," Mr Tolly said.

"Not 'alf." Fingers massaged one of his stumps. "In an' out the gulag like a flippin' yo-yo. Land's End to John o' Groats, you ask any o' the fuzz, beaks, screws, who Okky Daintry is, they'll tell you."

"Nothing nasty though," Aunt Bridget said.

"Nah, wouldn't hurt a fly, Okky. Goes in for an 'oliday, he says. When the weather gets a bit cold-like or 'e feels a bit run-down. In the gulag he's warm, well fed, gets 'ospital treatment, new clothes, builds his-sel' up for the months ahead."

"Which is all very interesting," Aunt Bridget said drily, "but I think we're wandering from the point, *as usual*."

"Just one thing." Mr Tolly was puzzled. "Why Okky, Max?"

"Like you said," Max crossed an immaculate knee, "he's got form, no fixed abode, who's to know? He'd not mind, we'll make it up to him when he comes back. All that hair, shouldn't be too difficult." His face changed, his mouth fell open in a leer: "'Lo, missis. Bladdy cold 'aday." He sniffed and sucked spit from his teeth. "Cor, I'm sweatin'. Any chanst o' a sambwidge? Bitta jamb?" Sniff. "Gor bless yer, missis. Jus' like my ol' mum. Straight up." He scratched an armpit.

Harry could almost smell him.

"Max," Mr Tolly hung an arm round his neck. "I am breathless with admiration. It's brilliant."

"Thank you." Max smiled. "It's nice to be appreciated. But then, we're all brilliant in our own little ways."

"So we are," said Aunt Bridget. "But you," she pointed, "should be back on the stage."

"How often ve tell him?" Huggy shrugged. "He never listen."

"I'm very happy here, thank you," Max said. "I don't tell you to leap back into a wrestling ring, do I? I don't tell Bridget to go back to Oxford."

"Neither you do," said Aunt Bridget. "The theatre's loss is our gain. I can't wait to see the new Okky Daintry. How long till you're ready, Max?"

"A couple of days?" he said. "Need to get a move on. Monday maybe?"

"Excellent." Aunt Bridget polished a smudge from her glasses. "Now the other matter, that bank job we've been thinking about for some time."

"The Western Standard here in town," Dot said. "The night of the Summer Fair."

"'Bout time we turned that place over," Fingers said crossly. "Flippin' manager keeps lookin' at me like I'm a thief or somethin'."

110

"Vell, darling," Huggy said gently. "Perhaps he have a point, no?"

"It's me pension! Blimey, 'f a bloke can't cash his pension without 'e gets the ol' third degree, thumbscrews, lights in the eyes—"

Sometimes Aunt Bridget despaired. "If we could concentrate for one minute," she said, "I was about to say that I think we should put the bank job on hold for a while. I know you're all looking forward to it, and it's going to be an absolute sensation, but with this business of Eddie Carver suddenly coming up, I think we should focus our attention on that."

There were cries of disappointment: "Ah, no! . . . Come on! . . . I've got the nitro! . . . It'll be fun!"

"I know, I know. And we *will* do it, I promise. But who knows what information Max is going to pick up, or where it will lead. And we've got to have a clear run. If we start trying to do two things at once somebody might end up in chokey again – for real, not like Max – and I just couldn't bear it."

The grumbles subsided.

"Do you think we have a chance, Aunt Bridget?" Harry said. "Of getting his treasure, I mean."

"I don't know about *we*," she said, "but yes, as much as anybody else. More, maybe. And one thing I do know, if we succeed it'll be worth ten times what we'd get from the Western Standard Bank."

"Megabucks," Fingers said.

"Absolutely right. Millions."

"Enough for the Africa project?" said Mrs Good, who sat repairing a pair of Harry's jeans.

"Yes, I hope so, Goody."

"What's the Africa project?" Harry asked.

"Surely you've heard about that," said Auntie Florrie.

He shook his head.

"Goodness, it's one of our biggest schemes." She kicked off her shoes and curled her legs beneath her in the horrible corduroy armchair. "We always planned, if we got a really big haul, to build a hospital for some of the village people in central Africa."

"And wells for clean water," Dot said.

"And a school," said Aunt Bridget.

"You can see what it's like on TV." Mrs Good looked up. "Poor souls, they've got nothing."

"So we thought we'd like to do our little bit to help," said Auntie Florrie.

"But it's not just building these places," said Aunt Bridget, "that's the easiest part in a way. We have to keep them running: a doctor, nurses, teachers, schoolbooks. So we need a really *big* haul for that."

"Like Eddie Carver," Harry said.

"With any luck." She looked at him over her granny glasses. "It would be nice, wouldn't it."

Harry tried to picture it. "Yes," he said.

Chapter 11

Okky in the Gulag

"What's that smell?"

Harry was eating his morning muesli. He looked up from the *Telegraph* sports pages.

"What smell?" Mrs Good wrinkled her nose. "The toast?"

"No, something dirty, like—"

She joined him. "Oh, you're right." She looked around her clean kitchen. "What is it?"

"Mornin', missis!" An appalling figure stood in the doorway. "Any chanst 'f a cuppa tea? Coupla rashers an' slice o' fried bread?" Spittle sprayed from his lips. With a thick tongue he licked his chin.

"Max! You're disgusting! What *are* you wearing?"

The once-famous Shakespearean actor was dressed in an assortment of decaying jerseys, jackets and body-warmers tied round with rope, corduroy trousers it was best not to think about, and burst boots. A rampant grey beard and shock of hair that hadn't seen a comb in months reduced his face to a leathery circle of brown. A set of broken teeth, furred and yellow, obscured his own.

"What do you think?" He shambled into the middle of the

floor and struck a pose like a model. "And from Dior we have the latest in—"

"You stink!"

"I know, but it'll wear off a bit. Least I hope so, I'm gagging. I wrapped them in a bit of mouldy carpet and buried them in old whatsit's manure heap down the road. A bit riper than I intended." He regarded her anxiously. "Apart from the pong, though, what do you think?"

"Apart from the pong?" She blinked as if it stung her eyes. "Okky to a T. Let's hear the voice again."

Max leered at Harry. "'Lo, young sir. Fancy a life in the woods, do yer?" It was a wheezy voice as if it took Okky a lot of effort. "What is this life if full o' cayer, We 'ave no time to stand an' stayer?"

Harry stared, entranced.

"Terrific, Max." Mrs Good shook her head. "If *I* can't tell the difference, I'm sure no magistrate will."

"Good," Max said, back in his own voice. "Now, about that bit of breakfast."

"Not in my kitchen," she said firmly. "You can take a chair outside. Here, put this old newspaper on it."

The dirty old tramp patted Harry's cheek as he passed. "Have a good day."

"You too." He looked up. "What are you going to do?"

"Ah!" Max tapped the side of his nose. "Secrets."

Harry lay on the lawn with a carton of juice. School was over for the day and he had changed into jeans and a red T-shirt with an eagle swooping across the chest. The geese were absent, having waddled off through the wood to the lake.

Auntie Florrie sat beside him in a deckchair. A broken

straw hat protected her from the sun. That month's edition of *Hot Rod* lay on her lap.

At half past ten that morning, while Harry was at gym, Max had provoked and then assaulted a portly businessman in the High Street. Auntie Florrie, who had driven him into town with the windows open, had enjoyed it greatly:

"You should have been there," she said. "It was a scream. I was shadowing him along the pavement – you know, the way you do – and all the people were stepping aside to avoid touching him. Then suddenly here's this fat – I don't know, solicitor or businessman – coming towards him, talking into his mobile, ever so stuck-up and pleased with himself. Just from the look of him the sort you'd like to shove a grapefruit into his face. Max goes up to him, touches his forelock: "Scuse me, sir."' She tried to copy the voice. "'Spare a few coppers for a cuppa tea?' The man ignores him and steps round, so Max goes after him. 'D'you 'ear what I said?' The bloke's annoyed, makes a face. 'Do you mind,' he says and tries to get past again. But Max wouldn't let him. 'Get out my way,' the man says, all blue striped suit and fat cheeks, hair glued across the top – years younger than Max, forty maybe. 'Only arsked yer f' the price 'f a cuppa tea,' Max says and makes that face of his, all furry teeth and tongue poking out. The geezer gets angry and people start to watch. Of course, that's exactly what Max wants. 'I'm on my way to an important meeting,' the man says. 'If you don't step aside I'll call the police.' 'Ooooooohh!' Max says. 'I'll call the police!' Spit flying in all directions. 'What's so special about you, can't give a few coppers t' a bloke down 'n 'is luck?' The man stands his ground and takes out a hanky to cover his nose. 'This is outrageous,' he says. 'I'll tell you one more time—' 'Listen, mister,' Max says. 'I'll tell yer what's ou'rageous. You stood there like Lord Muck in yer fancy suit an' me 'thout the price 'f a cuppa tea an' a sambwidge.' And he pokes him in the waistcoat. 'Porky!' he says. 'Frog-face!' And the man's so startled he falls over backwards. An' his phone smashes to bits on the pavement, an' he hits his head, an' Max is going through his pockets looking like Rumplestiltskin. It was brilliant."

"What happened then?" Harry sat up.

"Well, the bloke starts to fight back and hits Max across the ear. So Max pokes him in the eye. And the next minute there's a right old ding-dong. Then passers-by join in, an' by the time the fuzz arrive there's twenty or thirty men all piled in there like a rugby scrum, and women pulling them by the hair and hitting them with their shopping bags – really gorgeous! I took a photo, one for the album."

"But what about Max?"

"Oh, they took him off in the paddy wagon. Shouting his head off, having a marvellous time. Knocked some coppers' hats off on the way. Come up before the beaks in the morning, I expect."

Adults behaving badly – Harry loved it. But not for the first time in his year at Lagg Hall he was puzzled. This was his family. Here was Auntie Florrie in her sun-hat, Aunt Bridget working on an article for *Mathematical Review*, Mrs Good preparing a delicious dinner for ten, Nutty tidying the herbaceous border, Mr Tolly rehearsing for a TV spectacular. They were, without exception, kind-hearted people who dedicated themselves to helping others. And yet Max had just assaulted an innocent businessman and several policemen in the High Street. They were planning a bank robbery. They were criminals who wished to acquire the loot of a notorious gangster – a murderer! Was this all right? Was it acceptable, today, to rob the rich to help the poor? Was it a good thing to break the law to build a hospital for people who otherwise would die? To provide a school for people who without it would never even learn to read and write? To give them clean water? Harry hoped so, but it was very confusing.

Due to an outbreak of summer flu Max could not appear before magistrates until Wednesday morning. By chance this was an in-service day for Harry's teachers so he had the day off, but no matter how he pleaded, Aunt Bridget would not allow him to go with her to the court. So instead he gave the boat a fresh coat of paint, brushed Chalky and Socrates until the hair flew, and waited for her to come home at teatime.

She dropped an armful of library books on the kitchen table. Among them were *Jack the Gripper* and *Snakes of the World* which Harry had requested. But now he had no time for books:

"What about Max?" he wanted to know. "What happened?"

"Give me a minute." She flopped down on a chair. "Be a good boy and make your auntie a cup of coffee. Not that instant rubbish, a decent cup."

He put on the kettle and reached for the cafetière. "Biscuit?"

"One of Goody's sultana oaties. Thanks."

She soon revived.

Harry nibbled a biscuit and sat opposite.

"He really should be back in the West End," Aunt Bridget said. "What a performance! He pleaded guilty and the chairman of the bench, this old bat in a green hat with a white silk rose, gives him three months' probation, bound over to keep the peace. Well, that's no use to Max, he wants a few days in clink, doesn't he. So he says, you'll not believe it: "'Ere, missis. I love yer 'at. Does somethin' to a man, an 'at like that. 'Idden passions, I reckon that 'at means. 'Ow about you an' me steppin' out when yer finished?' And he makes that face, you know, the leery one with his tongue hanging out. 'See where we end up, know what I mean?' And he taps his nose and gives her the dirtiest wink you ever saw."

Harry laughed.

"I don't like to think some of the things you're learning in this house," Aunt Bridget said. "Anyway, to finish the story, the woman – a dreadful creature with a face like a skull – she turns scarlet and speaks to the clerk of the court. 'Contempt of court,' he says straight out. 'Seven days. Maybe that will teach you a bit of respect for the bench, Daintry.' But seven days aren't long enough so Max says, 'Respect! She's the one should show a bit o' respect, comin' into court wiv an 'at like that an' stirrin' up a man's feelin's. Gettin' me all upset.' 'Fourteen days,' the clerk says. 'Thank you, your honour, your lordship,' Max says, good as gold. Then he blew a kiss to the ghoul in the hat," Aunt Bridget smiled, "and they took him below."

"What'll happen to him?"

"He'll go off to Cony Hill – least I hope so. Not much good if they send him to the Scrubs or Strangeways. No, it'll be Cony Hill. We'll give him a couple of days to suss out the situation, speak to Eddie, then I'll pay him a visit."

"Can I come?"

"No, you can't. You have to make an application, to start with. And they check your fingerprints. You are *not* having your dabs on a prison computer."

118

"Well, if I can't go to prison, can I have another biscuit?"

Aunt Bridget gave her horsy smile and pushed them across. "Now tell me about your day," she said.

There were notices, posters, warnings on the wall. Auntie Florrie and Aunt Bridget sat at a long counter, not unlike those you see in a bank or post office, separated from Max by a thick sheet of perspex. He looked cleaner than the last time they had seen him. Now he wore thick serge trousers and a navy jersey with *HMP Cony Hill* across the chest. Luckily the glue he had used for his wig and beard was strong because both had been washed.

"'Lo, lovely ladies." He grimaced lest anyone was watching. "Come all that way from Lagg 'All jus' to see ol' Okky? Brought me a bit o' baccy, 'ave yer? Give it t' the screws, they'll pass it on 'f I'm lucky."

"How's it going, Okky?"

"Burned me cloves. Made me take a barff, wash out all me 'elfy grease. Ovverwise OK, I s'pose." His tongue licked far down his chin. "Good grub. Fink I might give one o' the screws a little tap, make it a monf." He glanced round to be sure they weren't overheard and leaned close to the grille. "I've been talking to Eddie. As me, I mean. In his cell. He's very sick. Used to be built like a bull, remember, thick neck, strong arms. Looks more like a ghost now. Refuses to go to hospital, so they're letting a doctor come in to treat him here. Got his own things about him, a few books, a little privacy." Max spoke in a whisper. "He knows a bit about us – the Wrinklies, I mean. I asked him about the loot, straight out. He went berserk, you should have seen him. Threatened to tear my heart out and eat my liver."

"Still got the old charm then."

"Everybody's been getting on to him, I reckon. Thought I was after it like all the rest. So I told him what we were doing, what we wanted it for: the sick people, give the kids an ed –" He broke off, staring across the room, and vanished back into Okky Daintry: "Bladdy screws, rip off yer parcels soon 's look at yer."

Aunt Bridget and Auntie Florrie resisted the temptation to turn round. Mad Ruby and Gestapo Lil had entered the room. Moments later they came into view. Ruby wore her customary black. Lil was sexy in sunglasses and a gold summer suit with the jacket over her arm. Prisoners broke off talking to their wives to shout and whistle at her. In seconds the room was like a zoo. Contemptuously the pair walked to a place at the end of the counter and sat down. Priestly joined them beyond the perspex divide.

Somehow, although he had been in prison for six months, he was as portly and pompous as ever: a medium-sized pig with ginger hair brushed across a balding dome, a ginger moustache, cheeks that quivered, hot-tempered eyes and a little mouth with moist red lips that looked as if he spent all day eating quails' eggs and buttered asparagus. After brief greetings they fell into earnest conversation.

"I wonder what they're talking about," Auntie Florrie said.

"I don't know why," Max said, "but I've got a feeling he might be planning a break-out. This business of Eddie. The whole prison's humming. Round him like flies round a jam pot. If Percy waits till the end of his stretch he's going to be too late. He wants out."

Aunt Bridget glanced round. "You say Eddie *knows* about the Wrinklies?"

"More like guesswork. He knows we were behind Percy's arrest, of course. But he'd kept track of various jobs and donations. Put two and two together. So I told him. It's all right, he's not going to split." Max blew the whiskers from his lips. "What's he want money for now? Brother dead. His kids hate him. Can't take it with you; no pockets in a shroud. I said to him: 'What are you going to do, then, give it to one of those women been ripping you off all your life? Let it rot back into the ground? That makes it all worth while, doesn't it, that's really sensible. Why not give it to us? Let us *use* it. Give your horrible violent life some point, do something that matters.' 'Like what?' he says. 'Build the Eddie Jones Memorial hospital,' I told him. 'Cure people of leprosy. Help kids to walk. Stop them dying.'"

"What did he say to that?" Aunt Bridget asked.

"Nothing much, nothing I want to repeat anyway. Just gave a kind of roar and threw his dinner plate at me."

"But after?"

"I think he liked it. He wants to talk to you anyway. He says give him a few days to think about it. Tell her to come in next Wednesday."

"You mean," Auntie Florrie pushed back her curls, "he might just tell us where it's hidden?"

"I don't know what he means. Probably doesn't know himself. But from what I can make out he's got no other plans. Perhaps he wants to make peace with the big man upstairs."

Aunt Bridget nodded. "Deathbed repentance."

"Tell us about Percy," said Auntie Florrie.

"Eddie can't stand him, calls him Uriah Creep. He comes sniffing round Eddie's cell, that little mouth of his pursed up with sympathy, eyes shining with greed. I can tell you one thing, though, he doesn't like Eddie seeing so much of Okky Daintry." Max slipped back into character: "Bin givin' me some very unfrien'ly stayers. An' me the sensitive type."

They looked along the counter to discover they were being watched. Prisoner Priestly, his fiancée and his mother were staring in their direction.

"Oh dear, oh dear!" Okky sprayed the partition. "Will yer look at 'em: the ginger porker, mutton dressed as lamb, an' the black widder spider."

"Wouldn't I just like to go along there and slap their chops," Aunt Bridget said. "Take no notice. Bad luck we all had to come on the same afternoon. Fingers crossed they think we've just come because Okky's a lonely old man who used to camp in the woods."

But Priestly, Gestapo Lil and Mad Ruby were curious. Their heads came together. Percy told them how much time the old tramp had been spending with Eddie Carver. And now he was talking to the enemy. Repeatedly they looked along the line of visitors.

"You're sure he doesn't know who you are?" said Auntie Florrie.

Max shook his shaggy head. "Okky Daintry, that's me. Man o' the woods."

"Watch your back anyway," Aunt Bridget said.

"Fink yer need tell me that, sweet'eart?" he wheezed. "Don't you worry 'bout ol' Okky. He knows 'ow to take care of his-sel'."

Twenty minutes later it was time to leave. As they rose, Auntie Florrie spotted Ruby talking to one of the guards. They stood apart from the other visitors, out of sight of the surveillance cameras. She slipped a hand into her pocket and took out her visitor's pass. Something came with it, a little brown packet. She passed them to the guard. He examined the pass and handed it back then coughed and felt for a handkerchief. The packet was gone.

What was it – drugs? Had Percy started taking drugs? Was he dealing?

Ruby returned to the others. The guard returned to his post at the door. Apart from accusing him and attracting unwelcome attention, there was nothing Auntie Florrie could do. If only Mr Tolly were there, she thought, he could pick the guard's pocket.

"Bye, then, Okky," Aunt Bridget said, raising her voice a little. "Try not to fret. Come back to see you in a day or two."

"Bye, my lovelies!" He blew an expansive kiss. "'Ere, gotta message for Mrs Good, 'er that makes the steak and kidney pud. Tell 'er, Okky is willin'. Got that? Like Mr Barkis. Go a'ead an' book the church. I'm gonna sweep 'er orf to a life o' luxury an' puddens in the woods. Heh-heh!" He laughed, tongue down his chin, and blew his nose into his jersey.

They came away.

That was Saturday.

On Sunday afternoon Harry went rock climbing with Dot.

Chapter 12

Wreckers Crag

The Parish Church of St George and St Dunstan was a mile away across the fields, two by road. Often Harry walked but this Sunday he went by car, sitting in the front of the new Rover. Aunt Bridget, Mrs Good and one or two others were regular attenders, the rest went occasionally. Harry had no option. And though he might often wish to do something else, he enjoyed it. He liked the beautiful stone church with its leafy graveyard and surrounding meadows. He liked the cool and quiet, the young vicar, the hymn tunes, the carvings, the light through the stained-glass windows. Even though he did not always understand the psalms or follow the sermon, when he got home he always felt better for having been.

Then there was the big Sunday lunch with roast beef, Yorkshire pudding, gravy – his favourite taste of the whole week – and usually some kind of trifle to follow.

On this particular Sunday, while the rest sipped coffee, Harry left the table and ran upstairs to pull on jeans and an anorak because Dot was taking him rock climbing at Brandy Cove, just up the coast from the port of Fairhaven.

From the top of his tower, though not the windows of the

house, the sea was visible. Twenty miles away it formed a strip, sometimes dark, sometimes glittering, above the treetops.

They went in the Rover, Dot peering through the wheel and driving even more slowly than Nutty. The climbing gear – ropes, karabiners, helmets, Vibram-soled boots and the rest – lay in the trunk.

After half an hour, as they reached the crest of a hill and the blue sea opened before them, Dot said, "Let's not go to Brandy Cove, people watching us with binoculars. Let's go to Wreckers Crag for a change, it'll be quieter." And so, as they reached the crossroads, she turned left instead of right and ten minutes later drew up on a grassy plot above the cliff. It was backed by woodland. Before them gorse, brambles and an occasional stunted oak tree sloped down eighty metres to the cliff edge.

Sunday drivers and families who wanted to picnic on the beach preferred Brandy Cove to the wilderness of Wreckers Crag. That afternoon it was deserted, though if Dot had paid more attention to the driving mirror as they bumped along the potholed lanes, squeezed in by hedges, she might have noticed that they were being followed. Two hundred metres behind, never drawing closer, a red Aston Martin tracked them through the increasingly lonely farmland. As they stopped above the cliff, it too swung to a halt, hidden among trees. Two people got out, a man and a woman. Furtively they crept foward and peeped through the branches.

Harry and Dot pulled on their climbing boots, collected helmets and coiled rope, and started down a track that led to the stony beach. The wind had freshened, a line of cloud gathered above the sea.

Harry said, "Why's it called Wreckers Crag?" It was the first time he had been there.

"Back in the old days, when ships carried tea, tobacco, wine up and down this coast, the smugglers put ashore at Brandy Cove." Dot squeezed past gorse bushes. "But sometimes on wild nights they flashed a light from the cliff here. Ships thought it was the harbour light at Fairhaven and sailed in. Got smashed up on the rocks. Wreckers pulled the cargo out of the surf. Carried it up this path on ponies."

"Very steep."

"Had to whip them on."

"What about the sailors?"

"Drowned. Some got shot. Lots of stories about it. And ghosts: poor sailors screaming, drunken wreckers with their torches, ships breaking up."

They reached the foot of the track and emerged from the bushes. It was a stony bay; wild sea rocks covered with pools; tremendous cliffs with fulmars wheeling their stiff-winged circles overhead.

"We're not going up *there*!" Harry was horrified.

"No, no. You're not ready for that yet. Too exposed. See further along." Dot pointed. "That crack? There's a way up there. Not too hard at all."

The waves broke on scoured rock as they crossed the shore. Long weed trailed in the gullies.

"Ready then?" They stood at the foot of the climb.

Harry dropped the coil of rope and looked up. It was high but did not look impossibly difficult. "OK," he said and pulled on the simple harness.

Dot was ready before him. Carefully she checked the clips and ropes. "Right, we'll do it in two stages. I'll climb as far as that shelf, see, and bring you up behind me. Then we'll go on to the top."

Harry nodded. He loved these outings with Dot.

"Good boy." She patted his cheek and started to climb.

A diminutive figure, Dot had been one of the leading rock climbers of her generation with many first ascents of the great cliffs of Europe and the Himalayas to her name. From mountains she had graduated to the State Circus in Paris as an acrobat and stunt woman. From there it was but a short step to becoming a cat-burglar whose exploits had captured headlines across the Western world. In France they called her *La Mouche de Marseille*. The English papers named her Dotty Skylark. And in Chicago, where drug-crazed revellers had seen her pixie face at a window on the sixty-seventh floor, she was known as Tinkerbell.

Harry watched as she scaled the cliff above him, feet firm, little fingers knotted in the crevices. He twitched the rope free of a tuft of grass. She reached the halfway stage and tied herself to the rock.

"Taking up the slack." The line tightened. "Right, in your own time."

Harry reached up, set his foot on a flake of stone, and began to climb.

Twenty metres above him Dot looked down, the rope securely over her shoulder. "More to the left. That knob there – no, just above it. Good."

Steadily he made progress.

The fulmars were nesting. A short distance below Dot he came face to face with one in a cranny. Harry was fascinated. The bird drew back and opened its beak in warning. Unsure if he would get a painful peck, he reached towards it. His intention was to brush the spotless breast and slip a hand beneath to feel the eggs or possibly chicks. With no warning the fulmar strained its beak wide and a jet of fluid shot from its throat. Harry was splashed all over – his hand, the side of his face, his collar. It *stank*!

"Ugghh!"

"What's wrong?"

"This bird! It sicked stuff all over me."

Dot laughed. "Teach you to leave it alone."

He rubbed his hand on his trousers. Took out his handkerchief and scrubbed his face. The smell clung. It filled his nostrils like rotting fish oil.

"Don't be such a baby, you're not hurt. Probably good for your skin. Come on up."

Harry gave the bird a resentful look and resumed climbing. Two or three minutes later he joined Dot on the ledge.

"Here, tie a line round this projection. I'll knock in a piton." She tapped a spike into the wall and made certain he was secure. "Never take chances, even when you're resting."

Side by side they looked out to sea. The bank of cloud was closer. The waves had taken on a steely hue. "I hope it's not going to rain," she said.

Some of the birds now flew beneath them. Harry watched as they circled to nesting mates, failed to judge it perfectly and dropped away to try again.

"I love these moments," Dot said. "At least I do when my companion doesn't stink like a box of dead crabs." She rooted in her rucksack and found two bars of chocolate cream.

"Thanks." Harry peeled back the silver paper.

A scatter of pebbles rattled past. They looked up. High above them, at the edge of the cliff, a bush was moving.

"Sheep or something." Dot watched for a few seconds and took a bite of chocolate. "Goody gave us a flask of tea and some cake and stuff. We'll have it at the top."

A few minutes later they rose. "I'll go on. You secure?"

Harry checked. "Yes." He led the rope over his left shoulder and round his right arm.

"Leave the piton, I'll collect it another time." She glanced up. "Here we go."

He watched as she started up the crack, feet braced on either side, raking out moss and ferns to secure handholds. Steadily she climbed away from him and in five minutes was hauling herself over the brink to the clifftop. Harry wondered if he would ever be able to climb as well.

She shouted down. "Great fun! Just give me a minute to find a belay. There's a tree here I'll. . . Oh!"

There was a sound of scuffling and raised voices. Harry stared up. The bushes tossed violently. Words reached him:

". . . boy's down there, he'll . . ."

". . . deal with him, you just . . ."

". . . ahhh! You little . . ."

". . . better. Pull it tight, she's . . ."

Gradually it quietened. "Dot, what's happening?"

No reply.

"Dot? . . . Dot?"

The leaves stirred. A head emerged. It was Gestapo Lil, sliding forward on her belly. Her hair was dishevelled.

A second head joined her. It was GBH.

"I can't stand heights. Give me the willies." He looked down. "Oh, look at him down there. Oh, my God!" He withdrew.

Lil was made of sterner stuff. "Come on up," she said.

Harry looked at the rock face between them. Climb that without Dot? He looked past his boots. All at once it seemed a long way down. The waves broke on hard rocks. He imagined falling, the thud of impact, his body broken. He clung to the cliff.

"You hear? Come on up."

"I can't."

She tugged the climbing rope. He was pulled off balance and gave a cry.

"I can't!" he said again.

"Yes you can. You'd do it if that titchy whatshername was with you."

"But she's not," he said. "I'd fall."

"Well I'll hold the rope." She pulled it tight.

Harry was dragged to his tiptoes. "Stop!" he shouted. "Stop!"

The rope fell slack. Terrified she would pull him off the ledge, he released the rope and clipped his harness to the piton Dot had hammered into the rock. "I can't climb up," he said. "I just can't."

She thought about it. "Well tell us about Eddie Jones."

He was silent.

"Eddie Jones," she repeated. "Eddie Carver. You know who I mean. In Cony Hill. With my Percy. And that old tramp."

Harry's brain raced. So she didn't know about Max.

"Your batty aunts were there yesterday. What for?"

"I don't know what you're talking about."

"Don't give me that. They were in seeing that disgusting old man. What's it all about?"

"How do I know where they went yesterday? I was out on the bike. I never heard of any old tramp."

"So you say." She jerked the rope savagely and found it loose. "Oh, very clever! He's called Ollie Dainty. Not very dainty if you ask me. Camps in the woods. What's his connection with Eddie and all those aunts and other geriatrics you live with?"

"I don't know. Honest."

"Ah, honest! I know what *honest* means."

When Harry didn't reply she wriggled back and soon reappeared, standing this time and carrying a rock the size of a labourer's boot. Tendrils of hair blew about her face. Her nails were blood-red against the stone. She raised it above her head. "Are you going to tell me? Or do you want me to feed your brains to the seagulls?"

"How can I tell you what I don't know?"

"Ahhh!" She flung the rock but not at him. Harry saw it shatter on the stones below. When he looked back she had gone.

Dot, meanwhile, lay in a small clearing fifteen metres from the cliff edge. She had been attacked from behind, blindfolded so that she did not see her assailants. A gag was in her mouth, her hands and feet were tied. For good measure, GBH had tipped out the contents of her rucksack and pulled it over her head. Having nothing else to do at that particular moment, he sat on the grass, opened Mrs Good's sandwiches and poured himself a cup of tea.

Cloud covered the sun. The wildflowers were dimmed. A chill wind blew his hair. GBH pulled up the collar of his jacket.

Gestapo Lil beckoned him out of earshot. "Little rat won't talk. Have to get it out of this one."

"Rough stuff?"

"If necessary. Take the gag off."

131

It was soon done, the rucksack replaced.

"I wouldn't scream," Gestapo Lil said. "There's no one to hear you. If you do, well, my companion will have to stop you, won't he?"

Dot grunted.

"Good, we understand each other." She crouched close. "Now, Eddie Carver and that old tramp. You know the one I mean – in the gulag. You've got a choice. Tell us about it or we'll sling you over the cliff."

"What about Harry?"

"Dangling on that rope like a spider. Tried to climb and came off. When we dump you, he'll go down the same time. Look like an accident."

"What do you want to know?"

"Everything."

So Dot told them. About Okky Daintry. And Max. And Eddie Jones. And Aunt Bridget going to meet him. Everything.

A few spots of rain came on the wind. GBH brushed grass from his trousers and slid the knife round his belt. "'Bout time one o' you in that nut-'ouse come clean," he said.

Gestapo Lil smiled, catlike, with satisfaction. "Well, well. Very interesting. Max Beauguss, eh? And clever-knickers going in to see Eddie on Wednesday. Now Percy will know what to do."

"Harry!" Dot struggled beneath the car rug. "We have to—"

"Oh, don't worry about him, he's safe enough," Gestapo Lil said. "Clipped to that spike you hammered into the cliff. Couldn't fall if he wanted." She pushed through bushes to the cliff edge. "Still there?"

Harry scowled up. "What's happening?"

"Your little friend's been telling us about – oh, lots and lots of things."

She pulled up the rope and returned to Dot. "Now, where's the car keys?"

"Harry—"

"I told you, he's safe – for the moment, anyway. I'll ask you again, where are the car keys?"

"Up at the car."

"What?"

"Hidden by the front wheel."

"GBH, go and check."

"Oh, thanks," he said. "So much for anonymity. Why don't you go, Miss Lavinia Lucretia McScrew of Felon Grange? I'll have another sandwich."

He unwrapped it and threw the paper on the grass.

"And whose dabs are all over that?" she snapped.

He sighed and picked it up. Hand in pocket, he climbed the slope to the Rover.

"Yeah, they're here." He waved the keys.

Gestapo Lil was in a mood for vandalism. The ground sloped downhill from the car to the top of the cliff. Dot and Harry were well to one side. "Check it's out of gear," she called. "Let off the handbrake."

GBH thought about it. There was nothing he liked better than a bit of violence and destruction. "Hey, Wreckers Crag! Right on!" Good humour restored, he leaned across the seat and did as she said. The door clunked shut.

He set his hand against a wing and pushed. The car did not move. He pushed harder. The heavy Rover rocked and fell back. For added safety Dot had jammed a stone beneath a rear wheel. GBH kicked it away. With a whisper the car rolled forward.

But the front wheels were turned to one side. With no key in the ignition the steering locked. Instead of ploughing straight ahead and over the cliff, the powder-blue Rover swung in a gentle arc, bumped across some tussocks and came to rest parallel to the shore.

"Brilliant!" Gestapo Lil called through the rain which was now falling steadily. "Just what I had in mind. Very exciting."

"Sarky cow!" GBH climbed into the driver's seat. The tyres slithered and skidded on the wet grass as he backed to the car park to start again.

This time he ensured the wheels were straight and left the ignition switched on. Carefully he wiped the steering wheel, walnut dash and the rest clean of fingerprints.

It was as if the beautiful car *wanted* to commit suicide. GBH had barely stepped out, had not even had time to shut the door, when it set off, brushing him aside. Gathering momentum, it headed straight downhill towards the cliff edge, eighty metres away, bucking over ridges, ploughing through a thicket of bramble.

"Hey! Yeah!" GBH shouted with excitement.

The door flapped wildly. A mound threw the wheels to one side, the steering wheel spun. The bright car bounced on. Almost directly in its path stood an oak tree, blown all one way by the wind. It missed by centimetres. Birds whirled from the branches. A thicket of yellow gorse and wild briar lay ahead. Hidden beneath was a ditch, remnant of an old fortification. The wheels dropped, the bottom of the car scraped earth, the bonnet buried itself in thorns. Ten metres from the cliff, the Rover hammered to a halt.

Deeply disappointed, GBH ran to look. Though every door was unlocked, there was no way in without scratching himself bloody. And even if he could reach the controls, the car was stuck. It would take a tractor to pull it out of there. Picking at his damp trousers, he returned to Gestapo Lil.

"Can't be helped." She scraped a rat's tail from her eyes. "Still, it'll keep them here for a while. Time to go home. We've got what we came for."

GBH slung the thermos and what remained of the picnic over the cliff.

"What about prints?"

"Rain'll get rid of them," he said.

"Good, no evidence."

Dot had freed her hands.

"Less of that!" Gestapo Lil pushed her sprawling and dragged her arms behind.

GBH tied them again and hauled her to a sitting position.

"Here's what we're going to do," Gestapo Lil told her. "We'll leave you the rope. Stay there for five minutes, then you can work your way loose and bring up rat-face. Start before that and we'll take it with us. He'll be stuck down there for hours."

"Yes, all right." Dot was placating. "What about the car?"

"Forget the car, the car's stuck. Five minutes. And I mean five, not one." She turned to GBH. "Let's get out of here. I'm soaked to the skin. And I'm sick of this shrivelled-up old fairy."

The rain danced on puddles in the lane. Heads bowed, they walked to the Aston Martin, two hundred metres away. Gestapo Lil backed out of the trees. They drove off.

Dot heard them go. Head in the rucksack, she did not stir. Five minutes was not up.

Far below her on the dripping crag, Harry, too, heard the engine. Above him all was silent.

"Dot?" His anorak was sodden, his jeans clung tight. The cold made his voice shake. "Hello?"

Rain beat against him from the sea. His world had shrunk to a circle of grey. Harry rubbed drips from his face and looked below. The waves were louder. In his imagination he saw the drunken wreckers, the drowning seamen that Dot had told him about. They peopled his loneliness. For the hundredth time he tested the piton and looked up again.

"Hello?"

There was no reply.

Chapter 13

The Gunpowder Plot

Harry lay in the big white enamel bath. A flotilla of plastic ducks and crocodiles bobbed by his toes, a white and red cabin cruiser chugged past his knees. Slowly the cold ebbed from his bones.

There was a tap at the door and Mrs Good came in.

"Warmer now?"

"Yes, thanks." He sank deeper in the water. "How's Dot?"

"Still upset but she'll be all right."

"It wasn't her fault. They must have been watching the house."

"Of course it wasn't her fault." Mrs Good sat on the bathroom chair. "But try telling her that."

"She was brilliant," Harry said. "Climbed down to take me up. I couldn't have done it by myself."

"In all that rain."

"It was freezing."

"I don't know how you did it, either of you. I know I couldn't. I'd have just died up there. Taken a crowbar to get me to move a finger."

He smiled. "It wasn't that bad."

"They're frightened after a shock like that you'll never want to go again."

"No, it'll be OK." Harry made waves. "Not this week, though."

"Oh! Well, your Aunt Bridget wants you to go tomorrow. If the rain stops, that is. Take the day off school."

Harry was astonished. "Say that again?"

"She's very definite about it. Doesn't want you to get scared. Like getting straight back on a horse after you've fallen."

He sank to his nose. Watched her across the water. Went right under.

"What do you think?"

He took a shaky breath. "Yeah, all right. What about Dot?"

"Says it depends on you. Wants Florrie to go with you."

"To the same place? Wreckers Crag?"

"I'm not sure. Take a picnic anyway." She pulled a big white towel from the rail. "Ready?"

"In a minute. What about the car?"

"No real harm done. Bit scratched, of course, bump in the wing, crack in the exhaust. Nutty can't wait to get his hands on it."

"How'd they know we were there? Auntie Florrie, I mean."

"Guesswork really. When you weren't back by tea, people thought you must have got a puncture or something and the rain was coming on so Huggy and your Auntie Florrie drove over to Brandy Cove. When you weren't there Huggy remembered Dot once saying she'd like to take you to Wreckers Crag sometime." She fished out the ducks and crocodiles. "You can see it from the cove if you know where to look. And you know your Auntie Florrie's got eyes like a hawk."

"She could see us from Brandy Cove?"

"Not you, maybe, but the rain had eased up and she could see something blue on the clifftop. So she got the binoculars off the back seat and saw the car. Very close to the edge, she said. Gave her a terrible fright."

"It must have been about the same time we got the farmer," Harry said. "He was great. A big red Fordson, let me ride in the cab. Pulled it out no bother."

"And gave all four of you tea in the farmhouse," Mrs Good said. "Let Florrie phone home. The rest of us were getting worried."

"I'd like to be a farmer," Harry said. "Ploughing fields and looking after calves." He rose, streaming water, and stepped out on to the bath mat.

Mrs Good wrapped him in the towel. It was the first time she'd been allowed to do this for many months.

"You'd be good at it," she said. "Yes, you'd make a good farmer. But we'll see. Plenty of time before you need start thinking about that."

Harry let himself be mothered. This was something his own mother had never done, partly because bathtime coincided with cocktail time, but more because she was never there. Keeping the young Harry Barton clean had been one of Gestapo Lil's duties. Affection and fun did not feature largely in her regime. From the age of six, bathtime in Hampstead had been: "Go on, be quick. Don't waste hot water and don't wet the floor. You're up there to wash yourself, not play games. Wipe the bath out when you're done, there's Ajax in the cupboard. Put the towel and your dirty clothes in the washing machine. When you've finished you can make me a cup of tea."

Lagg Hall was different. Mrs Good finished rubbing his hair. All spiky, Harry regarded her through the soft white folds:

"Are they going to the police? Tying Dot up and leaving me stuck down there; trying to put the car over the cliff."

"Your aunties would like to, but it's just your word against theirs again, isn't it. Like when they set fire to the place, and chased you out of Felon Grange. I know you saw the pair of them over at Wreckers Crag, and Dot heard them, of course, but where's the proof?"

Harry sat on the side of the bath while she dried his toes.

"Then you'd have to be interviewed again, and make a statement, and be called a liar by them over there. Go into court if it got that far. It's the last thing anybody wants. And then, of course, there's Max."

She relinquished the towel and Harry finished drying himself.

"He's just lied in court, hasn't he, made a fool of them all. It's in a good cause, I know, but it's still perjury and impersonation and common assault. If it came out, think what a field day the papers would have, him a famous actor and all. They'd put him away for years, poor man. And the reporters would be round here, ferreting away, sticking their noses in."

"What's happening, then?"

"They've been talking about it downstairs. I know you've had a fright – and Dot too. But there's no serious harm done and they don't want people asking questions. So your Aunt Bridget's going to try and do a deal: we'll take no action if they'll keep quiet about Max. It's not as if they've got anything to gain by it, Dot told them everything."

"About Eddie Carver – and the treasure?"

"Whatever they wanted to know. She was worried sick about you."

"I was OK."

"But Dot didn't know that. She thought you were dangling on the end of a rope with all those rocks down below you. Poor soul, it's a wonder she didn't go out of her mind."

Harry wrapped the towel round his waist and pulled out the bath plug.

"I'll look after that. You go and get dressed."

"Thanks, Goody."

"You're welcome, love. There's nobody in this house wouldn't do a lot more for you than that."

Steam eddied into the corridor as he opened the door. Though the house was warm, the air felt cool against his skin as he made his way to the attic. Rain battered on the skylight. Dry jeans and a jersey lay on his bed.

Soon he was dressed. A warm smell of cooking met him as he descended the stairs.

Tangle had been foraging in the wood. Head on one side, tail wagging, he stood watching as Harry crossed the hall.

"Hello, Tangle." He bent to pat him. "Uggh!" Tangle's coat was sodden and icy to the touch. He jumped up, muddy paws against Harry's knee. "Get off!" It was too late, pawprints stained his clean jeans, the cold seeped through. Unabashed, the ragged mongrel looked up with bright eyes. "Come on, then." Harry turned towards the kitchen. "Let's get you dry. How about a *biscuit*?"

It was a word Tangle knew well. He gave a little leap and trotted ahead.

Harry wondered if there might be a biscuit for him too, one of those chocolaty ones with chunks of ginger. After all, as he could tell from the chatter and alcoholic vapours that drifted from the living room, the rest were having their pre-prandial snifters. He could hardly be expected, after such a shattering experience, to live on *air* until dinner. It was worth a try anyway.

By morning the storm had passed. Auntie Florrie drove Harry and Dot to the seaside where, beneath blue skies and fluffy white clouds, they made a second ascent of Wreckers Crag and presented the farmer and his wife with a gigantic box of chocolates.

On Tuesday, for Harry, it was school as usual. But that evening, while he was doing his homework at the kitchen table, an event occurred at Cony Hill Prison which dominated the front page of newspapers across the country and by breakfast time was being investigated by national television.

It was followed, less than twenty-four hours later, by a second event at the prison, also widely reported and scarcely less sensational.

What happened was this:

On Tuesday evening, only hours before he was due to meet Aunt Bridget, Eddie 'Carver' Jones fell down a long iron staircase and broke his neck. No longer the muscular bull of his prime but reduced to a skeletal savage with over-large teeth, he was dead when warders reached him.

Carver had many enemies, in jail as well as out. What had happened no one was certain, or at least no one would say, though within seconds the upper rail was packed with prisoners. Among those watching was Colonel Percy Priestly. When questioned by warders and the prison governor, he could shed no more light on the incident than any other inmate. "Such a waste of a life," he opined, shivering with pleasure at the memory of the quick push he had given Carver, and the sight of the notorious gang leader plunging headlong to his death. "So much violence and plotting. Perhaps if he had spent more time reading the Good Book, his end would have been more peaceful." Piously he raised his eyes to the ceiling. "As ye sow, so shall ye reap."

Within the prison and without, speculation about the size and location of Carver's treasure rose to fever pitch. There were rumours and counter-rumours. Flowerbeds were dug up. Garages were ransacked. Gang members were strung up by their thumbs. It got nowhere, for the simple reason that following the murder of Dart only one person knew. And now he too was dead.

Three days later the funeral cortège of Eddie Jones, elder son of Jack and Ethel Jones, scrap merchants, of Peckham, passed through the streets of London. Police and other interested parties were present in abundance. Hoodlums, heavies and men in black hats came to pay their last respects. Batteries of flash bulbs left them dazed. Awkwardly, in the crematorium, they set their hats on their knees, felt for cigars they dared not smoke, and kept their eyes open during the prayers just in case. After the last chorus of *Onward Christian Soldiers* had died away and the coffin, heaped with heart-shaped wreaths and scarlet roses, had slid through the crimson curtains to wherever coffins go in a crematorium, they gathered in stony-faced groups. Some, it was said, slugged an attendant and dragged the coffin out of the furnace just as the flames were igniting. Having no screwdrivers or jemmies in their funeral attire, they shot off the lid in the belief that a plan, detailing the whereabouts of Eddie's fortune, was about to be incinerated with him. They were mistaken, nothing resided in the coffin but Eddie's corpse dressed in a dinner jacket and looking, one reported afterwards, as if their efforts amused him and he was about to spit in their eyes.

The second occurrence to capture the headlines and bring Cony Hill Prison to the attention of the nation, took place the very day after Eddie's plunge down the staircase. To the police, the prison authorities and the media, the two events did not at first seem connected. To the residents of Lagg Hall, however, the link was as strong as the chain on a pair of handcuffs.

It started at eleven o'clock on the Wednesday morning. At about the same time Harry, in the middle of a mountain of extra maths which he had been given for not paying attention, was caught finishing a funny drawing of Mr Weldon. This was serious, but much more serious was the little brown packet Colonel Percival Bonaparte Priestly had taped to his leg beneath his uniform trousers. The bent screw had passed it on.

Earlier that morning, although he was perfectly fit, Priestly had reported to the sick bay complaining of stomach cramps. Since he had rarely been ill previously, the doctor thought he was genuinely unwell and signed him off duties in the kitchen. Now, in a corner of his cell, he pulled up his thick serge trouser-leg and tore off the surgical tape. A dozen hairs came with it. He yelped and looked round with watering eyes. He had not been observed.

Swiftly but carefully he unfolded the paper. A small pile of grey-black powder lay within. It was not drugs, as Auntie Florrie had guessed, at least not in the usual sense. It was gunpowder – a mixture of sulphur, charcoal and potassium nitrate – tipped from a number of shotgun cartridge cases in the kitchen at Felon Grange. If Priestly had laid it on a stone floor and hit it with a hammer, he would have blown his hand off. This was not his intention. Quickly he tipped it into a cup and threw the paper from the barred window. There was a small washbasin in his cell. Greatly frightened, he half filled the cup and swirled the gritty black liquid round and round. Finally, with a shaking hand and a prayer that he would not die, he raised it to his lips and drank it down. It tasted disgusting. He rinsed his mouth, rinsed the cup and lay down on his bunk.

It did not take long for the gunpowder to take effect. A prison guard who was searching a cell a short distance away heard a choking cry, a groan, a howl. He ran along the iron landing. Priestly was writhing on his mattress. His eyes were aflame, his nose ran. Unable to control himself, he was sick on the floor.

The guard blew his whistle for assistance. The prison doctor was summoned. He remembered signing the prisoner off. His skin was a bad colour, his heartbeat was irregular. At once he had him carried by stretcher to the sick bay.

The doctor did all he could. Had he been practising during the 1914–1918 war he would have recognized the symptoms of gunpowder poisoning. But this was a young doctor, not yet thirty. He had never heard of it. Throughout all those years of medical school and hospital training it had not even been mentioned.

Lunchtime came and went. The patient's condition deteriorated. He was put on a drip. Sweat poured down his piggy face. His skin was bluish-purple. He struggled for breath. Sometimes he hallucinated, shouting and hitting out at invisible objects.

The doctor feared for his patient's life and in the late afternoon an ambulance was summoned to take Priestly to St Luke's Infirmary at the far side of the city. He was handcuffed, even though scarcely conscious, and accompanied by two guards. One was unusually tall. The second guard, a stocky man, was chained to the prisoner.

At short notice a room had been made available in a ward on the third floor. At once the patient was put in an oxygen tent, a fresh drip was attached to his hand.

An hour passed, and then another hour. Priestly's colour improved, his heartbeat stabilized, he breathed more easily. By visiting time it was apparent, even to the bored and unsympathetic guards, that he was past the worst. The oxygen tent was removed. Limp as a dead hamster, prisoner Priestly lay on the pillow. His bloodshot eyes, the only part of him to move, slid around the room.

They were cut off from the rest of the ward. The door was shut, the curtains drawn. No name was displayed in the slot outside. The only people to enter were doctors, nurses, and one of the catering staff with dinner for the guards.

Some time after eight the door opened briskly and a doctor strode in without knocking. She was a small woman with brown skin – Spanish, perhaps, or Egyptian – and walked with a limp. Coarse grey hair was coiled in a bun on the back of her neck, she wore heavy-rimmed spectacles and had a wart on her upper lip. She was accompanied by a nurse, a young woman with dark hair and a bosom that went before her like the prow of a sailing ship. She had suffered some accident because a strip of sticking plaster was attached to her left eyebrow and the eye beneath it was bruised. It was not the sticking plaster or bruising, however, that occupied the guards' attention. The tall guard pulled himself together and read the name tags pinned to their uniforms: Dr Marcia Fazzi and Staff Nurse Tina Mackay. He glanced at his watch and entered the details in his notebook.

Gestapo Lil suppressed a smile, she liked her role as a nurse. But it was Ruby who was the actress. She took her place at the patient's side. With rubber-gloved fingers she checked his pulse. She lifted an eyelid, looked down his throat with a spatula, tucked a thermometer beneath his arm, and examined the chart at the foot of the bed.

"Ver' good. Right, nurse, now we get him down'a the renal unit. Where's the wheelchair?"

"Right outside, doctor." Nurse Mackay adjusted a strap.

"Right outside'a?" In her years with the Mafia, Ruby had played many parts. She had been a doctor the time she rubbed out Manny Schultz in Milan. "What good is it to my patient right outside? We need it in here! Come on, we haven't got all night. I want'a get home even if you don't."

"Here, hang on." The shorter guard was still chained to the prisoner. "Where d'you think you're taking him?"

"For tests'a. Where you think we take him, wind-surfing?"

"Sorry, doc. He don't leave this room."

"Not without the say-so of the prison guv'nor," said his companion.

"Well, you go ring him. Me, I fed up. I go home. He die — that OK by me." She started for the door.

"Just a minute. These tests, important are they?"

"You, you are guards, you guard him. Me, I am doctor, I try cure him. He, he sick man, he need tests'a. What you

147

think, I overpower you? You six foot four. Me, five foot – almost." She raised her eyebrows in a question. "Now, you want I treat him? Or you want I go home?"

They glanced at each other and down at the helpless figure in the bed. "OK, doc. But the bracelets stay on."

"Bracelets, earrings, you paint his toenails for all I care." She turned away. "Come on, nurse. We waste time."

The chair was wheeled in. Clumsily the sick man was assisted from his bed. A blanket was spread across his knees. Dr Fazzi, limping heavily in her built-up shoe, led the way from the room. Nurse Mackay jumped as one of the guards patted her bottom. The other guard pushed the wheelchair.

They left the ward and circled the landing to the lifts. Most were for general use. One was labelled *Theatres: Treatment*. A bored theatre orderly was lounging alongside. He was a man in his thirties with tinted glasses, lank red hair and designer stubble. A faint smell of chloroform clung about him. The guards were surprised to see that, like Dr Fazzi and Nurse Mackay, he wore surgical gloves.

A notice listed the various departments. Idly one of the guards read it while they waited.

Nurse Mackay pressed a button. Somewhere beneath them doors closed. Machinery whirred. The numbers above the lift doors were illuminated: B – 1 – 2 – 3. It stopped. The doors slid open. The little group followed the wheelchair inside.

The orderly raised weary eyes.

"Basement," said Dr Fazzi.

"Here," the guard said. "That notice out there says renal's on the fifth."

They took no notice. The orderly punched button B. The doors rattled shut.

Chapter 14

The Ambulance and
Whortleberry Yawkins

The guards had no time to protect themselves. The lift had barely jerked into motion when the elderly doctor whipped a cosh from beneath her skirt and smacked the tall man across the side of the head. He gave a jerk, a sigh, and collapsed like a toy skeleton.

At the same moment, Nurse Mackay sprang at the shorter guard, punching and scratching. They tumbled to the floor. Dragged by the chain, Priestly fell on top of them. So did his wheelchair. So, wielding her cosh, did Dr Ruby.

GBH, who fancied himself in his red wig and theatre scrubs, sprang into action. Swiftly he punched a button labelled *Emergency Stop* and pulled a bottle of liquid from his pocket. From a second pocket he took a wad of white lint. The heady fumes of chloroform filled the confined space as he slopped the bottle on to the pad and struggled through the melée.

Ruby's cosh flailed up and down. In the excitement of the fray she hit Gestapo Lil by mistake. Stunned, she fell across the shorter guard's face, suffocating him. GBH heaved her aside and leaped on the man with his wad of chloroform. Though one hand was chained, the guard fought back. GBH socked him with his fist and jammed the wad across his mouth and nose. The heavy anaesthetic did its duty. The guard slumped into unconsciousness.

It was just in time for there had been a little accident. In the urgency of the moment, GBH had thrust the bottle of chloroform into his breast pocket without securing the top. It had come off. His jacket and T-shirt were drenched. GBH felt his own brain start to reel. For a few more seconds he pressed the pad to the guard's face then fell back and gasped for oxygen in the chloroform-impregnated air.

Of the four men and two women in the lift, only Ruby remained in possession of her senses. Hauling bodies this way and that, she thrust her little brown hand through the guard's clothes, searching for the key to the handcuffs. It was not in his jacket pockets, nor his trouser pockets. She found it attached to a clip on his belt. In a moment she had released her fat son.

They needed air. She pushed the wheelchair upright, climbed on to the seat and pushed open the escape hatch. A hospital mouse keeled over as a ball of anaesthetic vapour surged through the lift shaft.

Slowly they recovered. Priestly was restored to his chair. Gestapo Lil fingered a lump the size of half a tomato under her cap. Mad Ruby returned the cosh to its Velcro fastening.

The guards were given a few sustaining whiffs of chloroform.

"All ready?" GBH released the red stop button and the lift continued to the basement.

At eight-thirty in the evening all was quiet. The unconscious guards were hoisted to hospital trolleys and covered with sheets. Gestapo Lil and GBH wheeled them into a darkened operating theatre. Then, accompanied by his medical team – the limping doctor, the sexy nurse and the chloroform-saturated orderly – Priestly was wheeled through corridors, fire doors and out to the ambulance bay.

It was an area of red asphalt with bushes in tubs and the bright glass of the infirmary soaring above. Seven vehicles stood ready, one with the rear doors open and twin metal ramps hooked to the sill. Towards this they made their way and pushed the wheelchair aboard.

"Hey! What do you think you're doing?" A paramedic called from the window of the restroom. "Wait there." He came striding from the door in his green uniform. "That's my ambulance."

"We have to get this patient home." Ruby turned to face him. "They need'a his bed."

"Not in my ambulance you don't, doc." He was a powerful-looking man with a pleasant face and blond hairy arms. "No one told me."

"No? Well I telling you."

"Where's the authorization?"

Ruby was lost. She did not know the procedures. "To take this patient three mile? Rubbish! We back in ten minutes."

"You know the rules. Anyway," he read her name tag, "Dr Fazzi? Never heard of you."

"Well, now you have'a. Can we get going?"

"Nurse Mackay?" He stared at her sensational bosom and wrinkled his nose at the clouds of chloroform rising from GBH. "Never seen you neither."

Everything hung in the balance.

"What ward's he from?" The paramedic jerked his thumb at the figure in the wheelchair.

Hospitals are busy. In the whole building only one single room had been available.

"3F," Ruby reported instantly.

"3F!" The man laughed. "That's gynaecology. Having a kid, is he?"

Paramedics work in teams of two. His bearded partner watched from the restroom window.

"Anyway, seen you before, haven't I?" He stared at Priestly. "Yeah, you were that bloke come in teatime, terrible colour. I brought you from Cony Hill. You was in prison! Hey, what's going on? What you tryin' to—"

GBH swung a raking fist and caught him on the cheekbone. The paramedic was knocked halfway across the bay. A loud shout came from the restroom. His partner vanished from the window.

"Quick!" Ruby took charge. "Get aboard. GBH —"

He knew what to do. In a second a knife was in his hand. The blade flashed out. He plunged it into a tyre of the next ambulance in line and ran to the cab of their own vehicle.

"Get out o' there." The paramedic stumbled in pursuit.

GBH swung the knife at him and scrambled into the driver's seat. They had planned to hot-wire it. There was no time. And no key.

He jumped down and sprang at the dazed paramedic. The man fell easily. GBH put a knee on his chest. "The key! Gimme the key!" He pricked him in the neck. "I'll do you! I swear I will!"

The second paramedic arrived.

"Keep back!" GBH stared at him. "I'll stick your pal!"

He came no closer. The frightened paramedic pulled the key from his pocket.

Dragging him by the chest, GBH retreated to the cab. In a single movement he dropped his captive, sprang into the driver's seat, slammed the door and snapped the lock shut.

The bearded paramedic was at the window, hammering, shouting.

"It's that guy from the jail." The fallen man struggled to his feet. "They're making a snatch."

GBH turned the key in the ignition, groped for the gears and stamped on the accelerator. The ambulance shot forwards. Priestly's wheelchair shot backwards. Ruby caught it as it was going out the door and clung tight. The paramedic grabbed the driver's door handle. It was torn from his grasp. Picking up speed, the ambulance took off across the hospital car park. A man with an arm and leg in plaster stood right in the way. His eyes popped. With a cry he fell aside.

GBH had never driven a van before, let alone an ambulance. He was not very good at it. Trailing the ramps with a noise like a train crash, he cut a swathe through the car park. Visitors' cars were bulldozed aside. Doors were bashed in, wings ripped off, headlights shattered. By luck more than good management, he reached the hospital gates and veered out wildly into the road. The tyres squealed. The ramps were thrown off. Those in the back were flung against cupboards. Apparatus crashed to the floor.

Headlong they raced down the road. GBH searched the dashboard and pressed a switch. The flashing emergency lights came on; the headlights flashed alternately. He pressed another, the siren began to wail. They were doing sixty within the thirty-mile-an-hour limit. Ruby and Gestapo Lil pulled the doors shut.

GBH stared in his wing mirror, looking for signs of pursuit, dreading the lights of a police car. None came. The road behind was empty. One of the ramps had hit a bus. The traffic had come to a standstill. He turned a corner. Then another corner. He switched off the emergency signals. All was calm. Nothing disturbed the city evening.

Had they pulled it off? He could hardly believe it. Was the boss free?

He was. And five minutes later the ambulance drew up in a backstreet among warehouses. One wing sent a dustbin flying. A scraggy cat fled in alarm. GBH switched off the headlights.

It was dusk. What streetlamps there were had been broken by vandals. An elderly blue Ford stood in the shadows. It was a hired car. GBH had parked it there before going to the hospital. Though they appeared safe for the moment there was no time to lose. Mad Ruby opened the boot of the car and took out a can of petrol and four plastic bags. These contained their everyday clothes. In the back of the ambulance they stripped off their uniforms, wigs, padded bra, rubber gloves, built-up shoe, false wart, spectacles, everything that connected them with the parts they had played. Priestly was helped out of his hospital gown into joggers and a jersey. Gestapo Lil assisted him from the ambulance to the waiting Ford. She slid into the back seat beside him.

"Oh, Percipops!" She took his hand.

"Oh, Lavvy-Poo!" They kissed tenderly. He looked into her face. "What's happened to your eye?"

"Eh? Oh!" She took out her handkerchief and rubbed off the fake bruising. "There!"

He laid his piggy head on her shoulder.

"How do you feel, precious?"

"Awful," he said.

"Never mind, we'll soon have you better. You're free now. I'll look after you."

"Mmm," he said and popped his thumb into his mouth.

Ruby and GBH, away from this touching scene, piled everything on the floor of the ambulance and doused it in petrol. Swinging the can, they sloshed the sides, and the blankets, and the medical equipment so carefully maintained to save lives. Both were on a high, they loved destruction.

"Right, matches." Ruby held out her hand.

"I'll do it."

"No you'll not. You're driving – better than you drove the ambulance, I hope. Give me the matches."

With bad grace he passed them over.

The air was heavy with petrol fumes.

"Are you ready?" She struck the match and threw it forward. With a *whop!* and a *whoosh!* that lit the alley to the chimneys, the ambulance exploded into flame.

"Yeah! Fantastic!" His eyes shone like a boy's on Guy Fawkes' night.

"Is good, no?"

"Gorgeous! Feel the heat."

"All gone. No need worry about forensics. One match – whoosh! Up she go."

But it wasn't safe to stand watching. "Come on. We got'a get out of here."

Reluctantly they jumped into the Ford and took off down the potholed lane. As they reached the street the first spectators were gathering, attracted by the blaze. Though several, afterwards, remembered the car and even recalled that

155

there had been passengers, no one paid the slightest attention to the number plate.

Harry lay reading. Aunt Bridget had bought him a volume of real-life adventures. He had finished Shackleton's voyage from Elephant Island to South Georgia. Now he was among snakes and piranhas in the Amazon jungle, searching for the lost Fawcett expedition.

The distant sound of police sirens slowly entered his consciousness. He set down his book and listened. It must be urgent. Had his aunts or one of the others been up to something? He didn't think so. It must be some other emergency.

A ruby-eyed moth started flying again, clicking against his lampshade, casting its shadow round the walls of the attic. Reading was impossible. Tangle watched it through slitted eyes, took a deep breath and went back to sleep. Harry turned out the light.

Down in the living room the rest were having a nightcap. For some it was Ovaltine, for Auntie Florrie it was a Highwayman's Friend with a dash of cherry brandy. All eyes were glued to a thrilling heist movie, but after a lifetime of crime their ears were attuned to the wail of a police siren. Auntie Florrie, whose senses were particularly acute, had the hearing of a bat. Even though the note be as faint as a gnat in an iron foundry, she picked it up unerringly.

"Oh, my goodness! Here they come!" She spilled her drink down the front of her dress. "What have we been doing? Is everything hidden away?"

Aunt Bridget heard it too. "Florrie, darling, we've done nothing. Not for ages. They're a million miles away."

"Oh, you know what I'm like. Are you sure?"

"Absolutely. You know as well as I do." She rescued what was left of her sister's drink. "Go and mop yourself down and refresh this – whatever it is." She sniffed the glass and took a sip. "Oh, very good. While you're at it you can make me one. And stop worrying."

When Florrie had gone she said: "I suppose no one *has* been up to anything?"

They shook their heads.

"Perhaps we all need a holiday."

"Max deserves one anyway."

"I couldn't agree more. Champagne weekend at the Savoy, yes? We'll pack him off the minute he gets out. What about the rest of us?"

"Can't do nothin' till we get this Eddie Carver business sorted out," Fingers said.

"Von vay or another."

"That's right, 'Uggy. Don't feel too 'opeful meself, this time. What d'you reckon, Bridget?"

"Who knows?" She shrugged. "Never say die. Let's see what Max's got to say next time we—"

"Listen." Mr Tolly held up a hand.

The police siren, never close, had faded.

"See, they're not coming here."

"Must be going like the clappers. Wonder what's the hurry."

Fingers gave his gappy grin. "Mebbe someb'dy knocked off Felon Grange. All that new gear."

There was a chorus of approval.

"Hey, that's an idea. Why don't we—"

"No!" Aunt Bridget said firmly. "Forget it! Anyway, who

says there's been a crime? You know what the fuzz are like, enjoy putting on a bit of a show. Sirens, lights – gives them a kick. Probably just some farm boy had too much to drink. Thanks, Florrie." She took the glass her sister handed her.

"Maybe they get invite to barn dance," said Huggy.

"Perhaps it's a car crash," said Mr Tolly.

But there *had* been a crime, a serious crime. And though there wasn't a barn dance, there was very nearly a serious car crash.

The governor of Cony Hill, as might be expected, was furious at what had occurred. The audacious snatch from hospital of prisoner 5060376, better known as Colonel Percy Priestly, did not show his guards or his prison in a very good light. And so, as soon as the situation became clear, two fuzzmobiles packed with police officers were dispatched to Felon Grange, the home of the prisoner's mother, Mrs Ruby Palazzo, and his fiancée, Miss Lavinia McScrew.

It was fifty miles distant. Blue lights flashing and sirens shattering the night, they streaked down the motorway and turned off on to the country lanes. Two miles from their destination, rounding a tight bend at sixty, they came face to face with a battered farm truck. Luckily the truck was well over to the left and chugging along at thirty. The driver, a man named Yawkins, was forced across the verge and half into a ditch. In boiling dust the police cars climbed a bank, ripped through undergrowth, and crashed back on to the tarmac. Stems trailing and leaves whirling high, they sped on their way. There wasn't a second to lose.

Had the police stopped, as they should have done, they might have wondered why the cab of a dirty old truck smelled of expensive perfume. They might have been surprised, looking in the ashtray, that such a disreputable figure as Whortleberry Yawkins smoked Davidoff cigarettes. They might have enquired what he was doing so far from home at that time of night.

But the police did not stop.

Farmer Yawkins blinked to recover from the dazzle and dismounted from his cab to inspect the damage. To his surprise the only dents were those rusty old friends which gave his truck its character. It was a relief because the last thing he wanted was to need a garage and be investigated by the police – or anybody else. It would not be difficult, he saw, to reverse back on to the road. A happy drool ran down his chin. He wiped it away and watched the blue lights speed across the side of a hill. They dipped from sight.

Whortleberry Yawkins, or Baba, as he was better known, was a big, soft-bodied man of forty with a cherubic face, untended hair and crazed blue eyes. He reached into the cab for a bottle of cloudy cider and popped the stopper with his thumbs. Eyes on the stars, he took a throatful and snapped the bottle shut. It was an action as automatic as smoking a cigarette. As he replaced the bottle on the seat he smelled the perfume. These days Baba rarely came into contact with women. It had been nice driving all the way out here scrunched up against that pair of beauties, specially the blonde one. As for his nephew who had travelled in the back! What was it they had called him – GBH? Why GBH, for God's sake? His name was Phil. Anyway, the back of the truck was the best place for a piece of rubbish like him.

An owl hooted. A fox barked from the hill, dry and clear. The night was full of hunters. Hunters in blue, an' all, Baba thought. Hunters in fast cars. "But they'll not catch un," he confided to a nearby bush. "'Cos he bain't here, see. He's back in the old house at Scrumpy Bottom, sleepin' off the effects o' that gunpowder." The starlight glinted on his wet lips. "Look for a hundred year, they'd never find un there."

Smiling, he climbed into his cab and bumped back to the narrow road. Carrying passengers, a rare occurrence, had required him to rearrange things. He switched on the inside light and replaced them in their familiar disorder. Taking a tape of Tchaikovsky's *First Piano Concerto*, he slipped it into the stained machine beside him and turned up the volume. The great chords crashed across the fields. Cattle turned their heads. Rabbits raced for cover. Singing along, Baba threw the truck into gear and resumed his journey. It was thirty-five miles to Cider House Farm – Scrumpy Bottom as it was known locally – the dilapidated straggle of buildings that Baba called home.

It would be nice to have company.

"And where were you while all this was going on?" Gestapo Lil confronted the police with eyes like chips of ice.

"It wasn't our job."

"Where were the guards then? I suppose there were guards."

"Yes, there were guards."

"Well what were they doing? Down the corridor chatting up the nurses, I suppose."

They stood in the hallway. Felon Grange was three-quarters furnished. Paintings hung on the magnificent staircase. A polished oak dresser and other pieces of furniture stood against the walls.

"And he was poisoned?" Ruby's eyes burned. "I don'a

believe it. Who poison my son? Why he take'a poison? How he get poison in the jail? I gonna see my solicitor. Why you not take'a better care of him?"

Uniformed officers kept watch outside the house. Two detectives interviewed the occupants. One was a fresh-faced young sergeant, the other a chief inspector with sleek hair.

"Don't give us that. Think we spend all day sticking bananas in our ears. Think we don't know about you lot here at Felon Grange?" The inspector gave a crooked smile. "Three people, two women and a man, exactly matching the size and age of the people in this house, entered the infirmary, assaulted the guards, snatched a convicted felon, stole an ambulance and burned it out. You'll go down ten years for this. You're on the computer, all got form, here and in Italy. Why not make it easy for yourselves. Tell us where he is and it'll count in your favour."

"You want we tell lies? Sure, what we got to lose? Here, I give Police Benevolent Fund a cheque for ten thousand while we're at it."

"Pounds," said the sergeant, "or Mafia lire?"

"Oh, you're so sharp. Watch you don'a cut your throat while you're shaving."

Although it was barely ten o'clock, they had changed into their night attire. It had been a close call. The rattle of Baba's truck had hardly faded down the drive when the police were hammering at the door. Gestapo Lil wore a slinky cream dressing-gown with a froth of red lace. Her hair hung loose.

"I wish he *was* here, my Percy. See off the likes of you. But he's not. Thanks to you I don't know when I'll see him again." Tears gathered in her eyes. "In the hands of some horrible gang. I don't know if I'll *ever* see him again."

"Oh, come *on!*" The inspector rolled his eyes. "Give me a break!"

"You think he here in this house?" Mad Ruby said. "OK, go ahead, look. We nothing to hide, we not even care about search warrant." She strode to the dresser. "You want look in stables also? Here, take'a the keys."

She threw them at the young sergeant. They fell to the polished floor.

"You find him, you take him. You prove we been in the hospital," she held out her wrists, "here, put on the cuffs. You find we use'a the cars, OK, take them too. The engines stone cold. We not been out since this morning."

"Where were you, as a matter of interest?"

"When, this morning? Five minutes ago? Last Christmas?"

"This evening."

"This evening?" She shrugged. "Here. There's work to do. We furnish it, in case you not notice. Then we watch video."

"Not the TV?"

"Programmes all'a rubbish. What the name of that movie we watch?" she said to GBH who sat in a chair out of the limelight. "Hey! You! I talking to you."

"Video?" GBH slept in his underwear. For the police he had wrapped himself in a pink candlewick bedspread with tassels. "*Hang 'em High.*"

"That'a right. And a cartoon."

He yawned. "*Bugs Bunny and the Great Escape.*"

"That a joke?" The inspector stared.

"No, was good movie. Very funny, like yourself. How I joke when you let'a my son poisoned and snatched by some crazy gang?"

GBH covered his hairy legs. "Gotta fag?"

The inspector said, "It *was* you, the three of you. I know it and I'm going to prove it. Them disguises you wore, they're going to turn up. Forensic'll have a field day."

"Disguises?" Ruby raised her eyebrows. "Like Mickey Mouse masks'a? You mean people walking round hospital in Mickey Mouse masks and nobody—"

"No, like wigs and warts and specs. Designer stubble." He crossed to GBH and felt his jaw.

The tough guy smiled. "Sorry, darlin', you're not my type."

"You just shaved?"

"So what, gonna arrest me? I always shave at night. Can't be bothered in the mornin'."

"Oh, you're all very clever." The chief inspector was getting rattled. "All very smug. But you mark my words, you're going to make a mistake. And when you do," he jabbed a forefinger, "I'll be there."

"Oooooh!" GBH said. "I'm scared!"

"What a very unpleasant man." Barely up to the inspector's shoulder, Ruby pulled her dressing gown tight.

"He doesn't like people who are innocent," Gestapo Lil said. "Or guilty, I expect. Take no notice, they'll soon be gone."

Two of the uniformed officers had drifted into the hall.

"Come on then." The young sergeant took charge. "Since we've been invited, let's take a shufti. Don't expect we'll find anything but you never know."

"I got a magnifying glass somewhere," Ruby said. "It help you find clues."

One of the constables said, "There's a priest's hole in the library. That business at New Year, remember."

163

"Chock-a-block," Gestapo Lil said. "Stacked to the ceiling. Better bring your handcuffs." She started along the corridor. "Come on, I'll show you. Don't want you smashing the place up."

"There's the old keepers' sheds out in the woods an' all," GBH shouted after the retreating figures.

"And the cellars," the sergeant's voice drifted back. "And the coal bunkers. And the lofts in the stables. We know."

They took their time: looked through bureaux, climbed up to the attic, checked videos, peered into the washing machine, winkled their torches into unlit corners. Apart from brands of shower gel, makes of underwear and tastes in reading, they learned little except that, as expected, Priestly was *not* there, there was no evidence of disguise, and the people at Felon Grange were not short of money.

It was not yet midnight when they took their leave. "We'll be back."

"Come for dinner."

"Missing y'alreaaddy."

They watched the policemen cross the portico and descend to their cars. Moths fluttered about the coach lamps. Gestapo Lil waved goodbye. GBH banged the door shut and shot the bolts.

A visit from the police had been expected. Indeed there would have been something wrong if they *hadn't* turned up, which was why that fool Yawkins had sent them crazy with his snail's-pace driving. All the same, they had made it – just.

Well pleased with the way things had gone, they retired to the kitchen. The stove was dirty with spills. For three days no one had washed any dishes.

"That'll be your first job tomorrow," Gestapo Lil told GBH. "Clean this place up, it's a pigsty." She examined her face in the mirror. "Put the kettle on and make a pot of tea."

"I don't want tea. Make it yourself." Bedspread hanging like a cloak, GBH took a beer from the fridge and threw the tab at the sink. It fell on the tiles. "I'm not a skivvy, that's women's work." He sucked away the foam. "I don't work for you anyroad. Now he's out and staying with my Uncle Baba, I work for the boss."

Mad Ruby and Gestapo Lil turned on him. There was about to be a major explosion. Luckily at that moment the phone rang. Ruby glanced at the clock. Who was ringing at that hour? What had happened? Apprehensively she picked up the extension.

"Hello?"

It was her son, Gestapo Lil's fiancé, the escaped prisoner.

"You've got to get me out of here," he cried.

In the background she heard laughter and the crashing notes of a piano.

"The man's a lunatic!"

Chapter 15

Fisherman's Tryst

Following the violent death of prisoner Jones on Tuesday, and the snatch of prisoner Priestly a day later, all visiting was cancelled at Cony Hill. Even though Aunt Bridget was desperate to speak to Max, the jail was sealed tight as Fort Knox while the governor and his staff searched every cell, every workshop, every corner of the recreation area, and conducted enquiries. They discovered nothing, and on Saturday morning a limited form of visiting was resumed: twenty minutes and a single visitor for each inmate.

Aunt Bridget was lucky, she was one of the first, and at eleven o'clock presented herself at the prison gates.

"It was just awful," she reported to the others later that day. "They searched us: looked in my handbag, patted me under the arms, made me empty my pockets on to a table – everything."

"No need to tell us, love," Fingers said. "We've bin there, remember."

"I know, but one forgets how *grim* it can be sometimes. All the screws watching you with narrow eyes, shouting when there's no need to, rattling their keys, banging the doors."

They sat at the picnic table beneath the giant chestnut tree on the lawn. Pencils of sunlight pierced the canopy of leaves. A squirrel bounced along the edge of the wood.

"It makes me so determined," Aunt Bridget said. "No matter *what* happens, none of us is *ever* going back inside."

"Don't get yourself all upset." Mr Tolly took her hand.

"And Max will be out in a few days." Mrs Good topped up Aunt Bridget's coffee and dropped a ginger parkin, of which she was very fond, on her plate.

"Thanks, Goody." She blinked hard. "Silly me."

"Not at all," Huggy said. "You our number-von favourite nice voman. But now ve get on." She set her elbows on the table. "Vhat Max have to tell you?"

"You're right." She adjusted her granny glasses. "Well, much to his surprise – and mine, too, I have to say – during his last few days Eddie seems to have undergone some sort of transformation. Max says he became quite – I was going to say fond, but fond's not the right word, he was a wicked, evil man – sorry for him anyway. They had one or two quite long talks and Eddie showed a side of himself you'd never guess at. Growing up in the streets the way he did, trading from the back of a lorry, he never saw many flowers, apart from outside a florist's, a few doors along from their junk yard. Tough guy like him, he couldn't admit to liking flowers but he loved that shop. So when he grew up and got a place of his own, he made a walled garden where no one could see him, and he could plant and smell the flowers to his heart's content."

Aunt Bridget nibbled her parkin. "And furniture, he loved good furniture. And art galleries, except he never bought paintings. Paintings were vulnerable. Paintings were for stealing, not having them stolen."

"He felt the same about banks," Auntie Florrie said.

"That's right. And do you know why he hated banks? When he was a boy his father handed over his entire life's savings to some manager to invest. The man was a crook, one of the nasty sort, ran off with every brass farthing. Left them penniless. So after that his father turned all his money into gold – just in case there was a fire – and hid it in the attic. Eddie's done the same."

"Hidden it in the attic?" Harry cried.

"If only." His aunt smiled. "No, never trusted banks. Turned his money into gold and hidden it away somewhere."

"And he was going to tell you where on Wednesday, only—"

She shrugged. "We'll never know now. But what I *do* know is that Priestly was sniffing around there like the nasty old stoat he is. One time Eddie caught him listening outside the door and went after him with a chair. Would have knocked his brains out, Max says. The screws had to drag him off. Hard to realize this was the same man as liked growing his sweet peas and azaleas. But Priestly must have heard them discussing the Africa scheme, and me going in to see him, and maybe Eddie doing something good with his money, because it was Priestly pushed him down the staircase – the very night before I went in. Couldn't bear the thought he might tell us where the treasure's hidden. The governor never found out but all the prisoners know, common knowledge on the landings."

"And now Eddie's dead and Priestly's on the loose," Mr Tolly said.

"Where do you think he'll have gone, Aunt Bridget?" Harry said.

"Who, Eddie or Priestly? I've got a pretty good idea where Eddie's gone. But Priestly, who knows. Not Felon Grange anyway."

"So is that it?" Absent-mindedly Mr Tolly pulled a bouquet of feathers out of Harry's ear. "Max had nothing useful to tell us?"

"Oh, far from it. He found out where Eddie used to live."

"The valled garden!" Huggy said at once. "He bury it in the valled garden!"

"Unfortunately not. Apparently that's been dug over so often it looks like a turnip field. Anyway, he had to leave that house. Last time he was divorced his wife got it and Eddie went to live with his brother. He'd been divorced too, ripped off by his wife. They'd both had enough of marriage so they set up together. Big house in Hampstead."

"I used to live in Hampstead," Harry said. "Before I came here."

"So you did," Aunt Bridget said. "Anyway, Dart didn't share his brother's love of gardening, but he did share another passion. They were both crazy about fishing. Packed the car and went off every chance they had. Even called the house after it."

"Antidote to the lives they lived during the week," Auntie Florrie said. "Monday to Friday burglary, extortion, beating up shopkeepers, terrorizing the west side of London, drowning people in barrels of eggs. Then off at the weekend to grow geraniums and stand on riverbanks catching trout."

"I wonder where they went," Mr Tolly said thoughtfully.

"Eddie never said."

"Psychos if you ask me," Fingers said. "What did they call this 'ouse, anyway?"

"*Fisherman's Tryst.*"

Harry was startled.

"What's wrong?"

"Did you say *Fisherman's Tryst?*"

"Yes, why?"

"In Honeysuckle Wynd?"

It was Aunt Bridget's turn to be surprised. "How do you know that?"

"It's just round the corner from where I stayed. I used to go there."

"You used to—"

"When I lived with Gestapo Lil. Mr Jones. He had this great big fish pond in the back garden. White Daimler. Fig tree against the wall."

"You knew him?"

"Sort of. He used to give me nuts."

"Nuts?"

"Yeah, he kept this box of salted almonds on the front seat. I used to go round there when Gestapo Lil wasn't watching."

"But why didn't you say?"

"Well *I* didn't know who he was. Lots of people are called Jones. He was just this man round the corner."

"Couldn't have been Eddie," Fingers said. "He's been inside since 'Arry was a toddler. Must've been Dart."

"Dart Jones who was shot?" Harry said sadly. "He was a nice man."

"To you maybe."

"I fell in the pond once," he said. "Gestapo Lil would have killed me. He took me inside and dried my clothes in the machine so she never found out."

"That was nice of him."

"Yeah. It was freezing. He gave me this huge bath towel and we sat by the fire in a kind of den. Smelled of cigars. Big stuffed salmon in a case."

"Stuffed salmon." Fingers was thoughtful.

"An' a rack of rods – salmon, trout, spinners. Taught me to play poker."

Mr Tolly said, "I wondered where you picked that up."

Fingers said, "Tell us about the pond."

"It was full of these big red carp, trailing fins. . . Oh, they didn't fish there or anything."

"I didn't mean that. A big pond, you said, at the back of the house. Was it very deep?"

"Not where I fell in. About a metre. But you couldn't see the bottom."

"That's enough questions," Aunt Bridget said. "The rest will keep. But see what else you can remember, Harry."

"I can remember everything," he said. "It was only last year."

"And you can take us there?" Auntie Florrie said.

"Not from here," Harry said. "But once we get to Hampstead, yeah, no bother."

"Good boy," Dot said approvingly.

Four people drove down in the Merc: Aunt Bridget and Huggy in the front, Harry and Fingers in the back.

At a little before eleven they parked in a quiet side street and walked the last few hundred metres. As they passed the many-gabled house where Harry had spent the first ten years of his life, he pointed it out to the others.

"Big place for just the two of you," Fingers said.

"Yeah." Harry shivered to remember what had gone on in those fine high rooms, left by his globe-trotting parents in the hands of Gestapo Lil: the daily confrontations, the punishments, her whip and knuckleduster, the hours of housework she had forced him to do, her thefts, the lonely child he had been. Now – he took Huggy's hand as they turned the corner into Honeysuckle Wynd – there wasn't a happier boy in the whole of Britain.

Two minutes took them to their destination. *Fisherman's Tryst*, in this very expensive part of London, was a fine brick and half-timbered building which stood well back from the road behind hedges and a front garden set with trees. Harry led the way up the drive and opened a gate in a wisteria-covered trellis. The others filed through. Carefully he shut the gate behind them and turned to face the back garden.

It looked like a building site. Someone had been there before them. The pond which Harry knew had gone. In its place was a hole that might have been gouged out by a digger, two thirds full of muddy water. On every side the manicured lawns were fouled with heaps of gunge and pond weed. Mixed in with it were the fish, beautiful gold and scarlet carp with trailing fins and tails. Several had been half eaten by some cat or urban fox.

Aunt Bridget stepped close to examine them. "They've been dead for a day or two."

"Who do you think it was?" Harry said.

"Who you think?" Huggy responded. "Percy Pig Priestly, that who."

"Must have come over right after 'e got sprung," Fingers said. "Couldn't have done all this by himsel', though, not even wi' that GBH helping him. Expect he rung up some of his old mates an' promised 'em a share. Dropped round after dark wi' shovels and rakes an' done the business."

"D'you mean he knew about the pond?" Harry said.

"Certainly he did. Eddie's fence, wasn't he? Must have been here loads o' times. Prob'ly been drooling over what might be lying down there for years."

"The loot, you mean?"

"What else? First thing struck me when you told us about it. Big fish pond, what better place to hide a few bags an' boxes? Course he had the same idea. Stands to reason. Wouldn't dare try nothin' while Eddie an' Dart were alive. Now they've gone," he shrugged, "well, things are diff'rent."

"And he was eavesdropping, remember, when Eddie was talking to Max," Aunt Bridget said.

Harry looked at the fish, mouths gaping, eyes crusted. Two, somehow, had survived. Aimlessly they circled in the brown water.

"D'you think they found it," he said, "the treasure?"

"'Ere in the pond, you mean?" Fingers said. "Course not."

"How d'you know?"

"Dear, oh dear! Use your porkies."

"Porkies?"

"Pork pies, eyes."

Harry gazed around. "What am I supposed to be looking for?"

Fingers shook his head. "An' 'ere's me thinkin' you're gettin' the 'ang of it. If they'd got it out 'ere there'd have been no need to break into the 'ouse, would there."

And now Harry saw that the wood was splintered round the lock of the back door. He walked over and examined it.

Fingers joined him. "Used a jemmy. Don't know what the trade's coming to – no finesse." He pulled down his sleeve and turned the handle but the door seemed to be locked. "Give it a whack, there's a good lad."

Harry banged the door with his shoulder. It crashed back. He looked round in alarm.

Aunt Bridget had brought gloves. She handed a pair to everyone and led the way into the house. Harry shut the door at their backs.

It was a fine house. Despite their reputations, Eddie and Dart had taste. Good, if not valuable, paintings hung on the walls; fine furniture stood on Bokhara rugs. The den where Harry had sat by a blazing fire was panelled with oak and still smelled of cigars. The lounge, a man's room, had leather armchairs, cased fish on the walls and a large television. The cellars had been opened out and extended to form a room with a bar, easy chairs and a full-sized billiard table.

Violence had enabled Eddie Jones and his brother to live comfortable and outwardly-respectable lives. Similar violence – murder, in fact – had brought those lives to an end. And now the brothers were dead, the violence had been turned upon their house. The billiard table was ripped from end to end. Broken bottles of five-star brandy littered the carpet. The pictures were shattered, the furniture destroyed.

Other rooms had received similar treatment.

"Know why they done this?" Fingers said.

Harry was appalled. He shook his head.

"Spite," Fingers told him, "'cos they couldn't find what they were lookin' for. See?" He pointed to the shattered display cases, the disembowelled salmon. "Struck me the second you told us yes'day. Stuffed salmon – missin' treasure. Aha! Not a bad place to stash 'alf a kilo o' nice sparklers, few bags of uncut diamonds. But the gelt weren't there, and it weren't in the fish pond. They were miffed. So they took it out on the 'ouse."

Harry looked down at the stuffing, the imitation weed on which the great fish had rested. A little brass plaque was attached to a fragment of frame. He picked it up and read: *Salmon, 46lbs 10ozs. Caught by Mr Edward Morris Jones on* . . . followed by the date and some river he had never heard of. He dropped it with the rest.

A squashed box of chocolates stood on the sideboard. Huggy popped a strawberry cream into her mouth.

"Fingers." Aunt Bridget called from the landing. "Here's the safe."

"Ah, now you're talkin'!" Followed by the others, he trotted up the thickly-carpeted staircase.

Aunt Bridget stood in the master bedroom. It, too, held the aroma of expensive cigars. Harry imagined his old friend smoking in the king-sized bed.

"What do you think?" she said to Fingers.

The safe had been forced, the door stood open. Scattered papers and two or three empty jewellery boxes from Asprey and Cartier lay on the floor.

"Dear, oh dear!" Fingers crouched to examine the lock. "Bad as the back door. Must've taken 'em half the night. Cold chisel, see." He indicated the curled, bright steel and looked over at the window. "Triple glazing, just as well. Must've sounded like a shipyard."

"Good safe, though," Huggy said.

"You must be jokin'. Daffy Duck job. Surprised villains like Eddie an' Dart never fixed themselves up wi' somethin' better than this."

"You could have opened it? Vithout the chisel?"

Fingers looked all round. "Sorry, love, who are you talkin' to?"

"Vell, could you?"

"'Uggy, darlin', this is Fingers. Remember? Blimey, my mum give me safes like this to play with in my pram."

Harry said, "Maybe they reckoned people would be too scared to break in."

"One-way ticket to the chicken farm. Could be." Fingers straightened. "Prob'ly never kept much at 'ome anyway, got another safe somewhere else. Not goin' to keep millions in 'ere, anyroad."

"No room if it gold," Huggy said.

The bedroom overlooked the back garden. Aunt Bridget stood by the window examining papers. Harry gathered up a few pages and did likewise. They meant nothing to him: bank statements for a few thousand, share in a racehorse, letters. A name caught his eye, Yussuf Aziz.

"Aunt Bridget," he said. "Auntie Florrie once said something about your Uncle Aziz. He used to be Eddie's accountant or something."

"Yes?" She didn't look up.

"Was his first name Yussuf?"

"Yes," she said, still reading. "Not a real uncle, though. Just a friend from the old days. Lovely man, not like the rest of that crew."

"There's a letter here from him."

"Let's see." She dropped the sheet she had been reading.

"Not much, just something about a *tax return*," Harry said, uncertain what that was.

"Mm." Aunt Bridget read it carefully and tucked the paper into her pocket. "I was thinking we ought to pay Uncle Aziz a visit. Since we're down this way perhaps we could go today."

Fingers looked wistfully at the empty jewellery boxes. "I wonder what info Priestly an' his pals got."

"Time will tell," she said. "Not much we can do about that."

Huggy crossed the landing and looked down on the road. She was beginning to feel anxious. "Time ve go. Already ve chance our luck."

"You're right." Fingers helped gather the papers into a small sheaf. "Take this lot wiv us an' scarper."

It was the voice of experience. Perhaps even a sixth sense. They descended to the hall. Harry went into the kitchen and found a Tesco bag for the papers. A minute later they stood back in the garden.

"Gloves," Aunt Bridget said.

They dropped them into the bag. After a last look at the devastated pond, Harry led the way through the trellis to the front of the house.

A neighbour, shampooing his new Jaguar, looked up as they emerged. The house, he knew, was unoccupied. The owner had been murdered.

"Lovely car." Aunt Bridget was cool. "Have to give my old Beetle a wash when we get back."

He smiled uncertainly and watched as they walked off along the pavement. Chains of foam ran down his metallic-blue pride and joy. Deciding it was none of his business, he returned to work.

It was not the last of their alarms for before they had even reached the corner a police car swung into view. Uniformed officers occupied the front seats. To their horror it drew up alongside. The window slid down and a pleasant young policeman smiled out. "Good morning."

They stopped. "Good morning."

"Do you live round here?"

"Not far," Aunt Bridget said.

"Would you know which house is *Fisherman's Tryst*? Posh street like this, they haven't got numbers."

"Oh, I think it's er –" In two minutes they could be in the Merc and away. "That one down there." She indicated a house near the end of the leafy road. "With the white gateposts. Not too sure mind."

He looked where she pointed. "Thank you."

"Trouble?" she said.

"Neighbour rang up. Said she'd seen some people hanging round the back. Thought we'd better check it out." He looked past her. "Your friend all right, is he?"

The blood had drained from Fingers' face. Close to fainting, he clung to Huggy's arm.

"Not been well," Aunt Bridget said. "Better after he's had his Sunday lunch."

"Tell me about it." The policeman raised a friendly hand. "Thanks for your help. Bye-bye."

The window slid up. The fuzzmobile drew away.

"Oh, my vord!" Huggy exhaled. "Come on, ve vaste no time. Fingers!" She pulled her sleeve from his catatonic clutch.

His eyes focussed. He recovered quickly. "Cor! Kiss me quick and call me Charlie! I thought we'd 'ad it that time." Shifting his grip to the front of her jacket he started across the road, dragging Huggy behind. "I'm gettin' too old for this caper."

Harry ran to catch them up.

"Stop it!" Aunt Bridget hissed. "Slow down. Harry, wait. Fingers! Act normally."

They assembled on the pavement opposite. Sober as a party of churchgoers, they rounded the corner and walked on past Harry's old home to the Merc. Aunt Bridget took the wheel. Harry sat in the front and guided her through narrow streets away from Honeysuckle Wynd. Emerging into the Sunday traffic she turned left, then right, then left again, then right again. Reaching the main road, she put her foot down.

By the time the policemen realized they had been directed to the wrong house, had explored the back garden of *Fisherman's Tryst*, discovered the forced entry, and spoken to the owner of the Jaguar, Harry and his companions were miles away.

"Where now?" he asked.

"Oh, never mind," Fingers called from the back seat. "Just keep driving, Bridget."

"I think I want to go to Oxford," she said, turning into the lane for the M25.

"Oxford!"

"Why Oxford?"

"It's where Uncle Aziz lives," she said.

"What about lunch?" said Harry.

"Took the words right out of my mouth." She glanced sideways. "See if you can spot a nice pub."

Chapter 16

Killer Dogs

Frogwood St Peter, about nine miles from Oxford, is one of the prettiest villages in England. Centuries-old brick and stone houses, several thatched, stand higgledy-piggledy around the village green and rushy duckpond. The pub is half-timbered, the store full of gossip. Magnificent trees dapple the lanes with shadow.

An old farmer directed them to the house of Uncle Aziz: "A couple of hundred yards down there past St Michael's and round the corner, right on the edge of the village." He stumped off. "Best place for it an' all. Never ought to have been allowed."

It was the strangest house Harry had ever seen, surrounded by triple-spiked railings, an electric fence and security cameras. Two bold notices, one either side, were displayed by the electronically-controlled gates. One, painted upon the image of a glacially-pure mountain, proclaimed the name of the house to be *Nanda Devi*. The second notice, red and black on white, announced:

Danger!
These Premises are
Patrolled by Guard Dogs.
Keep Out!

The garden, if garden it could be called, was an acre of stone slabs, large and small, white and pastel shades, set here and there with dwarf ornamental trees. The house itself, right in the middle of this airy space, was built entirely of glass; vertical glass and glass set at angles, a house like an arrangement of prisms. The farmer's reaction became clear. How the planners had allowed such a house in a traditional Oxfordshire village was a mystery.

They walked to the gate and Aunt Bridget pressed the intercom. Immediately, before there was time for an answer, a wave of small dogs, fifty at least, flooded across the slabs. They were terriers, mostly Yorkies with their coats cut short, but among them a scattering of chihuahuas, griffons, Westies and Scotties. Growling and yapping, they faced the visitors through the electric fence.

"Guard dogs!" Harry smiled.

"Yes?" The intercom crackled and spat.

"Uncle Aziz?"

There was a pause. "Who's that? What do you want?"

"A voice from the past, Uncle. Bridget Barton. With one or two friends."

The noise of the dogs rose to a crescendo. The words from the intercom were lost.

"What was that?" she shouted.

"I said, how do I know it's Bridget?"

"Well, come and see. Look in one of your screens." She waved up at a camera. "Not a blaster in sight if that's what this is all about."

There was a long pause. "Bridget! Long time no see! Hang on, I'll be right out."

The figure who emerged from the house was small and brown-skinned with a bald dome and halo of frizzy white hair. He wore a loose Hawaiian shirt, shapeless shorts and leather sandals.

"All right, all right, all right!" he shouted at the hysterical dogs. "Shut up! They're friends! Ali Baba!"

The noise was scarcely reduced. A dozen dogs looked round.

"Ali Baba!" He shouted the words of command. "Ali Baba, you cretins! Ali Baba, for God's sake!"

At last they fell silent. Tails wagging, they gathered round his skinny legs.

"Bridget!" Beaming with large false teeth, he came to the electric gate, opened a control box and confidently pushed a succession of buttons. Nothing happened. He thought for a moment, counting on his fingers. "Ah, I remember, seven-five not five-seven." He pushed the buttons again, mouthing each numeral as he keyed it in ". . .three, seven, five." With a flourish he finished and pressed *Activate*. There was a terrific bang and a blue flash. The gates burst open, so violently that if Harry had been standing any closer, they would have broken his arm. The dogs scattered. The startled face of Uncle Aziz appeared through a cloud of smoke. He fanned it away. "Are you all right?"

They assured him they were.

"Ach, that nothing," Huggy said. "Vhen you live vith Fingers, every day it is like var just broke out."

Uncle Aziz didn't understand. "Damned code." He glared at the blackened control box. "I never used to have this trouble. When Mr Jump was away last week I couldn't get out for three days."

"Who's Mr Jump?"

"The electrician. Have to give him a ring when we go in. But never mind that." He advanced down the steps, arms wide. "Bridget Barton! My number-one favourite crook of all time! How are you?"

"Fine, Uncle Aziz. Just fine."

They embraced.

"A social call, I hope. You're not visiting me after all this time with nasty questions?"

"Of course not," she said affectionately. "You should know me better than that. Though since you mention it, there are just a couple of things. . ."

Uncle Aziz was enjoying the company. He leaned back in his chair and swung a sandal from his big toe.

Harry said, "What's *Nanda Devi*?"

"I beg your pardon?"

"The name of the house."

"Oh, Nanda Devi. It's a very high mountain in the Himalayas. My mother was born in the Delhi slums. From the top of a tall building she could see this pure, beautiful thing on the horizon. So different from the gutters where she lived. So when I had the money to build a place of my own, I tried to make it a bit like my mother's dream."

"Were you born there?"

"No, I'm from Wolverhampton."

"It's a gorgeous house, Uncle," Aunt Bridget said. "So original. Who designed it?"

"I did. Forty years an accountant and all I ever wanted to be was an inventor. Ridiculous really."

Harry gazed at the glass panels above his head.

"Angled so they act like mirrors," said Uncle Aziz. "We can see out but people outside can't see in. Not even at night with the lights on."

They sat in the lounge. It was like reclining inside a crystal, with a scarlet grand piano, very comfortable blue, green and yellow chairs, a shell-pink table, mauve television set and electrically-heated glass floors covered with rugs in jazzy colours.

"All bullet-proof," said Uncle Aziz. "Has to be, the people I met working for Eddie Jones. Here," he pulled an enormous revolver from beneath a cushion and passed it to Harry. It was the sort of gun Indiana Jones would have used. "There's some spare sheets of glass round the back. Try it if you don't believe me."

Harry took it gingerly. "Is it loaded?"

"Course it's loaded. What good's a shooter if it's not loaded?"

It was heavy. Blue steel with a rosewood handle.

"He's not used to guns." Aunt Bridget took it from him. "Weapons of any sort. None of us are." She slid on the safety catch and set the revolver out of harm's way. "Not a word to Goody about this, Harry. She'd have a fit."

"But couldn't I just try it on a bit of—"

"No."

"To see if—"

"No."

When Aunt Bridget said *no* like that she meant it. Harry looked out at the garden. Already Mr Jump was working on the gates. A boy, too, had appeared, walking round the flagstones with his head lowered and a pair of long-handled rubbish collectors in his hand.

"Who's that?"

Uncle Aziz followed his gaze. "Oh, that's David."

"What's he doing?"

"Mm? Oh, he's my poop sergeant."

"Poop sergeant?"

"Well, when you've got as many dogs as I have, you need to keep the place hygienic. Comes round twice a day."

Harry made a face. "What a rotten job."

"Think so? All the local children are clamouring for it. Call themselves the poop troop. Waiting list as long as your arm."

"You're kidding."

"Why? It's not hard work. Pick up the doggies' presents, scrub the spots with disinfectant. Two hours a day."

"I wouldn't do it."

"No? Hundred quid a week?"

"What!"

"Have to keep the workers happy. I can afford it. Only two conditions: they've got to do the job properly and be reliable. Miss once, they're out. Plenty ready to step into their shoes. Parents are dead for it. Teaches them responsibility; doesn't interfere with their schoolwork; money put aside for university when the time comes."

Harry watched David, a year older than himself, as he walked round the garden. New Walkman, expensive Reeboks.

"I happy in house like this." Huggy snuggled into her chair.

"Thought you were 'appy at Lagg 'All," Fingers said.

"Oh, ja. Lagg Hall home. But this different. Nice. I like ver' much."

Harry said to Uncle Aziz, "What have you got so many dogs for anyway?"

"What does it say on the gate? Protection, same as the shooter."

"But they're just little terriers."

"Think I should get a couple of Rottweilers? I tried that. Somebody fed them steak and sleeping pills. Would have topped me if it hadn't been for the alarms."

"What happened?"

"Believe me, you don't want to know. Anyway, these little fellas are much better."

Harry was not convinced. "Look."

One of the Yorkies squirmed on its back while the electrician rubbed its tummy. A Westie stretched its paws up his leg, looking for attention.

"Ah, but they know Mr Jump and David. I introduced them." Uncle Aziz had an idea. "Here, come with me."

Harry followed him down a corridor. Through open doors he saw bedrooms and a glittering kitchen, all hidden by angles of the glass. Right at the end was a workroom.

"Put these on." Uncle Aziz handed him a pair of thick leather trousers and a leather jacket. "A bit on the big side but you can turn up the cuffs."

Harry did as he was bidden. They were hot and heavy.

"Now these." Uncle Aziz passed him a pair of boots, a face mask, a leather balaclava and finally gloves.

He felt as clumsy as a deep-sea diver.

Uncle Aziz accompanied him to an outside door. "Bridget," he called, "and you others. Come and see this."

They appeared in the corridor.

"Oh, my vord!" Huggy blinked. "You dressed up like Fingers make von of his explosions."

Aunt Bridget said, "What's happening?"

"He was asking about guard dogs," Uncle Aziz said. "Right, son? Wasn't convinced these little chaps could do the job. Now," he said to Harry, "when you came in you were with me, so you were safe. See what happens when you go it alone. Try to reach the gate."

Harry looked. It was thirty metres away. Behind the wire face mask his eyes were scared. What had he let himself in for?

"Don't worry." Uncle Aziz bared his big teeth in a smile. "There'll be enough left to bury. I've got a shoebox somewhere. Your auntie can take you home in that."

Harry hoped it was a joke. He gritted his teeth. "Bye, Huggy. Bye, Fingers. Been nice knowing you." Pushing the door wide, he flapped out into the garden.

For the first few paces the little dogs didn't notice. Then one barked. The rest looked round. The terrier by the gate sprang to its feet. Next second the flagstones were a blur of racing demons. Their yapping and snarling drowned out the afternoon. Like a flood they surged against Harry's legs, rose to his hips, leaped to his chest and shoulders. Terrifying teeth were in his face. Claws raked at his arms and neck. From boots to balaclava they hung from his body. Harry struggled to keep his balance. The weight was too much. He fell. They were all over him, fifty dogs, like ants on a caterpillar. Daylight was blocked out. The people at the door could not see Harry at all. He cried aloud.

"Enough! Stop it! Ali Baba!" Uncle Aziz strode among them. "Ali Baba! Ali Baba!" Seizing the terriers by the scruff of their necks, he flung them aside.

Harry lay panting. Terrified.

But unhurt.

"You OK?" Uncle Aziz helped him to his feet. "Friend!" he said to the excited terriers. "Friend. Good dogs. Friend. Ali Baba."

In twos and threes they returned. Tails began wagging.

Nervously Harry put down a hand. Bright eyes looked up from fringes. A Westie yipped, showing how pleased it was to be noticed.

"Take off the gloves."

Harry did so. Tickled the friendly dogs behind the ears. Crouched to rub their chests.

He removed the mask and balaclava.

"Heh-heh!" Uncle Aziz gave a skip. "Well, what do you think?"

"I'm not going to break in," Harry said. "That's for sure."

"Eddie Jones," said Uncle Aziz. "How did I know? I've been expecting a call – but not from you, Bridget."

"Sorry, Uncle." She smiled sheepishly. "I'd not have bothered you, really I wouldn't, and it's lovely to see you. I should have come ages ago. But we do need a lead of some sort and you're our last hope."

They had returned to the lounge. A girl of sixteen or so, wearing a tight top and hotpants, brought in a tray loaded with tea and cake and cherry scones. Harry thought she was very pretty. As she left she trailed fingers through his hair. He blushed scarlet.

"Behave yourself, Jenny," Uncle Aziz said sharply. "Shameless young hussy!"

She blew him a kiss from the door and was gone.

"My housekeeper's daughter." He smiled fondly. "Don't be misled by that little performance, she's got a mind like a razor. Just won a scholarship to Trinity College. Reads maths for fun. Bit like you, Bridget."

"Thank you, sir, she said. More years than I care to think about since I looked like Jenny."

But Harry was still tingling from those fingers in his hair.

Uncle Aziz busied himself among the teacups. "So are you going to tell me what it's all about?"

Aunt Bridget glanced at the others. "All right. We want to track down this treasure he's supposed to have hidden away somewhere."

"Oh, Bridget! You disappoint me. Every crook in the country's looking for that."

"And half the police and half the rest of the population, I should think," she said.

"Which would give a cunning old fox like you a chance to sneak in somewhere else behind their backs."

"Well we're not," Aunt Bridget said. "We're after Carver's dosh like everyone else. But *unlike* everyone else, we don't want it for ourselves."

"Bridget, no!" Huggy and Fingers were startled.

"It's all right," she assured them. "A nest of scorpions couldn't drag a secret out of Uncle Aziz."

So while they sipped tea and dropped crumbs, Aunt Bridget told her old friend about the Wrinklies.

"My darling girl!" Uncle Aziz took her hand as she finished. "I've read about these brilliant jobs in all the papers. *And* the secret donations – there was one just the other day. But it never crossed my mind you were behind it all. What an absolutely marvellous idea."

"Thank you," she said. "We're all very dedicated. Anyway, Max – he's our actor friend – found out where Eddie and Dart lived. We've just been over to have a little look-see, and Harry found a letter with your name on it. So here we are."

Fingers said, "Tell 'im what we want the money for."

"We want to build a hospital in the African bush," she said.

"For people who haven't got doctors and medicines," Harry explained.

"A school also," Huggy said. "And vells so the vomen not need valk all day to fetch vater."

"Biggest job we've tackled." Fingers leaned forward. "Need a big 'aul this time, see. Reckon if we can get our 'ands on Eddie's fortune, it might be enough."

"Marvellous," Uncle Aziz said again.

"Max got himself arrested," Aunt Bridget went on, "so he could get into Cony Hill and go to work on Eddie face to face. And it was all going so well! Then Percy Priestly pushed him down those steps – and that was that."

"The papers never said. So that was Piggy?"

"It certainly was."

"Not his usual style. He was more the secretive type, working behind the scenes."

"Not any more, he's getting bolder." Aunt Bridget dabbed some crumbs from her plate. "Anyway, as far as I can see, that's the end of the line for us. So we've come to see you, Uncle. You must have been his accountant for – what, ten or fifteen years."

"Something like that, I suppose." Uncle Aziz scratched a skinny brown knee. "Money into offshore accounts, fiddled his taxes, backhanders to people in the bullion markets – no end to the shady deals I did for Eddie Carver. But all the violence! Every year it got worse. It made me sick. I'd had enough of it. When he went inside it was my chance to get out. So I vanished for a few years, just to be on the safe side. Then I built this place and – well, here we are."

"Offshore accounts?" Aunt Bridget raised her eyebrows. "I thought he didn't trust—"

"That was in the early days, before it was all gold, gold, gold. And diamonds, of course."

"But is there anything left in those offshore—"

"Oh, you can forget about that. Empty as Harry's plate there." He passed him a cream sponge. "The fuzz and the Inland Revenue cleaned him out like a dose of Epsom salts. I couldn't find you a nickel if my life depended on it."

"And I don't suppose you have any idea where he hid all that gold, gold, gold?"

Uncle Aziz shook his head.

"So you can't help us at all?" Aunt Bridget was despondent.

"I didn't say that. I said I didn't know where to lay my hands on any dosh."

A single Westie was allowed inside the house. It wandered from chair to chair hoovering up the crumbs.

"There's a lock-up the far side of Oxford," said Uncle Aziz. "At least it was still there a few months back."

"A lock-up!"

"Oh, you'll not find what you're looking for. No suitcases full of fifties. Just a place Eddie and Dart kept a few things they wanted out of the public gaze."

"What sort o' things?" Fingers said.

"There was a hot car, I remember that. Big safe. Few odds and ends." Uncle Aziz looked from a window. "I don't go out much, never quite sure who might be waiting down the lane. But if you're interested, why don't we go round and have a look."

"Place will have been ransacked by now surely."

"I shouldn't think so. Only three people knew about it as

191

far as I'm aware: Eddie, Dart and me. There was a chap from the Bristol Butchers followed them one time but, well —" He made a face.

"But what?" Harry said.

"He never go home for his tea," Huggy said. "Some qvestions you no ask."

Harry shut up.

"I suppose Dart'll have made a few changes," said Uncle Aziz. "But *I've* certainly not touched it, and for the last seven years Eddie's been inside."

Aunt Bridget finished her tea and rose. "Come on, then, what are we waiting for?"

Huggy sat firm. "Ve vait vhile I enjoy this most mouth-vatering fruit cake. You vant plan X *mark the spot*? It been there seven year, it no vanish seven minute."

"Yeah," Fingers agreed. "Good tea an' all. I'll 'ave another drop o' that thanks, Aziz, mate." He held out hands like broken starfish. "Tune up the nerves in me fingertips for openin' that safe."

Uncle Aziz poured. "We'll take my car."

"Perhaps you vant go on ahead," Huggy said to Aunt Bridget. "Pat the little doggies in the garden."

Aunt Bridget looked out. The scrubbed slabs steamed in the sunshine. Two or three Yorkies, bright-eyed and silky, wandered by the gate. "I think I'll wait," she said. "They'll have to make do with Pedigree Chum tonight."

Chapter 17

The Lock-Up

There were two cars in the garage, a red Mini and a blue Rolls-Royce Corniche. Both were bulletproof.

"We'll take the Rolls." Uncle Aziz climbed into the driving seat and kicked off his sandals. "Come on, we get in here."

"Harry, I want you in the front," said Aunt Bridget. "Plenty of room for the rest of us in the back."

They were quickly settled. Uncle Aziz pressed a button and the steel door rolled up. They slid out into the leafy lane. The door hummed shut at their backs.

"Let's take the scenic route." Uncle Aziz turned left and left again and soon they were out in the rolling hills of the Oxfordshire countryside.

Although the speedometer dial was graduated up to 150 miles an hour they drove slowly, rarely exceeding thirty. Butterflies rose from the verges as they passed. Fat cattle grazed in the meadows.

Harry loved the huge, expensive car. He ran his hand over the upholstery. Beside him the bare-legged, gnome-like figure of Uncle Aziz sat hunched over the controls.

Aunt Bridget tapped Harry's shoulder. "Look." Ahead of

them and far away, the city of Oxford had come into view. "See the colleges. That tower, just to the left of the trees, that's Magdalen, right next to my old college. And the four spires close together, that's the Bodleian Library. And that globe, that's the Radcliffe Camera. And the Tom Tower at Christchurch."

He looked where she pointed.

"It would be nice if you went there one day."

Study at Oxford? Harry couldn't imagine it. All the same, as the grey walls of the university vanished and reappeared, vanished and reappeared beyond hedges and patches of woodland, he thought how fine they looked and how he might quite like to study there one day.

But Oxford is not all dreaming spires and students in scarves and pretty girls in punts on the Isis, it is an industrial city, and as they descended from the farmland Harry was disappointed to find himself among shabby houses and pubs and shops with metal grilles over the windows. Cardboard and papers lay on the pavements, somebody had been sick the night before. Slowly the inhabited suburbs gave way to warehouses. They crossed a canal. A gasworks appeared above dusty trees. It was a wasteland. For a hundred metres they drove alongside a rusty mesh fence, then Uncle Aziz turned through a high, broken gate into an abandoned lorry park. Three boys kicking a ball stopped to watch as the incongruous Corniche crossed the cinders and disappeared between sheds. Beyond lay a hidden corner of weeds and overhanging branches. Uncle Aziz drew up and groped for his sandals with a horny toe.

"Watch the nettles." He opened the driver's door, but before he stepped out he reached into the glove compartment and took out a small automatic.

"What?" He saw Harry staring. "Just in case, son, just in case. When you've seen some of the things I've seen, met some of the people I've met, you don't want to take any chances."

"Like *Nanda Devi*," Harry said, "and the dogs."

"You've got it." Uncle Aziz patted his arm and dropped the firearm into a deep pocket of his shorts. "Be prepared, like the Boy Scouts."

Harry wasn't sure that the motto applied to carrying automatics, but he said nothing and they dismounted into the weeds and puddles.

A two-minute walk took them to a black steel door in the breeze-block wall of a warehouse. The paint was peeling, the edges of the door grey with ancient cobwebs. There were three keyholes. Fingers dug into his holdall and squirted them copiously with WD-40. Uncle Aziz struggled with a bunch of keys. They would not turn. Huggy pushed him aside: "Here, let me have a go." One after another, squeaking with protest, the locks yielded to force. The hinges, too, were rusted. The door cracked open and stuck. Huggy grasped the edge of the door and *pushed*. Reluctantly it screeched wide. They followed Uncle Aziz into the chill, stale-smelling shadows.

The lock-up was spacious, six metres high, ten or so broad and fifteen metres long. Three 150-watt bulbs with metal shades hung on long flexes. One was fused but two flooded the space with light. Harry stared around. Everything was covered in dust. A forest of one-arm bandits and pinball machines stood by a wall. Roulette tables were piled into a corner. There were coat racks and wine racks, chandeliers, rolls of carpet, unopened cases of whisky, bundles of fishing magazines, several pieces of antique furniture, framed paintings, old coats, the entire back of a bar, and a barrel Harry didn't like to think about which was half full of eggshells and rock-hard gunge. Even after all those years it smelled bad.

The largest and most dramatic object in the lock-up was a car, a Maserati convertible with white-gold paintwork and a brown hood. It stood nose to the wall, surrounded by junk. The tyres were flat, the hood mouldy, the tax disc years out of date. Despite this, and despite the fact that he had just been driven round Oxford in a £200,000 Corniche, it was the most exciting car Harry had ever seen except on a screen. But it wasn't just the fabulous style that grabbed his attention, it was the bullet holes. From bonnet to boot the body was riddled, vicious holes now rusting round the edges. The windows were starred, the hood pierced. Tufts of stuffing sprouted from holes in the cream leather upholstery. And it was stained. Streaks and handprints and dry, blackened pools of what must once have been blood.

"Now you see why the Rolls is bulletproof." Uncle Aziz stood at Harry's shoulder.

"What happened?" he said.

"Stepney Steelfitters trying to muscle in. Dart and Eddie had given a couple of their mob the treatment, so the Fitters set up an ambush for them coming out the dog track. Dart had stayed behind to talk to some bookies but they got Eddie in the chest and the legs." He shivered. "Poor Paddy took most of the shots."

"Was he killed?" Harry said.

"He was twenty-one. Looked more like fifteen in his coffin." Uncle Aziz moved away. "His wife had just had a baby."

Fingers had discovered the safe. He struggled to move a fruit machine out of the way to get more room. "'Ere, 'Uggy. Give us a hand."

She lifted it aside. And then two more.

"That's better, let the dog see the rabbit." He rubbed his palms. "This is more like it. I said they'd 'ave a better job than that useless tea-caddy in the 'ouse."

Aunt Bridget said, "I won't even ask if you can open it, Fingers, darling. How long, that's all?"

"Depends 'ow long you're goin' to stand there blockin' the light." He unzipped his holdall.

"Oh, my vord. He going to blow up Oxford!"

"Use yer loaf." Fingers looked up. "'Ow can I use jelly when we just started searchin' the place? Blow you up, more like, all yer sarky cracks." He pulled out a stethoscope and clipped it into his ears. "Fifteen minutes, set yer watches. Now push off, the lot o' you." He crouched to the lock.

"Artistic temperament." Aunt Bridget mouthed the words and drew the rest away. She saw Harry staring at the Maserati. "Come on, leave that, you'll give yourself nightmares. We've got work to do."

"What?" He joined them by the pinball machines.

"Build a hydrogen bomb. What do you think?"

"Find Eddie Carver's treasure."

"Well that would be nice but let's start by looking for a clue."

"Like what?"

"Come on, Harry, you're not normally this obtuse. How do I know? Hotel bills, petrol receipts, souvenirs, anything. A road map with a big red X on it could be useful."

"Shall I start with the car?"

"Bloodthirsty child! No, I'll do that. You get on your hands and knees and look in the corners."

So Harry crawled between boxes and underneath tables. He found cigar butts and labels from packing cases, spider webs and empty booze bottles. His only discovery of interest was a large desiccated rat. He blew off the dust. A find so splendid was not to be wasted so he backed out and tapped Huggy on the shoulder. The screech she produced on finding the shrivelled rodent in her face would have done justice to the *Flying Scotsman* with a full head of steam. It was all very gratifying.

"You vait!" She shook her fist. "I get you back."

Harry grinned and set the rat aside to collect when they left. There were lots of things he could do with a dead rat.

Aunt Bridget and Uncle Aziz, meanwhile, had been hunting through abandoned coats and containers and the pockets of the Maserati. They drew a blank. Everyone waited for Fingers.

"Ahh!" He spun a wheel, listened carefully, and spun it back. There was a click. He gave a heave. The heavy door of the safe swung open. "And for my next trick –"

Uncle Aziz stared in disbelief.

"'Ow long?" said Fingers.

Huggy checked her watch. "Seventeen minutes."

"Seventeen! Blimey, I must be slipping."

"No you're not," said Aunt Bridget. "You're a genius."

"Yeah, well." Fingers shrugged. "That's true, o' course." He pushed the safe door to its widest and peered inside. "Few sparklers. Oh, yes, very nice." He passed them back.

Aunt Bridget took a diamond and emerald tiara and two or three necklaces in her long hands. She set them on the table beside the rat. They were followed by some brooches and flashing rings.

"My God, Bridget!" Uncle Aziz furrowed his brow. "Do you do this often?"

"Not really," she said airily. "Maybe, what, five or six times a week?"

"Five or six times a *week*!"

"Just teasing. No, this is a bonus. Thanks to you, dear Uncle." She smiled, then her hand flew to her mouth. "Oh, but what am I saying? This isn't ours at all, it belongs to you."

"Me? I don't want it."

"But it's you who worked with Eddie. You who brought us to this—"

"That side of my life is history and it's staying that way, thank you very much. I'd rather carry a cobra home than one of those necklaces. If you want them, take them, they're yours."

"Well, if you're sure, Uncle. We didn't come looking for goodies at all. But if you don't want them, we'll certainly take them and—"

"Snappers-up of unconsidered trifles," Fingers said.

Uncle Aziz was lost. "What?"

"Something Bridget says sometimes. Shakespeare, I think." He held a necklace to the light. "Nice stuff anyway."

"Lovely," Aunt Bridget agreed. "Every little helps. Thank you, Uncle. But it's not what we came for. Anything else in that safe, Fingers? It's big enough."

Harry could see a blue glint of metal.

"You're not going to like it." Fingers reached into the bottom and when he turned his arms were full of weapons: pistols, a rifle with a telescopic sight, two dismantled machine guns. He dumped them on a pool table. "'Ang on, there's a few more."

Aunt Bridget surveyed the pile of arms and made a face. "You're right, I don't like it." She turned, "Huggy, do you think you could find something to spike them with, smash up the mechanisms?"

"Ja, absolutely. I look."

Fingers rooted in his bag. "'Ere y'are." He produced a metal punch and a small hammer. "See if they'll do you."

"I hate guns," Aunt Bridget said. "Look at that Maserati over there. And you driving round in a bulletproof Rolls. Think how much better off the world would be if they'd never been invented."

"Eddie and that crowd," Uncle Aziz said, "they'd just have used knives instead."

"Perhaps you're right." She sighed. "Anyway, what else have we got in there, Fingers?"

There was plenty: old ledgers, an empty leather satchel, fishing flies, a pair of heavy gold cufflinks monogrammed EJ, a lunch box, a set of darts, a box of crystal champagne flutes that somebody had stamped on, and a ripped-up marriage certificate.

"Blimey," Fingers said. "What a load of old rubbish."

"I drew this up." Uncle Aziz flipped through one of the ledgers. "Made it up, more like. Hardly a word of truth in it." He pushed it away and took another. "What a way to waste your life."

"No clues then?"

"'Fraid not," he said. "Just figures. Sorry."

"Well, that seems to be that," Aunt Bridget said. "And just when we were doing so nicely: from Eddie to Max, to

Fisherman's Tryst, to you, Uncle, to the lock-up, to – nothing. The chain comes to an end." She brushed off a cobweb. "Still, *nil desperandum*. Back to the drawing board. See if we can't come up with—"

"Aunt Bridget." Bored with the grown-ups' talk and the columns of figures, Harry had wandered across the lock-up. Idly he opened drawers which had already been searched. Behind the other furniture stood a small hall table, beautifully inlaid with scrolls and acanthus leaves. It stood face to the wall, jammed in by a wardrobe, beer kegs and assorted junk. From the back you could not tell it had a drawer but Harry, crawling on his hands and knees, had seen it. He heaved the heavy wardrobe aside and cleared a space to turn the table round. The drawer, eight centimetres or so deep, opened easily. Within, to his disappointment, lay a long out of date telephone directory, two crumpled cigarette packets, a third half full, a tube of menthol sweets dissolved into syrup, and a dirty ashtray. Another blank, Harry thought. Leaving the sweets, he dumped the rest on the top and peered into the back of the drawer. Something had worked its way into a corner. He took it out and felt a surge of excitement.

"Aunt Bridget."

It was a pocket diary from twelve years earlier, the year before Harry was born. There was a picture of a fisherman on the cover with a salmon leaping at the end of his line. Above stood the words *Fisherman's Diary*.

"Harry, you marvellous boy!" Aunt Bridget took it from his hand and glanced at the table.

"Stood in Eddie's hall when he lived in Chalfont," Uncle Aziz said. "Before he broke up with his wife and moved in with Dart – his third wife that would be. He was fond of his furniture, Eddie. No room in the house, I suppose, so he bunged it in here."

"Not nicked then?" Fingers said. "Worth a bit, that table. And that bureau over there."

"Shouldn't think so, not when he had them in his home."

Aunt Bridget was looking through the diary. "No name," she said. "Recognize the handwriting?"

Uncle Aziz looked past her shoulder. "Yes, that's Eddie's."

"Well," she turned a few pages and read the entries. "This needs studying." She slipped the diary into her pocket. "We'll take the directory too. So thanks to you, dear Uncle Aziz, and my brilliant nephew, the hunt goes on."

"'Ere, what about me?" said Fingers. "Weren't for me, we wouldn't 'ave all them sparklers to take away wiv us."

"Qvite right." Huggy had finished spiking the guns. "And veren't for me, Harry never have love-ly surprise." Before he could move, she tweaked out the neck of his T-shirt and dropped in the dead rat. The withered corpse slithered down his bare back and lodged at his waist.

"Ah!" Harry tore at his clothes. "Ah! Ah!"

"Serve you right," said Huggy.

Chapter 18

Whitewater Hall

"Whitewater Hall," said Aunt Bridget. "It has to be. I've been over it and over it. Everything fits."

"Tell us again," called out Mr Tolly. "I mean, those bits about the fishing."

Aunt Bridget flicked through the pages of the diary that by now she almost knew off by heart. "Right, are you listening?"

It was the following evening, Monday, and everyone had gathered in the dining room for a meeting. The work on the lounge was finished, the ravages of fire consigned to history, but it stank of fresh paint and the new carpet and furniture hadn't been delivered yet. Harry slouched horizontally in a ginger moquette armchair. He had been playing with Tangle in the woods, not going too deep in case of unwelcome visitors from Felon Grange. His face was streaked with dirt, his knees were green and his fingernails black. Idly he cleaned them with his Swiss army knife.

On a red plush settee beside him, Auntie Florrie nibbled a pretzel and washed it down with a slug of Bosun Blinder. She saw Harry watching. "Don't look at me like that, you're as bad as Goody."

He raised his hands. "I never said a word."

"I've spent the whole day fitting that new transmission system to the Merc. A girl needs some little treat to make life worth living. Anyone would think I was a raging alcoholic, just because once in a blue moon I enjoy a tiny—"

"Ahem!" Aunt Bridget cleared her throat pointedly. "Could we talk about this later? Might it be possible, just once in our lives, to stick to the matter in hand?"

"All right." Auntie Florrie blinked her baby-blue eyes. "Dear, oh dear! What a fuss."

"As I was saying," Aunt Bridget raised the slim diary, "Whitewater Hall. Every two or three months Eddie goes down there for a bit of fishing."

"Went," said Auntie Florrie.

"All right, *went* down there for a bit of fishing." Aunt Bridget gave her a frosty glance over the top of her glasses. "Usually there's just the note to remind him, but once or twice he's made some little comment afterwards. Like this, listen." She read, "Friday, February 23rd: *To Sandy at Whitewater*. And then, in a different pen, *Snow during night, not taking. Bloody freezing*."

"Vhitevater meaning Vhitevater Hall," said Huggy.

"Where else could it be?" said Aunt Bridget. "How many other Whitewaters do you know? It's a great stately home. Half the country must have been there one time or another, paid the entrance fee and gone round as tourists. I know Florrie and I have, several times: the big house, the gardens, the wildlife park, tea rooms. For someone like Eddie Jones from Peckham with a taste for the good things in life and daft on his fishing – well, it's got the big lake, the river, a titled earl. He'd have loved it."

"What does it mean *not taking*?"

"The fish weren't biting."

"And who's Sandy?"

"The last owner," said Aunt Bridget. "Died a few years ago."

"So ve not can ask him."

"No, but by sheer chance I know the present Earl," said Aunt Bridget. "Gunther Warwick-Scott, lovely man. He used to be one of my students. Inherited the title when his uncle passed away."

"What title's that then?"

"What do you think, Angel, Tsar of Russia? Earl of Whitewater, of course."

Harry said, "Did he used to play rugby?"

"He did, as a matter of fact. Why?"

"Mr Weldon told us about a famous player called Gunther what-you-said."

"Warwick-Scott."

"That's it, he captained the Lions. Everyone called him Gunther the Grunter because of the noise he made in the scrum."

"He captained Oxford too." Aunt Bridget smiled. "Strong as an ox. He became quite a star."

"Aye, that's all very well," Angel interrupted. "But it's gey queer to call a man wi' a name like yon 'Sandy'."

"If you'd been paying attention," Aunt Bridget said, "I told you he's the *present* owner. His uncle, the seventh Earl, the one he took over from, was called Sandon."

"How do you know that?" said Auntie Florrie.

"I looked him up in Debrett. And then I phoned Gunther this afternoon."

"And did he know," Auntie Florrie hid a cocktail burp, "about Eddie Carver?"

"Never heard of him."

"Didn't know that his uncle, the seventh Earl, was a pal of one of the nastiest gang leaders in England?"

"I didn't tell him that but no, he didn't. You're right, though, they must have known each other quite well, else he wouldn't be calling him Sandy or have gone down there so often."

"Long way for a day's fishin'," Nutty said.

"Oh, he stayed overnight. Sometimes two or three nights." She returned to the diary. "That was February, right? Now listen. May 3rd: *Fishing, Whitewater*, and added later, *Beautiful fish, 13lb 10ozs, conditions perfect.*"

"That's some fish! What do they catch there, salmon?"

"Salmon's sea fish," Nutty said. "Sea rivers, anyway. Place like that it'd be brown trout – rainbow trout if he stocks it."

"Pike," somebody said.

"Maybe it's his total catch for the day."

"Could be," Aunt Bridget said. "Your guess is as good as mine. Anyway, a month later, June 14th: *Whitewater a.m. Dart arriving dinner.* And the next day: *Heavy rain, sheltered in S-H*, two exclamation marks. *Poor Sandy, what an innocent*, exclamation mark."

"What's S-H?" Auntie Florrie said.

"I think it has to be the summer house."

"That little place down by the lake?"

"I think so, don't you? It's in exactly the right place. If it came on to rain heavily that's where they *would* go, isn't it? Right by the water; somewhere to sit; sheltered from the *hoi polloi* by all those azaleas and rhododendrons."

"Didn't they," Auntie Florrie tried to remember, "didn't they call it a *gazebo*?"

"Amounts to the same thing. A bit of a fancy word. Don't you think Eddie Jones would call it a summer house?"

Her sister shrugged.

"Assuming you're right," said Mr Tolly, "what theory have you come up with, Bridget?"

"Well, my guess is that Eddie went to Whitewater one time, as a tourist like the rest of us, and fell in love with the place. Upwardly mobile chap like that, it would be right up his street. So he made it his business to meet the Earl and his wife, say invited them down to London for dinner and a show, and got himself invited back for a bit of fishing. Sandon was hard up: it was Gunther's side of the family had the money. So maybe Eddie slipped him a few quid now and again. Anyway, he must have made himself agreeable because every few months back he went—"

"And hid the stuff when he was down there!" Dot cried.

"The proceeds of his robberies, yes."

"In the summer house!"

"That's my reading of it," said Aunt Bridget. "Why all the exclamation marks? Why the reference to Sandy being an innocent? My guess is that the three of them were fishing away that day when it came on to rain, so they went into the summer house to shelter. And there was all that loot, right under their feet. Eddie grinning away to himself: *Poor Sandy, what an innocent*. It's exactly what he'd think."

Tangle trotted in from the kitchen licking his chops. Harry tickled him with a bare toe.

"Vell," said Huggy. "Vhen ve go to Vhitevater? Dig up this summer house?"

"Treasure!" Dot said.

"Gold!" said Harry.

207

"Saturday night," said Aunt Bridget in her more businesslike fashion. "Gunther's invited me for the weekend. Harry, you're coming too. So on Saturday, if you're agreeable, I'd like Dot, Huggy and you, Mr Tolly, to drive down and put up at the *Candlemaker's Arms* in the village."

Mr Tolly looked at the others. "I'll ring in the morning and book rooms."

"Better you use false names," said Huggy.

"Golly, that's a good idea," he said. "Maybe I should use a false address too."

She threw a cushion at him.

Aunt Bridget said, "Harry's got a busy week ahead of him. He breaks up on Thursday, as you know, for his summer holidays. Before that there's – what's happening, Harry?"

"Sports day tomorrow," he said. "And the class party on Wednesday."

"That's right, and on Friday you're coming down with me to Whitewater."

"Oh, but I was going to the baths with Akku and Charlie on Saturday."

"You've got the whole holiday for that."

He made a face. "Will I have to get all dressed up?"

"It's us he wants to see, not our clothes. Don't be so negative, you'll enjoy it. He's got a son your age."

"Little Lord Fauntleroy," Harry said.

"Maybe, wait and see." She turned to the others. "So that will give me all day Saturday to spy the lie of the land. Then I'll meet you in the grounds round midnight ."

"Sounds good to me," said Mr Tolly.

"Ve take the gold back vith us, ja, to the *Candlemaker's Arms*?" Huggy said.

"Depends how much there is. We might have to hide some and come back for it later. Maybe bury it ourselves."

Dot did a couple of back-flips with excitement.

"That's if everything goes to plan." Aunt Bridget sighed. "It never does but who knows, one day there might be a miracle."

Mrs Good said, "If we can talk about tomorrow for a minute. Max is due out of Cony Hill at nine. He's still Okky, remember, so I'm meeting him at the gate with one of his famous 'puddens', then off to the splendid *Drunken Dragon* for a shower, a change and a big reception breakfast. It means an early start but I want you all there, no lie-ins tomorrow. Poor man, after what he's been through in that horrible place, all in the interests of this treasure you're after, it's the least we can do. I've baked a Welcome Home cake for teatime, and Harry's iced it and covered it with candles. Then of course there's the celebration dinner tomorrow night."

"And off to the Ritz a couple of days later for a champagne weekend," Mr Tolly said. "Almost makes it seem worthwhile."

"It does not," said Fingers. "The man's a hero."

"I know we're all talented," Aunt Bridget said, "but I can hardly take it in how brilliant he's been. He deserves an Oscar."

"Ve make bonfire ven it get dark," said Huggy. "Burn his Okky clothes."

"You could get some fireworks." Harry sat up.

"Good idea," Huggy said. "Ja, I vait after school, after sports day. Ve go the toy shop in town."

"That's a thought," said Mrs Good. "How many of us are going to the sports day?"

Hands were raised. "Me . . . of course . . . what sort of a question's that?"

"Wouldn't miss it for the world," Fingers said. "I want to see Dot give that 'eadmaster another 'andbagging."

Amid the laughter Mrs Good glanced at the clock and rose. "Right, Harry, upstairs to the bathroom. If you're quick you can come down in your pyjamas and have a cup of cocoa. See the end of that video you were watching last night. Come on, on your feet. Chop–chop."

Harry went.

Whitewater Hall was one of the great stately homes of England. As Aunt Bridget drove up the two-mile drive and Harry glimpsed the vast grey pile between towering sequoias, he could not believe he had been invited to stay as a guest.

"No need to get dressed up," Aunt Bridget had reminded Goody. "His nice jeans and a T-shirt are perfect."

They crossed an ornamental bridge over the river which fed the lake, and circled the sunken garden. Whitewater Hall rose before them with its broad flights of steps and raised terrace, pillars, pediments, hundreds of windows, dozens of chimneys and balustraded roof.

Aunt Bridget cast an appraising eye. "Nice place, eh?"

Harry didn't reply. Even though he was himself an honourable – the Honourable Eugene Augustus Montgomery Harold Barton, a string of names he hated – he was awestruck.

A smart blue helicopter with orange insignia sat on a lawn, roped off from the public.

"Keen on flying, Gunther. Had his pilot's licence even when he was at Oxford."

They turned from the tourist-dotted carriageway on to a

domestic drive between bushes. A chain blocked the way. On it, a dangling notice read:

NO ADMITTANCE
STRICTLY PRIVATE

"Out you get," said Aunt Bridget.

Every moment expecting to be grabbed at the neck by a uniformed footman, Harry unhooked the chain to let her through, replaced it and got back into the car.

Toot-toot! They drew up in a cobbled courtyard with sheds and drainage pipes and green wheelie-bins. A boy around Harry's age came running from the door.

"Dad!" He called back to the house. "They're here."

"All right." A voice came from within. "I'll just be a minute. Bring them in." There was the sound of a lavatory flushing.

Shyly the boy approached the car. Harry liked him. "Dad says, will you come in."

"Goodness," Aunt Bridget spoke from the driver's window. "It's easy to see whose son you are. Michael, is it?"

He nodded, blushing.

"Well I'm Dr Barton. I used to be one of your dad's tutors at Oxford. And this is Harry."

"Hi." Equally shy, Harry looked past her bony shoulder.

"Hi," said Michael.

A broad, beefy man with rosy cheeks and a shock of fair hair came striding from the door. "Come on, Mike, I thought you'd have them in the house and glasses of whisky and squash in their hands by this time." He finished fastening his trousers. "Bridget! Ma-arvellous to see you!" He drew her from the car and planted a fat kiss on her cheek. "And this must be the famous, rugby-playing Harry you were telling me about. Hello, there, young-un. What say if we punt a ball about on the grass after lunch? Try not to kill any of the tourists – not good for business." He laughed. "Tell you what, Mike can look after you for now, show you your room and that, and I'll take care of your gorgeous auntie. Best lecturer ever to set foot in Oxford. Got me through, I can tell you that."

"Don't believe a word he says." She opened the boot. "He got a first."

"Thanks to you, that's what I'm saying," said the cheerful Earl of Whitewater. He turned to his son. "Mum's just popped down to Tesco's. We'll have coffee when she gets back."

Harry pulled out his suitcase and followed Mike into the house. His room was on the first floor: flock wallpaper, a blue-and-white duvet and a view of the lake.

"What d'you want to do first?" Mike said.

"Dunno." Harry shrugged. "Whatever you think."

So Mike took him to the snooker room.

Harry had a great time. Mike went to Eton but if he'd gone to Barleymow Junior School he'd straightway have become one of Harry's best friends.

After lunch, as Gunther had promised, they took a rugby ball to a far lawn. For an hour they kicked to one another and passed and sold dummies and tried to bring each other down with flying tackles. Gunther, two stone heavier than in his playing days, was soon red-faced and gasping. "Not bad, not bad at all," he wheezed as they returned to the house and he gave Harry a photo of himself scoring a winning try against the All Blacks. At Harry's request he autographed it. *To Harry,*

Akku and Charlie, he wrote, *three great boys, with best wishes from Gunther W-S.*

Then, while Gunther showered and joined Aunt Bridget, Harry and Mike, grass-stained and with dirty hands, wandered through the tremendous public rooms, giggled at the collection of what-the-butler-saw machines, played table football, drove through the wildlife park with one of the rangers, rowed on the lake and scrounged chocolate éclairs from the woman in the tea-shop. The day ended with dinner in a cosy dining room, smaller than the one at Lagg Hall.

"Having a good time?" Aunt Bridget found Harry sitting up in bed with a forty-year-old *Rupert* annual.

"Brilliant."

"Mike's a nice boy."

"I wish he lived nearer." Harry let the book fall shut. "Aunt Bridget, is it OK digging up the treasure in the summer house? I mean, Gunther and everyone are being fantastic. It feels really mean, creeping round in the dark behind their backs."

"I know, I know." She sat on the bed. "But I keep thinking what we want the money for: all those African children who can't have a lovely time like you and Mike. And I don't know *how* to tell him now. It would spoil everything."

Harry nodded. "Perhaps we could share it, take half and leave him the rest."

"Some of it anyway. Great minds think alike."

"And it's not really his money, is it," Harry said. "It's just on his land."

"It's not in any way his money," Aunt Bridget said. "He knows nothing about it – or Eddie and Dart Jones."

Harry made a tent with his feet. "What are you going to do?"

She sighed. "I can't see the point in saying anything until we know if the treasure's actually there. If it is, well, let's play it by ear from then."

Harry thought about it and felt better. "And we'll send them a big box of chocolates when we get home, whether it's there or not."

"The biggest." She kissed his forehead. "And invite Mike for a holiday if you'd like that."

Harry smiled. "That would be great."

She stood. "Incidentally, when I go out to meet the others tomorrow night, I hope you don't, in your wildest dreams, think you're coming with me."

Harry looked her in the eyes. "Course not, Aunt Bridget."

"I mean it, Harry."

"I know," he said.

Chapter 19

The Gazebo

Aunt Bridget was out of sight. Harry pulled the back door shut and flitted across the moonlit yard. He peered round a stone pillar. For a second he saw her high-shouldered figure silhouetted against a dewy bank then she turned between trees and was gone.

It was quarter past midnight. After an idyllic Saturday, during which Gunther had taken them up in his helicopter, swooping above the lake and far-off countryside, Harry had found it hard to stay awake. Eventually, as the clock struck twelve, Aunt Bridget came to satisfy herself that he was in bed and asleep, as he knew she would, turning back the duvet to ensure that the shape beneath was her nephew and not an arrangement of pillows. Harry breathed deeply and kept his eyelids still until she was gone, then rose and pulled on the darkest clothes in his suitcase.

Now here he was, tracking her through the hundreds of acres of moonlit garden which surrounded Whitewater Hall. He reached the point where she had vanished. The wood was dark. A pheasant called. He heard a rustle and froze. What was it: a badger? a keeper? a killer? his aunt? The sound was not repeated. Harry started down the edge of the wood.

The lake lay below him, four hundred metres away, silver in the light of the half moon. Was this, he wondered, why the estate was called Whitewater, or was it, as Aunt Bridget had told him, because of the white northern light, the beds of waterlilies, and the cherry orchard that covered part of the shore?

Keeping to the shadows as much as possible, Harry made his way downhill. The rich scents of the summer night came to his nostrils. His trainers and the bottom of his jeans were sodden with dew. Without a sound a roe deer emerged fifty metres ahead. It was followed by a fawn. For a minute they stood looking around, then crossed the lawn into bushes at the far side. Harry walked on, and in five minutes came to the banks of rhododendron which circled the landward side of the summer house. Treading on the sides of his feet, he crept round.

The summer house, or gazebo as Gunther and Mike called it, stood on a small knoll fifty metres from the shore. It was an octagonal building more than two centuries old, so delicate that it seemed a puff of wind must blow it away. Fragrant honeysuckle and fat white clematis twined around the pillars and balustrades. Lit by the moon, it had the appearance of a building in a fairy tale.

Aunt Bridget was right, Harry thought, this was where Eddie, Dart and the late Earl of Whitewater had sheltered from the rain. Directly below the summer house a wooden jetty projected into the lake. A path edged with white stones led from this to the short flight of steps at the entrance. It was the obvious place.

No one had arrived yet. Aunt Bridget was meeting the others in a different part of the garden and bringing them on.

Harry looked round for a hiding place. Beyond the grass a low bank of earth dropped to the pale stones of the lakeshore. Between this bank and the jetty was a triangle of black shadow. Harry slithered down and disappeared. He made himself comfortable – and waited.

All was still. A fish jumped. He turned his head and saw the widening ripples. When he looked back, four figures had appeared at the far end of the bushes. As they came closer he made them out: the tall, stick-like figure of Aunt Bridget; Huggy, solid as a Russian bear; Mr Tolly, a big man, his shining dome hidden by a cap; and Dot, small as a child. For professional criminals they were making a lot of noise.

". . . feet are *soaking*!" Mr Tolly sneezed. "At this rate . . . dose of pneumonia."

"Will you shut up!" This was Dot.

"Vhat you expect you vear gymshoes." A fallen branch snapped with a loud crack. "Oops, sorry."

Mr Tolly was carrying a spade, Huggy what looked like a metal detector. Harry was surprised. To the best of his knowledge there wasn't a metal detector at Lagg Hall. Perhaps it was a new purchase. They clashed together.

"For goodness sake!" Aunt Bridget hissed. "Look, here we are. Up you go. And be quiet!"

They mounted the steps and vanished into the summer house. Harry strained his ears and heard a chink of tools. They were still talking but more softly now. The narrow beam of a pencil torch appeared. It moved about. He glimpsed hands, metal, jackets. A winking red light shone in the darkness. Someone had pressed the test button on the detector. A loud *beep-beep-beep* shattered the silence. Harry was startled. Figures crowded round the machine. The noise ceased. Phrases reached him:

". . . thought you could work it . . . else do you suggest? . . . dig up the whole . . . like a potato field! . . . Oh, shut up!"

The almost invisible figures parted and one – Mr Tolly, he thought – began sweeping the detector in wide arcs across the floor.

The grass at the verge was untrimmed. Harry watched between a tuft and a jagged, seeding thistle. He did not have to wait long. In less than a minute the flashing red light reappeared, the noisy bleeper pierced the night. A hand was clapped over the light but the noise continued. Shapes rushed forward. The machine was silenced.

". . . heaven's sake! . . . *want* the fuzz to . . . 'bout there."

They were excited. The torch was trained on the floor. Figures gathered round. One fell to its knees:

". . . like fresh cement . . . you don't mean? . . . way of finding out."

A glint of steel came and went in the torchlight. Harry heard a chink, a scrape, a little splitting noise. He had visited the summer house during the day and knew the floor was tiled. Had one been lifted? It was impossible to tell what was happening. He squeezed his eyes and looked away to ease the strain. What he saw made his heart leap. A hundred and fifty metres away a man was making his way downhill towards the lake. The rhododendrons hid him from the four in the summer house. Frantically Harry scrambled along the shore until he could no longer see the intruder, then clambered up the earth bank and raced across the grass.

"Aunt Bridget!" His voice was a hiss. "Aunt Bridget!"

The light went off. There was momentary panic. Then a voice: "Harry? Is that you?"

"What are *you* doing here?"

"Never mind that." He ran up the steps. "There's someone coming."

"What! Where?"

He pointed.

"How far off?"

"Getting close."

"Oh, my vord!"

"Leave this. Into the bushes. Quick!"

They tumbled over the rail. The ground was three metres below. Aunt Bridget twisted an ankle. Mr Tolly winded himself. Ignoring the hurt, they scrambled beneath the rhododendrons. The branches tossed wildly. Harry squashed a slug under his hand. Dot got a twig in her eye. Huggy got a nest of crawly things in her hair.

They were just in time. The leaves had barely stopped shaking when a man in gaiters with a shotgun over his shoulder came into view.

"The keeper," Aunt Bridget breathed.

They watched through the leaves.

He was young and singing softly: "*I can't get no – no-no, no – I can't get no – Satisfaction!*" He broke into a little dance, twitching his shoulders, jigging in his country boots, and completely failed to notice the wet footprints on the steps of the summer house. The jetty lay before him. He strolled down and stood looking over the lake. His lighter flashed. Wreaths of cigarette smoke drifted about his head.

At last he was gone and they emerged from their hiding place.

"Ugh!" Huggy hunted for a comb to rake the beasts from her hair.

Harry scrubbed the slime from his hand.

Dot felt her watering eye.

Mr Tolly took deep breaths.

"Well, Harry." Aunt Bridget tested her ankle and found she could walk on it. "I can't say I'm pleased you didn't stay in bed as you were told – but thank goodness you didn't."

"Ja," Huggy agreed. "This time you save our pork for sure."

"Bacon," Dot said.

"Vhat?"

"The word is bacon. He saved our *bacon*."

"Sausages, mushrooms, vhatever. He save us, that all that matter." Huggy planted a powerful kiss on Harry's hair. "Good boy."

"And now back to work," Aunt Bridget said. "I suppose one of us had better keep a lookout."

"I'll do it," Dot volunteered. "Harry's done his bit."

So Harry joined the searchers in the summer house.

The floor was covered with hexagonal tiles, red and fawn. Three had been lifted so far, right in the middle. At once Harry saw the fresh cement.

"D'you think someone's been here before us?"

"Certainly *somebody* has. The question is who – and why and when? Let's hope it's not the Priestly mob."

Now they had made a start the tiles lifted easily. Harry stacked them to one side.

"Right," said Mr Tolly when they had bared roughly a square metre. "Let's dig down a bit."

The surface was hard-packed sand. Beneath that lay soil. He started in the middle and had shifted only a dozen spadefuls when the blade hit something hard. The effect was electrifying. Everyone gathered round. The narrow beam of the torch lit tumbled earth. Mr Tolly probed with a jemmy and discovered the outline of whatever lay buried. Carefully he scraped the earth aside, dug beneath, and lifted it on the spade.

It was a rectangular box with a peaked lid and made of yellow-bronze metal. Aunt Bridget took it in her practical hands and brushed off the soil.

"Is that it?" Harry said eagerly.

The lid was hinged. She opened it. Harry craned his neck to see. Within lay not the diamonds, rubies and fat gold coins of his imagination, but a kilo or two of grey-white powder.

"What is it?" He was puzzled. "Drugs?"

Aunt Bridget shut the lid and handed him the box. She pointed to a small metal plaque with an inscription. Harry angled it to catch the light.

Sandon Geoffrey

Seventh Earl of Whitewater

1907–1985

"What does that mean?"

"It's his ashes," Aunt Bridget said.

"His – ugghh!" Harry got such a fright he dropped the casket. The top burst open. The seventh Earl spilled out over his trainers and cascaded into the hole.

Harry was horrified. Huggy guffawed loudly and clapped a hand over her mouth. The rest were laughing too. Mr Tolly returned as much as he could into the casket. The rest he dug into the ground. It vanished in moments.

"Earth to earth," Huggy said. "He not mind, he still under the summer house vhere he vant to be."

Carefully Mr Tolly reburied the casket. "There, no harm done, no one the wiser."

But Harry was shaken and went to stand at the water's edge. The thought of the late Earl's ashes all over his feet gave him the creeps and he waded out, swishing his trainers in the water. Dot had not seen what happened and walked down to the jetty. When Harry told her, she burst into giggles.

"It's not funny," he said. "It's awful!"

"Not to me," she said. "I think it's a hoot."

And in a while Harry began to laugh too.

When he returned to the summer house, Aunt Bridget was sweeping the metal detector across the floor. Harry took over while she joined Huggy and Mr Tolly who had given up trying to replace the tiles. The earth was uneven. It was hopeless. The job would have to be left to the experts.

Abruptly the red light started flashing again, the noisy *beep-beep-beep* rang out across the night.

"How do I stop it? How do I stop it?"

"Switch off. There! There!"

The machine fell silent. Harry stared out into the moonlight, looking for keepers, listening for shouts and the thud of running feet. They never came. The only sound was the quack of a duck far across the lake.

Mr Tolly fell to his knees and inserted the blade of his pocket-knife between two tiles. Carefully he levered then moved on round. In a minute a tile popped up. The rest came easily.

Harry stared down. Had he discovered Eddie Carver's treasure?

Huggy began to dig. Nothing appeared. The pile of earth grew. Mr Tolly ran the detector over the hole. The metal was still there. They removed more tiles. Huggy dug on. The mound of earth was up to Harry's waist. At last there was a chink of iron. He held his breath. Huggy took the torch and stepped down into the hole. They waited. With disgust she hauled out a few links of heavy chain, eaten away by rust, and threw them on the tiles.

Harry took the machine and moved on. The summer house had one more secret to reveal, an old penny among the sand. He slipped it into his pocket as a souvenir.

Aunt Bridget shone her torch across the ruined floor of the summer house. "Oh, dear! Still, we'll pay for it somehow. And I had such hopes."

"What about outside," Harry said, "in the grass?"

"I suppose." Aunt Bridget sighed. "Or at the end of the rhododendrons. Or under that oak tree. Or ten paces towards the rising sun on Midsummer's Day."

"It was just an idea," Harry said. "It's worth a look."

"I'm sorry." She squeezed his shoulder. "You're right, of course."

So they examined the outside of the summer house and Harry ran the metal detector over the surrounding grass. Three times it burst into life. Three times, refusing all help, Mr Tolly dug a deep hole. In the first he discovered a broken bit of tractor, in the second a Woolworth's brooch, and in the third a yellow oil drum that Huggy thought was an unexploded land mine.

Aunt Bridget examined her wrist watch and looked back at the mounds of soil. "Leave them," she said. "I have had enough. We're doing this for other people, let somebody else shoulder a bit of the work. It's time we were in our beds."

"Sorry, Bridget." The weary Mr Tolly gave her a hug.

"I'm the one should say sorry," she said. "I was so sure."

"You do your best," Huggy said.

"We all do that, all the time." She smiled regretfully. "Come on, Harry, let's get a bit of shut-eye. The sun will be up in half an hour. It's getting brighter already. See you all back at Lagg Hall."

"Night-night." Clutching the earthy tools, Dot, Huggy and Mr Tolly set off back to the car and their rooms at the *Candlemaker's Arms*.

Harry and Aunt Bridget climbed the long hill from the lake to Whitewater Hall. A path ran through the woods. She limped on her twisted ankle.

"Will you be able to drive?" Harry said anxiously.

"When we go home? Yes, it's the left, it'll be fine with a dressing."

"What a mess we made!"

"We did a bit. Nothing broken though. No harm done. Ow!" She trod on a stone. "Gunther'll get an anonymous letter of apology and a bundle of used notes through the post in a day or two. The labourers will get a couple of bottles of whisky. They'll get over it."

But that was yet to come. At breakfast Gunther was angry.

"Twice!" he exploded. "Once was bad enough – but twice! In a week. What's so special about poor Sandon's ashes? And this time they've stolen half of them. What do you think it is – some kind of witchcraft? Cats' entrails in the wood?" He cut off a corner of fried bread and smothered it in egg.

"Terry was round there twice during the night and he saw nothing. Whoever it is, they're cunning, that's for sure."

"I've told you," Mike said. "They've got a map, like *Treasure Island*. Pieces of eight. A crock of gold."

"If it's a crock of gold no one told me about it. There was no crock of gold there when we buried Sandon's ashes – the first time *or* the second." He looked across the table. "What do you make of it, Bridget?"

"I don't know what to say." She dabbed her lips with a damask napkin. "This is the *second* time?"

"That's right. When was it before, Mike?"

"Tuesday," he said.

"Not even a week then. Didn't make so much mess, the first lot, just dug up the ashes and pushed off. Terry bagged a few rabbits that night, we think the shooting disturbed them."

"Nobody saw anything?" said Aunt Bridget.

"Yes, a young fellow at the road-end was walking home in the early hours. He said he saw four very suspicious-looking characters. Two men and two women, quarrelling. That could have been them. Drove off in a black Range Rover. At least he thought it was black, you can't tell in the moonlight."

"Were they carrying anything?" Harry stifled a yawn.

"He said not."

"So they didn't find any treasure then?"

"You boys and your imagination! You're as bad as Mike." Gunther packed his fork again. "If there *was* any highwayman's booty or whatever under the gazebo we'd have found it when Sandon died. I had the whole floor relaid."

Harry glanced at Aunt Bridget. She kept her eyes lowered, spreading honey on a slice of toast with mathematical precision.

225

"Dad." Mike changed the subject. "Can I miss church this morning and go to evensong instead?"

"Why?" his father said. "No, don't tell me. You want to take Harry down to have another look at those What-the-Butler-Saw machines. Nothing but heathens, the pair of you. There'll be plenty of time to look at your naked ladies *after* church."

"It's not naked ladies," Mike said. "We're not all like you, Dad. We want to have a table-footie tournament."

"A likely story! What do you think, Bridget?"

Harry knew what the answer would be.

"Church first, table-footie afterwards," she said.

He wiped his plate with a corner of bread.

Chapter 20

The Swimming Party

"Sorry, darlings," Aunt Bridget said. "It simply wasn't there. Never has been. When Sandon, the seventh Earl, died, and his ashes were buried in the summer house – or gazebo, as they kept calling it – Gunther had the whole floor relaid. There was nothing under it then and it's been untouched until Priestly and that lot dug it up last week.

"You're sure that's who it was?"

"A group of four, Gunther was told. Two men and two women. Quarrelling. A black Range Rover. It has to be."

It was late afternoon the following day, Monday. The sun blazed in a blue summer sky and they had assembled again in the shade of the chestnut tree.

"And I was so sure," Aunt Bridget went on. "Everything fitted: the reference to Sandy at Whitewater, the fishing, the exclamation marks, all the other details. I've been looking at the diary again this morning and I just can't see where we went wrong."

"Perhaps they dug it up for some reason before Sandon died," Mr Tolly said. "Moved it somewhere else."

"That's possible, of course."

"Or maybe Dart dug it up when his brother went into

Cony Hill and they realized he would never be coming out."

"No, that's not right, because Sandon died first." She picked at a mark on the picnic table. "I simply don't know where we go from here."

Harry said, "Is that the end of the search then?"

"What? Absolutely not. Just have to put on our thinking caps again. With eight of us, all bright as buttons, surely somebody can come up with a brainwave."

"A big fat clue," Dot said.

Harry was counting. "It's not eight," he said, "it's nine. There's me."

"Mm." His aunt tightened her lips. "We'll have to see about that. You're getting a bit too involved in our shenanigans for my liking."

Harry wore his swimming shorts and lay full length on the grass. He cupped his chin in his hands and didn't reply. It was not the time to argue.

Aunt Bridget looked at Max, who had returned that afternoon from his weekend at the Ritz. "I feel particularly bad about it because of you, Max," she said. "All you had to put up with in Cony Hill."

"That's all right, lovely lady," he wheezed in his Okky voice. "It's not your fault." He leered and licked his chin. "'Ere, 'ow 'bout me an' you goin' a walk in the woods this evenin'?"

"Dirty old man!" Aunt Bridget laughed. "Anyway, I thought it was Goody you had your eye on."

"Oh, it is, 'er an' all." The spit flew. "An' 'er treacle puddens." The words came oddly from a man in Savile Row slacks and a silk cravat.

"Two-timer," Aunt Bridget said. "Anyway, the answer's no. Too much to do."

"What's that then?" The voice came from Auntie Florrie. A little apart from the others, she lay in a deckchair and lifted her face to the sun.

"You know perfectly well, Florrie," said her sister. "The heat's addled your brains. And what *do* you think you look like!"

Auntie Florrie had hitched her skirt above her knees and slipped her arms from the sleeves of her dress. The sun had melted her customary heavy mascara and lipstick. Drowsily thinking they were suncream, she had massaged them in with her fingertips, giving her pools of blackness for eyes and a mouth like the bride of Dracula. "Oh!" She stirred langorously, making herself comfortable. "You mean the Summer Fair."

"Of course I mean the Summer Fair. Life doesn't come to a dead stop because we haven't found Eddie Carver's millions — yet! No *way* are we forgetting about it, but here and now there's the fair to consider. Saturday the twenty-eighth — that's only six days away. I've been so tied up with Whitewater and everything, I haven't given it a thought. Nutty, you said you'd take charge of all the arrangements. How's it coming along?"

"Fine, hinny. It's all in hand. We're enterin' the float competition, like last year. I've asked Mr Jenkins for the lend of his old hay cart. Harry an' me's takin' Chalky round to pick it up in the mornin'."

"What's the theme this year?" said Max.

"Wreckers Crag," Nutty said. "Harry's idea after climbin' up there wi' Dot. Angel's designed a cracker of a set. We'll start buildin' it soon as we get the cart round."

"Is there a part for me?"

"Hardly leave out wor star o' stage, screen an' telly, could we? Aye, ye'll have a big juicy role, dinna fret."

"What is it?"

"Policeman," Nutty said. "After yer couple o' weeks inside, yer just the one to play it. Old-fashioned cop wi' a stovepipe hat an' a pistol."

"Couldn't be better." Max laughed. "I can fancy that. From the Old Vic to a hay cart. Willie Shakespeare would have approved. What about costumes?"

"You remember when Harry came down as the Green Lady?" Mrs Good looked up from the fluffy pink cardigan she was knitting.

"How could I forget it?"

"Well, you wouldn't believe the stuff in those old trunks up in the attic: dresses, coats, make-up, you name it. A few alterations and a couple of trips to Oxfam – we've got just about everything we need."

"Do people know what parts they're playing?"

"Aye, but we're leavin' the actin' to the expert," Nutty said. "Let's get it set up first, then it's over to you."

Max rubbed his hands. "It's good to be back."

The grass made Harry's chest itchy. He jumped up and brushed off the bits. "Huggy, would you come down to the lake," he said.

"Ja, sure." She looked up. "Vhy?"

"I want to swim right across," he said, "but it's a bit scary in the middle. Long weeds and stuff. I thought you might row beside me."

Auntie Florrie struggled upright. "What's the water like?"

"Great," he said. "Quite warm over the sandy bits."

"Sounds lovely," she said. "I think I'll come with you. Can you wait till I get my costume?"

Mrs Good fanned her face. "Do you know, I wouldn't mind a dip myself."

"Lovely," Fingers said. "Come on, everyone. Let's make a party of it."

And they did, all eleven, jumping off the little wooden jetty and paddling in the shallows in an assortment of shorts, costumes and underwear that made Mrs Good laugh until she had hiccups. The Lagg Hall woods rang with their shouts. Harry swam to the far shore and came back in the boat. Tangle brought a stick from the wood, barking for someone to throw it. The startled geese watched from a distance. With a flash of green and scarlet, Morgan swooped overhead and landed on a branch.

"Aark!" He ruffled his feathers. "Give us a fag."

Huggy looked up, seventeen stone of muscle in a wrestling leotard. "Hello, you disgusting, horrible parrot."

Morgan regarded her with an unfriendly eye and waggled his tail. A big job whizzed past her shoulder. He gave a piercing wolf whistle. "What a smasher!"

Huggy laughed and bombed into the water from a high rock.

Angel made a painting. *The Swimming Party* by Angus McGregor – which was Angel's Sunday name – became that year's sensation at the Royal Academy autumn exhibition. Enormous sums of money were offered but it wasn't for sale, and when the show was over Angel presented it to Auntie Florrie who hung it at the head of the stairs. Of all the paintings and forgeries that flowed from Angel's topsy-turvy studio, *The Swimming Party* was Harry's favourite.

And that evening, as he and Tangle climbed the attic stairs at ten o'clock, he thought he had never been so happy: lots of laughter, lots to do, people he loved. As he pulled off his T-shirt his shoulders tingled with the day-long beating of the sun. He turned his back to the peeling mirror and saw dusky-red behind the tan. His hair, already fair, had been bleached another shade lighter. He brushed it with his fingertips, ducking his head to see, and reached for his pyjama jacket. The skylight was ajar to let out the heat of the day. Little sounds penetrated from the night. Harry threw back the duvet and crashed on to his mattress. His mind was too full to read. He was too tired. He switched off the lamp. Tangle made himself comfortable at the foot of the bed. "Night-night," Harry said and turned on his side. Memories of the swimming made him smile. He thought of the hay cart he would fetch with Nutty the next day; and Chalky and his friend Socrates, the grey donkey, out in their paddock.

Had Harry known that this was one of the last carefree days he would enjoy for some time, that within a week he would be a prisoner, and that within a fortnight he would have to swim for his life, he might not have fallen asleep so quickly.

Chapter 21

Summer Fair

The cart was filthy. Mud clung to the wheels. Hens laid eggs in the straw and muck that gathered in the corners. The paintwork was chipped.

Harry loved it. As he sat holding the reins at Nutty's side, and the good-natured Chalky clip-clopped along the lane, he felt like a gypsy king.

They parked the cart near Nutty's workshop and at once Harry got busy with a hose and scrubbing brush. By coffee time it was clean, and by early afternoon dry enough to begin painting.

Harry worked as Angel's assistant. His principal job, since Angel was the greediest man in the world, was to provide an unbroken supply of tea, cakes, cookies, and whatever other delicacies he could wheedle out of Mrs Good in the kitchen. In the times between, he blocked in the dogs and dragons and gorgeous flourishes that flowed from the artist's brush. They started at the shafts, painted up to the headboard, down to the enormous wheels, and back along the sides to the tailgate. By teatime on Wednesday it was finished, a riot of shapes and dazzling colour.

"Angel, that is fantastic!" the others said as they gathered round. "Brilliant . . . ought to go in a museum . . . buy it from Mr Jenkins . . . a genius!"

"Aye, ye're right," he said complacently and chewed his ragged moustache. "I dinna suppose one o' ye would happen to hae a sweetie or a biscuit aboot yer person? I canna live on air, ye ken. Yon laddie eats like a horse. A morsel hasnae passed my lips since —" His dirty fingers encountered a half-chewed toffee in the corner of a trouser pocket. Angel adored toffees. He threw a snot-stiffened handkerchief, a snail shell, some fragments of charcoal and other debris on to the grass and turned his pocket inside out. The lopsided, tooth-marked delicacy was covered with pencil shavings and bits of fluff. He tore it free and popped it into his mouth. "Mmm."

"Oh, Angel!" Mrs Good made a face.

"What's the matter, it's good." He munched. "Tell me again, what was that ye were sayin' aboot genius?"

Nutty and Mr Tolly, meanwhile, had been building the scenery to Angel's design, and as soon as the paint on the cart was dry it was hoisted aboard. It was a dramatic setting. Foaming waves crashed head high. The bows of a tremendous sailing ship with broken spars and rigging had run on to rocks. A towering cliff vanished into the sky-blue awning. Though it looked solid, the whole structure was made of cardboard, cloth and the lightest of timber so that it wouldn't be too heavy for Chalky to pull. As soon as it was nailed firmly into place a whole team, under Angel's supervision, set to work with paint and brushes.

By Friday everything was finished and that afternoon Max called for a full dress rehearsal. There would be seven on the float. Dot, who had worked with horses in the circus, handled the reins. She was dressed as a Victorian coachman in a top hat with ribbons and a cloak she had found at Oxfam. The six in the tableau were Harry, the ship's boy; Fingers, a drowning seaman; Huggy and Angel, two bearded and ferocious wreckers; Auntie Florrie, a weeping wife; and Max, a peeler, or old-style policeman, in a black uniform with silver buttons.

They had practised their parts but Max was a stern director. "Come on!" he shouted at Harry. "You're a deck boy. You're terrified. You're going to be drowned, for God's sake. You sound like a schoolgirl that's seen a spider. Put some guts into it." He strode on to Fingers. "What are you, a windmill?" And to Huggy: "What are you punching your chest for? You're meant to be a wrecker, not King Kong."

She shook her fist. "You vatch it, Max Beauguss, or I fetch you von!"

"Suits me," he said. "I'd *rather* be dead than try to direct you lot."

But in the end they got it right, and then it was Saturday.

Harry was up with the sun. Munching a biscuit, he pulled on wellies and fetched Chalky from the misty meadow. The friendly horse stood by the sheds, every now and then giving a shiver as Harry combed and sponged and brushed him until his white coat gleamed and his mane and tail flowed in cascades.

Goody cooked a special breakfast: bacon and sausages and fried eggs and fried bread for the busy day ahead. The sun broke through as they were eating, casting a streak across the tiled floor and scrubbed kitchen table.

The rest of the morning was spent putting finishing touches to the float and costumes. At eleven-thirty Mrs Good served squash and sandwiches at the picnic table. At twelve Harry put Chalky between the shafts. Nutty tied an old straw hat to Chalky's head to keep off the sun, and decorated his harness with flowers from the garden. Then it was time to dress. Mrs Good took photos. And at one they set off, rocking down the drive through the wood and rattling along the country road towards town.

They sat on the side, and walked when they came to a hill to help Chalky. Cars slowed as they passed. Windows were lowered:

"Looks great . . . see you in town . . . good luck!"

They waved back and at two o'clock arrived at the big field on the outskirts of town which was the assembly point. It was full of floats, mostly on the backs of lorries. As Harry looked around he saw Robin Hood and his merry men, an operating theatre, gorillas in a jungle, astronauts in silver bikinis. They were awfully good, he thought. What chance did *Wreckers Crag* have against such opposition?

At half past two, preceded by the town's brass band, the procession of twenty-seven floats set off. Numbers had been drawn from a hat and *Wreckers Crag* was tenth in line. Ahead of them, posturing on the back of a beer lorry, lads from the local rugby club had dressed as a harem with long wigs, heavy lipstick and boobs on the point of exploding. On the float behind, lady teachers from the High School had dressed as St Trinian's schoolgirls in gymslips and torn fishnet tights. With abandon they drank from bottles marked *Gin*, smoked like chimneys, and cuddled boyfriends.

They made Harry laugh but there was no time to think

about it because now they were driving through the crowded streets. Dot had left the driver's seat and stood barefoot on Chalky's back, cracking her long whip above the heads of the crowd. Auntie Florrie stretched arms towards the stricken ship and pressed a handkerchief to her eyes. Fingers struggled in the frothing waves. Huggy and Angel, grinning ferociously, waved swords and dragged a crate from the sea. Max, resplendent in a stovepipe hat and magnificent moustaches, called on them to surrender. He had borrowed a big Captain Hook pistol and fired it repeatedly with tremendous bangs and flashes and clouds of smoke. Harry, meanwhile, high in his crow's nest, clung to the rigging and cried aloud. He wore britches chopped off below the knee, a ripped shirt and a red rag at his throat. His face was streaked with greasepaint to look like dirt. He had gelled his hair and set it in tangles.

"Help!" he shouted again and again, his voice growing hoarse. "Help! Man the lifeboats!"

As he looked across the crowd he saw Akku and Charlie waving like mad. Elsewhere he spotted Mr Foggarty, his headmaster, and Mrs Good on the balcony of the library. Nutty, who would dearly have liked to come, had stayed behind at Lagg Hall in case of intruders.

As it turned out the house was in no danger – unless escaped prisoner Priestly was rash enough to go visiting in broad daylight – for Harry saw the other three residents of Felon Grange in the forecourt of a garage. GBH was filling the Range Rover with diesel while Gestapo Lil in an outfit of green silk, and Mad Ruby in her customary spider black, stood stretching their legs. Idly they watched the procession pass by. But as *Wreckers Crag* came abreast of the garage, Gestapo Lil clutched her companion's arm and pointed.

Harry felt his blood run cold.

They bared their teeth. Mad Ruby shook a little clenched fist. GBH released the pump handle and looked round.

Harry shouted to Auntie Florrie: "Look, it's Gestapo Lil!"

"Where?" She looked where he pointed.

GBH snatched a sponge from a bucket of water and hurled it with all his might. It was a lucky shot. The wet sponge hit Max on the ear and knocked off his tall hat. Ruby and Gestapo Lil danced with delight.

But Max was the true professional. "Ignore them," he cried and picked his hat from the floor. "You're on stage. Come on!"

Harry took a deep breath and leaned far out of the crow's nest. "Help!" he screamed. "Help! The ship's going down!"

Their assailants were hidden by a big Esso sign and the end of the garage.

"Throw down your weapons and give yourselves up!" Max roared at the wreckers and discharged his pistol.

"Never! Ha-ha!" replied Huggy in a savage bass. She brandished her club.

"My husband!" cried Auntie Florrie. "My boy! My darling!"

"Aarrgghh!" Fingers struggled in the foam.

Were they the best float? It was impossible to tell, but as Chalky pulled them through the streets it seemed to Harry that more cameras twinkled for them than for the others and the cheering rose to a crescendo.

The result was announced at half past four. The floats had

been drawn up, nose to tail, around three sides of the main square. The mayor, wearing his chain of office and surrounded by dignitaries, emerged from the town hall and stood at the top of the steps.

"My word!" he began. "What a treat! I think you'll all agree, there aren't many towns in England could put on a show to match Cobford. I said to my wife just this morning—"

Harry's attention wandered. From his perch high above the crowd, he searched for familiar faces and examined the fireworks strapped to the face of the town hall. At nine o'clock, just after it got dark, there was to be a big display. It was the climax of the day. He had been looking forward to it for weeks.

The mayor was coming to the end of his speech: ". . . done us proud . . . what price Hollywood, I say . . . *everyone's* a winner." He waited for applause. "But now the results you've all been waiting for. In third place – *Naughty Girls*." The principal teacher of maths from the High School, hair in pigtails, fag between her fingers, gym tunic hanging off one shoulder, went forward to collect the prize. "In second place – *The Operating Theatre*." A mad-looking surgeon with a bloodstained saw in one hand and a human leg in the other, pushed through the crowd. "And the winner of the first prize and a cheque for one hundred and fifty pounds, a worthy winner, I'm sure you'll all agree, is –" he paused. Harry could hardly breathe. "*Wreckers Crag* from the senior citizens of Lagg Hall. Plenty of life in the old dogs yet."

It was a popular result, there were shouts and cheers, but Auntie Florrie was gobsmacked. "Senior citizens!"

"Damned cheek!" Fingers said. "Look at 'im, he's about a hundred an' fifty years old 'imself."

"Hey, fatty!" Dot's cracked voice rang out above the crowd. "Who are you calling senior citizens?" Throwing off her coachman's cloak and hat, she sprang into a dazzling display of acrobatics – handstands, backflips, corkscrews, cartwheels – from one end of the float to the other, ending in a triple somersault from the top of the headboard, and stepping barefoot on to Chalky's back to take the ecstatic applause.

Angel, meanwhile, in his long wrecker's boots and sou'wester, mounted the steps to collect first prize: the cheque, a shield and a bottle of champagne.

"Aye, ye picked the right one," he said to the mayor. "The rest are rubbish."

A smell of sausage rolls and other savouries drifted from the town hall. The committee were having an early buffet. Angel adored sausage rolls.

"Thank ye very much." Clutching his prizes, he headed through the door to see what was on offer.

"No," the mayor called after him. "No, Mr er –"

But Angel was gone.

There were four hours to kill before the firework display, plenty of time to drive home, change, have tea and return in the car. But that wasn't the plan at all. On Fair Saturday everyone remained in costume, for at half past seven there was a fancy dress parade, and after the fireworks there would be dancing in the square.

So while Dot led Chalky away for a drink of water and nosebag of oats in the assembly field, and the rest peeled off jackets in the sunshine and went to find a cup of tea, Harry pulled on his trainers and set off to find Akku and Charlie. With so many people around, it was felt, he would be in no danger from Gestapo Lil and the rest of that crowd.

He met his friends by the octopus at the funfair, as arranged, and spent a fortune.

"Cor!" Charlie said as he paid for his third go on the dodgems. "Need to knock off a bank the prices they charge here."

Harry remembered the job at the Western Standard that Aunt Bridget had planned for that very day, but had postponed because of the hunt for Eddie Carver's treasure. "We should try it some time," he said. "What d'you reckon?"

"Don't be stupid," Akku said. "What car are you having?"

"Black one." Harry looked for it. "Number thirteen."

Charlie was already sitting in a red. He had chosen it three times in a row. "United! United!" He punched the air.

Akku shook his head sadly. "Don't be too hard on him, he's normal in some ways." He headed for an identical red car, but there was all the difference in the world. Akku's car was Arsenal.

At six they had to leave. Their money was gone and Harry had to meet the rest for a pub meal at the *Crosseyed Ploughman*. It was a nice place with ancient beams, waxed wood and hops round the bar. Two tables had been reserved and soon the ragged deck boy was tucking into scampi in the basket, with apricot strudel and ice cream to follow.

When Mrs Good and the hawk-eyed barman weren't watching, Fingers slipped him a glug of beer. "Real ale," Fingers told him. "None of your chemical muck."

Harry drank it, grimaced and wiped the foam from his lips. "It tastes terrible!"

"No it doesn't." Fingers took a long swallow. "Lovely!"

Max won the fancy-dress competition, not because his costume was better than anyone else's, but there was something about the way he glowered, and looked sideways with slit eyes, and discharged his pistol, that meant you couldn't take your eyes off him. Max was the most sinister policeman *ever*.

Then Dot went to look after Chalky because it was time for the firework display.

The square was packed like Cup Final day. Standing among the crowd, an eleven-year-old boy like Harry would have been lost behind the shoulders of the men in front. They looked for a better spot and found one at the far side of the square. An ornate drinking fountain, five metres high, stood on the pavement. Harry climbed up and stood on the basin.

"Here," said a man whose piggy daughter was whining because she had not thought of it first. "That's not hygienic."

He shouldn't have tapped Huggy on the shoulder. "Not hygienic," she growled. "You say my grandson is not hygienic!" She reached towards him with clawed hands. "I pull off your head and stuff it down the drain. Then you see vhat is not hygienic."

The man gave a sort of yelp and scuttled away, dragging his daughter behind.

"Veedy little man!" Huggy shouted after him. "The fountain not vorking anyvay."

At that moment the street lights in the square were

switched off and the firework display began. It was fantastic, better even than Harry had hoped. It started with a salvo of rockets that streaked into the sky and exploded into dandelion clocks of gold, diamond and multicoloured stars. It was followed by a second salvo, and a third, the detonations so loud you could feel them. The night sky was full of lights and crackles and curtains of fire. On platforms and the level area at the top of the town hall steps there were fountains and volcanoes. Whistlers zig-zagged across the sky, their demented *wheep-wheep-wheep* so scary that children covered their ears. The trees and buildings that surrounded the square flickered green and orange. A statue of John Bull was drowned in a cascade of white and crimson stars. A rack of giant Catherine wheels blazed and smoked. Yet more rockets whooshed towards the moon. The crowd craned their necks. Two thousand faces were illuminated. Cries of wonder were lost in the explosions. All too soon, as the grande finale, a spluttering message burst into fire, high across the face of the town hall:

UNTIL NEXT YEAR
GOODNIGHT . . . SAFE HOME

A curtain of stars, thick as a waterfall, spilled twenty metres to the steps. The crowd, lit by the golden glow, burst into spontaneous applause.

The street lights came on again. Everyone was smiling. Excited children chattered like birds.

Harry's position on the drinking fountain, a metre above everyone around, made him the most noticeable person on the pavement. He did not see the three furtive figures who stood watching him from the corner of a lane a short distance behind. When he turned to jump down, they hid their faces and melted into the shadows.

But there was a closer observer. No one paid any attention to the shambling, baby-faced Whortleberry Yawkins who stood crushed against them by the crowd. Harry smelled him, smelled his unwashed clothes and the cider on his breath. He glanced up and met the man's mild blue eyes, caught his shy smile, saw the cloudy bottle from which he was about to drink – and instantly forgot. His mind was too full of the fireworks.

"Well," Auntie Florrie put her arm around his shoulders. "What did you think of that, you dirty, ragged boy?"

"Great!" he said. "I loved the rockets. What's happening now?"

"To us or you?" said Aunt Bridget.

"All of us."

"Well, *we're* going to the beer garden in the park."

"Then on to the dancing," Max said.

"Exactly," she said. "You, Harry, are going home."

"Oh, but Aunt Bridget! Couldn't I stay on? Please! Look," he pointed to some rowdy children with their parents. "I bet they're staying."

"I bet they are," she said, "but you're not. You've had the float, the fair, the fancy-dress, the fireworks – oh, all the f's. Now it's the grown-ups' turn, without the children."

He made a face.

"I know, I know. I know all the arguments but the answer's the same. Goody's going to drive you home. Poor Nutty's missed the whole day and he built most of the float. You can tell him all about it."

As Whortleberry pressed close to listen, he trod on Max's toe.

Max looked up sharply. "Do you mind."

"Sorry." Whortleberry bobbed his head and backed away.

"Tell you what," Mrs Good said to Harry. "We'll look in and see Chalky on the way. See how he got on with all those bangs and flashes."

When the grown-ups were united like this it was no good arguing. To a chorus of "Night, 'Arry . . . you vere brilliant . . . see you in the morning, sailor-boy," he followed Goody from the square.

Unnoticed, Whortleberry slipped away and joined the three who were waiting for him in the lane.

The Rover stood in a floodlit car park, prizes hidden beneath a rug on the back seat. Mrs Good drove to the field on the edge of town and for five minutes they talked to Dot and Chalky. The sweet-natured horse lived a quiet life and had been very frightened by the fireworks. Harry stroked his neck and gave him some fruit pastilles from the bag in his pocket. Then they set off home.

Though Harry would not admit it, he *was* tired after the long day. As they drove at forty miles an hour between the fields and by the moonlit river, he felt his eyes closing. Had the journey been longer he would have fallen sound asleep, but in ten minutes the Lagg Hall woods rose before them and Mrs Good turned from the road into the long drive.

The headlamps cut a swathe through the trees. Suddenly she braked. Harry was thrown forward against the seat belt. A branch blocked the drive. How had that got there? There hadn't been a wind. Perhaps it had just rotted and fallen. But the leaves on it were green. He felt a quick shiver of fear and

245

at the same moment became aware of movement at the side of the car. Black figures in the moon shadow. The front doors were yanked open. Powerful torches flashed in their faces.

"It's that biddy what does the cooking."

"And the little rat himself."

"Back's empty."

"Good, we make it quick, avoid'a violence."

Mrs Good struggled. "Who are you? Get your hands off me!"

"You stay right where you are, dear. It's not you we're after."

Harry recognized the voices: GBH, Gestapo Lil, Mad Ruby Palazzo.

A vehicle swung in from the road. One headlamp was dazzling, the other dim, like a drooping eye. Harry heard the rattle of an old diesel engine. It drew up. The lights were cut. He saw that it was a battered farm truck.

Someone grabbed him by the collar. He struggled and shouted.

"Shut up!" A fist clumped him across the side of the head. A thick arm reached past to release the seat belt. Clumsily he was dragged from the car.

Harry kicked out. "Help! Help!"

A hand covered his mouth. He bit it hard.

GBH cried with pain.

A second thump made Harry's head reel.

Somebody was fiddling with his face. He smelled Gestapo Lil's perfume. A strip of carpet tape was slapped across his mouth.

He kicked out again, twisting with effort, but only met air.

They threw him to the ground and grabbed his legs, forced them together. In moments the tape was round his ankles.

He flailed about him with his fists and hit somebody in the eye. Another smell, sweat and cider, a newcomer. They rolled him over and pressed his face into the dirt. His arms were dragged behind, his wrists secured by the plastic tape.

Still he struggled. "Unnnh! Mmmm!" They were the only sounds he could make.

Now that he was helpless they bound him more tightly, wrapping the tape around his knees, all the way round his chest, trapping his elbows against his sides. To make doubly sure his mouth stayed shut, they rolled the tape right round the back of his head.

"Who's there?" Running footsteps approached from the direction of the house. Nutty had been watching television. He wore a new bib and brace. The headlights of the Rover caught his bald head. "Stop, whoever you are."

"No, you stop'a. Right there."

Nutty came on.

The blast of a shotgun startled the woods. Birds crashed away through the treetops. Harry strained his neck and saw the sawn-off in Ruby's hands. Nutty was shocked but did not appear to have been hit.

Then GBH took Harry's shoulders, the moon-faced, cider-smelling man took his feet, and he was carted away like a roll of carpet. "One – two –" With a heave they slung him over the side into the back of the truck. With a painful crack he landed on his shoulder.

GBH jumped up beside him. The second man got into the cab. The door banged shut.

"Harry!" Mrs Good was shouting. "Harry!"

There were confused footsteps on the gravel. He heard a scuffle. Voices were raised. There was a second gunshot.

Then the engine shuddered into life and the truck was moving, backing down the drive to the main road. Harry saw the branches passing overhead. They swung out on to the tarmac. The truck stopped, gears ground.

It drew away.

Harry was a prisoner.

Chapter 22

Scrumpy Bottom

The chain was rusty and ten metres long. Originally it had been used to tether a bull but for the past two decades had hung from a nail in one of the outbuildings. Now Whortleberry had found a use for it. One end was looped round a crooked beam and threaded through an iron ring. The other end was attached to a pair of handcuffs. These were fastened around Harry's wrists. The chain gave him freedom to move between his bed, the living room, the kitchen and the bathroom. The toilet was a bit difficult to manage but it was possible. He could even, had he wished, have taken a bath in the filthy tub.

When he arrived the evening before, Harry had been attached to one handcuff only. During his year with the Wrinklies, however, he had acquired certain skills. At the first opportunity he had taken a spike from a kitchen drawer and picked the lock. Whortleberry Yawkins, whose farm this was, had caught him by the shirt as he was vanishing through the window. "Not going already," he had said, overpowering Harry with his bearlike strength and bearlike BO, which left him gasping. "I was looking forward to a bit of company." And kneeling on him on the kitchen floor, he handcuffed

Harry's wrists across his stomach and removed the tool drawers to an unreachable corner of the room.

Cider House Farm – or Scrumpy Bottom, as it was known locally – where Harry was being held prisoner, had for the best part of a century been a thriving concern. Whortleberry's father, Jos. A. Yawkins Esq, had been a hardworking and successful cider producer, like his father and grandfather before him. In the twenty years since his death, however, the farm had fallen into disrepair and decay. The fine flavour of *Yawkins Old Special*, a byword for excellence, was remembered by only a handful of drinkers and a row of flyblown certificates screwed to the landing wall. For Whortleberry – Baba, as he was called – had no interest in cider, except as liquor to feed his addiction, and the brew he made was so powerful, cloudy and bad that it had addled his brain. At one time the farm had welcomed visitors: now the apple trees were cankered and twisted, the roof of the cider house was falling, woodworm had infested the mill, rats ate the fallen fruit and made nests beneath the abandoned vats. In the past there had been cattle, too, and horses, but now the whole five hundred acres – meadows, orchards and yards – were returning to the wilderness. Grass grew waist-high, bushes much higher, and in the late summer the air was thick with wasps. Baba liked it. It was the way he wished his farm to be.

The house was as neglected as the rest of the property and came as no surprise to the three or four visitors who, in the course of a year, forced their way along the stony, boggy, overgrown track that led to Scrumpy Bottom. Yet Baba was by no means a poor man. He was, in fact, worth the best part of a million, but money meant nothing to him, except as a secret and something not to spend. The window frames were rotting. One window, which had collapsed, was covered by boards. A sheet of corrugated iron had been nailed to the roof to cover a patch of missing pantiles. When a gale blew, it filled the house with a rattle like thunder.

Baba was not short of company, though not of the human sort. He had two dogs which he loved, a Border collie and a matted Old English sheepdog. Feral cats inhabited the barns. Hens, sheep and an occasional pig wandered in from the yard, though generally the lounge and bedrooms were forbidden territory. The animals were nervous, for their reception was uncertain. Sometimes they were made welcome, spoken to affectionately, given crusts, carrots, a handful of cereals. Other times they were driven from the house by shouts and missiles – cups, coal, carving knives. And eventually, when the time was right, they became Whortleberry's dinner.

During his father's time, the hub of Cider House Farm had been the kitchen with its Aga cooker and table that could seat a dozen. Baba preferred the lounge, a spacious room with bay windows that in the past had overlooked an immaculate garden, apple orchards and the countryside beyond. In the evening, standard lamps had cast a glow over polished furniture and comfortable, chintz-covered settees. Good books lay about. The crystal sparkled. Now years-old bird droppings streaked the window panes. The view was obscured by lichen and self-seeded trees that pressed their leaves against the glass. The same chintz, stained with cider and strewn with dog hairs, covered the settees. The same pictures, in the same places, hung on the faded walls. From time to time Whortleberry brushed the floor, shook the covers, hacked back the growth. Otherwise, he scarcely noticed.

Those who met Whortleberry Yawkins, who saw the madness in his misty blue eyes and smelled his crumpled clothes, would never have guessed that he had a secret passion. In the lounge were the three items of furniture that fed it. One was an old piano, pulled into the middle of the room. The second was an enormous, fingermarked television, placed where he could see it from the piano stool. The third was an elderly music centre with large speakers. Shelves were heaped with dusty videos – films going back to the silent era – and tapes, discs and gramophone records of great music.

On his rare forays into the city – for which he added a layer to the scum that ringed the bath and put on the cleanest clothes he could find – Whortleberry had two destinations. The first was a renowned music shop where he stood for a full hour struggling with the desire to buy a beautiful, thirty-thousand-pound Steinway grand piano. The second was an electronics emporium where he spent nearly as long staring at enormous plasma television screens and state-of-the-art music centres. He could afford them easily. He longed for them, he drooled over them. One day he would buy them. But not today. Contentedly he set off home, turning from the motorway on to the small and smaller roads that thirty miles later passed the end of the scarcely-visible track that led to Scrumpy Bottom. Smoke rose from the old pick-up truck as he climbed a long hill. Halting to let the engine cool off, he reached to the passenger seat and popped the stopper on a new bottle. The window was open, a fresh wind blew from the fields. He turned the tape in his player and pressed *start*. The soothing notes of the second movement of Beethoven's *Emperor* piano concerto washed over him. Whortleberry settled in his seat, leaned his head against the rest, and shut his eyes. Automatically he took a sip.

Cider fed Baba's shapeless body, the piano fed his soul. It was hard to believe, looking at him now, that at the age of nineteen Whortleberry had been a rising star at the Royal Academy of Music. The piano prizes were his. Orchestras and concert halls competed for engagements. He seemed destined for a glittering career – but scrumpy had put an end to all of that. His greatest pleasure these days was to run old movies with the sound turned off and improvise music to accompany the drama, as cinemas had done in the years before the talkies: soft for the love scenes, jaunty for the comedy, sinister for the villains, and crashing for the murders. He played with his mouth working and his cider-crazed eyes glued to the screen. Night after night, sometimes at three in the morning, sometimes in his underwear with a bottle at the end of the keyboard and owls shrieking as they killed rats about the barns, he played accompaniments to *Graveyards of Blood*, *Gone with the Wind* and *Dolly the Dancing Dinosaur*, whatever matched his mood of the moment.

It was one such interlude, on the day Percy Priestly was snatched from hospital, that had caused him to ring home and call Baba a raving lunatic.

That evening, eighteen days earlier, after driving Gestapo Lil, Mad Ruby and his nephew back to Felon Grange, and narrowly avoiding being written off by a police car in the process, Baba had returned to Scrumpy Bottom where Priestly had been taken to recover from his gunpowder poisoning. The plan was for the escaped prisoner to lie low there for a few days and when the heat was off move closer to home. It was rare for Baba to have a guest, even rarer for him to have an audience. The opportunity was too good to miss. And so, having set the table with a loaf of bread, a tin of corned beef, and a gallon of mind-altering cider, he had launched into a selection of his all-time favourites.

It was a virtuoso performance. Priestly was astonished. For ten minutes he listened with admiration. But Baba did not stop after ten minutes, the music went on. An hour passed. And then a second hour. Priestly thought he would go crazy. "For God's sake!" he cried as the crashing chords of a gun battle filled the room. "Enough's enough! Give it a rest."

Baba turned mad eyes upon him and waved a bottle. His chin shone with spittle. "Ah, ha-ha-ha-ha-ha-ha-ha!" he said. It made the colonel's blood run cold. He was rescued at two in the morning.

Despite this setback, there was no denying that Scrumpy Bottom was the perfect hideaway. And so, when the kidnap was set up for Harry and a safe house was needed, GBH was sent to inform his uncle.

It went like clockwork. Baba's truck, with muddied number plates, was hidden at the roadside. Harry was captured. Bound and gagged, he was flung aboard.

Followed by Gestapo Lil and Mad Ruby in the black Range Rover, Baba drove first to Felon Grange. They drew up at the moonlit portico. Colonel Priestly, who by now had installed an infrared warning system in the drive and spent much of his time at his old home, came down the steps to meet them.

"Got him, good." He leaned over and poked Harry with a hand holding a fat cigar. "Horrible child! See how *you* like being dragged off and kept prisoner in chains and handcuffs."

"Uhhh! Nnnn!" Harry responded.

Priestly tapped his ash in Harry's hair. "If I had my way you'd be trussed up like a turkey and slung in the coal cellar."

"With rats and maggots," added Harry's one-time nurse.

"You all so soft'a," said Mad Ruby. "What wrong with concrete boots? So easy, any hardware store sell you quick-setting cement. Two hour maximum. Take him to bridge. Splash'a! End of problem."

"Here, no need for that sort of talk." Baba was horrified. "Keep him safe at Scrumpy Bottom was what you said."

"Yeah, right." Priestly smiled with fat lips. "But we don't mind paying for a few little – extras."

"Uncle Whort'll do what we agreed an' that's all there is to it." GBH dropped the tailgate and heaved Harry out the back. "Come on, let's get him in the driver's cab."

With a few knocks he was manoeuvred into the passenger seat. Harry thought he was going to fall out. "Hassen uh see weh." He rolled his eyes.

"All right, give us a chance." They had brought the car rug from the Rover. GBH draped it over Harry's head then pulled down the seat belt and clipped him in. "No need to advertise where you're takin' him," he said to his uncle. "Watch he doesn't fool you, that's all. He might be just a kid but he's slippery as an eel."

"If he tries any funny stuff give him a leathering," said Gestapo Lil. "He understands that."

"Sleeping pills," said Mad Ruby.

"He'd better be there when we come down tomorrow afternoon," Priestly warned, "that's all I can say."

Baba got back into the cab. "Nice company you're keeping, Phil," he said to his nephew.

They retreated to the steps and he started on the fifty-mile journey to Scrumpy Bottom.

Harry was given a downstairs bedroom. He was sure he would never sleep. One of the cats had left a dead baby rabbit on his pillow. The blankets were covered with dog hairs that made him sneeze. The mattress felt damp. The handcuffs were uncomfortable.

A few metres down the corridor Baba played on and on, sometimes singing to accompany himself or shouting at the television: "Go on, let him have it, the fat slob! . . . Dear me, you don't half fancy yourself, darling." The bull chain made it impossible to shut the doors.

At last the piano fell silent. Harry breathed a sigh of relief. But not many minutes later the music was replaced by snores. Baba was sleeping on a settee: at least, Harry had not heard him climb the stairs. He lay thinking: he would give him a while to go right under, then creep out and explore the house. See if he could find some way to unlock the handcuffs. Pick Baba's pocket for the key. He turned over and shut his eyes.

And when he opened them again it was daylight.

For a moment he did not know where he was – then he remembered. But something had woken him. What was it? Some noise. A scream. He shivered and clutched the bedclothes to his throat. The sound was not repeated.

He was just about to get up when the door moved. Harry froze. A dog looked in, a slim Border collie. It lifted its nose as if scenting him. He greeted it: "Kk-kk. Hello, boy." The dog ignored him and retreated.

Harry pushed back the blankets and swung his feet to the

carpet. His waist itched. He pulled up his shirt and saw that he was covered with red bites. Some insect. He spotted a tiny dot and looked closer. It vanished. Fleas! Horrified, he shook his shirt, pulled off his trousers and turned them inside out, flapped them up and down. Fleas! Ahhh! Clutching his clothes and dragging the chain, he fled through to the kitchen.

The spots itched like mad. He clawed his leg and his back. His skin became inflamed. The red spread from one spot to another. He started on his chest – then stopped. Heavy footsteps approached up the corridor. Harry backed away and stared.

Baba came through the door. He wore the same clothes as the day before, the clothes he had slept in. But it wasn't his crumpled clothes, or wild hair, or rank smell that caught Harry's attention. For in his hand Baba carried a rusty cleaver, the blade red with blood. For a moment neither spoke. Then Baba said:

"Been killing a pig. Thought we'd have a bit o' pork tonight. Fancy that? Bit o' pork with nice crackling, apple sauce, roast taters? Find a few rasps?" He clattered the cleaver into the sink and rinsed the blood from his forearms. "What is it? Cat got your tongue?"

Harry didn't reply. His eyes were on the cleaver, the edge bright with whetting.

As Baba dried himself on a rancid towel, he seemed to notice for the first time that Harry's shirt hung from the handcuffs and his legs were bare. "What you got your pants off for? What's all those marks on your skin? Some allergy is it? Got the lurgy?"

"Fleas," Harry said and struggled against tears.

The scales fell from Baba's eyes. The curtain which separated his fantasy life from reality was torn down. This wasn't a game. The three-quarters-naked boy who stood before him wasn't the villain he had been painted: wasn't some thug to be 'given a leathering', 'flung down the cellar steps', 'fitted with concrete boots'. He was frightened, and no wonder. He was upset. He was brave.

And he was in Baba's charge. He looked at Harry's inflamed skin; saw the ship's boy rags he was wearing; saw the filthy state of the kitchen. His cheeks burned.

"Look, it's all right," he said. "You're quite safe." He tried to put a comforting arm round Harry's shoulders.

Harry backed away.

"Can't say I blame you. But you are, really."

His matted English sheepdog trotted in from the passage.

"They're the culprits," Baba said. "Aren't you, Teddy, you disgusting brute. Dog fleas, see. Don't bother me. Pickled skin, I reckon. Different a young lad like you. Still, soon put a stop to that."

He went out to one of the barns and after a few minutes returned carrying a cardboard cylinder with a rusty tin lid.

"Derris powder," he announced, reading the peeling label. "Dynamite. This'll soon put a stop to the little beggars."

Harry hugged his bare chest. It was cold in the kitchen.

"Have to get you some clothes an' all." Baba coughed and he was engulfed in a stink of cidery breath. "Wait here a minute. See what I can find."

Harry rattled his chains. "I haven't got much choice."

Baba paused in his tracks. "No, I suppose not. I'll be right down."

He hurried upstairs and rummaged through the drawers in his bedroom. Everything was worn, stained, dirty. He sniffed a shirt and turned his head away. Clean clothes? There were none. What about a bedspread? Then he remembered his father's clothes, the suits in the wardrobe of what had once been his father's bedroom – the room, in fact, in which he had died. His father had been smaller than Whortleberry, his clothes wouldn't fit or they would have been worn long since. He went through and pulled open the mirrored door. A stale smell of moths and shoes and dead cigars wafted out. There hung his father's suits, untouched for over twenty years. He remembered them well: the silver-grey, the navy with a red thread, the tweed favoured by farmers. The cloth was chill to his touch. Still, a good shake-out, he thought, an airing, and one of them would do. He hesitated, then pulled the navy from its hanger. In a drawer he found a singlet, some neatly folded socks and a pair of droopy underpants. He returned downstairs.

Harry had found a tablecloth and draped it round his shoulders.

"That's no good, here." Baba turned his deck boy trousers the right way round and sprinkled the inside with derris powder. Did the same to his shirt. "Right, you can put them on again." He offered the can. "Want to put some inside your pants?"

Even insecticide was better than fleas. Harry turned away and did so. The dust stung his nostrils.

Baba set a light beneath the greasy kettle and found a brick-hard loaf of bread in a cupboard. Briskly he ran it under the tap and set it in the oven to crust up again. He rinsed a spoon and scraped the fur from a jar of marmalade. Inside ten minutes breakfast was ready.

Harry watched the preparations with dismay, but to his surprise the hot bread and marmalade were excellent. So was the tea with caked dried milk.

While Harry ate, Baba was a whirlwind of activity. He switched on the immersion; raked out the ancient ashes and lit a fire in the Aga; shook the moths' wings from the suit and hung it in the sunshine; dragged Harry's bedding and the loose covers from the lounge into the yard; filled a huge tub with water and slopped in a liberal quantity of disinfectant that in the old days had been used to sterilize the vats; and sprinkled the settees, beds, carpets, corners and crevices with the derris powder.

"Come on," he said as Harry finished his second mug of tea and fifth slice of bread and marmalade. "You can give me a hand. I'll loosen one of them handcuffs. Mind, if I catch you trying to escape again, I'll give you a good leathering, like the lady said."

Harry hesitated. Did he want to stay moping indoors, or get outside and do something? "All right," he said.

"Are you giving me your word?"

Harry said, "No." Then he thought about it. He did not believe Baba would give him a beating, he was too kind. In fact Harry quite liked his strange, shambling jailer, though he wished he did not smell so bad. In an odd way he felt sorry for him. "All right," he said.

So Baba removed the handcuff from one wrist and shifted the chain to a ringbolt in the yard. Later he moved it to the branch of a tree, then the post at the foot of the banisters, so that Harry could help with the work.

It was the busiest day the farm had seen for many years. They steeped all the bedding in the disinfectant and stuffed it into the rarely-used washing machine. Did the same with the loose covers, some towels and Baba's clothes. Caught the struggling dogs and forced them into the tub. Rinsed their arms and heads to remove the splashes. Hosed off the dogs. Washed the accumulated dishes and cleaned the bath. Hoovered the dirt and powder from the beds and carpets. And carved up the slaughtered pig into joints, wrapped them in polythene and packed all but one into an ancient deep-freeze in the barn.

When they had finished, Harry took a bath. Afterwards Baba painted his flea bites – there were sixty-three – with a bottle of crusted iodine. Then Harry pulled on Josiah's singlet and navy blue suit. The underpants would have fitted two boys his size and hung past his knees. He fastened them with a safety pin. Braces supported the pinstripe trousers. Harry turned up the legs and sleeves and considered himself in a cracked cheval glass not unlike the one in the attic at home. He liked his image. All he needed was a shirt and fedora to look like a Chicago gangster.

He returned to the lounge and looked from the window. Hens pecked in the orchard. A breeze blew the rags of moss that hung from the apple trees. Their clean clothes and bedding fluttered in the sunshine.

"Place looks good." Teddy – who as an Old English sheepdog had been named after Edward Elgar, the English composer – gave a yelp as Baba tugged a comb through his matted hair. "I should have cleaned up ages ago. Months. Years."

It looked better, there was no denying. The swept hearth and blazing fire gave it a homely look. Harry thought of the lounge at Lagg Hall and compared the wallpaper and window panes of Scrumpy Bottom. It had a long way to go yet.

"I suppose you'll be wanting lunch," Baba said. "Means I'll have to go to the shop in the village. Take half an hour."

Harry said, "Those trees growing against the window. Give me a saw and I'll cut them back while you're away. Let a bit more light in."

"Yeah, cut through that beam up there while you're at it. Good idea. I'll give you the chain saw, make it easier."

Harry made a face.

"What we'll do instead," Baba set down the comb, "is this." He shortened the chain round the beam and snapped the second handcuff round Harry's wrist. "Then I know you'll be here when I get back, right?"

Harry flopped on to a settee.

"Anything you don't like?"

He shook his head. "Yeah, being a prisoner."

The pick-up drove away. The black and white collie, whose name was Pete – short for Peter Ilyich Tchaikovsky, whose *First Piano Concerto* was one of Baba's favourites – trotted into the room. He had hated the disinfectant and still stank of it, but now his coat was flea-free, tick-free and almost dry. Harry made a fuss of him, the way he did with Tangle, and Pete pressed against his legs.

The heat of the fire made his flea-bites unbearable. He moved away, clawing his shoulder bloody. Pete followed, seeking more attention.

Harry looked round the room. Was there *no* way to pick the handcuffs, unhook the chain? Poker and tongs lay in the hearth. A jumble of books, cloths, playing cards and other useless junk filled the drawers and cupboards. He thrust his fingers down the sides of the chairs and found dust, a magazine, a few small coins.

Then his eyes fell on the fire. Could he heat the chain until the iron glowed white-hot and pliable? Could he break it with the poker? Harry did not know but it was worth a try.

He jerked the bull chain along the beam to get some slack and buried a few links in the heart of the fire. Sticks lay at one side of the hearth, a ragged coal scuttle at the other. He heaped the fire high. The flames began to roar. His face was scorched. Harry moved aside, waiting for the blaze to reach maximum heat.

He sat on the carpet, wrists together and back to the wall. Pete's head rested on his knee. Harry stroked his soft ears and Pete blinked with pleasure. The dog could have lain like that all day but abruptly he sat up. His head turned towards the window. For seconds he listened. A ridge of hair rose along his back. His lip curled, showing his teeth. With a growl he ran from the room.

Harry stared towards the window and a few moments later heard the noise of a car. It was drowned by a chorus of barking from Pete and Teddy. He rose, trying not to disturb the links of chain in the fire. The dogs stood facing the overgrown track. Harry caught a glimpse of red. His heart stopped. It came closer. He saw it clearly. A two-seater, sleek and expensive. It was a car he knew well. An Aston Martin.

It belonged to Gestapo Lil.

Chapter 23

Baba Triumphant

Car doors banged. Harry looked from his chain to the window. The barking rose to a crescendo. He heard voices then a loud yelp of pain. Pete ran past on three legs, one paw hanging. His cries faded across the orchard. Teddy was silenced.

"Damned dogs!" It was a man's voice, high-pitched, petulant, Priestly. "Ought to be put down, the pair of them. If I had a gun with me I'd do it myself."

"Quite right, Percy. Savage brutes." Harry knew both these voices. The icy, crystal tones of Gestapo Lil had pursued him through life. "Keep a hold of that stick, there might be more inside. We know there's a little rat."

"There'd better be. *And* a dangerous lunatic."

"Dangerous? Do you think so?"

"You've seen his eyes. Mad as a hatter. His smell will knock you dead at ten paces. Pure poison gas."

"And he's the man looking after Harry." She clapped her hands. "Marvellous!"

After a moment Priestly said, "Where's the truck?"

"Oh, no! You don't think—"

"Come on."

"Harry?" High heels click-clacked across the yard. "Harry Barton!"

Harry stood by the fire. Shadows darkened the sunlit passage at the far side of the room.

"He's not in the kitchen."

"Or the bathroom."

"Ah!" Gestapo Lil stood in the entrance. "Here he is, Percy. The boy himself." Smiling nastily, she advanced into the lounge. "Still in one piece, more's the pity."

She was immaculate as ever. On this summer afternoon she wore a corn-yellow suit with snake-green accessories: earrings, necklace, crocodile handbag and knee-length boots. Her eyeshadow, too, was green. Her lips and nails were deep blood red. Her hair, the same shade as the suit, was braided and coiled in a chignon.

"What are these clothes you are wearing?" she said contemptuously. "You weren't wearing them last night. You look like a clown."

Colonel Priestly followed her into the room. Although he was on the run, her fiancé had made no attempt to disguise himself – this day, at least. Freed from prison, he was revealed as a stout, strutting little man with red cheeks and hot-tempered eyes. Despite the July sunshine, he wore the tweed suit with loud checks that Harry remembered from the year before. A gold chain crossed his waistcoat. Gold rings were on his fingers. A gold tooth winked in his smile. It was nearly as much gold as Eddie Carver. Unlike his murdered boss, however, Priestly wore spectacles, had thinning ginger hair which was oiled flat, and a ginger moustache.

"Well." He cracked the stick against his leg and crossed to the hearth. "What are you doing? Trying to melt the chain?"

Harry didn't reply.

"Ignorant young fool, do you know nothing? Do you think it'll melt in there?" He raised the stick to give Harry a backhand swipe.

Harry darted out of reach. The white-hot chain was pulled from the fire and skittered across the carpet. Blazing coals came with it. Gestapo Lil sprang aside. The high heels made her clumsy. Harry's chain hit her on the ankle. She was not burned but the green crocodile boots, for which she had paid three hundred pounds just the day before, were ruined. At the same time, little fires were starting all over the floor. Flames ran up the front of a settee. The air filled with smoke and the stink of burning wool. Harry stamped on the fires, smothered the flames on the settee, picked up coals with the tongs and threw them back into the hearth. Priestly had no intention of damaging his handmade brogues. Instead, he clasped a handkerchief over his mouth and hurried to the kitchen for a jug of water. All he could find was a milk jug. It extinguished a single coal. By the time he returned, the fires were out. Smoke rose from blackened holes in the once-beautiful carpet. Beneath the chain it still smouldered. Priestly tipped his jug of water. The hot iron fizzed and spat.

But Gestapo Lil had no eyes for the carpet, did not care about the blaze there might have been. "My boots! Oh, Percy! Look what he's done!" A pattern of chain marks ran across both feet. Wherever the white-hot metal had touched, the leather was burned to a crisp. The boots were beyond repair. Her eyes rose to Harry. "Right, you! You've asked for it this time." She snatched the stick from Priestly's hand. "By the time I get through with you, you'll—"

"What do you think you're doing?" Baba stood in the doorway. A cider bottle was in his hand. He had been drinking. Amid the panic no one had heard his return. "What's all this smoke? What's going on?"

"What do you think? It's him!" Priestly pointed with the milk jug. "Nearly set the house on fire. Hadn't been for us, the whole place would have gone up."

"That's not true," Harry said.

"See what he did?" Gestapo Lil extended a foot. "Ruined! I'm going to teach him a lesson he'll not forget."

"With that?" Baba nodded at the stick.

"Well I'm not going to poke it up my nose."

Baba had revised his opinion of Gestapo Lil. He did not like her. "Leave him alone."

"What! I should say so."

"Let me put it another way." He drained his bottle and grasped it by the neck. "If you lay a finger on him, I'll bash your brains out."

She was startled.

So was Harry.

"Who do you think you're talking to?" Priestly blustered.

"You if the cap fits," Baba said. "I said I'd keep him here and I will. He's a good lad, good company. Helped me clear up. But if you think you're going to come into my house and start knocking him about, you can think again."

"What I think is, you'd better mind your own business," Priestly said. "What I think is, you'd better remember what I told you the last time I was here."

"What was that then?"

"You're off your trolley. You ought to be put away. One word from me and the social services will be round here with the padded van before you can say fruitcake. All it takes is a phone call."

"Ah, but you won't."

"Won't I?"

"No, you won't." Baba drew a clasp knife and tested the blade with his thumb. "'Cause if you so much as think about it, you might find yourself in a deep hole somewhere out there in the orchard. Ha-ha-ha. Her an' all." The spittle ran down his chin. He wiped it off and returned the knife to his pocket. "Or the deep freeze. The boy and me just put a pig in there this morning. Plenty o' room for a couple more. That right, Harry? Lonely place this."

Harry's blood ran cold.

"'Sides," Baba went on, "you seem to forget you're on the run. Cops are on the lookout. We've seen you. We know who you're knocking around with. I got your prints all over a jar o' cider from the last time." He nodded to the yard. "Car tracks out there. Number plates. Couldn't wait to tell me how clever you'd all been getting out of prison an' that hospital. So you'd better not try coming it round here, neither of you. Specially since you've started burning holes in my dad's Persian carpet. You can pay for that. An' don't start blaming the boy again 'cause I don't believe you."

They were silenced.

Baba rarely made a speech that long. The spittle flowed freely. He went to the kitchen and returned with a fresh bottle. "Now I'm going to have a half-hour at the piano, I haven't touched it all day." He settled himself on the stool. "If you're going that suits me fine. If you're staying you can make some tea and sandwiches for us all. I've been to the shop." He ran his fingers over the keys.

"Give me the key to the handcuffs," Priestly said.

"The boy's staying here."

Baba's back was towards them. Before Harry could warn him, Gestapo Lil snatched up a vase and ran forward. CRASH! It shattered across the back of Baba's head. If the china had been thicker it would have knocked him senseless. But luckily for him and unluckily for Gestapo Lil, it was made of Chinese porcelain and did little damage.

Baba gave a roar that was half anger and half drunken laughter. He swung from his seat. Gestapo Lil fled to her fiancé's side. It did not save her. Baba grabbed her by the wrist.

"You're a dangerous woman. For two pins I'd put you across my knee and give you a right good hiding. It's what you deserve." He threw her to the carpet. "Now behave yourself, I'm warning you."

Harry could hardly refrain from cheering.

"And you can pay me for that vase as well. I hope you've got plenty in your piggy bank because it was Ming." Rubbing his head, Baba returned to the piano stool. "Now sling your hook, the pair of you, or make them sandwiches. The boy's not leaving this room and there's an end of it. I wouldn't let you two in charge of a foaming dog, let alone a young lad." He took a long pull on the cider and looked over his shoulder at Harry. "Watch my back, all right?"

Harry looked from one to the other. He nodded.

For a minute Baba tinkled the keys, then launched into a thunderous Rachmaninov prelude.

Gestapo Lil clutched her fiancé's arm and pulled herself to her feet. Her face was scarlet. Tears of humiliation ran down her cheeks. They retreated to the end of the room.

What was going to happen next? Harry was scared. Beyond the window he saw movement. Pete had returned from the orchard and stood looking uncertainly towards the house. His front paw hung a few centimetres above the ground.

Harry crossed to the piano. "Mr Yawkins." He tapped him on the shoulder.

Baba looked round. "What?" The mad cider look had come back into his eyes.

"I think you should come – I mean go – outside. Pete's been hurt."

"Pete? Stupid mutt! What's he done to himself this time?"

"Well, he's not done anything to *himself*. It was –" Harry looked across the room.

"What?"

"When they first came. He was barking."

"What are you saying?"

"They hit him. That's why they've got the stick."

"Hit him with a stick!" Baba lurched to his feet. The stool fell. "Hit Pete! You bloody, bloody –" he shouted. "You –" He rushed from the room.

Priestly and Gestapo Lil stood rooted to the spot. Whatever they may have intended, Baba settled the matter. When he found Pete whimpering in the yard with his leg gashed open and badly bruised, he went berserk. Shouting hysterically and hardly knowing what he did, he ran back into the house. "You cruel, bloody –" Tears of rage filled his eyes. The spittle flew. "Out! Out! Get out of this house!"

Priestly raised the stick in self-defence. Baba wrenched it from his grasp. "Get out! Before I kill you!" The stick thudded on their backs. They put up arms to protect their heads. Priestly's Rolex was shattered. Stumbling and crying aloud, they were driven from the room, down the passage, across the yard to the car. "Ahhh! Ow! Get off!" Risking broken fingers, they pulled open the doors and scrambled inside. The stick hit the windscreen. They snapped the locks shut.

"Bloody madman!" Priestly's glasses hung from one ear. He looked up.

Baba bared his teeth and whacked the Aston Martin above the window. The metal buckled; the stick broke. He flung what remained at the bonnet and kicked the door. The paint split. He kicked again and beat his fist on the roof.

Priestly shouted at his fiancée: "Come on, you fool! Get a move on."

"Don't call *me* a fool," she snapped back. "You're the one brought us to this madhouse."

"Never mind that." He flapped his hands. "Just get us out of here."

"All right! All right!" She switched on the ignition and flung the car into gear. His waving hand hit her in the face. "Will you stop that. You really are such a pig sometimes." Angrily she trod too hard on the accelerator.

The wheels spun. The tyres squealed. Slewing and snaking, the car shot away, bounced off an ancient horse trough and careered on up the track. A scatter of grit hit Baba on the legs. A rock lay by his foot. He flung it after the retreating car. By good luck it hit a rear light. The plastic shattered and fell to the ground.

"That's right! Get out! Get out and don't come back."

Harry watched from the window. He loved it. Baba stood like a triumphant ogre, shouting and shaking his fist until the car was lost along the overgrown track.

At length he turned and saw Harry at the lounge window. Gruffly he looked away. "Pete?" he called. "Pete?" Then looked back and smiled shyly.

Harry saluted him with handcuffed arms.

Baba waved back. The smile became a grin. Then a big belly laugh. "That saw them off, Harry boy. Eh?" He belched. "They'll not be back for a while."

Pete had fled. The violence frightened him. Baba went searching and found his collie looking from the doorway of a barn. He was shivering.

"Come on, then. Poor boy."

Pete limped forward placatingly, belly low, tail between his legs.

"All right, lovely. No one's going to hurt you. Let's see what those nasty people have done to a good boy." Tenderly Baba examined the wound, moving aside the hair to see the split flesh and a glimpse of bone. "Brave boy." He stroked the dog's head. "It's the vet for you. Have to get that stitched. Up you come." He lifted Pete in his arms and carried him to the house. "Yes, yes. I know." He shut his eyes as Pete strained to lick his whiskery face. "Pooh! You stink of that old disinfectant. Just as well, seeing what's happened. Vet doesn't want your old fleas hopping round his surgery, does he."

Harry made the long-awaited sandwiches while Baba bathed the wound with dilute iodine and bound it with a towel.

"Lucky you come," he said. "Clean towels, no fleas and that." In quick succession he swallowed half a cup of tea, bit into a ham sandwich and washed it down with a glug of cider. "Mind, if you hadn't come, I don't suppose he would have been hurt in the first place. Carpet wouldn't be burned. I wouldn't have a lump on my head. Car wouldn't be all bashed up."

"It's not my fault," Harry protested. "I didn't ask to be kidnapped and brought here. Do you think I want to be chained up, threatened with a hammering?"

"I didn't say that," Baba said. "I only said *if* you hadn't. Dogs would be scratching. I'd be stretched out on the settee over there, snoring my head off probably. Happy as pigs in muck, all three of us. That right, Teddy?" He slipped his shaggy companion a corner of sandwich.

"I don't even know where I am," Harry said.

Chapter 24

The Cosh and the Smile

They returned at six and brought a puppy. It was enchanting, a Dalmatian with big paws, bright brown eyes and a floppy, bouncing friendliness.

"It was lost," Gestapo Lil explained, leading it from the Range Rover on a length of cord. "Wandering on the railway line, miles from anywhere. Percy risked his life going down to rescue it."

"Didn't want to think it might get hurt," he said brusquely. "Nice little thing."

The truth was rather different. The puppy belonged to a seven-year-old girl who adored it and had been taking it for a walk in the park. Gestapo Lil had pushed her over and stolen the puppy. And far from risking his life, Priestly had spent the afternoon in a country hotel, drinking brandy and smoking cigars. He had been in little danger since the hotel belonged to Rotten Reg, a criminal associate from the old days.

"Know you like dogs," he said now. "Thought you might give it a good home."

Teddy and Pete, his leg stitched and bound by a tight bandage, investigated the new arrival.

"Things got a bit out of hand this afternoon." Gestapo Lil presented Baba with a large box of Belgian chocolates. "Wanted to say sorry."

"Don't believe them," Harry called from an open window. "They're probably drugged. I bet she's got a cosh or a pistol in her handbag."

"What an imagination." She laughed merrily.

Harry was wrong about the chocolates but he was right about the handbag: it was a cosh.

Baba did not know his visitors so well. Moreover, he had reached that stage in his cider-swamped Sunday when chocolates, an apology and a puppy were hard to resist.

"All those black spots." He watched the Dalmatian romping around the yard. "Looks like a piece of music. I think I'll call him Crotchet. Or Quaver. Have to think about it."

The chocolates were gift-wrapped. He dropped the pretty paper on the ground and examined the cellophane. It had not been tampered with. He tore it off. "Come on into the house. Try a drop o' cider then Harry'll make a pot of tea."

"No!" Harry called. "Don't trust them. Watch your back."

His urgency filtered through to Baba's brain. "What's he talking about? Not *got* anything in your bag have you?"

"Of course I haven't." She drew the handbag to her side.

"Boy thinks so. Let's have a look."

"No. Get off! Stop it!"

He wrenched it from her grasp. The handle tore from the green crocodile leather.

"Percy!" she cried.

Munching a white chocolate truffle, Baba rooted inside. "Ahh! What's this?" He produced the cosh, a nicely-balanced American blackjack of heavy rubber filled with lead shot, and a loop for the wrist. He turned it to read the manufacturer's label:

S. P. Litskull : Chicago
By Appointment
Suppliers to the Mob
Medium

"Well, that's not very friendly." Baba tapped it lightly against his head and winced. "Ooohh! We'll get rid of that, I think." He drew back his arm and flung the cosh far across the overgrown orchard.

With excited wuffs Teddy and Pete, followed by the willing pup, bounded off in pursuit.

"No! No, you cretins," Baba shouted after them. "Leave it! Leave it!"

They ignored him. A panting, happy Teddy laid the cosh by his feet and looked up expectantly.

"No!" Baba said firmly and dropped the saliva-covered cosh into his pocket. "I said you were a dangerous woman." He passed back the damaged handbag. "No more nasty surprises, I hope."

"It's ruined!" Gestapo Lil examined the torn leather. Like her matching boots, it had been bought the previous day and was *very* expensive.

"Better that than my head." Baba selected a truffle dusted with cocoa powder. "Good chocolates these."

They followed him into the house.

"Right." Priestly clamped the cigar in the corner of his mouth and fixed Harry with his piggy eyes. "You know what we've

come about. Eddie Carver. What can you tell us? And don't
say you know nothing."

They sat at the kitchen table with a big flagon of cider and
a cherry cake Baba had bought at the village store. It was the
first time Harry had tasted Baba's milky, devastating booze. He
liked it.

"I don't know what you're talking about," he said to
Priestly. "Who's Eddie Carver?"

"Don't give us that. We know exactly what you've been
doing, where you've been, who you've been talking to.
Think those mad old aunts of yours and their batty friends
would keep *shtum* when they know we're holding you?"

"You're lying," Harry said. "You always lie. They've told
you nothing."

"Is that so?" Priestly thrust his hot-tempered face into
Harry's. Harry saw the sheen of oil on his ginger moustache;
the little red veins in his eyes; smelled the tobacco and brandy
on his breath. "Well, let me enlighten you. We know Eddie
was talking to Okky Daintry, or should I say Max Beauguss,
in Cony Hill. I saw them." He jabbed a forefinger into Harry's
chest. "We know someone put you on to Eddie and Dart's
pad in Hampstead." Another jab.

"Round the corner from that dump where I wasted half
my life looking after you." Gestapo Lil looked up from fitting
a black cigarette into a long jade holder.

"Right," said her fat fiancé. "And that put us on to the
summer house at Whitewater. We got there first too, only
when we dug it up there was nothing but funeral ashes—"

"Which wasn't what we had in mind—"

"Exactly. Then you got there somehow – probably
something you found in Eddie's house – and dug them up all

over again. Right so far?" Jab–jab. He sat back and sucked life into his dying cigar. "So what we want to know, if you've got any thoughts of seeing those *dear* old aunties again, is where do we go from here?"

Harry's heart was thudding. Apart from Uncle Aziz and the lock-up in Oxford, they seemed to know everything. But he had learned something: Priestly, too, had come to the end of the trail.

"Where, eh?"

"I don't know," he said.

"What if I say I don't believe you," Priestly said. "That aunt of yours, Bridget Barton, she's got something up her sleeve, I can tell. Wants us to think she's told us everything but she's holding something back, isn't she, cunning old cat. What is it?"

There was nothing. Not that Harry knew about. He remembered a trick that in the past had driven Gestapo Lil crazy: pretending a secret that wasn't there. He opened his eyes wide with innocence and gave a smile so small his lips didn't move. "I don't know," he said and shook his head. "Honestly."

It worked like a dream. "I know that look, the lying little creep!" She banged her fist on the table. A plate somersaulted and smashed on the red-tile floor. "He does know." She strode round the table and fastened her nails in the lapel of his suit. "Tell us."

Oiled by the cider, Harry's brain worked like lightning. "Maybe you should ask somebody else."

"Somebody else?" Priestly said. "Who?"

He didn't reply.

"Who?" Gestapo Lil yanked him to his feet. "Who should we ask?"

"Another of that bunch?" Priestly leaned forward. "Which one? Max Beauguss?"

Harry was in familiar territory. For years he had been manhandled by Gestapo Lil. It was almost a game. He was sure Baba wouldn't allow them to hurt him. He smiled and said nothing.

"That other one, Florrie Fox?" Priestly said. "Fingers Peterman? Turning traitor is he?"

"Who said it's one of us at all?" Harry said.

"Not one of you? What are you talking about? Who else could it be?"

"Who else?" Gestapo Lil rattled him by the jacket and raised a hand.

Baba growled.

"Who d'you think?" Harry said rashly. "You're so stupid. Who's not here and not one of us?"

"What's he talking about?" Priestly said.

"I know." Gestapo Lil let Harry go. "It's that mother of yours. And GBH. That's who he means." She swung back. "Isn't it?"

Harry looked her in the eyes.

"Ooh, I couldn't half give you a wallop," she said. "That look."

"He's leading you on." Priestly ground out his cigar. "My mother would never—"

"Wouldn't she? For that sort of money? Her and that precious GBH you're so fond of? They're thick as thieves."

"D'you think so? I've never noticed any—"

"Oh, come on, Percy. Even you can't be that blind. The way she's always phoning that family of hers over in Naples. Jabbering away in Italian. Ringing off whenever you come into the room. What d'you think they're talking about, the Queen's hats? You can't stand her anyway, always bossing you about. If I had a quid for every time you've said 'why doesn't the shrivelled old witch get on her broomstick and take off' I'd be—"

Baba was listening. "You want to watch her," he told Priestly. "See what she's doing, trying to drive a wedge 'tween you and your mother. Number one, that's who she's interested in. Left you in the doo-doo when the cops picked you up last New Year, didn't she? Who was it ended up in clink? You want to think about that." He wiped his chin with the flat of his hand and rubbed it on his trousers. "Going to lay into Harry over there with a stick. Smashed a vase over the back of my head. She's a dangerous woman, how often have I got to tell you? Maybe it's her the boy's talking about."

"Me?" said Gestapo Lil.

Her fiancé didn't reply.

"Percy?"

Everyone looked at everyone else.

Harry lifted his glass with both hands and took a long draught of cider. It was all very satisfactory. If only he could get his hands on some lockpicking tool, or better still, the key of the handcuffs.

The cider hit his brain like a sock filled with feathers. The room slipped sideways.

Harry giggled.

Chapter 25
The Raid on Felon Grange

It was 2 a.m.

The old Mercedes swung from the road and started up the long avenue of beech trees. It was in high–power mode but moved slowly, purring past the ghostly silver trunks. The headlamps were switched off. Auntie Florrie leaned over the wheel, peering into what little light came from a low crescent moon.

There were three others in the car: Fingers, to cope with unfriendly locks; Dot, in case climbing became necessary; and Huggy, to subdue Gestapo Lil whom they had come to kidnap.

"Stop!" Fingers had his arm out of the window, in his hand a little gizmo to detect the beams of security devices. It flashed and bleeped softly.

Auntie Florrie drew up. Fingers got out and traced the beam to its source. In a minute the device was immobilized.

"Lucky I brought it with me."

They drove on.

"There. " Dot pointed between the two in front.

The massive bulk of Felon Grange rose before them. Auntie Florrie slowed to a whisper and drew up under trees by the forecourt. Nutty had sprayed the car dark blue and removed the bulb of the inside light. They clambered out and eased the doors shut. On tiptoe they crossed the pink tarmac, grey in the moonlight, and passed the fountain. The pillared portico rose before them. They mounted the steps and vanished into deep shadow.

The door was sturdy, built to withstand intruders. Dot shone her torch while Fingers tackled the keyhole with a heavy-duty probe. In less than a minute the bolt snapped back.

"Genius," Huggy whispered.

But the door was bolted on the inside.

"Blimey," Fingers said. "Don't trust nobody."

They fanned out to examine the windows, Dot and Huggy one way, Fingers and Auntie Florrie the other. All were locked. They turned corners. Dot tapped Huggy on the arm. A window on the second floor stood a hand's-breadth open. Huggy nodded. Dot ran lightfoot to a long drainpipe, dipped her hands in a bag of chalk, and began to climb. In moments she was hanging from the gutter high above the ground. Hand over hand she swung along until the open window was directly beneath her. A coil of light rope with a hook at one end was over her shoulder. She hooked it over the metal gutter and let it tumble to the ground. Gripping the rope with her feet and tough little hands, she descended to the sill of the open window.

The curtain was drawn. What lay beyond? Dot listened. All was silent. She crouched and put her nose to the gap. A scent of aftershave and sweaty socks drifted from within. A man's room. Was it occupied? She inched open the curtain. Still no sound, then a mutter made her heart leap. Instantly she swung aside. The noise was not repeated. The man was talking in his sleep. It was not Priestly, Dot guessed, his room would be on the first floor. Besides, the voice was too deep. It had to be GBH.

The window slid up easily. She pushed back the curtain and shone her pencil torch round the room. No dressing table or electric fire stood beneath her. With a neat squirm she slid through the gap.

GBH, forty-five centimetres taller than Dot and more than twice as heavy, lay in the bed. Black hair covered his chest. A naked arm, tattooed and muscular, rested on the duvet. Beside it was a scatter of magazines. Dot saw Batman and Dennis the Menace. On top of these lay the war comic GBH had been reading before he went to sleep. This was his favourite reading material. The page was covered with shouts, screams, explosions and bodies, as a snarling US Marine blasted the Vietcong with grenades and a machine gun. In contrast to this ugly violence, a toy badger with most of its hair missing was cuddled beneath his chin.

Dot crept past a chair strewn with jeans and underclothes and let herself from the room. She found herself in a vinyl-floored corridor spread with rugs. A narrow flight of stairs descended to the richly-carpeted first floor. Snoring made a door rattle. Priestly was taking a big risk by sleeping in his own bed. Dot flitted past and came to the head of the grand curving staircase that led to the entrance hall. She ran down.

The hall was spacious and magnificent. As she crossed to the front door, a figure emerged from a corridor on her right. It shot back. Quick as a mouse, Dot vanished into a shadow so intense she could not see her hand before her eyes. She waited in fear. Why was there no hue and cry?

"Dot? That you?" It was Fingers.

She stepped out.

"Dear, oh dear!" he said. "What a fright you give me. My tripes turned to water. How'd you get in?"

"Top window open. You?"

"Door round the back."

Dot groped in the darkness and took his hand. She felt the comfortable knobs of his missing fingers. "Professionals, that's what we are, darling. Where's Florrie?"

"Front door, I 'spect."

A chequebook lay on the hall table. Fingers slipped it into his pocket. "Never turn down the chance of a chequebook or a free drink. First thing my old mum ever taught me."

They opened the stained-glass door of the lobby, went through and slid back the bolts. Huggy and Auntie Florrie were waiting on the threshold.

"Oh, my vord! You both so brilliant!" Huggy wrapped them in her embrace.

They shut the doors at their backs.

"Now, vhere this vicked bitch, this Lily Gestapo ve come kidnap?"

"First floor," Auntie Florrie whispered. "Third door on the left, that's what Harry said. There's the bathroom where he hid on the right, then just past it the bedroom where he saw her watching that video and painting her nails."

"What about Ruby?"

"Along the other way."

"And GBH?"

"Top floor," Dot said briefly. "Priestly's here as well."

"In the house?"

She put a finger to her ear. The distant snores vibrated in the silence. "That's him."

"What a racket!" said Auntie Florrie. "Sounds like an old banger with a hole in the exhaust."

Dot led the way upstairs and turned along the corridor. Pencil torches pierced the darkness.

Fingers pushed open a door on the right. "Bathroom," he breathed. "Jus' like 'Arry said."

They listened outside the third door on the left. Huggy pressed her ear to the panel. Priestly's snores from a nearby bedroom disturbed the silence. "Vhy he not shut up," she said impatiently. "You vant I go in there and fix him?"

"Behave yourself," Dot said. "How would that help? It's Gestapo Lil we're after. Do a swap for Harry."

Fingers eased the door open. At once they smelled perfume. "Recognize it?"

Auntie Florrie shook her head.

"*Poison*," Dot said and giggled.

They filed into the bedroom. It was pitch black. Fingers opened one of the curtains. It made little difference, the moon was on the far side of the house. Now they could hear the regular breathing of the figure in the bed. Auntie Florrie flashed her torch about the room. It was as Harry had described: the dressing table, television, small armchair. The king-size bed stood with its head to the wall and projected into the middle of the carpet.

Fingers took a roll of broad masking tape from his holdall and nipped off a length with his teeth.

The sleeping figure stirred. An arm in a nightgown appeared. All was shadows.

"Ready?" He mouthed the word.

Huggy tiptoed to the side of the bed. Fingers stood opposite.

"One, two," he held up widely-separated fingers. "Three!"

Huggy ripped back the duvet and grabbed the sleeping figure by the shoulders. Before she could scream, Fingers slapped the tape across her mouth. All was confusion. An arm lashed out and hit Fingers in the eye. Flailing legs struck Auntie Florrie in the stomach. She was winded. Her torch flew across the room and landed beneath the curtain. Subdued cries filled the darkness:

"Ahhh! Oh! Mmmmmm! Uh-uh-uh-uh!"

Huggy took charge. She pinned the struggling figure to the mattress. "Dot, the duvet!" The bones beneath her hands were birdlike. She was surprised then cast it from her mind, most of her opponents were built like a rhinoceros. The others tied the thrashing arms and legs and a minute later the figure on the bed was wrapped up like a parcel in the cosy duvet.

"Oh, my goodness!" Auntie Florrie rescued the torch and rearranged her curls. "What a fighter!"

"Yeah, well." Fingers held his watering eye and viewed the violent bundle with the other. "Knew that, didn't we. Fings 'Arry told us."

The snores from Priestly's bedroom were uninterrupted. Auntie Florrie straightened the pillows and wished they had brought a sack or a blanket. It would have been more elegant: the bed neatly made, Gestapo Lil gone, no sign of their presence at all. Still, there was something enigmatic about a missing duvet. She looked round at her friends and felt a glow of pride. The Wrinklies at their best.

Huggy swung the duvet to her shoulder. Dot peeped out into the corridor. Softly they crept away.

Back at Lagg Hall, meanwhile, no one could sleep and they had gathered in the kitchen. Mrs Good kept the kettle on the boil. A dozen times Aunt Bridget, high-shouldered and wearing a man's woollen dressing gown, went to the door and stared down the drive.

Twenty-seven hours had passed since Harry was snatched, the most terrible hours of Mrs Good's life. Her eyes were red with weeping.

"Will you stop blaming yourself, Goody," Max said. "How often do we have to tell you? It could have been any one of us."

Mr Tolly put his arm around her. "What were you supposed to do? Attack them with your bare hands and get yourself shot?"

"That Ruby would have done, an' all," Nutty said. "Standin' there with her sawn-off. Mad as a weasel with a beetle up its bum, that one. Put a bullet through you soon as look at you."

Mrs Good dabbed her eyes with a damp handkerchief. "I know, I know. But I just can't stand it. Harry there with those wicked brutes. Goodness knows *what* they're doing to him."

"Taking good care of him if they've got any sense." Aunt Bridget's eyes flashed behind her granny glasses. "If they don't, I'll not rest until I see all four of them put away for life – and I mean *life*."

"Absolutely." Even at three in the morning Max was elegant. His pyjamas and dressing gown were silk. It was difficult to believe that this man with his sleek black hair and manicured nails had been Okky Daintry. "Tell us again, darling. When you and Florrie went over to see them last night, what did they say, exactly?"

"So full of themselves," Aunt Bridget said. "Really, I'm a woman of peace but I could have done with a baseball bat. Gestapo Lil and Mad Ruby smirking away, and Percy saying that Harry was being looked after in some place we'd never find him in a million years." She ticked off the point on a finger. "Then if we spoke to the police we'd never see him again; there's a plantation in South America where he'd disappear for good." Another finger. "The difference between us and them, which we'd better remember, is that we care what happens to him while they don't. And finally, they'll give us three days to cough up enough information to lead them to Eddie Carver's treasure."

"Information which we don't have," said Mr Tolly.

"But try to get them to believe that," said Aunt Bridget. "They know we'd do anything to get Harry home. At the same time, we could be holding something back. They have no way of knowing."

"So they're putting the screws on," Nutty said.

"Which is why Florrie and the rest of them are over there right now, doing a snatch on Gestapo Lil," said Mr Tolly. "So we can do a swap."

"That's about it." Aunt Bridget covered her mouth with an anxious hand and cast troubled eyes at the clock.

Angel, who had remained silent, was sketching with a cheap biro on a roll of kitchen towel. A strip of dazzling likenesses of the people in the room straggled across the table. They were drawn in the styles of Picasso, Leonardo, Van Gogh. He glanced round with greedy eyes and reached for a slice of cream sponge. Only three remained. He had eaten the whole cake. The plate of biscuits was empty.

Mrs Good slapped his hand sharply and put it back.

"There'll be none left for the others. I don't know how you can, Angel, at a time like this."

"Have I no' got to keep ma strength up?" he protested. "Anyway, the laddie'll be fine. It's no' as if—"

"Sshh!" Max held up a hand. "They're here."

There was a scrambled exodus, a patter of slippers through the house and out the front door. Last in line and believing himself unobserved, Angel darted back and crammed the slice of sponge cake into his mouth. The whipped cream, irresistibly delicious, squirted over his beard and dripped on the table. Hastily he was scooping it up with a forefinger when a voice of doom called from the door:

"Angus McGregor!"

He spun round guiltily. Creamy crumbs clung to his lips.

It was Mrs Good in her sternest, most sergeant-major mode. "How dare you! How *dare* you, when there's people out there risking life and liberty so that we can get dear Harry back."

Briefly Angel thought about challenging her authority, then decided against it.

"Give your face a wipe and come on out with the others." She handed him the dishcloth. "And if I catch you doing anything like that again, *ever* —" She pursed her lips and stood aside to let him leave the kitchen first. When he could no longer see her face, she broke into a smile. Like the mother of a naughty boy, she loved him to bits. Besides which, there were two more cakes in the pantry.

The outside light had been switched on. The Mercedes, with its dusty dark-blue paint and false number plates, crunched to a halt on the gravel. As the quartet who had made the raid on Felon Grange stepped out, the crowd at the door raised a cheer. The doors slammed. All eyes were on the duvet perched on Huggy's shoulder. It bucked and struggled.

"Be still!" She slapped it on the bottom.

A midden would have been the best place to throw a woman as unpleasant as Gestapo Lil, but no midden was available. The kitchen floor was the next choice but this would have been a little crowded. So they all trooped into the sitting room. The last time she was there, Gestapo Lil had tried to burn Lagg Hall to the ground by throwing a petrol bomb through the window. Now she would be able to see how she had failed, how beautiful the room looked once again.

They gathered round. Huggy dumped her bundle on the carpet. The duvet fell open. They stared.

"Oh, my God!" said Aunt Bridget who never used such language.

Angel began to laugh.

The furious figure of Mad Ruby Palazzo sprang from the folds. She had been tied up in darkness and now the knots were coming loose. She tore the masking tape from her mouth. "I kill you!" Her black eyes fizzed, her skinny goat's legs danced beneath the nightdress. "If I had'a my gun, I blow you all to hell. When my brothers hear, they tear out your hearts."

"Very nice language, I'm sure," said Mrs Good.

"They cut out'a your tongues and eat them on toast."

"Yes, yes, we get the picture." Aunt Bridget turned to her sister. "What were you *thinking* about, Florrie? That old witch is no use to us. How could you make a mistake like that?"

"Not Florrie's fault," Fingers said. "It was pitch-black. We went straight to the room 'Arry told—"

There was time for no more. Only Dot, four foot nine and six stone three, stood between Ruby and the door. Judging a woman so small would be easy to overcome and the other

Wrinklies would be slow off the mark, she snatched a toasting fork from the wall and made a dash for freedom.

It was a mistake, for Dot's reactions were like quicksilver. As Mad Ruby sprang at her, stabbing with the sharp brass toasting fork, Dot leaped aside, bounced off the back of a settee, and brought her down with a scissor-grip round the throat. The fall broke them apart. But Ruby was not called mad for nothing. Her chance of escape lost, she flung the fork at Dot like a trident. It whizzed past and stuck quivering in the front of a new piano. There was a gasp from those watching, but Dot was unfazed. During her years with the circus, she had frequently stood in as the assistant of a drunken knife-thrower while his regular assistant was in hospital. She had been a high-wire artiste, climbed skyscrapers, and swung like Quasimodo about the dome of Notre Dame Cathedral. Dot was used to flirting with death. Moreover, had Ruby been better informed, she would have known that none of the Wrinklies, not even Huggy, kilo for kilo, was tougher than Dotty Skylark. And so, when Ruby made her next charge, kicking and scratching and screaming, Dot was ready for her. "Oh, is that the way you want to play it," said the tiny old lady.

"Dot, don't," said Auntie Florrie.

She was too late. Already Dot was in full flow, a whirlwind of flying judo, spins and somersaults from which occasional fists and feet emerged to knock her murderous opponent from chair to sofa and back again. Even though Ruby was bigger and had been the aggressor, it was an uneven contest, and she was lucky to have suffered nothing worse than a bleeding and blocked nose when Huggy stepped in to break it up.

"She's a badwobbad!" Ruby pushed Huggy away. "Why you dot keep her locked up?"

291

"*She's* mad?" Nutty raised bushy eyebrows. "I think ye got somethin' a bit mixed up there, hinny."

Dot threw herself into a chair. "I enjoyed that. Haven't had a scrap for ever so long."

"Good," Aunt Bridget said drily. "Well, now it's over perhaps we can sit down like rational people and decide what to do next —" she eyed her sister — "in view of this unexpected change in our plans."

Max came to Auntie Florrie's aid. "I can't see it makes much difference." He smoothed his thin moustache. "We want to do a swap for Harry, right? They went to kidnap Priestly's horrible girlfriend and came back with his gruesome mother instead."

"They'd changed bedrooms," Fingers explained.

"Whatever," said Max. "It's a swap, that's the point. Mother or girlfriend, what's the difference? He'll want her back."

"Are you sure?" Mr Tolly toyed with a deck of cards, aces came and went.

"He by boy." Ruby dabbed her nostrils with a tissue. "Ob course he wa't his babba."

"He can hardly go to the police," Max went on. "So all we've got to do is keep the old bat locked up until a couple of us go over there and do the deal. Meet some place for the swap-over and —" he gestured with a theatrical hand.

"Bob's yer uncle," said the more down-to-earth Nutty.

"I suppose so." Aunt Bridget chewed a lip.

"Well, it sounds good to me." Mrs Good rose and straightened her dressing gown. "Even a horrible man like that wants his mother home. And we'll get dear Harry back. Now," she looked at the four who had been to Felon Grange.

"What about *a cuppa tea an' a slice o' cake*, as Worzel Gummidge used to say? Then bed." She looked at Mad Ruby. "You will make sure she's safe, won't you, Huggy? I wouldn't like to think of her walking round the house in the middle of the night with a carving knife."

"No vorry." Huggy grasped Ruby's arm with a hand like an attachment on a JCB and smiled with tombstone teeth. "I make sure."

Chapter 26

Ruby Meets Her Match

"You've done what?" Colonel Priestly had been disturbed in the middle of breakfast. A napkin was tucked into his collar. He hadn't shaved.

"I'm sorry, am I not speaking clearly?" Aunt Bridget repeated the words slowly: "Kid-napped your mo-ther."

"Kidnapped my mother? What are you talking about?" He dabbed his lips. "My mother's upstairs in bed. Having a lie-in."

"Are you sure?"

"Of course she is."

"How do you know?"

"Well, she's always –" He looked at Gestapo Lil who stood by his elbow and then up the stairs. "Mamma?"

There was no reply.

"Mamma!"

GBH appeared on the landing, a towel round his neck.

"Not you, you fool. You're not my mother."

"Oh, right." The man disappeared.

"I'll go up." Gestapo Lil wore a slinky red dressing gown and sunglasses. Her honey-blonde hair hung loose. She turned hidden eyes upon the callers. "Pathetic. Just pathetic!" She started up the long staircase, swaying her hips like Marilyn Monroe.

Priestly watched her go: portly, bug-eyed, middle-aged, ginger, balding. He wasn't much of a catch, thought Aunt Bridget. At least his mother was a fighter. And although Gestapo Lil was vile, you had to admit she was stylish. Some men, she guessed, might even find her dishy. What a woman like that could see in froglike Percy Priestly was beyond her. And despite the alarm in the drive, why was he taking such a risk, living almost openly in his own home? Had the local fuzz been paid off? Had he got some commissioner from Scotland Yard in his pocket?

Auntie Florrie eased her arm. She had got a small tape recorder strapped to her ribs and it was uncomfortable. A lead was threaded through her bra to a tiny mike hidden in a buttonhole of silk flowers.

"She's not there." Gestapo Lil called over the banisters.

"What?"

"No sign of a break-in or anything. But the duvet's gone and she's not there."

"Have you tried the bathroom?"

"Don't be stupid, of course I have. She's gone."

Aunt Bridget raised her eyebrows.

"What have you done with her?" Priestly tugged the napkin from his neck.

"Nothing," she said. "Yet."

"What do you mean?"

"Let me explain."

"Yes, I think you'd better." He stepped forward with clenched fists. His face was red.

"Don't threaten me," Aunt Bridget said calmly, "or I'll knock you down."

"She will too," Auntie Florrie said. "She used to box for

Oxford, you know. When we were in Holloway she was middleweight champion."

Priestly retreated to his former position. Gestapo Lil joined him.

"Perhaps now we can all behave like civilized people." Aunt Bridget sat on a hall chair, her back ramrod straight. "You have snatched our nephew, Harry Barton. We'd like him back."

"Hah!" sneered Gestapo Lil.

"We, in our turn," continued Aunt Bridget, "have kidnapped your mother. We want to do a swap."

"A swap?" he repeated and thought about it. "My mother for that little toerag we've got chained up and hidden away at –" He stopped himself in time.

"That's right."

"A swap?" He glanced at Gestapo Lil and began to laugh. "A swap!"

"What's so funny?" said Auntie Florrie.

"You cannot be serious." His laughter redoubled. His chins shook.

Gestapo Lil, too, was laughing. She clung to his arm.

"My mother for –" He wiped his eyes. "Keep her. Please."

"What?"

"Listen," he said. "We'll do a deal."

"Percy?" Gestapo Lil looked up.

"No, it's all right. I'll tell you what," he said to Aunt Bridget. "I'll give you a thousand pounds and you keep her locked up in your attic over there. Down in the cellar. Somewhere she'll never get out."

"And throw away the key," said his fiancée.

"Rid of the old bag at last." He kissed the top of her head. "Good idea?"

"Two thousand pounds," she said, "and they can get those people in Liverpool to crate her up and send her off to that place in Bolivia."

"The plantation, you mean – or the tin mines?"

"You know, surrounded by jungle," she said, "with cannibals and piranhas to stop her escaping. Mind you, *she'd* probably eat the cannibals!" She broke into a peal of laughter and pushed up the sunglasses. "Oh, Percy!"

In the early morning and without her make-up, she looked ten years older. Auntie Florrie touched the tape-recorder to make sure it was still in place.

"You do realize we're talking about your mother," Aunt Bridget said.

"Who else?"

"The Hag of Naples," Gestapo Lil said contemptuously.

"And after we've got all we want out of the brat, we'll ship him off too." Priestly looked at his visitors. "Unless, of course, you've remembered anything interesting about Eddie Carver."

Aunt Bridget was lost for inspiration.

"Ah, well." He smiled and looked round for his chequebook. "Is it one thousand pounds or two thousand pounds?"

Gestapo Lil looked them up and down. "If I were you, I'd make it two thousand," she said. "Then you'll be able to buy yourselves some new clothes."

"Thank you for the advice." Auntie Florrie extended a forefinger and poked her in the eye.

"Well," said Aunt Bridget as they returned to the Rover. "No swap for Harry but what a feast of information. Did you get all that?"

"I hope so." Auntie Florrie felt under her arm and switched off the tape recorder.

"I wonder what the fragrant Ruby's going to make of her ever-loving son."

"Not to mention his girlfriend."

"No love lost between that pair." Aunt Bridget lifted her face to the sun. "Couple of quarrelsome cats."

"Hissing and clawing at each other." Auntie Florrie unlocked the car. "I wouldn't like to be in Priestly's shoes."

"He'll survive," her sister said. "Unfortunately. Mind if I drive?"

Auntie Florrie tossed her the keys. "Give me a chance to take off this horrible machine."

"Try not to frighten the rabbits."

"Oh, you're so cheeky sometimes."

As they started down the drive, Auntie Florrie hitched up her jumper.

"I don'a believe you." Ruby was tied to Huggy by a rope. "My boy never say those things. He love his mamma."

"I'm afraid he did," Aunt Bridget said.

"You're lying!" She spat. It didn't reach Aunt Bridget and landed on the kitchen tiles.

Huggy jerked the rope. "You vant I lock you in the cellar like your so-loving boy vant?" she said. "In the dark – vith the cockroaches and the rats? The size of cats, some of them."

Mad Ruby gave a shudder. She had a horror of rats.

It didn't go unnoticed.

"Then behave," Huggy said. "And vipe that up." She handed her a paper towel.

Reluctantly Ruby did as she was told.

"It's true what Bridget's telling you," said Auntie Florrie. "Every bit."

"I don'a believe you neither."

"What if we play you a tape then?" Aunt Bridget fetched the machine from the dresser.

"A tape?"

"We made it this morning. Over at Felon Grange like I told you. Florrie had a microphone in her clothes."

Ruby didn't want to believe it. "Tapes can be fixed, say what you want'a. You got that actor here, Max . . . something."

"Oh, for goodness sake!" Aunt Bridget was exasperated. "Huggy, will you get this woman to sit down and shut up for once in her life."

"Ja, sure." Huggy dragged Mad Ruby to the table and forced her into a chair. "Shut up! Von vord, I gag you again. Truss you up like the Christmas chicken. You hear!" She scowled. Her muscles bunched. She cracked her fingers with a noise like trees breaking off.

Ruby was silent.

All eyes were on Aunt Bridget as she slotted in the tape and pressed the *play* button. She had run it to the section she wanted:

A swap! Priestly's laughter filled the kitchen. *You cannot be serious . . . keep her, please . . . thousand pounds and you keep her locked up . . . in the cellar . . . rid of the old bag at last.* It was a cheap machine, the static hissed and crackled, but the voices were clear. *. . . crate her up . . . that place in Bolivia . . . min you, she'd probably eat the cannibals. . .*

"That's enough! Enough!" Mad Ruby swept the pla from the table. Mugs and a mixing bowl went with it. floor was awash with coffee and flour and broken china

From a spot by the sink the voices ran on. . . . *talking about your mother . . . who else . . . the Hag of Naples. . .*

With a shriek, Ruby ran round the table and jumped on the machine. The plastic shattered.

. . . my chequebook . . . pounds or two thousand pounds . . . were you I'd make it. . .

She jumped again. Ground her heel. The recorder squealed and was silent.

It wasn't enough. She pounded her feet. Screamed in Italian. Picked up the remains and hurled them across the kitchen. By chance they hit the mirror which exploded in a shower of bright splinters.

"Well," said Mrs Good, who did not approve of such tantrums. "If you ask me, a woman in your position needs all the *good* luck she can get, never mind seven years of *bad*."

"Way that went up," Fingers sucked his teeth, "I reckon it's more like seventeen."

"Safe when she's a hundred and twenty then," Dot said.

Huggy felt responsible. "Here," she threw down a cloth and thrust a dustpan and brush into Ruby's hands. "You von angry voman. But you know who *really* angry – me!" She poked herself in the chest. "Now sveep up, and sveep up good!"

"Go on like this," Fingers said, "she'll have the whole house spring-cleaned by teatime."

But Ruby was beyond reason. She threw the dustpan and brush across the floor. "You want it cleaned up? Clean it up'a yourself! Who you think you're talking to?" She jerked the rope from Huggy's hands. "Me, I go kill that bitch fiancée of my boy. Turn'a my Percy against his mamma!"

"You vant kill Gestapo Lil," Huggy said. "Me, I vant sit on your head. Come here."

"Before you do, Huggy," Aunt Bridget intervened, "perhaps we can settle up with Ruby about the mirror."

Ruby looked at her. "The mirror?"

"Yes, that was a nice mirror and you've broken it. Who's going to pay for it, that's what I want to know."

"You kidnap me and you want I pay for a broken mirror?"

"Well somebody's got to. When Percy gave us that two thousand pounds we didn't count on a broken mirror. Oh, *and* a tape recorder. What would they cost – fifty each? That's two thousand one hundred."

Mad Ruby was lost. "What are you talking about?" She appealed to the others. "What is she talking about?"

"It seems straightforward enough to me," Aunt Bridget said. "Percy's given us two thousand pounds, right, but you've just done all this damage. Who's going to pay for—"

Ruby took the bait. "My son give you two thousand pounds? I not believe you. What for he give you two thousand pounds?"

"For delivering you to those people in Liverpool," Aunt Bridget said. "It was all on the tape. You really haven't been paying attention."

"Liverpool? What people in Liverpool?"

"The ones who'll be shipping you off to that place in Bolivia," Aunt Bridget said patiently. "Your loving son gave me their address." She thought. "Course it couldn't be by ship the whole way. The last few hundred miles would have to be on foot through the jungle."

"My Percy want you send me to Bolivia?"

"To work on this plantation he's interested in. Drugs, I suppose, or cotton. Or down the tin mines, of course."

"You're lying again. Send his mamma to the tin mines? I don'a believe you."

Aunt Bridget shrugged. "Suit yourself." She took a slip of paper from the dresser. "Here's his cheque, maybe that'll persuade you. Half now, half when he hears you've arrived."

"Let me see that."

It came from the chequebook Fingers had lifted from the hall table at Felon Grange. Angel had forged Priestly's signature from the scrapbook of handwriting – politicians, crooks, police officers, magistrates and the like – which Aunt Bridget had compiled throughout her life. It was indistinguishable from the real thing. A Scotland Yard expert could not have told the difference.

To *Bridget Barton*, it read, the sum of *One thousand pounds only*, signed, *Percival B. Priestly*.

Ruby examined it closely.

"This is the second cheque." Aunt Bridget passed it across. "Dated November, you see. He reckons that should be plenty of time. Three or four weeks from now you'll be landed in Salvador – that's the port they usually use. Then a couple of months through the jungle – quite mountainous in that part, I believe, takes a while. Fever, too. Mosquitoes. Snakes. Alligators. But most of them make it, he says, so you'll probably be all right." Aunt Bridget smiled. "Who knows, once you're settled in you might even find yourself a new husband among the fieldworkers."

"Or the tin miners," Dot said.

"Why not? A bit muddy, but I'm sure some of them are very nice men. Can't be many women out there, you can probably have your pick. So it's not as if it's the end of everything. Just, I don't know, a change of lifestyle."

"You don'a mean it."

Aunt Bridget shook her head sadly. "We weren't the ones started all this. It was you lot kidnapped Harry. We want him back. So we took you in exchange, except your loving son won't do a swap. Doesn't want you back at all, it seems. So what are we supposed to do about it? After all the trouble we've been to, we deserve to get *something* out of this fiasco. And you haven't been terribly nice to us, you must admit: trying to set the place on fire, shooting at Harry, hanging around outside his school, snatching him in the middle of the night, insulting us, trying to kill Dot with a toasting fork. You can't blame us for wanting to get our own back, and two thousand pounds is better than nothing. At least it will get you out of the way. Of course, if Percy and Lavinia had a change of heart that would be different, but from the way they spoke I can't see much chance of that happening. So why *not* send you to that work camp in Bolivia?"

Mad Ruby was appalled. She meant it! This scarily clever woman was as ruthless as she was. Here were the cheques to prove it. She handed them back.

"I can think of a reason," she said.

Aunt Bridget's heart was thudding. She pretended to be uninterested. "What's that?" She went to a jar on the shelf and popped a toffee into her mouth.

"Do you want to hear or not?"

"I can't imagine what you've got to say that might be of the slightest interest. Anyway, Huggy wants to sit on your head. Or are you going to lock her up in the cellar after all, Huggy? There's this huge fellow comes out sometimes," she said to

Ruby. "We call him Rattenstein. Scares me to death. You never saw such a monster." She munched. "Oh, silly me, you won't be *able* to see him, will you? The bulb's gone."

"Ja, I take her down. I respect the seat of my trousers too much to sit on her face." Huggy moved in. "Come here, you."

Ruby hit out. Backed into a corner. Snatched up a soup ladle. It did no good. Huggy disarmed her and threw the little woman over her shoulder.

Dot opened the cellar door.

"No!" Ruby shrieked and hammered her thin fists on Huggy's back. "No! Percy's not the only one knows where the boy's being kept."

Aunt Bridget stopped chewing. "I beg your pardon?"

Huggy halted at the entrance. Beyond her the cellar steps descended into darkness.

"I know where he's being kept," Ruby gabbled. "I know the name of the farm. I can take you there. I know everything about it."

"I don't believe you. You're trying to pull some trick. We'd go there and find a couple of machine guns stuck up our noses. Go on, Huggy. Take her down."

"No, I do know! Really! Please! Aahhhh!"

Ignoring her screams, Huggy hitched Ruby on her shoulder and started down the cellar steps.

"Perhaps she really does know something," Mr Tolly said. "Unless she's a very good actress."

"Yes, I tell'a you," she shouted. "I tell you."

"Well, if you think so, Mr Tolly," Aunt Bridget said. "All right, Huggy, we'll give her another chance. Up you come. Let's hear what she's got to say."

But as the horrors of the cellar receded and she was set back on her feet, Mad Ruby's brain began to function. "Of *course* I know where he being kept. Yes, I tell you. Show you on the map. I *take'a* you there. But in return you got to let me go."

Aunt Bridget considered. "What do the rest of you think?"

"Not until we've got 'Arry," Fingers said.

"Safe," said Auntie Florrie.

"Of course not," Ruby sneered. "Not even you that stupid."

"If this some trick," Huggy growled, "I tie your feet round the back of your neck. I take you down cellar vith the rats. You not get out till they gnaw you to vhite bones."

Ruby shuddered and pulled her nightgown straight. "No trick. You get'a the boy, I get'a go free." She held out her arms. "You give me some clothes."

"I think we can arrange that." Aunt Bridget looked round. "All agreed?"

They nodded. "Yeah. . . Right. . . Get Harry home where he belongs."

"Splendid," she said. "Come on, then, let's go into the other room. It's more comfortable."

They drifted from the kitchen.

"Goody, darling." Aunt Bridget turned at the door. "Any chance of a cup of tea? I'm dry as a dead vulture in the desert after all that."

"Well done, Bridget," Mrs Good said. "But you really are very naughty. All those lies, frightening her like that."

"It worked though, didn't it. And they've got Harry, for goodness sake."

"Indeed they have." She filled the kettle. "Coming up in two shakes of a lamb's tail. Bit of shortbread?"

"Lovely." Aunt Bridget gave her a wink and was gone.

"Rats in my nice clean cellar!" Mrs Good said to Nutty who had stayed behind. "The idea!"

Nutty, who was very fond of Mrs Good, crept up behind and gave her a kiss on the ear.

"Stop that!" she said, not entirely displeased, and slapped him on the arm. "You're getting altogether too fresh these days, Nutty Slack. Make yourself useful and nip down to the cellar while I clear up this mess. Fetch me one of them nice cauli's from the vegetable rack. I think I'll make some cheese sauce and we'll have it with the beef tonight."

He switched on the light and descended the steps. The air smelled of apples. The scrubbed floor and whitewashed walls of the cellar were bright as a bedroom.

Chapter 27

Caisteal an Uisge Ghil

By lunchtime Harry's hangover had subsided to a headache and he was hungry.

"Help yourself," Baba said. "I bought loads of stuff yesterday."

So Harry put two fillets of battered cod and a big tray of oven-ready chips into the Aga and heated beans in a saucepan. He wiped the kitchen table and found a cleanish tablecloth at the bottom of the drawer. By the time he had spread it with place mats, cutlery, glasses, a jug of water and a vase of flowers he picked by leaning through the window, it looked like a respectable Saturday lunch.

"Not for me," Baba said, glass in hand.

"Ah, come on." Harry pulled him from the settee and along the passage.

The fish was almost ready. Mouth-watering aromas filled the kitchen.

Baba nodded. "Yes, all right. You've done well." He put a hand on Harry's shoulder and kissed the top of his head. "I should have got married and had a boy like you myself."

"Why don't you?" Harry said. "You're not that old."

"Maybe not that *old*," Baba sat at the table. "Not like your regular run of men, though. Queer in the head." He held up the cider. "Done for my brain."

Harry stood waiting to dish up.

"Never much good talking to women at the best of times." Baba looked around. "What woman would want to live here anyway?"

Harry was more positive. "You could get it fixed up. Buy yourself some new clothes." He hesitated. "Have a bath."

"Heh-heh-heh!" Baba wasn't offended. "You're a good lad but it's a bit late now."

Teddy and Pete stood drooling at the unfamiliar smells that emanated from the Aga. Baba rubbed their muzzles and wiped his hand on his trousers.

"Happy enough here with my old pals, aren't I?"

"But don't you miss," Harry gave an awkward shrug, "people?"

"Sometimes, course. That's why it's so nice to have a young chap like yourself staying for a few days."

A faint smell of burning reached Harry's nostrils. He rushed to rescue the lunch.

The cod was delicious. For pudding they had blackcurrant cheesecake with ice cream. And Harry rounded the meal off with coffee and a chocolate biscuit.

Baba was not accustomed to such a substantial lunch – to *any* lunch, in fact. Overcome by the effects of the food, he retreated to a sun-rotted hammock in the orchard and fell asleep in the shade of the canopy. In the heat of the afternoon the birds were silent. Baba's snores rose above the hum and rustles of insects in the long grass.

Harry, meanwhile, washed the dishes and tidied up. For half an hour, using everything from a kitchen knife to a buckled fork, he strove to pick the lock of his handcuffs, but the two links of chain kept his wrists so close that he could not get the proper angles. Disheartened, he went through to the lounge and sat at the piano. He couldn't play, at least not properly, but he enjoyed the sound of the notes and picked out a couple of tunes with a forefinger. Although he had a voice like a crow, Harry liked songs you could sing, and he was in the middle of *How much is that doggy in the window* when a chorus of barking disturbed the peace of the afternoon. He stopped playing and listened. The barking continued. He had heard no car. Perhaps it was a stray cat. Or a fox. Or intruders – not Priestly and Gestapo Lil again!

"Shut up!" came a slurred shout from the orchard. "Pete! Teddy! Be quiet!"

It made no difference. The barking came closer. It entered the house. There was a noise of scampering, slipping claws in the passage.

"Wow! Wow! Roof!"

Harry recognized that bark. His heart skipped a beat and he swung round on the piano stool. The next second, like a woolly bullet, Tangle came hurtling from the shadows and leaped into his lap.

"Tangle!" Harry clutched him with chained hands and tried to bury his face in Tangle's hair. But Tangle wriggled like a corkscrew, trying to lick every bit of Harry's skin he could reach, and torn between having a spectacular fight or making friends with the dogs that had met him in the farmyard.

When Teddy, Pete and Crotchet, as he became known, saw Tangle in Harry's arms, they decided to be friends. And the next moment Auntie Florrie came through the door, wearing a pretty, off-the-shoulder summer frock and carrying a pickaxe handle. She was followed by Fingers, Aunt Bridget, Huggy and, at the end of her rope, Mad Ruby Palazzo.

"Oh, Harry! My darling, are you all right?" Auntie Florrie, impetuous as Tangle, ran to the piano and smothered him in her embrace.

I was all right a minute ago, Harry thought, and struggled to escape the clouds of Chanel, sticky lipstick, and strong arms that crushed him to his auntie's bosom.

"I like the suit," Aunt Bridget said. "Very Al Capone. Where did you get that?"

"Chained up like a flippin' bullock!" Fingers pulled a set of probes from his pocket and examined the handcuffs. "Someone give me a quid every time I opened one of these, I'd be a millionaire."

The cuffs fell loose and Harry rubbed his chafed wrists. "How'd you get here? I didn't hear a car."

"Left it up the track," Auntie Florrie said. "Came on foot, commando style. Didn't know what sort of reception we'd be getting. Great fun!" She looked around. "Where is everybody?"

"Everybody?" Harry said. "He's sleeping out there. That's him snoring."

"Who is it then?" Fingers said. "That GBH?"

"You vait here." Huggy passed Mad Ruby's rope to Aunt Bridget. "I go rearrange his arms and legs, ja?"

"No," Harry said. "No, it's not GBH. It's the man that lives here. It's his farm. His name's Whortleberry Yawkins – 'cept everyone calls him Baba. He's some *relation* of GBH, I think, but he's all right. He's –" He touched his head.

"Whortleberry Yawkins?" Aunt Bridget said. "I've heard that name before."

"He plays the piano," Harry said. "You should hear him!"

Aunt Bridget shook her head. "No. No, but it'll come to me. A long time ago. There can't be two people with a name like that."

"Vhatever," Huggy said. "He keep you prisoner, is bad. I vant speak this Vortleberry vhat-you-said. Vhy he not here, anyvay? Vhy the dogs not vake him up?"

"He's been drinking cider," Harry said. "Had a big lunch." He led the way out to the orchard.

Baba sprawled in the hammock. He had kicked off his shoes. Buttons were unfastened. A triangle of belly peeped through his shirt. A shining stream of saliva ran down his chin.

"I remember!" Aunt Bridget pointed at the unconscious wreck with his baby face. "When I was at St Hilda's. Every November a chamber orchestra from the Royal College of Music used to come up for a weekend of parties. We gave them dinners and accommodation, they gave us a concert for St Cecilia's Day. One year he came up, Whortleberry Yawkins, a big ungainly chap. Played one of the Mozarts. What a pianist! Quite the star of the show. I've often wondered what happened to him."

"Vell," Huggy was unimpressed. "Now you know. Vhat happen, he become a kidnapper. Chain up children in his dirty, smelly house." She kicked the hammock. "Hey, you! Vake up! Ve vant talk!"

Harry, assisted by Fingers, made tea and afterwards, at Aunt Bridget's request, Baba played Beethoven's *Appassionata* sonata.

"That was absolutely wonderful," she said. "Thank you so much."

Baba stared at her, his emotions in a turmoil.

"Now, you've got the address," she said. "And there's the phone number, see. You're to come over whenever you like. You've got *friends* at Lagg Hall. There's hot baths and the best cook in England. You'll always be welcome. Remember."

Harry said, "Play them that bit you made up for *Star Wars* the other night. You should have heard him," he said to the rest. "It was brilliant. Here, I'll get the video."

"Not right now, Harry," Aunt Bridget said. "Maybe some other time. We've got to be going. Besides, Mr Yawkins has given us enough treats for one day."

Mad Ruby rose from the settee. She was scratching, Harry was delighted to see. A flea – with luck more than one – seemed to have escaped the extermination. "Now you give me lift to the phone box." It sounded more like an order than a request.

"I beg your pardon?" said Aunt Bridget.

"I said, you give me—"

"Yes, I heard what you said. But I'm afraid we don't like you. We've kept our side of the bargain. Goody and Florrie have fixed you up with a set of clothes. You're free to go. But in view of the fact that you kidnapped Harry and have kept him chained up here for the best part of two days – an act, may I say, that would get you ten years minimum in the slammer – you're hardly in a position to ask favours."

"Clothes!" She plucked at a purple blouse with frills and tight matador pants in green velvet. "You call these clothes! I hate them!"

So did Goody and Auntie Florrie. They had been bought at Oxfam for Christmas charades.

"Well, give them back," Aunt Bridget said. "Perhaps Mr Yawkins can fix you up with something better."

Baba grinned wetly and sided with the tall lady who

remembered the old days. "I think you look very nice," he said to Mad Ruby. "Purple and green with red shoes, very nice, yes. Are you married?"

"What?"

"I thought you might stay and keep me company. After the boy goes. Just for tonight. The others will be back in the morning – the ones you came with the first time."

"Are you out of your mind? Stay here? In this stinking dump? I rather cut off all my hair and—"

He caught her by the wrist. *Click!* The handcuff snapped shut. "Just for one night, you'll be quite safe. A bit o' company. Mouthful o' cider." He wiped his chin. "You can have his bed. It's quite clean, we de-loused it."

"Let me go!" She tore at the handcuff. "Take it off'a."

"Vhy for you complain?" Huggy caught Baba's rolling eye and smiled. "Vhat sauce for the goose—"

"We've got to be going," Aunt Bridget said. "Goody and the rest will be getting worried.

"Goodbye," Harry said.

Baba took his hand in a big paw. "Here," he went to the kitchen and returned with a litre of the dynamic cider. "You can drink it when you get home."

"No he can't." Aunt Bridget set it firmly on the table. "He'll get juice. Thank you all the same."

Baba escorted them to the yard.

"Remember," Aunt Bridget raised a forefinger. "We're expecting you at Lagg Hall in the next few days. If you don't come, I'll be over to root you out."

Auntie Florrie said, "We've got the new piano."

"So we have, I'd forgotten. So you're to come over and show us how it should be played."

Tangle had made friends with Teddy, Pete and the pup. Now it was time to leave. Tail high, he trotted ahead up the overgrown track.

Harry's trousers trailed on the ground. He looked behind and raised a hand.

Baba waved back.

And when Harry looked again, all he could see of Cider House Farm was the red-rusted sheet of tin on the roof and a chimney with lopsided pots.

A skylark was singing, soaring and tumbling above the abandoned fields. They stopped to listen. Harry shaded his eyes.

Abruptly the bird swooped back to earth. Other sounds had alarmed it: a high scream of abuse from the house, and the crashing notes of a piano.

"Dear, oh dear! Bit of a ding-dong going on back there," Fingers said. "Got 'is work cut out dealing with that one. She'll eat 'im alive, given 'alf a chance."

"No she'll not, he can look after himself." Harry told them how Baba had driven Gestapo Lil and Priestly from the house.

"Really, Harry." Still holding the pickaxe handle, Auntie Florrie picked her way round a puddle. "The people you keep company with!"

He laughed, and two minutes later the old Merc, Harry's favourite car in the whole world, appeared through a gap in the bushes.

Bad weather blew in from the west. For two whole days, cloud hung in the branches of the Lagg Hall woods and beating rain turned the tracks to mud.

Tangle moped about the house. Morgan deserted his lonely

314

tower and found a perch in the hall. Chalky and Socrates retreated to their dry shed. Even the geese seemed fed up.

Harry's computer was in his room in the tower but the electricity had been switched off for the repairs. Aunt Bridget let him use her laptop.

"One hour a day," she said. "That's quite enough. People matter more than machines. I'm not going to have you stuck over a screen from morning till night."

Which meant two hours a day, Harry thought, if he planned it right.

He loved working with computers. That first morning he played a game which involved rescuing a martial arts princess from a planet where the temperature ranged from nuclear core to absolute zero. In the evening he surfed the web, finding out about piranhas in the Amazon, parrots in Africa, cider, and real-life pirates. Finally, hoping no one would catch him, he clicked on to Brigitte Bardot, a film star from a million years ago, whom Harry thought looked very pretty.

The next day, with puddles on the lawns and rain bouncing off the roofs of the cars, he took a mug of hot chocolate to the dining-room table and switched on the laptop again. He had been thinking about the new rugby season, and surfing the web was delighted to find a site about the British Lions which several times mentioned his friend Gunther Warwick-Scott – Gunther the Grunter.

This led Harry to thinking about Whitewater Hall. Munching an apple, he made a search. It didn't take long. To his delight it had its own website: *www.whitewaterhall.org.uk*. He clicked on to it and after a few seconds, abruptly, there before him was a full-screen photo of the hall in all its splendour. There lay the lawns where Gunther had punted the ball about, the lake where he had fished with Mike, the summer house they had dug up in the middle of the night.

Harry moved the pointer around, scrolled up and down, fascinated by everything that appeared. First he clicked on to *Introduction*, a brief outline of what Whitewater Hall was, the county in which it was situated, what it had to offer visitors, the hours of opening and prices of admission. It was cheerful, the text dark blue against a background of Whitewater daffodils nodding on the lake shore.

Next he investigated *Location*, which provided lots of geographical and geological information, and precise details of how to reach Whitewater Hall.

When the *Map* came up it seemed all wrong and at first Harry thought it must be a mirror image. North was not where he expected it to be, and distances were not what he remembered. He was lost until, by an effort of the imagination, he fixed on key features and turned everything round in his head. Then he knew where he was and spent ten minutes exploring the estate where he had spent such a happy weekend.

The next click took him into the *History* of Whitewater Hall. The text now was darkest green against a shifting background of ivy-clad walls and gorgeous staterooms. Harry's apple was almost finished. Elbows on the table, he nibbled the green bit round the stalk and read the account before him:

Whitewater Hall, Harry read, *one of the great stately homes of England, is among the finest examples of the collaboration between the architect John Nash and the landscape gardener Humphry Repton. It was commenced in 1798, and incorporates elements of a design suggested by the wife of the builder, Sir Pieter de Witt.*

Sir Pieter was a descendant of that Johann de Witt who had fled from Holland in 1672 to escape persecution by William of Orange. The British branch of the family flourished, and by the time Sir Pieter assumed the title in 1793, it owned estates in France, Belgium and England, and was extremely wealthy.

In 1796, Sir Pieter married Lady Isabel Rattray, youngest daughter of Lord Goole of Strathgoolie in Perthshire. At the time of her marriage, Lady Isabel was just seventeen years old. She was, as may be seen from her portrait by Sir Henry Raeburn which hangs in the Crimson Drawing Room, a shy and beautiful young woman. It was to be a long and happy marriage. To please his young wife, Sir Pieter engaged Nash to build a house which contained references to Caisteal an Uisge Ghil (Castle of the White Water), the Scottish home of her childhood, which she had loved so much. It was not possible, in an English estate, to create the rushing river which gave the Highland castle its name, but Nash and Repton did their best by damming a river to the north-east of the house and creating an extensive lake which would reflect the white light of northern skies, and by planting cherry orchards and water lilies along the shore. In addition, as an echo of the Scottish baronial style, Nash built into his design a —

Harry stopped reading. The blood drained from his face. Whitewater! There was a *second* Whitewater! He stared at the words on the screen, not taking them in. If there was a second Whitewater, then. . . He set his apple core aside, wiped his fingers on his shirt, and scrolled back to the beginning.

There it was, Perthshire! Castle of the White Water! He hadn't been mistaken.

Harry rushed to get pencil and paper and wrote it down in case he couldn't find it again on the computer, then went back to *search* and typed in the other names he had discovered:

Caisteal an Uisge Ghil, whatever language that was – Gaelic, he supposed. It referred him back to the website.

Strathgoolie: geographical information.

de Witt: historical details but nothing relevant.

John Nash: page upon page of architectural history.

Rattray: there it was again, Caisteal an Uisge Ghil (Castle of the White Water), Perthshire, Scotland.

Harry switched off the laptop. "Aunt Bridget!" Clutching the torn-off scrap of paper, he ran through the house. "Aunt Bridget!"

Chapter 28

Gunther Draws a Map

"Hello? Gunther?"

They gathered round the telephone.

"Goodness, what a quick ear you have. Yes, it's Bridget again. . . Fine, thank you. . . Yes, he is too. Thriving, you might say. Getting up to all sorts of. . . What's that? . . . Say that again. . . Fell and broke his arm? Oh, poor Mike! How did that happen? . . . Yes, well boys do that sort of thing, don't they. But listen, I've got a question for you. . . Oh, you're so cheeky sometimes. . . Well it's this, do you know anything about a castle up in Scotland? Its name's in Gaelic, something like Kaysteal an Uska Gill. It means Castle of the White Water. . . You do!" She looked up at the others. "You did what? . . . Spent all your summer holidays there!" She clapped a hand over the mouthpiece and listened for a long time. "With who, did you say? . . . Your Uncle Sandy. . . Yes, it sounds a wonderful place. Now listen, Gunther. Are you going to be at home for the next few days? I'd like to come down and talk to you. . . Yes, about this Kaysteal an — oh, you'll have to teach me how to say it properly. . . No, I can't tell you what it's all about. Not just yet. . . Of course I will. So is it all right to. . . What? You're going away

319

when? . . . On business, yes. . . For a fortnight? Then it'll have to be today. . . Two hours or so. . ." She looked at her watch. "Half–twelve, one o'clock. . . Lunch? That sounds lovely. Perfect timing. . . Bring Harry?" She looked across, wrinkling her brow in a question. He nodded eagerly. "Yes, he'd love to come. . . Yes, he is. . . Well don't tell him that or he'll get big-headed. . . Yes, me too. See you in a couple of hours. . . Right, 'bye."

She put the phone down.

"What was that he said about me?" Harry asked.

"He says boys who ask questions that are none of their business should get a kick in the seat of the pants."

Harry struck a wrestling attitude. "You'd have to fight me first."

"Hah! Shrimp! You fancy your chances, don't you."

"Not really," he said mildly. "Have I got to change?"

"Wouldn't hurt to wipe that chocolate tash off your top lip. Turn round. Yes, you'll do fine."

Mrs Good disagreed. "Indeed he will not. Upstairs this minute, Harry, and give your face and hands a good wash. There's fresh jeans and a polo shirt by your bed. And give me those shoes. You are *not* going visiting looking like that."

Harry added his name to the graffiti on Mike's plaster.

"Is it still sore?"

"It itches." He poked with the blunt end of a knitting needle.

"Mike, stop it!" his father said. "You'll break the skin, then it'll go septic."

"Oh, but Dad!" He scratched vigorously and withdrew the knitting needle.

After a family lunch in the kitchen, they had withdrawn into a sun-lounge away from the tourist trail. The clouds had opened to a beautiful afternoon. Occasional trespassers wandered by, hoping, perhaps, for a glimpse of the Earl of Whitewater. It was unlikely they would recognize him, Harry thought, in his bare feet, scruffy shorts and old check shirt.

Aunt Bridget opened her laptop on a coffee table and turned to *My Documents*, where she had typed in various details and questions.

"Right." She drew a deep breath. "It's very good of you, Gunther. Sorry about the secrecy, but I really will tell you all about it as soon as I can."

"That's all right." He drew on a small after-lunch cigar and blew smoke at the ceiling. "What is it you want to know?"

"It's something Harry turned up on your website this morning."

"To do with Uncle Sandy's place, I gather, not Whitewater Hall at all."

"I hope you don't mind."

"Course not."

She pointed to the name on the screen. "Maybe you can tell us how to pronounce it for a start."

"OK. Cash–chl," he said.

"Cash–chl," said Aunt Bridget.

"An oosh–kuh."

"An oosh–kuh."

"Yeel."

"Yeel?"

"That's it."

"Cash–chl an Oosh–kuh Yeel."

"Spot on," Gunther said. "Only a bit faster, of course."

Harry read it off the laptop: Caisteal an Uisge Ghil. "It doesn't look like that," he said.

"Wait until you hear a lot of Gaelic speakers together," Gunther said. "You'll think you're in Albania."

"A bit pathetic we can't even pronounce the name of the place." Aunt Bridget adjusted her granny glasses. "How did you come to spend all your holidays there?"

"With Uncle Sandy," he said, "I told you. Well, he's not my uncle really, just some sort of distant cousin. Don't ask me, you'd have to go to an archivist. Sandy's side of the family's gone straight down the male line for centuries, no problem. My side's had more changes of name than changes of socks. Nothing but girls, distaff side every time. And Sandon, of course, didn't have any children, so it came to me. Mike there's the first male heir there's been for – well, ever, as far as I know."

"But you kept in touch – with the Rattrays, I mean."

"Oh, yes, the blood's still there. And Caisteal an Uisge Ghil's the most marvellous place for a holiday. Uncle Sandy, too. The loveliest man in the world."

"Sandy?"

"Alexander."

"Alexander Rattray?"

"Oh, do you want the whole thing? He's much more than just that: Colonel Alexander Moncrieff Rattray, MC, DSO, late Argyll and Sutherland Highlanders, Lord Goole of Strathgoolie." He caught Harry's eye and smiled.

Aunt Bridget typed the details into her computer. "A most distinguished man."

"Absolutely. And poor as a church mouse. How he keeps that place going I've no idea. Falling about his ears but he won't take a penny from me. Scottish pride! Rather see the place in ruins than be beholden to anybody."

"What about family?"

"Oh, he had a son. David, a few years older than me. A great chap, my hero when I was a boy, but he got killed. Broke his father's heart. He'd got in with one of the big motor companies, mad to get the world water-speed record. Not jet or rocket, power-driven. Hit a log on Loch Ness. Never found the body."

"How terrible!" Aunt Bridget hesitated. "Then what about the inheritance? After all those years, centuries."

"No one's quite sure. It's up to Sandy, of course. He'd like a Rattray but there isn't one. I suppose he might leave it to Mike, here, or possibly me. Which in a way would be a good thing because we'd have the money to put it to rights – or at least stop any more of it falling into the loch."

"Into the loch? An old Scottish castle on a loch. A rushing river. It sounds very romantic."

"What have I been telling you? You look at your Scottish calendars, it's all there: the grey castle, the mountains, eagles, salmon, stags. You'd love it. I'll have to take you sometime." He eyed her keenly. "Unless, that is, you've got plans to go sooner."

Aunt Bridget smiled non-committally.

"Ah!"

"We'll see," she said. "This loch you're talking about, what's it called?"

"Loch na h-Iolaire."

"You said that deliberately."

"No, that's what it's called, Loch of the Eagle. I think it refers to the ospreys – you know, the fish eagles. But it could mean golden eagles, they've got both."

"Say it again."

"Loch," he said phonetically, "na hew-lur."

"Loch na hew-luh."

"Almost," he said. "Pronounce the r: hew-lur."

"Loch na hewlur."

"You've got it."

"How on earth do you spell that?"

"Well, Loch na –" he broke off. "Look, why don't I just draw you a map of the place, it'll be easier. Mike, be a good chap and fetch me a sheet of paper. And something to rest on."

Harry ran off with him. They were soon back.

"Thanks. Now," the Earl of Whitewater shifted to a low stool beside Aunt Bridget and rested a clipboard on his big bare knees, "this is the River Goole, right, running through the strath. Heathery hills on each side. Up there to the north you've got Ben Mór Ruadh," he wrote it in. "That means the big red mountain. And down here to the south – " he sketched in a whole range of smaller peaks. "Mountains all round, really. Now the river flows on and right here, half a mile or so before it reaches the loch, it starts down this terrific gully. Rocks each side, roaring water, deep pools. That's where the castle gets its name – Uisge Ghil, the white water. Then it reaches the bottom and flows on out into the loch." He wrote the name: Loch na h-Iolaire.

"Loch of the Eagle." Harry kneeled at his side. "Let's see how you spell it."

Gunther held it out and added to his drawing. "There's an old oak wood along the shore here – great place for mushrooms – and the King's Crag right above it. Little cliffs all over the place but this is a big one. And the jetty and the old boathouse. And Highland cattle. And Lady Island in the loch here."

"Lady Island?" Harry said.

"I'm sure it's got a Gaelic name but that's what they call it. Now the track – there's no road to the castle, you know, just this stony track – runs along the south side of the river here." He drew a dotted line. "That's where people leave their cars when they come for the salmon fishing. Reckoned to be some of the best in Perthshire."

Salmon! Harry remembered the smashed cases at *Fisherman's Tryst*, the fish ripped to pieces on the carpet. Had they come from the River Goole? He glanced at Aunt Bridget.

She sat ramrod straight. Whatever she may have been thinking, her face displayed nothing.

"Great days," Gunther was saying. "Oh, we have good trout fishing and coarse fishing here, but nothing compares with being out on a good salmon river in the Highlands."

"I suppose people pay quite a bit for the privilege," Aunt Bridget said.

"Absolutely. Height of the season, these days, about seven hundred pounds a week. That's for a single beat, you know, with a ghillie. Or out on the loch. It's Uncle Sandy's main source of income. That and the grouse shooting. And the deer stalking, of course."

"It must add up to quite a bit."

"Well, yes. If he lived in a council house he'd be rolling in it. As it is, it's about half as much as the poor man needs to keep the chimneys from crashing down through the roof."

"I suppose most of the fishers stay – well, where? Is there a village?"

"With a very nice fishing hotel, the *Highlandman's Arms*. About nine miles away."

"Not in the castle then?"

"He's not equipped for it. Wouldn't pass the regulations these days. Besides, it's his home. Would you like strangers sitting there in the evening, pushing back the single malt? Wandering along to the bathroom in the middle of the night? I know I wouldn't. He did occasionally put people up in the past but he didn't like it."

Aunt Bridget gazed from the window.

Harry wondered if she would mention Eddie and Dart Jones, or a summer house, but she didn't.

"The castle's on the north side of the river." Gunther drew it in. "There's a bridge goes across the gorge. Old as the castle. Right time of year you can look down and see the salmon leaping."

Head on one side, he considered his map and added a few details. "And that's about it, I guess." He handed it to Aunt Bridget and stood up. "You're being very mysterious. I can't wait to find out what it's all about."

"Well, you'll have to learn patience."

Mike watched her with big eyes.

"Can you be trusted to keep your trap shut, young man?"

He looked at his father.

"Well, can you?" Gunther said.

"I think so."

"Think's not good enough. Sorry." She switched off the laptop, slipped the map inside and snapped it shut.

"I mean I *can* keep a secret," he said.

Aunt Bridget smiled. "I'm sure you can, Mike. And you must be very curious, but this isn't a game. It's real life and we're deadly serious. I'll tell you this much: it might be about money, quite a lot of money. Money that could be used to build a hospital for sick people in Africa, and a school for children who aren't as lucky as you and Harry. Money that might help your Uncle Sandy to repair his castle." With sharp blue eyes she regarded him over the top of her glasses. "And that's all I'm going to tell you for the moment. And it's a *big* secret."

Gunther said, "I know that look. You used to look at me like that during tutorials. Scared me to death."

"Really? Quite right too. Chasing pretty girls all over Oxford when you should have been studying the books I set you."

"You don't believe that, Mike, do you?" He looked down at his son.

"Yes," Mike said.

His father laughed aloud and caught him by a wrist. "You don't need to worry about Mike," he said to Aunt Bridget. "If he says he'll keep a secret, he will."

Mike tugged at his father's fingers, trying to get free.

"Why don't you boys run off for half an hour," Aunt Bridget said. "Then we've got to be going."

"Go out on the lawns," Gunther said. "Get yourselves some exercise."

But Mike and Harry had plans of their own. They wanted to see how far a nice smile might get them with the lady who ran the teashop.

"Right, Dad." Mike looked at Harry. They giggled and ran from the room.

"Young energy!" Gunther flopped on to the sun-faded cushions of a settee.

"He's a nice boy," Aunt Bridget said.

"I think so. So's Harry."

"Yes, we're both very lucky." Aunt Bridget lifted her coffee cup and saw that it was empty. "I was thinking. It was quite a coincidence when you were their age, having two uncle Sandies, one an earl, the other a lord, both living on estates called Whitewater."

"How do you mean?"

"Well, there's your uncle Sandy that we've been talking about, up at Castle of the White Water in Scotland. I know he isn't your real uncle, just a distant cousin, but you call him Uncle Sandy."

"Yes, everyone calls him Sandy."

"And then there's your other uncle Sandy, who left you the estate here at Whitewater Hall."

Gunther was puzzled. "What on earth gives you the idea he was called Sandy?"

"But wasn't he?" Aunt Bridget was caught unawares. "I thought his name was Sandon."

"It was, but that doesn't mean he shortened it to Sandy."

"Am I getting mixed up?"

"I think you are. Poor chap had the most appalling string of names you ever heard: Sandon St John Geoffrey de Witt Tebag. He hated them. Used to call himself one of the Shropshire Tebags. Only one decent name in the whole lot, so he dropped the rest and called himself Geoffrey. We all knew him as Uncle Geoff."

"But you called him Sandon when we were here before." "Did I?"

"Yes, you talked about poor Sandon's ashes."

"I suppose I must have done then. Maybe I've got into the

way of it. People come asking about the family, you know, boring old genealogists. Want to trace us back to the primeval ooze. Drives me nuts. I call him by his official name then: Sandon, the Seventh Earl. But when he was alive it was always Geoffrey or Geoff. Never 'Sandy' anyway."

"Oh."

"Why, is it important?"

"No." Aunt Bridget shrugged.

But she was furious with herself. She, who masterminded every operation for the Wrinklies, who took meticulous care over the tiniest detail, had built up a whole profile on a careless assumption. *To Sandy at Whitewater . . . fishing, Whitewater . . . poor Sandy, what an innocent*: it had all fitted so well. But now she discovered that Sandon wasn't called Sandy at all, he was called Geoff. And the Whitewater they wanted, the Whitewater where Eddie had fished for salmon, stayed with Sandy and, she hoped, hidden his treasure in the summer house – *not* the gazebo – wasn't even in England, but over three hundred miles away in the Highlands of Scotland.

She shook her head. "Am I getting old, Gunther? Is my brain turning to porridge? Ask me a question."

It was a trick that had dazzled her students. "All right. What's the cube root of," he scribbled some figures, "185,193?"

She thought for a moment. "Fifty-seven."

"Definitely turning to porridge," he said. "How do you *do* that?"

She smiled.

"Another question: I was going to make some more coffee. Would you rather have tea?"

"The coffee was delicious."

"Coffee it is then." He gathered up the cups and was

heading for the door when he stopped and looked back. "You and I understand each other quite well."

"I think so. We always have."

"So you'll realize I've got a pretty good idea what you're up to."

"Yes, I've been a bit worried about it."

"Do you want me to hazard a guess?"

"I'd rather you didn't."

"Fair enough." He nodded. "I just want you to know that whatever it is, you've got my support. And if there's anything I can do to help—"

"You can say you forgive me about the floor of the gazebo."

"I had wondered if you were involved – but what on earth for? All part of this Uncle Sandy business I suppose."

She nodded guiltily.

"Don't worry, what you sent was more than enough. Place looks like new. The only person who was really upset was Uncle Geoff."

"That's a terrible joke."

"It's one of Mike's. I thought it was rather good."

"What a nice earl you are, Gunther."

"Stop flirting," he said.

"I can't help it, it's those hairy knees. Incidentally, since we're talking about the gazebo, I don't suppose—"

"There's one on Uncle Sandy's place?" he said. "I thought you'd never ask. Yes, on Lady Island."

"On the island?"

"Back in the old days the ladies liked servants to row them out on the loch and they'd take tea in the summer house. That's why it's called Lady Island."

"What sort of condition's it in?"

"Falling down like the rest of the place. And the island's completely overgrown, almost impenetrable. The sheep and the deer can't get out there, so while the hillsides are nibbled bare, the island stands up in the water like a bit of the Amazon jungle. Great place for wildlife. Often see otters. And there's an osprey nest in one of the pine trees." He indicated the tray. "I'll get the coffee."

"Thanks."

"Give Uncle Sandy our love." His voice drifted back from the corridor.

"If I see him. Haven't made any plans yet." She leaned back on the cushions. "What about boats?"

But Gunther was out of earshot.

Chapter 29

Hooligans

They cruised the streets of Cobford looking for a place to park.

"We haven't been to Scotland for years," Aunt Bridget said. "The roads will have changed. I really must get a new map."

It was five o'clock and town was busy. Although Hawthorn's, the excellent bookstore she wished to visit, was in the market square, they ended up parking by a muddy play area close to the river.

"Best we can do." She pressed the remote and the locks snapped shut. They started up a steep street that led to the town centre. "Anything you're wanting while we're here?"

Harry examined the coins in his pocket. "I might get a slush," he said.

It had been a busy day. Aunt Bridget had just driven for two hours on the motorway. Their minds were on other matters. If they had been more alert, they might have noticed the small, fierce, Italian-looking woman in black who emerged from a black Range Rover in the forecourt of a garage repair shop and stood watching their retreating backs.

Mad Ruby had gone to enquire about the repairs to the Aston Martin. Her night at Scrumpy Bottom, chained to the beam, listening to Baba's ravings and piano playing, and remembering the treachery of her son and his fiancée, had put her in a mood to chew off heads. Little expecting the reception that awaited them, Priestly and Gestapo Lil had driven over the next morning to threaten Harry. It was a violent reunion. Now, three days later, a fragile peace had been restored and she waited for a progress report on the damaged car.

Harry and Aunt Bridget passed from sight. How Ruby hated them! How she longed for revenge! Fifty metres away their shining new Rover stood unattended. How she longed to run along the street and smash the windows, batter the panels and break every lamp with a brick! Alas it was impossible. She was known in the garage. She could not run fast enough to make a getaway.

Raucous shouts rose from the playing field. Four teenage boys had torn a branch from one of the surrounding trees and were using it to attack a newly-repaired goalpost. One swung from the crossbar, bouncing to make it break. Ruby's heart surged.

"Back in a few minutes," she called into the workshop and drove off briskly.

The goal was a short distance beyond the Rover. The boy who seemed to be the leader of the group was aged about fifteen with a bold stare and spots round his mouth.

Ruby stepped from the car and beckoned.

He said something to the rest and they laughed.

She took a twenty-pound note from her purse and waved it gently by her shoulder. "Come here."

They left their game and trotted across the muddy grass. "You wanna be careful, ol' lady. Flashin' your money around wi' blokes like us in the neighbour'ood."

"Oh, you don'a frighten me," she said. "You want take it, take it. Or you wan'a do a little job and get a lot more?"

"Why don't we jus' take what you got right now an' forget the job?" He grabbed for her bag.

She pulled it out of his reach. "Because if you do, I *kill* you."

"You!" He laughed again. "Four foot o' nothin'? Don't you mean your great 'ulking brothers?"

"I not need my brothers. I know your ugly face'a. I hunt you down myself and shoot you like a dog."

"She's a nutter," one of the boys said.

"Who cares?" said another with dirty rat's teeth. "How much are you talking about, dear?"

"I not *your* dear, that for sure." She considered. "Four of you – twenty each. Eighty pound, and keep your traps shut."

"Make it a hundred," said the leader.

"All right, a hundred. But for that'a you do really good job."

"You haven't told us what it is yet."

"A hundred quid!" said one of the boys. "Here, I'm not toppin' no one."

"See that car?" She fixed her eyes on it. "That nice shiny blue Rover. Brand new."

They nodded.

"I want you smash it up," she said.

Was she serious?

"Trash it. Vandalize it. Windscreen, bonnet, tyres, the lot. Upholstery. Everything."

They realized she meant it. "Hey, yeah! Cool!"

"OK, then. Where's the money?"

"*After* you done the job."

"You kidding?"

"All right. Half now, half later." She took another thirty from her bag and passed it round. They held it to the light, stuffed it into jeans pockets. "I leave the Range Rover round the corner. Walk up to the church." She pointed.

"St Gabriel's."

"Whatever. Let me get out of sight before you start. I see you in the graveyard."

"No funny stuff," said the leader, "'cos if there is, we'll get you. Works both ways."

"You're so quick," Ruby said sarcastically. "I bet you're a real bright boy in school."

"Don't go to school no more," he said. "School's borin'. Waste o' time."

She drove away.

It was a quiet graveyard, no longer used for burials. The stones were grey with lichen, some lopsided.

She waited in a triangle of yew trees, hidden from the road. The hooligans were taking a long time. Perhaps they had just taken the money and scarpered. Then she heard voices and the pad-pad-pad of trainers.

"Where is she? . . . Old witch! . . . Must be here, her car's down the road."

She stepped out of hiding. The four boys joined her. They were panting, flushed, excited:

"Fantastic! . . . Reckon it's a write-off. . . I could make a career out of this. . . Wish we'd had a can o' petrol."

Young and boastful, they sought her approval.

"Think that old man'll be all right?" one said.

"What old man?"

"Fool with a walking stick and a fat Labrador. Tried to grab me. I had to push him over."

Ruby said, "You got away all right?"

"No prob." The leader was carrying an expensive black case.

"What's that?"

"Computer. Lying on the back seat under a jacket."

"I'll have that."

"Jokin', aren't you?" He knocked her arm away. "Fetch a few bob this will."

"Where's the dosh?" A boy pushed to the front. "Don't want to hang round here all day. Split 'fore the pigs show up."

Ruby handed over the second fifty. "How much for the computer?"

"It's not his, it's mine," said the rat-toothed boy. "I'm the one found it."

"An' I'm the one got it," said the older boy. "'Undred quid."

"A hundred? Fifty."

"'Undred."

"I not got a hundred." She checked her purse. "Sixty-five, see?" She showed him the lining. "That all I got."

"You can get it though, easy. 'Ole in the wall. 'Undred's nothin' to a woman drives a Range Rover."

It was extortion on his side; a once-in-a-lifetime opportunity on hers. Who could tell what information she might pick up from Bridget Barton's computer. "All right," she said, and wished she was carrying the sawn-off. "Come on, we go to the bank."

"Rest of you get lost," the big boy said. "And keep your lips buttoned. See you tonight."

They slipped away.

Side by side like gran and grandson, Ruby and her acne-speckled companion left the graveyard by a side gate and made their way to the nearest cash point.

At the same time Harry and Aunt Bridget were returning to the car. Harry sipped a mango slush. Aunt Bridget carried the road map in a Hawthorn's poly bag.

He stopped. "Look."

Mad Ruby and a thuggish boy he did not recognize were leaving a Barclay's cash machine across the road. The boy was tucking something into his back pocket. Ruby carried a slim black case.

"I wonder what she's been up to," Aunt Bridget said.

Harry gave a little shiver as if someone had walked over his grave.

"Everything's on it," Aunt Bridget said. "Everything! And there's nothing we can do about it. We've got to start now."

"To Scotland?" Auntie Florrie said.

"Of course Scotland, where do you think?"

They were in the kitchen. Nutty had been dispatched to fill the Merc with petrol and rouse a friend who owned a garage. They needed a second car. Fingers had gone with him.

"I hate to say it, but what about the fuzz?" said Max who had been touching up his roots and missed the start of the conversation.

"We've reported the damage to the car, but not who's responsible."

"What about the laptop?"

"Haven't decided yet. I mean, we know it's Mad Ruby but where's the proof? Where would it get us reporting her? It would be the end of Eddie Carver's loot as far as we're concerned. Not to mention that Priestly seems to have half the local force in his pocket, living in Felon Grange the way he does."

"After this he'll have gone back into hiding," Dot said. "Holed up with some villain that knows about computers."

"Which is why we've got to *go*," Aunt Bridget insisted. "Right away. Soon as Nutty and Fingers get back with the Merc and whatever else."

"I hope he get something big and comfortable," Huggy said. "Ve need sleep going Scotland. Ready for action."

"Tell me the last time Nutty let us down," Auntie Florrie said. "He's trying to get a four-wheel drive. Goodness knows what sort of tracks we'll find up there."

The roar of an engine announced its arrival. A vehicle less comfortable it would be hard to imagine. Nutty's friend had provided him with a Land Rover scarcely less battered than the car it replaced. It was brown, mud-stained, floored with filthy carpet. So many calves, sheep and farm dogs had clambered over the seats, it was hard to tell their original colour.

"What is *that*!" Max was appalled.

"Doesn't look much, I'll give ye that," Nutty said. "But it's the best he could give us at a minute's notice. Got a new engine, new tyres, an' it's just been overhauled. Belongs to a farmer the far side o' town. Canny car."

"Canny car!" Huggy said contemptuously. "You think I driving all the vay to Scotland in *that*, you off your head."

"Take no notice, Nutty darling, it's perfect. You're a

338

miracle worker." Auntie Florrie kissed him on the cheek. "It'll be like rally driving again. Can I have first go?"

"Rally driving! Miracle vorker! Hah! A miracle ve reach Scotland, you ask me." Huggy turned back indoors.

"We'll have to take turns," Aunt Bridget said. "Halfway in the Mercedes, halfway in the Land Rover. It's what we've got, anyway, and Florrie and Nutty know ten times more than the rest of us put together. They're the experts in our little gang, so let's get cracking."

"Who?" Max said. "Everybody? It'll be a bit cramped, don't you think?"

"I can't go, I've got this TV recording tomorrow." Mr Tolly had been practising for weeks.

"And somebody's got to stay here," Mrs Good said. "This is your sort of thing more than mine. I'll invite my sister for a few days."

"Everyone else then," Aunt Bridget said. "We'll not know who's needed until we get there, not for sure. Nutty and Florrie, obviously. And Dot – there might be some castle walls we need to climb."

"An' locks need openin'," Fingers said.

"And Huggy, of course." Aunt Bridget looked towards the house. "We could need her strength any time. Goodness knows who we might come up against: gamekeepers, the Felon Grange crowd. They'll not be far behind us, you can count on that."

"Forbye, a wee Sco'ish accent may come in handy," Max said. "I hope ye're no' plannin' tae leave me behin'."

"And I wouldn't miss it for the world," said Aunt Bridget. "So that's about—"

"Ahem!" A cough in the background made her turn. "I

think maybe ye're forgettin' somethin', Bridget Barton," came a high, peppery voice. "It's gettin' to be a habit wi' ye."

"Oh, Angel! I'm terribly —"

"It's a bit late for that. Yon poncy actor wi' his dyed hair an' *Brigadoon* accent. Why d'ye need that when ye've got a real Scot in yer midst? A Highlander *forbye*!" He glared at Max. "Angus McGregor, by name, from the Isle o' Skye."

People stood back to give him the floor. "I was workin' in ma studio. None o' you thought to ask old Angel aboot yon castle. Did ye, eh? Not even though my mother had the Gaelic an' I ken the place fine. I camped there in my caravan for a whole week."

"What!"

"Just so. When I was forgin' ma Landseers an' McCullochs. Grand bit o' romantic Scotland. National Gallery in Edinburgh couldna tell the difference. Snapped them up like hot bridies. Heh-heh-heh!"

"Did you meet the owner, Sandy Rattray? Lord Goole of—"

"I ken his title fine. No, he was still in the army. It was a long time ago, y' understand, afore Her Majesty give me a few years dinner, bed an' breakfast in Barlinnie. But I've still got a twa-three paintin's in my studio somewhere."

"Well let's see them."

"It'll take mebbe a few minutes." He looked at Mrs Good. "D'ye suppose there's any chance of a couple o' bits of yon caramel shortbread while I'm lookin'? Ma belly's cleavin' to ma backbone."

"I'm sure there is, Angel," she said. "And a big slice of that lemon cake you like so much. Just as long as it doesn't spoil your appetite."

He grinned with pleasure, hiding his crooked brown teeth with the back of a hand. The magnifying spectacles made his blue eyes grotesque. Fragments of pastry – Mrs Good tried to remember the last time they'd had pastry – were caught in his ragged beard.

"Give us a shout when you're ready," Aunt Bridget said. "Meanwhile, everyone else, let's pack our cases. How soon can you have dinner on the table, Goody?"

"There's just the veg," she said. "Half an hour?"

"Right then, suitcases in the hall in half an hour. All agreed? Ready to leave straight after dinner."

As they drove north, Harry couldn't wait.

Angel's pictures had given them a taste of what lay ahead. Stags locked horns on a wild hillside; an eagle ripped a hare with its sharp beak; misty landscapes rolled on forever. And there, in the midst, stood Caisteal an Uisge Ghil, tough little flowers and ferns clinging to crevices in its grey walls. Savage mountains rose above. The wind-ruffled loch lay at its feet.

It had been a hard job persuading Aunt Bridget to let him come:

"No!" she had said decisively. "No! Who knows what may happen, Harry. It's no good pleading. The answer's no."

But out of earshot, Auntie Florrie had put her foot down firmly. "I know, Bridget, I know. You're quite right: it's a wild part of the country, it might be dangerous, there could be fighting. But there is *no* way we can go off to the Scottish Highlands on a treasure hunt and leave an eleven-year-old boy behind. It would be plain cruel. We wouldn't even be going if Harry hadn't picked up that clue on your computer. The computer, may I say, that *you* left unattended in the car."

It was rarely that Auntie Florrie, with her taste for make-up, perfume, hairdressers and pretty clothes, expressed herself so forcefully. But Auntie Florrie had not won the Isle of Man TT three years in succession, and gone on to become Formula One champion, by smiling sweetly and being nice. Beneath her frilly exterior, Auntie Florrie was as tough as rugby boots, and when her eyes flashed as they did now, and her lips were set, she was a force to be reckoned with.

"Dot thinks the same as me – all right, as *I* do, if you want to put on your headmistress face. So does Fingers. And Max. Everyone I've talked to. You're outnumbered. So you can just go out there right now and tell Harry that you've changed your mind. He can come after all."

And so, as the two cars sped north up the motorway at a steady sixty-five miles an hour, which was the best the Land Rover could do on a long journey, Harry sucked a buttermint, looked out on the darkening fields, and hugged himself as he thought of the adventure that lay ahead.

Chapter 30

A Fishy Story

The *Highlandman's Arms* stood quarter of a mile from the village. It was an old sporting inn with ornate woodwork above leaded windows. The weathered brick frontage, which faced south, was half obscured by purple clematis. Rolling moor surged right to the car park.

Aunt Bridget had rung ahead and by the greatest of good luck a party of American tourists had been struck down by food poisoning in Edinburgh. This meant that not only could the *Highlandman* offer accommodation to nine people at short notice, but the best rooms were available.

They arrived at five, a very antisocial hour, with the sun rising above the mountains. A sleepy porter made coffee and showed them to their rooms.

To Harry's delight he was given a large room to himself with a four-poster bed, complete with curtains.

"Very nice." Huggy looked in. "You deserve it, vhat those nasty people did Scrumply Bottoms. You good boy. Ve not here at all, vere it not for you."

Fingers was yawning. "Dear, oh dear! What's wrong wi' me? Spent me whole working life on night shift. Never used to be this tired."

"You're not twenty-one any more, that's all," Auntie Florrie said gently. "We all need a couple of hours shut-eye."

So they went to bed and reassembled at nine for an enormous Scottish breakfast. Beyond the dining room windows the moors were bathed in sunshine. Grouse whirred above the heather. There wasn't a house in sight.

Harry loaded his fork with black pudding and fried egg. "Great, isn't it!" he said to no one in particular.

"Smashin'!" Fingers was on to the toast and honey. "A'most as good as 'ome."

Angel was too busy eating to reply. His lips shone with grease.

Aunt Bridget didn't hear. Back straight, she sipped black coffee and gazed into the middle distance. She was thinking.

After breakfast Auntie Florrie went into the village and bought an Ordnance Survey map. And a bit before ten, loaded with packed lunches and thermos flasks, they piled into the cars and set off for Caisteal an Uisge Ghil.

The first four miles, through forests and moorland, were by narrow road with passing places. Sheep wandered on the tarmac. The rain of recent days had swollen burns which gushed from the hills and plunged beneath hump-backed bridges. A solitary cottage stood on a knoll. A short distance further on, Auntie Florrie, who led the way in the Land Rover, swung right from the road on to a stony track. A wooden signpost emerged from the heather. Words were carved into it. Harry tried to read them but they were obscured by lichen and years of exposure to the wind and rain.

The Land Rover rocked as they climbed steeply across the side of a hill. Auntie Florrie was in her element, swinging the wheel sharply to avoid boulders, potholes and collapsing verges that could have sent them slithering into the ditch.

The track levelled then began to descend. At the highest point Auntie Florrie stopped to take in the scene and allow the Mercedes, which had to proceed more cautiously, to catch up.

Harry jumped down. The mountain wind blew in his face, carrying the scents of peat and heather. At his back the hill rose to a rocky summit. Before him, mile upon mile, the moors rolled on with dry-stone dykes, woods and a flash of lochs, until they were lost in the hazy distance. A thin, high-pitched *mew* made him look up. Two birds of prey were circling against the patched sky.

"Eagles?" he said.

"Buzzards." Back on his native soil, Angel was proprietorial. "Ye'll ken eagles when ye see them, son." He took a deep breath. "Ah, get all that Sassenach air out your lungs."

A short distance away a low, lithe animal shot across the track. It was carrying something in its mouth.

"Look!" Harry pointed but it was already gone.

"Stoat," Angel said. "Got a mouse to feed her babies."

Harry started after it. Abruptly he stopped. A big dragonfly, electric blue, rose from the ditch and hovered above the grasses. It darted from spot to spot then settled. He crept closer. It was a gorgeous creature.

The moors, which appeared so empty from a distance, were thronging with life.

The Mercedes drew up and everyone piled out.

Fingers clutched his collar, for the hillside was exposed and the day had not warmed up yet. "Where's this castle then?"

"About another three miles. Round the far side of the

hill." The map blew against Auntie Florrie's legs. She folded it and showed him. "See, along the river and down that rocky bit."

For a while they enjoyed the view then drove on.

The River Goole appeared below them, silver and blue, reflecting the sky.

They descended to the glen. A few cars — an elderly Bentley, a Jaguar, a Volvo estate — were parked on the verge, far apart and fitted with rod racks. Fishermen stood in the stream, thigh-deep in their waders.

Harry reminded himself that Eddie 'Carver' Jones, the vicious London gang boss, had frequently stood in those waters. Eddie Jones, whose biggest fish had been hacked to pieces on the floor of his Hampstead home. Eddie Jones, with a taste for drowning people in egg barrels. Eddie Jones, who had murdered Mad Ruby's husband and tried to have him canned and sold in the supermarkets. Eddie Jones, whose ill-gotten treasure they came to seek on Lady Island.

He shivered.

A different kind of fisherman, a heron, flapped up from the shallows, tucked its neck into its shoulders, and flew away with slow wingbeats.

A mile further on, the bright waters of Loch na h'Iolaire appeared through a gap in the hills. Though Harry had seen it on the map, it was bigger than he expected, four miles long by more than half a mile wide. Steep hillsides plunged to the shore on each side. It looked very deep.

They entered a patch of woodland, and when they emerged from the far side, the castle was in sight.

Caisteal an Uisge Ghil looked much as Gunther had described it and Angel had painted it, only now it was real.

For centuries Scottish lords had fought and hunted on the land where Harry now found himself. Within those massive walls they had feasted and entertained the nobility. How times had changed, he thought, as he drew closer in comfortable jeans and T-shirt, and popped the cap on his tube of Smarties. It was sad, for many of the ancient buildings were now in ruins. Some lacked only a roof but more had collapsed. Fragments of wall stood above mounds of rubble. Sheep and deer kept the grass short, but gorse had taken hold and birch trees sprouted between the stones.

In contrast to this romantic decay, the tower of the castle and the buildings on either side were spick and span. The walls in this part were freshly pointed. The bowmen's windows were trim black slits in the bleached stone.

The track began to descend. In a gorge alongside, the River Goole commenced its final descent to the loch. Beyond a low stone dyke the hillside dropped away into space. Harry craned his neck but it was impossible to see the bottom. He tapped Auntie Florrie on the shoulder:

"Can you pull up? I want to look down."

Max was terrified of heights. "Take no notice, drive on. Just take care."

Harry grinned. "Are you scared we'll go over?"

"Don't even say it."

"Not much of a barrier. They'd have to scrape us off the rocks like strawberry jam."

"Shut up!" Max said. "Horrible boy."

"All bones and lumpy bits."

"Oh, stop it!" His face was white.

Auntie Florrie said, "We'll be at the bridge in a minute. I'll stop there."

There was a small turning area and parking space for two or three cars. Harry ran to the bridge that crossed the ravine. It was arched and narrow. Standing in the middle, he leaned far over. The ferny cliffs went down and down to the rushing river. He gripped the lichen-yellow stones of the parapet and hoped the old bridge would not choose that moment to collapse. Upstream the gorge was deeper, but here the river was at its most spectacular. This was the crashing white water that gave the castle its name. Spray whirled high, creating fleeting rainbows. The roar of the torrent filled the air.

Harry dripped spit, watching to see it hit the river, but before it landed it was caught by a breeze and dragged away out of sight. He tried again, and as his spit fell, a salmon leaped, a great silver fish, lashing and struggling to get up the falls. It fell back. He could not believe his eyes.

"Auntie Florrie! Nutty!" They were coming towards him. "Quick! Quick!" They broke into a trot. "A salmon! It was jumping! Right there!" He pointed. "Honestly!"

A small crowd joined him at the parapet.

They waited.

Nothing happened.

"You sure, Harry? Are you just having us on?"

"No!" he said. "Really! I was just looking over and suddenly this—"

With no warning a salmon leaped again. It was followed by another – two big fish in the air at the same time. They fought to climb the falling water. One dropped back into the foaming pool. But the other reached the lip of the falls, hung in the speeding water for several seconds, then wriggled through and was gone.

"Terrific!" Aunt Bridget said. "What an effort! Just terrific!"

They watched for a few more minutes then looked about. Fifty metres beyond the bridge the track ran through an arch in what remained of the defensive wall. It was the entrance to the castle grounds. In the other direction, beyond the cars, the track continued downstream to the loch. Harry could see the wooden jetty and boathouse Gunther had marked on his map, and the oak wood with the tremendous crag hanging above it.

"What now?" Fingers lit a cigarette.

"Harry and I were the ones met Gunther and Mike, so we'll go to the castle and introduce ourselves. The rest of you –"

"We'll drive on down to the loch," Auntie Florrie said. "Have a look round. Spy out the island. See about boats."

"See you there. Shouldn't be too long." Aunt Bridget turned to Harry. "Come on, let's go and meet Lord Goole."

He pulled his clothes straight and ran fingers through his hair.

"You've got spit on your shoulder," she said.

He rubbed it in and trotted in the wake of his bony, long-striding aunt.

"Gunther was on the phone last night, as a matter of fact. Said you might be coming up this way."

"He was one of my students." Aunt Bridget sipped her coffee. "Long time ago now."

"Oh, it's not the first time he's spoken about you," Lord Goole said. "Holds you in high esteem."

"That's very kind of him," Aunt Bridget said, and wondered if Gunther's account had included *Sapphire*, the ladies' gang she had led during her years as an Oxford lecturer, and her subsequent five years in Holloway Prison.

"Some of those seminars you taught were the highlight of his time at Balliol, he says."

"Well, thank you. But if the truth were told, he hardly needed me."

"So you say, so you say. Anyway, you've been down to see him recently, I hear. Along with this young man. Made quite a pal of Mike, I understand."

Harry wiped shortbread crumbs from his lips. "We saw salmon jumping," he said.

"You and Mike? There aren't any salmon at Whitewater, surely."

"No, I mean just now, from the bridge."

"Ah! Yes, I believe there's quite a run on. Big fellas some of them." He smiled. "Good for business."

"We saw people fishing on the way down," Aunt Bridget said.

"On the beats by seven o'clock, some of them," Lord Goole said.

"They're certainly very enthusiastic," Aunt Bridget agreed. "We're staying at the *Highlandman*. By the time we went in to breakfast, the fishers had been long gone."

"I've got a four-poster," Harry said.

"Lucky you."

"We came up at short notice," Aunt Bridget explained. "Quite a crowd of us. The hotel had had a big cancellation, so we drove up overnight while the roads were quiet."

"Where are the rest?"

"Went on down to the loch. I hope that's all right."

"Absolutely. Why not?"

They sat in the castle kitchen, a huge room with a slabbed floor. The aristocracy seemed to spend most of their lives in the kitchen, from what Harry had observed. Lord Goole – Sandy Rattray – was a tall, thin old gentleman with long hands and a long, kindly face. He wore an open-necked shirt with a frayed collar and a baggy tweed suit with patches on the elbows.

His wife, a petite Frenchwoman named Yvette, came in from the garden wearing gumboots and carrying a pair of secateurs. She and her husband had met, Harry learned later, during World War II, when he was working behind enemy lines and she was a member of the Resistance. She had, it was horrible to imagine, been captured and tortured by the Gestapo. Until her retirement a few years earlier, she had been the local doctor.

"Oh, hello." She pushed her hair back with a wrist.

Her husband introduced them.

"I see Sandy's made coffee. Instant, I expect." She looked. "Yes, horrible! I make something drinkable."

Lord Goole tried to make up for his misdemeanour. "Here," he pushed the biscuit barrel towards Harry. "Try one of those in the shiny paper. The yellow ones. Chocolate marzipan. Awfully good."

Harry did as he was told.

"We're staying at the *Highlandman*." Aunt Bridget steered the conversation back.

"They'll look after you well," Lady Goole said. "You're lucky to get rooms this time of year."

"Popular with the fishermen, I understand."

"They do a special deal." Lady Goole spooned coffee into a cafetière. "When people come up for our fishing they want somewhere nice to stay."

Aunt Bridget took a gamble. "Did Gunther tell me you used to have people here?"

"A few, a long time ago." She smiled at her husband. "Sandy hated it."

"Don't remind me," he said.

"I bet you get asked, all the same. Rich businessmen, Americans, Japanese: give their eye teeth to stay in a beautiful old place like this." Aunt Bridget looked around. "Historic castle, views over the loch, not a road for miles – a real live Scottish lord."

"Absolutely right. And d'you know what they expect, some of them: flaming torches, bagpipes, a whole roast stag on a spit. Not to mention me dressed up like Rob Roy Macgregor and spouting Robbie Burns!"

"It's true." Lady Goole laughed.

"I mean, are they off their trolleys? Anyway, we couldn't, even if we wanted. Put people up, I mean. The roof on the South Tower's been declared unsafe."

"And it's our home!" Lady Goole swirled the kettle to take it off the boil. "Who wants strangers wandering all through the rooms?"

"Sitting there with their feet up. Boasting about how many *K!* they made on their last deal."

Two black Labradors trotted in. Absently he rubbed their ears.

"Queer folk," he went on. "One man, he stole all the toilet paper, not a sheet in the place. Another night, Evie went to the bathroom and bumped into this chap wandering the corridors in one of her nightdresses. Taken it from the drying cupboard. Said he was Lady Macbeth. Well, you can't have that sort of thing going on. Before you know it, they're going to be raking through the kitchen drawers for a cleaver."

Harry laughed.

"It's not funny, he was barking mad. Locked the bedroom door after that, I can tell you."

"Mike said something about a gangster," Harry said.

Aunt Bridget froze at his blunt approach but Lord and Lady Goole seemed untroubled.

"Oh, our poet," he smiled. "Poets, in fact. There were two of them, brothers."

"Poets?" Aunt Bridget said.

"Our little joke, but it's what they told us. Not that we ever saw anything they wrote, did we, Evie?"

"Nor were we ever likely to," she said lightly.

"Knew as much about poetry as I do about rocket engineering."

"One of them," said Lady Goole, "he ask if Walter Scott is the striker for Celtic."

"My wife's a football fanatic," Lord Goole explained. "But the oddest thing, you mentioning them just now, they've both been in the papers quite recently."

"Really?"

"Oh, yes. Both dead, you know, and quite violently. One shot in the street outside some gambling den. And the other fell the length of a flight of stairs in prison and killed himself."

"Some people are saying he was pushed," said Lady Goole.

"That's right. A couple of real villains. What were their names again? Your memory's better than mine."

Lady Goole put a small jug of milk into the microwave. "I know one was called d'Artagnan. The younger one, I think. His brother called him Dart. What was their surname now?"

"Something Welsh, was it? Williams? Morgan? Jones? That's it, Jones. Dart Jones."

"And Eddie. Eddie and Dart Jones."

"Oh, well done, darling! Well done!" He smiled and said to Aunt Bridget, "It's always such a relief to know one's not quite ready for the knacker's yard."

"I know the feeling," said Aunt Bridget, who was almost the same age and had a brain as fast as a computer.

"Well, they came for the fishing, must be twenty years ago now, and we put them up here. Don't ask me why, it just sort of became the regular arrangement. Anyway, they were dead keen. Couple of wide boys. Bit of cheek about them. Cockney chutzpah. Knew their way about. I liked them – to start off with anyway."

"Yes, *you* did, Sandy." Lady Goole passed round the coffee. "But I always felt there was a dark side. Never liked being left with them on my own."

"I remember you saying, and you were right. But when I went out on the river with them they were good company. Some of their stories maybe weren't for the ladies but – well, no great harm in that. Thank you," he spooned in the sugar.

"Not exactly what you think of as poets though," Aunt Bridget said.

"You said it." He gave a horsy laugh. "Dog tracks were more their style, I'd have thought. Billiard halls. Stuff fallen off the backs of lorries."

"But why did they pretend?"

"Dodgy scheme to get a bit of poaching on the loch. They'd got a beat on the river, d'you see. Other people had

354

paid for the loch, they had no right to be out there. And they could hardly ask permission. So one time they said to me: after the bustle and rush of London, would it be all right to take one of the boats out? See the moon. Commune with nature. Sometimes wrote a bit of poetry. Well, I mean! Come on, pull the other one!"

"And it wasn't always a fine summer night," Lady Goole said. "Sometimes it was March and freezing."

"That's right, it got to be a regular thing, you see. But I didn't mind, they were terrifically keen and obviously got a big kick out of it. Always brought Evie an enormous box of chocolates with a red ribbon, and a couple of bottles for me. Weren't doing any harm, what's a couple of fish here or there."

"Fish," Harry said. "Do you mean salmon?"

"Absolutely." Lord Goole explained. "If you're fishing up here a trout's called a trout, a pike's a pike, but if you say a *fish* you mean a salmon. Anyway, I told Jamie and Calum to let them be."

"Jamie and Calum?" Aunt Bridget said.

"Two of my keepers. Been with me for years. I think they saw them out there a couple of times. There's a spot the fish like round the back of Lady Island."

"And then one day, *pouf!* there's Eddie all over the papers. Pictures and everything. Gang boss arrested for murder. And what murders! Writing his initials in the skin of his enemies. Taking them to this chicken factory. Sticking them head first into a barrel of eggs. You know what they call him? Carver Jones! Eggy Jones! I say to Sandy, my God! You bring such people to my house. This could be me! You think I want to end my life as an omelette?"

He covered her hand with a loving claw. "But it didn't

355

happen, did it? And now he's gone. And Dart's gone. We need never think of them again."

Aunt Bridget caught Harry's eye.

He crunched the last of his marzipan biscuit. As Lord Goole had said, they were very good.

Chapter 31

The Swimmer

At lunchtime Lady Goole drove down to the landing stage with a pot of Scotch broth and mugs to drink it from.

They had been looking at two rowing boats which were chained to mooring posts. She said, "Would you like to go out on the loch? I think I've got keys in the car; if I haven't, it'll only take a minute to pop back and get them." It was impossible to explain that Fingers or Harry could have picked the locks in a moment. So they glanced at each other and sipped their soup while Lady Goole rummaged through the pockets of the old red Mini she was driving. "Yes, here we are," she said triumphantly, and handed the keys to Nutty who sat nearest with his shoes dangling above the water.

"We were just lookin' in the boathouse, your ladyship," he said in his broad Geordie accent. "Hope you don't mind but the doors wasn't locked or nothin'."

"Of course I don't mind," she said. "The ghillies keep the oars and one or two things in there. It's always open during the day."

"Only we were just sayin', that's a canny speedboat." He lifted his mug and did not notice her momentary silence.

"Yes," she said.

"Doesn't look like it's been out for years. Pity, bonny boat like that." He became aware that he was saying something wrong. "Oh, I'm not askin' to take it out, or nothin'. Ye've been very kind."

Aunt Bridget said, "Lady Goole's son was killed in a boating accident on Loch Ness."

"Oh, man, I'm sorry." His face burned with embarrassment. "Me an' my big mouth. Bridget never said. I'd no idea."

"How could you?" Lady Goole smiled. "Yes, the boat belonged to David. The company he was racing for gave it to him. It's been lying there since he died." She walked to the boathouse and pulled a door open. "Sandy was speaking about it back in the spring. Said we should really get rid of it. Except he's got a sort of half-feeling he'd like to try and get it going again. It's what David would have wanted. And maybe we could bear it again now."

A swallow dipped past her head. It had a nest in the old boathouse.

"He and Calum had a look but the engine – I don't know about these things. Choked-up, rusted, wet. Lying on the water all these years. Perhaps beyond repair. They couldn't get it to go, anyway."

Nutty's heart surged. This was his sort of thing. "I'll have a look at it if ye like. I mean, I don't want to put mesel' forward or nothin', but I've got a little bit of a way with engines."

"A little bit of a vay!" Huggy had hitched her skirt above her knees to catch the sun. "Lady Goole, you not listen to vhat he say. He fantastic!"

She smiled. "I'll tell Sandy. I'm sure, if you'd like to look at it, he'd be very grateful."

"I'll tell ye the truth, your ladyship, there's nothin' I'd like better in the world."

"It is very kind of you."

Harry listened to her musical accent.

"Only one thing," Nutty said. "Could we maybe move it round to the landin' stage here where there's more light?"

"Of course." She looked round the company of Wrinklies seated on the sun-warmed boards. "If you're free, would you care to come up to the castle, say around three, three-thirty? Just for a cup of tea, you know."

After she had gone Harry said, "She's so nice! I feel horrible, creeping round with secrets, planning to go out to the island and dig up all that money."

"If it's there," Max said.

"Even if it's not. I mean, she's brought soup and invited us for tea, and here we are wanting to steal all that treasure. It's not as if they're filthy rich, like the banks and that. They're dead poor."

"I feel the same," Aunt Bridget said, "just as we did down at Gunther's place. But if we told him about it, what's a peer of the realm supposed to do? Dig it up at midnight? Keep it for himself and hope no one finds out? Disgrace his family and old regiment by nicking the loot of a London gang boss, a notorious murderer? And him a friend of goodness knows who and a member of the House of Lords?"

"Dear, oh dear!" Fingers said. "Who'd want to be a member of the aristocracy?"

"Nightmare!" Dot pulled a foot back to touch the top of her head. "No fun at all."

"So we're going to dig it up instead," Aunt Bridget continued cheerfully. "And use it to save the lives of people who have no one to help them; and give an education to children who without it would never even learn to read and write. And if the law catches up with us — which it *won't*, Florrie, which it *won't* — I'm proud of what we're trying to do."

"And we'll keep some to help Lord Goole repair his castle," Harry said.

"Absolutely."

"Assuming it's there," Max said again and brushed a crumb from his immaculate trousers.

"It's there, all right," Fingers said. "Got goosebumps just lookin' across the water. Sure sign that."

Harry had finished. He scrunched up his sandwich papers and put them in the rubbish bag, then wandered down to the shore. Little flowers grew among the rocks. The water was tempting. "Can I go for a swim?"

"Let your lunch go down first," Auntie Florrie said. "Why don't you get a pair of oars and take one of the boats out."

"Good idea," Nutty said. "'Fore ye gan out on the lake, though, ye can give us a hand to tow the speedboat round."

"It's not a lake, it's a loch," Harry said.

"Same thing, cleverclogs. Haway."

Like a racing car or fighter jet, the speedboat was one of those objects that set the pulses racing. It had the perfect proportions and sleek, fast lines of a thoroughbred. A decade of neglect — dirt, dead insects, swallow droppings — had fouled the red and white paintwork, but that could soon be rectified. More importantly, what was the state of the engine?

The mooring ropes had hardened. Nutty worked them loose while Harry brought round a rowing boat and backed it to the entrance. Nutty threw him a line and he took a turn round a cleat at the stern. Then pulling hard on the oars, he towed the beautiful, filthy craft from the boathouse into the sunlight. Harry rowed well, for he often took the boat out on the lake at Lagg Hall. In two or three minutes he brought the speedboat alongside the landing stage and passed the towline to Auntie Florrie who looped it round a post.

"I never raced the boats," she said wistfully.

"Lord Goole's poor son did," Aunt Bridget replied.

The name *Red Sky* was painted along the boat's side in streamlined letters. Harry looked at Nutty in the cockpit, and thought about young David Rattray who had been the last person to speed round Loch na h-Iolaire; David Rattray who, in a different boat, had hit a log on Loch Ness at three hundred miles an hour.

Lord Goole had been watching from the castle and a few minutes later appeared at the far side of the river. He was on foot and they watched as he crossed the rickety rope bridge above the shore.

"Hello! Hello!" He gave his toothy smile. "Nice to see you all. Evie says don't forget half past three. She's up there right now, making some cherry scones."

He looked down at the boat. "You've brought it round then. Good to see it out again." He tried to continue smiling but suddenly his face crumpled and he had to turn away. He walked off a few paces and felt for a handkerchief.

They left him with his grief, and in a minute he turned back, blowing his old man's nose. His eyes were pink but his feelings were under control. "Sorry about that. It was my son's, you know. He was a fine fellow. Now," he stood on the edge of the stage and bent towards Nutty, still in the cockpit. "Hasn't been run for a long time. Not even started up. Engine probably rusted to hell, don't ask me."

"Aye, mebbes. But we'll not know till we've had a look, will we? Quality like this, might just need a bit of a clean-up. Are ye comin' down?"

Lord Goole took to Nutty, liked his plain way of speaking. "If I wouldn't be in the way."

"In the way? Man, it's your boat. Florrie, hold the stern steady while his lordship comes aboard." He stretched up a hand. "Here, catch a hold. Steady as she goes."

Awkwardly Lord Goole stepped down, nearly tumbled overboard, then recovered his balance.

"All right?" Nutty said. "Sit yersel' down there." He brushed a space clean with his hand.

Lord Goole did as he was told and looked around. He was enjoying himself.

"Beautiful boat – not that I know much about them, like." Nutty rubbed a hand along the transom, wiped dials with the tips of his fingers. "Look at that!"

Harry listened as they chatted, watched from the rowing boat as Nutty peered down into the engine. His interest waned. He pushed out from the landing stage and rowed along the shore to a spot where the rocks plunged steeply into the water. Just beyond, hidden from the others, was a white beach, studded with boulders. Behind it lay the bracken-covered hillside.

Harry rowed in until the bow drove up on the sand, then pulled off his shoes and socks and jumped down into the water. To his surprise, in the shallows at least, it was quite warm. A couple of heaves made the boat secure, then he set off exploring.

It was a great little beach: a stream tumbling through the bracken; a whole tree washed ashore and bleached bone-white by years of frost and sun; the desiccated remains of a heron.

He climbed some rocks to look around. A short distance further on, a herd of Highland cattle swished their tails in a rough pasture. They were gentle creatures with tremendous horns. Two had wandered down to the loch for a drink. The bright water dribbled from their muzzles.

No one was watching, so after Harry had circled the beach a second time, and struggled through bracken above head-height, and skimmed stones across the loch, he pulled off his trousers and waded out. The water felt lovely. First he went knee-deep, then past knee-deep until, bending to peer at his toes, he let the bottom of his T-shirt trail in the water. It felt horrible, so he pulled it off and threw it up the beach. Next thing, he was swimming.

The water had a peaty taste. After a while he stood, chest-deep, and looked all round.

Half a mile distant, the shaggy trees of Lady Island rose from the loch. Harry wondered if he could swim that far. Not right then, not alone. Boys drowned. But with someone rowing alongside. . . His stomach quaked, it was scary. All that dark water beneath him.

He returned to the beach and sat on a rock, letting his shoulders dry in the hot sun. Dragonflies darted above the stream. A family of mallard landed on the loch with a splash. His eyes kept returning to the island.

"Ha-rry!" His name drifted across the water.

He got dressed in the sand-free boat and a few minutes later was approaching the landing stage.

"Auntie Florrie?"

His wet hair and sodden underpants on the deck announced what he had been doing.

"Did I tell you not to swim straight after your lunch?"

"It was dead shallow."

He gripped the side of the speedboat. Nutty and Lord Goole were surrounded by plugs and leads and pieces of oily machinery.

Harry spoke past their heads. "If you or somebody come with me in the boat, can I swim out to the island?"

"All that way?" Auntie Florrie raised her eyes. "It's too far, Harry."

"No it's not. Please!" he said. "It would be great. Something to remember."

Lord Goole straightened. "I used to swim out there when I was a lad. Year or two older than you, mind."

"See," Harry said. "And if you're there with the boat and something for me to hang on to, I *can't* come to any harm, can I?"

She was unsure and looked round but Aunt Bridget was surveying Lady Island through the binoculars.

Fingers had stripped to his saggy vest, baring his scrawny arms to the sun. "Go on, Florrie, I'll come with you. You can see he's got his 'eart set on it."

"All right." She pointed at his wet pants. "Are you going to wear those again?"

"I've got my swimming shorts in the Land Rover."

"Go on then. I was fancying a little jaunt on the water anyway."

364

"We'll follow," Aunt Bridget said. "You game, Huggy?"

"Oh, ja!"

"Me too," said Dot.

Max sat in the shade, languidly fanning himself with a paper plate.

Angel wandered from place to place, munching the leftovers and recording details with a camera. He was planning a new Turner and maybe a couple of McCullochs. "This way, laddie." He tapped Harry on the shoulder. "Run your fingers through your hair, mess it up a little. That's grand." The camera clicked, and clicked again. "On ye go."

Harry climbed into the Land Rover. His shorts had fallen to the floor. He shook out the dust and sheep droppings. The shorts were blue with a pattern of stars like the Australian flag. He pulled them on and draped his clothes over a gorse bush to dry in the sun. The heat of the afternoon brought out the pineapple scent of the blossom.

Auntie Florrie and Fingers were drifting a few metres offshore. She had tied a line to the seat, ready to throw if Harry got into difficulties.

"Are you ready then?"

He padded to the edge of the splintery boards.

"Good to have a spirited lad around the place again." Lord Goole was watching. "You and Mike being such pals, you'll have to come up for a holiday some time. Give him a bit of young company. You can climb Beinn Ruadh over there. He'll show you that cave of his where he seems to spend half his time." He pointed. "In the King's Crag there, just above the wood. Can't see it from here."

"Like that, Harry?" Aunt Bridget said.

"It would be great," he said.

"Good. I'll put it to Mike." Lord Goole nodded. "Take care now. Give us a wave when you reach the island."

"How deep is it?"

"Loch's shallower this end. Deepest part you'll be swimming's about, say, seven metres? Watch out for rocks when you get close to the island."

"How deep in the middle?" He looked to where the mountain slopes came plunging down into the water.

"Ninety-four metres, that's what they tell me."

Really scary. Harry gripped the edge of the stage with his toes. He took a deep breath, set his teeth and launched himself into the loch.

It was great! Once he had got into his stroke, and come to terms with the beasts and other perils he imagined lurking in the black water beneath him, Harry loved it. A real challenge with a whiff of danger about it.

He duck-dived to about two metres. Abruptly the temperature dropped. On the surface it was bright and warm. Down there he felt a chill clutch of death and drowning, darkness on all sides. He clawed his way back to the sunshine.

The dive had given him a fright and he trod water.

"All right, darling?" Auntie Florrie stopped rowing. "Do you want the rope?"

"No, I'm fine." He kicked off again.

What wind there was blew up the loch, funnelling between the mountains. Tiny waves splashed in his face. Little by little the island drew nearer. Harry realized that he was going to make it – and he hadn't hung on to the boat for a rest, not once.

Suddenly a big, pale-coloured rock appeared, just below the surface. Too late to stop, he hit it hard and scraped the heel of his hand. Involuntarily he gasped and inhaled water. It started a bout of coughing. He doubled up. His legs went down. Fingers threw the rope. Harry was about to grab it then realized he could stand. Whooping for air and stuff coming down his nose, he leaned against the boulder.

"Brilliant, Harry! What a swimmer!" Auntie Florrie pulled into the shallows and clambered ashore.

Fingers tied the rope to a projecting branch.

The spasm passed. Harry looked back at the landing stage and waved. Distant figures waved back. Still coughing, he made his way up from the water.

They were on Lady Island.

In some ways a better name would have been Dog Island, for it was shaped like a dog's skull with its nose pointing down the loch; in addition there was a dogs' cemetery on the island where generations of Rattrays had buried their beloved pets. It could equally well have been called Bushy Island, for trees and scrub grew right to the shore, overhanging the water in some places. It was big enough – roughly two hundred metres long and a hundred metres wide – to contain many species: oak, rowan, birch, sycamore, crab apple, as well as several conifers. The tallest tree of all, a tremendous Scots pine with its roots anchored firmly in the topmost rocks, contained an osprey's nest. Loch na h-Iolaire, Harry thought, the loch of the eagle.

He looked back across the water to where the oak wood clung to the mountainside. Above it towered the mighty King's Crag. Sharp as a knife, a run of scree cut a gash through the trees. Harry was turning away when a black spot in the sunlit crag caught his attention. He stared and realized this must be the cave Lord Goole had spoken about. Mike's cave, ten or twenty metres above the top of the wood. If there was time when they got back, he decided, he would climb up and examine it.

But now, on Lady Island, they found their way blocked by the thick vegetation. Beneath the trees it might be more open, but here, where sunlight streamed in from the loch, they were confronted by a wall of leaves. They moved along the shore. Brambles, gorse and wild briar formed a barrier as impenetrable as coils of barbed wire.

"'Ere's a place." Fingers was in the lead. "If we climb over these rocks."

But Harry couldn't climb over the rocks. His feet were bare and there were thorns underfoot. Wearing only his swimming shorts, he would have been scratched bloody. "You two go on," he said. "I'll swim round till I find a better spot."

"You will do no such thing," Auntie Florrie said.

"But I want—"

"I know what you want." She kicked off her shoes. "Here, put those on."

"But what about—"

"I'll wait in the boat. Just sitting there in the sunshine, it'll be lovely. I'll see the island later."

Harry examined the shoes. They were red with a half heel and a little blue bow. "I can't wear these!" he said.

"Don't be silly, they're just something to protect your feet. We're not going to start calling you Mary."

They fitted quite well but Harry felt very peculiar, climbing over rocks in the Scottish Highlands, wearing nothing but his swimming shorts and a pair of his auntie's shoes.

Embarrassment was soon forgotten. This was an adventure.

By treading carefully and picking the brambles aside with the tips of his fingers, he managed to wriggle past the most vicious thorns. Not all, however, and soon his legs and sides were criss-crossed by scratches. They stung, and when Harry looked he saw two drops of blood running down his skin. He rubbed them off with the side of his hand and licked it clean. His blood tasted like iron.

Midges bit behind his ears. A horsefly landed on his arm. He slapped it sharply and the crumpled insect dropped to the ground.

Beneath the trees the way was clearer. There were ferns underfoot. Dappled sunlight shone through the leaves.

"Do you think there'll be snakes?" Harry tramped at Fingers' side.

"Oh, shut up!" Fingers said. "They give me the willies."

"I 'spect there will be," Harry said confidently. "Good swimmers aren't they? Prob'ly hundreds. Come across to the island where it's safer." He froze. "What's that?"

"What? Where?"

"There, look!" he pointed. "Oh, no, it's just a branch."

Fingers batted him across the shoulder.

There was no sign of the summer house. Ahead of them a series of small cliffs led to the highest point of the island. There was less vegetation here and they zig-zagged to the top.

Harry was a few paces in front and stopped in astonishment. Beneath him lay a scene of devastation. In the recent past a hurricane had roared up Loch na h-Iolaire. The sheltered trees had withstood it, but those before them, all the way to the dog's nose, had stood full in the path of the wind. Larch and spruce had been snapped clean off. Oak and sycamore had been torn from the ground and lay on their sides with roots exposed. They were not dead, for leafy branches grew on and seedlings sprouted about the shattered orange stumps of the parent trees.

Close to the shore, one of the first objects the wind had struck, lay the summer house – or what little remained of it. It was almost completely buried.

Chapter 32
The Stove and
the Speedboat

"**A**hoy, me hearties!"

Harry looked back at the loch. Aunt Bridget, rowing easily and feathering the oars as she had done when she rowed for the Oxford ladies, was approaching the island. In the boat with her were Dot and Huggy.

"Aye, there, Jim 'Awkins!" Aunt Bridget rested on her oars and squinted against the sun. "Oo's that ragged ol' mutineer alongside ye?"

"Ben Gunn," he shouted back. "Belay there, Long John, lest you want a broadside."

"Surrender," she cried, "or I'll 'ang the pair o' ye from yon pine tree. Leave ye to swing like tassels till the birds peck out your eyes an' your bones rot in the sun."

"Surrender? Never!" Harry loved it when Aunt Bridget played these games. He pointed an imaginary blunderbuss. "Bang! Bang!"

A scream, as if she had been shot, came from the boat.

"'Ere." Fingers was lost. "You gone doolally? What you all talkin' about?"

"*Treasure Island*." Harry returned to the present and shouted again. "Round the other side." He swung his arm in a wide arc and pointed.

They put their heads together. Dot waved back. "See you there."

Aunt Bridget turned the boat towards the dog's nose. Her sister pulled out from the island to meet them. They rowed on together.

The windswept summit of the island was covered with grass and wildflowers. Thyme and tormentil grew in crevices of the rocks. Harry's feet crunched on fish bones. He saw half a spine, some shrivelled heads and tails. Thirty metres overhead, the osprey's nest was black against the sky.

He longed to see an eagle. A dozen times since they set out that morning he had scanned the sky and looked again now. There were gulls high in the blue, swallows swooping for summer flies, ravens cawing about the great King's Crag – but no glimpse of the majestic bird he was seeking.

It would have been fun to descend from the summit in a series of jumps but Auntie Florrie's shoes made it impossible. Carefully he clambered down the rocks. Fallen trees and snapped-off branches were equally difficult to negotiate, but Harry had collected so many scratches that a few more made little difference. All the same, progress was slow.

Fifty metres from the summer house a small jetty had been built to assist the ladies in their long dresses when they came ashore to take tea. It was L-shaped and built of stone with a flight of steps leading down to the water, quite different from the wooden landing stage by the boathouse. For decades, perhaps the best part of a century, it had been crumbling, but enough remained to make it the best place to land on the island.

As the two boats drifted in, Huggy looked over the side. "Oh, my vord! The vater very deep. Dot, be careful, ve not vant you fall in."

"I can swim," Dot said cheerfully and leaped to the steps like a squirrel.

Aunt Bridget and Auntie Florrie threw up mooring lines which she wrapped round a rotted post, and a couple of minutes later, by good luck more than good management, all four were safely ashore.

Not long afterwards, Harry and Fingers appeared amid the chaos of fallen trees which covered that end of the island. Harry negotiated some roots, descended from a trunk, and came towards them through scrub and weeds.

"Oh, my goodness!" Auntie Florrie stood shoeless on the jetty. "Darling, look at you. We'll have to put some cream on those scratches. And insect bites. Oh, you poor boy."

Huggy said, "There von now. Stand still." She crept round and slapped it from his back. "Nasty ugly things, I hate them. And the little vons – they drive me crazy."

Even though his skin was aflame, Harry was determined not to make a fuss. "I'm fine."

"Course you are," Aunt Bridget said in the businesslike tone which was her highest form of approval. "Incidentally, I love the shoes."

"Don't," Harry said. "Just don't."

A short distance away, a group of small gravestones had survived the onslaught. He crossed to look:

Chancer, he read, *a faithful friend: 1838–1851. Djeilas, the beautiful. Finn . . . Meg . . . Jock.*

It was the dogs' graveyard. A few stones had fallen. Harry strained his muscles and heaved one upright. Beneath lay an ants' nest. The tiny insects swarmed hither and thither. A thousand eggs lay exposed. The ants began to pick them up and carry them underground to safety. This was *their* treasure. Carefully, grimacing to think how many he must kill in the process, Harry lowered the stone into place. It was too heavy and fell with a thud. He returned to the others.

"The dogs?" Aunt Bridget had been watching.

"Yeah."

"That's nice. Who's to say they haven't got their own little heaven." She turned to face the summer house.

It had been a fine building, wood and stone with a red pantile roof, unusual in the Highlands. It stood on a man-made knoll thirty metres from the water to protect it from winter floods. Occasional blossoms and a few tattered twigs revealed that roses and azaleas had been planted on three sides. It was easy to imagine how the castle ladies must have enjoyed coming here, sometimes perhaps with an easel and watercolours to paint the pretty building and the view down the loch.

Now it was a ruin. Perhaps the storm had ripped off the roof, perhaps it had been crushed by falling trees. Pantiles lay scattered around; a shard of glass winked in a ray of sunshine; fragments of paint – red, yellow, blue – adhered to an occasional timber. On top of all lay a fallen tree, its branches thicker than a man's thigh, leafy and rustling in the summer airs.

"Lady Goole did say the *castle* at half past three?" Auntie Florrie said. "I hope she didn't mean here."

Harry laughed, but Aunt Bridget glanced at her watch. "Which doesn't give us much time."

Dot was surprised. "I thought this was just a recce."

374

"Well it is, we didn't expect to be out here at all."

"Fings goin' our way for a change." Fingers clawed his bites.

"But since we are here —" Aunt Bridget looked over the top of her glasses. "Who knows, we might be only five minutes away—"

"From Eddie Carver's treasure!" cried Auntie Florrie.

"Well then, what are we all hanging around for?"

But Harry wasn't hanging around. He tumbled the shoes back into Auntie Florrie's arms and clambered barefoot into the branches of the tree. Two trees, in fact, and twigs of a third, all mixed up together. It was awkward, for branches which should have been horizontal were now vertical. All the angles were wrong. Thin and agile, he squeezed between, climbed up a bit, dropped down, and at length found himself standing on what remained of the floor of the summer house.

Dot had slipped through the branches as neatly as a sparrow and was there before him. "Fair old mess," she said. "Where do we go from here?"

The floor had been a work of art, an intricate pattern of red and gold hardwoods, set in a Celtic key pattern. It had long been in a state of decay. The beautiful blocks were stained with mould and slime, mostly dry at the moment. Creeping moss formed a carpet. But little remained, for the falling tree which demolished the upper part of the summer house had smashed on through the floor into the space beneath. Incongruously, right in the middle and gripped by branches, the stove had survived. It was an ornate, pot-bellied affair, surrounded by a hearth. Once it had been handsome but now it was being eaten away by orange rust.

All was confusion. Harry lay on his belly and peered down into the blackness under the floor. Shafts of sunshine and the brilliance of the afternoon made it impossible for his eyes to adjust. His imagination made up for it: every corner, every shadow, contained a bag, a box, a heap, a King Solomon's chest of treasure. He lowered his legs and prepared to wriggle past a thick branch into the darkness.

Abruptly he froze. What was that he had said so jauntily about snakes? There really were vipers in Scotland. He had seen snake-pits in films: David Attenborough, *Raiders of the Lost Ark*. And what else might be down there in the centuries-old blackness? And him in his bare feet. He pulled his legs back.

Aunt Bridget appeared among the branches and climbed down to join them. "What a tangle! Nothing so far, I take it." She looked into the hole from different angles. "On you go then, Harry. Thought you'd be down there already, sniffing round like a young badger."

Harry did not want to appear timid. "I'm not going down there," he declared boldly. "Might be snakes an' things."

"You're scared!"

"No I'm not," he said. "I'm sensible."

"Ah, *discretion is the better part of valour*. Quite right. Well, I'll tell you what. I'll do a deal with you. If you get bitten by a snake, I'll buy you a new bike."

"That's not much use," he said. "I'll be dead. That's a pretty safe bet."

"All right. Then I'll get you the best coffin money can buy. Can't say fairer than that."

He laughed.

"But there simply *aren't* any snakes down there," she said.

"They're frightened of you, anyway, and no one's died from an adder bite for decades. So are you going, or do you want Dot and me to have all the fun?"

Harry hesitated. "All right then. But a mountain bike. That red one in the Dawes catalogue."

"Wouldn't dream of anything else," she said.

A second time he lowered his legs into the hole – but it was scary! He rested a foot on the branch that had destroyed the floor, and stretched down into the darkness. The space was over a metre deep. His toes came to rest on something squishy. Mud? A dead frog? As the foot took his weight he felt something sharp beneath. A twig? Bones? A diamond brooch?

Harry stood in the space beneath the floor. It was chill, the dank wetness of a grave. His head and shoulders remained in daylight.

"Come on then." Aunt Bridget was getting impatient. "Stop faffing about. We haven't got all day."

"Goo' luck." Fingers looked through the leaves like a pixie who smoked too many fags. "It's there, take my word for it. Not jus' goosebumps now, I got the shivers."

"Hear that?" Aunt Bridget said. "What more do you want? Now are you *going*?"

He ducked beneath what remained of the floor and squeezed past the branch. In the confined space the reek of wet earth was strong. And now that he was out of the sunlight his eyes began to adjust to the gloom.

The summer house had been built on a stone foundation, banked up outside with tons of earth. Little by little it was collapsing: stones lay at his feet, the earth had spilled through. It was hard to move around for the space was criss-crossed by broken joists, rotted and worm-eaten. Slabs of flooring had fallen through, in places with the parquet still attached, and made some parts inaccessible. Right in the middle a stone structure, a metre or so square, supported the heavy stove above.

Harry stared around. A short distance away a pale object hung from one of the beams. He saw another. Was the treasure suspended in bags, he wondered, to keep it from the ground, to keep the rolls of banknotes dry? He squeezed past a jagged timber and added a scratch to his ribs. A subdued hum came from the nearer shape. Harry leaned forward. Things were crawling on the surface. They were wasps' nests. *Not* to be disturbed. He backed away.

Something else, different from the rocks and earth, gleamed in a corner. It was fungus, gross swellings and brackets like those that grow on trees.

Dot joined him. For ten minutes they crawled from end to end and side to side, heaving aside planks and those sections of collapsed flooring that were not too heavy.

The treasure was not there.

Streaked with dirt and cobwebs, Harry emerged into the daylight.

"Blimey! Look at him!" Fingers had joined them. "*Night o' the Living Dead*. Naked an' all."

"I'm not naked." Harry hitched up his swimming shorts and clambered from the hole.

"Nope, nothing." Dot bounced up and sat on the edge, swinging her legs. "Not that we can see, anyway. Need torches. Crowbar or something to shift the heavy bits. Even then," a huge spider crawled out of her blouse and she flicked it away, "I wouldn't count on it."

"Me neither." Aunt Bridget was looking at what remained of the floor. "Parquet like this, no way Eddie could have lifted it and put it back."

"Perhaps there was a hole already." Auntie Florrie stood on a branch. "Maybe they came in from the side."

"That's what I was wondering." Aunt Bridget turned to Huggy and Dot. "I don't like to ask this, but is there any chance you two would be absolute angels and stay on here when we go back? Give the place a thorough going-over. Make a bit of a clearance before we come back tonight with the saws and crowbars and everything. I'd stay myself but – well, I can't."

Dot did not want to remain on the midge-infested island, she wanted to go to the castle for tea, then drive back to the *Highlandman* for a shower and cocktails. "Course we'll stay, Bridget, love," she said cheerfully.

"Absolutely," Huggy boomed. "Ve become millionaires. Dot and me, ve run off to Monte Carlo, ja? Find ourself a pair of so-handsome boy-toys."

"You *are* good," Aunt Bridget said. "Can't promise the toy-boys, but we'll bring you a gourmet supper. About one o'clock? Survive till then?"

Harry broke in. "But the diary says it's here. If it's not under the floor, where is it? D'you think someone's got here before us?"

"It's always possible," Aunt Bridget said. "But I don't think so. They'd have left some trace. There's nobody been here for ages. And Priestly's still on the trail. And Fingers has got his famous collywobbles. No, I'm pretty sure it's still here."

"Well where?"

"I don't know. But I've got an idea."

He stared at her with intense blue eyes. "What is it then?"

"You know as much as I do."

He gazed all round. A horsefly landed on his chest, another on his leg. He slapped them dead. "I don't know."

"Come on, Harry. You're an intelligent boy. You've got a young brain. Keep looking – not at *me*! What can you see? Think!"

So Harry looked, and scratched his bites, and *thought*. "I still don't know," he said.

"You've *been* down there," Aunt Bridget said. "What's that behind you?"

An enlightened look spread over some other faces.

Harry turned. There was nothing behind him. Just the ruins of the summer house . . . and branches . . . and the old stove . . . and. . .

"The stove?"

"Go on."

"It's in the stove!" He clambered across. The fat iron stove was trapped in the fork of enormous branches. Harry pulled off the rust-red lid. "It's empty."

"Of course it's empty. What do you expect."

"But I thought you –" His eyes fell to the hearth. Aunt Bridget or someone had scraped back the dirt and twigs. The hearth was formed by two flagstones of red granite. "Under the hearth!" he cried.

"Worth a look, don't you think?" she said.

The stove had four stubby, ornate legs. Two rested on one slab, two on the other.

"Eddie and Dart could have pushed it across," he said.

"If they were strong."

"He was built like a bull, Eddie Carver. Isn't that what you said, Auntie Florrie?"

"And Dart. Powerful men."

"To push people into them egg barrels," Fingers said.

Harry grimaced. He rubbed his fingers over the flagstones and saw scratch marks.

"Who'd notice?" Aunt Bridget said. "Covered up the way they were with dirt and leaves."

Harry fell to his knees and looked beneath the floor. The stove and granite hearth were heavy. The pillar, if that's what it should be called, upon which they rested, was a box-like structure, four short walls built in a square. "D'you think it's hollow?"

"I should think so, don't you? Awfully thick to be solid stone. Built later."

"How do you know that?"

"Well look at the stove."

Harry did. "What about it?"

"Cast-iron stove like that, fancy legs, all those curlicues, pure Victorian. Put in to give the ladies a bit of comfort. Meant they could come out any time, not just the height of summer, and keep nice and cosy. Must have been lovely: see the daffodils, and the snow, and the autumn colours."

But Harry wasn't listening. He slid back into the hole and slapped his hand on the dirty pillar. "So d'you mean it's right in here – Eddie Carver's treasure?"

"Could be. Unless you have a better idea."

Without tools there was no way of breaking through. Harry emerged. The thirty-centimetre branches that gripped the stove were quite immoveable. "So is the plan that we come back tonight and—"

The roar of a powerful engine disturbed the peace of the loch — and immediately ceased. Its echo returned from the hillsides. A cloud of blue smoke was visible above the end of the island.

"Can I borrow your shoes again?" Harry climbed out through the trees and pulled them on. In two minutes he had scrambled round the shore to a spot from where he could see the boathouse and landing stage.

Nutty and Lord Goole were busy in the speedboat. Another cloud of blue smoke erupted and a moment later the roar of the engine reached him across the water. This time it lasted longer, five seconds at least.

"Terrific!" Auntie Florrie joined him. She had borrowed Huggy's size twelves. They swapped. The shoes were like canoes on his feet. Harry felt that with a bit of branch he could have paddled back across the loch in them.

Twice more the engine fired then settled to an irregular roar. Nutty ducked beneath the gunwale. The note became smoother.

"Will you listen to that," Auntie Florrie said. "Rolls-Royce. Still missing, mind, but beautiful! Takes me right back to the racing pits."

Over at the landing stage there was movement. Nutty had reappeared. A little swirl of water appeared at the speedboat's stern. Slowly it moved out into the loch. For a minute Nutty treated it gently, then the engine note picked up. The swirl became foam. The stern dug deeper. The bow lifted.

"A genius, that's what Nutty is," Auntie Florrie said. "A genius! Ten years in the boatshed and look at that."

The speedboat was beginning to fly. Nutty took it in sweeping curves, throwing up fans of water. It passed out of sight behind the island then reappeared, bows high, in a long straight run up the side of the loch.

"How fast will it go?" Harry asked.

"No idea. Hundred? Hundred and twenty? But he won't take it anywhere near that today. Needs stripping down first."

"Lord Goole's son was doing three hundred when he was killed."

"But that wasn't a normal boat, hardly even looked like a boat. It was built for one purpose only, to break the water-speed record. Hit that log and exploded into a million pieces."

Lord Goole saw them at the nose of the island. He raised a hand and called but his voice was lost in the noise of the engine.

Then Harry's prayers were answered. Nutty pulled back the throttle, turned the boat in a big circle and motored to the crumbling stone jetty.

Lord Goole threw up a rope and clambered ashore. "What a mess." He surveyed the tangle of trees. "Timber merchants tell me the wood's not worth the cost of getting it out, only answer's to burn it all and replant. The Forestry would come in and clear it up, of course, but I don't want them. They're after me to let them plant the hillsides, turn the place into a desert with all those damned Sitka spruces." He treated Auntie Florrie to his toothy smile. "Who'd be a landowner? No idea where I can put my hands on a couple of million, I suppose?"

Harry gasped but it was a chance remark. Lord Goole had no idea what they were doing on his island.

"Ah, well." His long face brightened. "All aboard the *Skylark*. Who's next?" He stood aside. "Come on, young 'un, you take my place. Then the lady."

Harry did not need a second invitation. He kicked off Huggy's shoes and stepped aboard. Lord Goole threw down the mooring rope.

"Better keep away from the fishermen," he told Nutty. "Get a bit narky. Come here for a bit o' peace, not to have speedboats taking their noses off. He rubbed his own rubbery nose. "Have a bit too much peace sometimes, I think."

"Hear, hear," Auntie Florrie said. "Come and join the others. I'm Florrie, by the way. Harry's other auntie."

"Florrie Barton?" Lord Goole was startled. "Not *the* Florrie Barton?"

"Oh, you say all the right things."

"But you were absolutely David's number-one hero. When he was a boy he had a big signed poster of you up on his wall."

"And I haven't changed a bit," she said. "Dishy as ever. But that's all history. Come and meet Dot and Huggy. And Fingers. Excuse his handshake. He used to look after crocodiles at the zoo, you know, feeding them by hand."

Lying blithely, she led the way towards the elderly quartet climbing down through the branches.

"She's some girl, your Auntie Florrie." Nutty went astern from the mooring and turned the speedboat to face the loch. "Might be a bit jumpy," he warned. "Engine's been fine-tuned. Haven't got the hang of it yet."

"It's great!" Harry said.

"Cuts out a bit an' all, just for a second but throws you forward, so get a good grip." He indicated a bar below the windshield.

Harry did as he was instructed and set his feet.

"Ready then?"

"Yeah."

The propeller churned, throwing up silt and weed. Bubbles slipped past. Nutty eased open the throttle. The boat picked up speed, beginning to bounce on the little waves that blew down the loch. Harry looked above the rim of the cockpit. The wind hit him in the face. Nutty went faster. The bows lifted. Water boiled white at the stern. A long wake spread behind them.

"Fantastic!" Harry shouted. The wind whipped his voice away. His eyes watered.

Wearing nothing but his swimming shorts, he began to feel cold. He ducked back into the cockpit and read the speedometer. Seventy knots! Nutty opened the throttle wider.

Headlong the red and white speedboat streaked down the loch.

Chapter 33

Night on Lady Island

It was Harry who spotted it.

They had left the castle in time to catch the hardware store in the village before it closed, and were on their way back to the *Highlandman* with a pickaxe, cold chisel and the rest – unusual purchases for elderly holidaymakers – when suddenly he shouted, "Stop!"

Auntie Florrie pulled in opposite the church and Harry jumped from the Land Rover.

"Just be a minute." He ran back down the road and peered round the corner of a brightly-painted guesthouse. A large sign, showing a prancing Highlander, a whisky bottle and a sprig of heather tied with a tartan ribbon, proclaimed that this was the *Scots Wha Hae*. A well-tended garden hid most of the car park from the road. Harry flitted to a spot from where he could see more clearly. He had been right. There, drawn back almost out of sight, stood a black Range Rover with security windows.

Perhaps there were many such cars. He jumped the stone wall and crept through bushes until he could see the number plate.

RIP 1!

Suddenly he was terrified. They were there! What everyone feared had come true. The Priestly gang had gone into the laptop; read the notepad; followed them up to Scotland. They knew everything: Gestapo Lil, Percy Priestly, Mad Ruby, GBH.

He looked round, expecting to be grabbed at any moment, then retreated through the bushes and raced back along the road.

The rest had gathered on the pavement.

"Well spotted, Harry!" Auntie Florrie hugged him tight and squashed her sticky red lips against his ear.

"Yeah." Unthinkingly, Fingers offered him a cigarette. "Might've saved the whole operation by that little bit o' detective work."

"So," Aunt Bridget said. "Before we set out tonight, we're going to need a bit of sabotage. All right, Nutty?"

"'Gainst that lot?" Nutty took Harry's cigarette and felt for matches. "My pleasure – an' they'll not even know anyone's bin there."

They resumed their seats and two minutes later were back at the *Highlandman*.

"Yes," the manageress told Auntie Florrie when she asked. "We did have a small group looking for rooms, but I'm afraid we couldn't accommodate them. We're always busy this time of year."

"They're people we know slightly," Auntie Florrie said. "A short ginger man."

"Yes, that sounds like them."

"A party of four."

"Let me see. Yes, there was the gentleman you mentioned; and a rather elegant blonde lady; and a small, foreign-looking woman."

"And one with a bolt through his neck." Max did a fleeting impression of Boris Karloff.

"I'm afraid I mustn't comment, but I know what you mean." The manageress smiled.

"Thank you, that's most helpful," said Auntie Florrie. "Actually, they're not people we *like* very much. If they should ask for us, could you possibly tell them we're not here."

"They did ask," said the manageress, "but I told them I was not in a position to say. We have eminent visitors from time to time and they expect privacy."

"What an excellent hotel this is," said Aunt Bridget. "Now I think we'll just go and freshen up. Then time for an aperitif. Dinner at seven-thirty?"

"The head waiter will show you the menu when you come down."

"Two of us won't be in this evening." Aunt Bridget explained the absence of Huggy and Dot. "Naturalists, you know. Mad keen photographers. Trying to get some dusk shots. Infrared. Badgers and barn owls, I think. Would it be too much trouble to make up a supper for them? Something tasty. Maybe with a little drop of wine?"

"Not in the least. I'll speak to the chef. We'll have it ready by the time you've finished dinner."

"You're very kind."

Harry stood at her shoulder, amazed by the ease and grace with which his aunts told lies.

For a long time he stood beneath the shower and let the water take the sting out of his inflamed bites and scratches. Afterwards, wrapped in a huge *Highlandman* towel, he lay on his four-poster bed and thought about the night ahead. It was hard to stay awake, but at seven o'clock, dressed in clean clothes and smelling of Savlon, he joined the rest in the bar. While they, with a view to the night ahead, sipped tiny gins and sherries, he drank two glasses of an unbelievably delicious non-alcoholic cocktail which the barman invented specially for him.

"Is it good?" asked Auntie Florrie.

"Fa'tastic!" he said, his mouth packed with crisps.

"You'll spoil your dinner."

"Mo I wo't," Harry said decisively.

Beyond the windows the moors turned red with evening. He blinked, weary after his energetic day and little sleep the night before. Aunt Bridget was watching him. Doubtless she was going to suggest an early night. He would have to put her right on that. Bed would be welcome, but if anyone thought he was going to miss out on whatever took place on Lady Island, they were out of their tiny minds. Even supposing he had to run the whole nine miles and swim across by night, Harry planned to be *there*.

To his surprise there was little argument.

Darkness arrived.

At half past nine Harry set out with Nutty, Fingers and Aunt Bridget to immobilize the Range Rover outside the *Scots Wha Hae*. Parked in a corner behind trees, as it was, nothing would have been easier: a pointed knife, four quick stabs. But Nutty would have none of it.

"Crude that, man," he said to Fingers. "Soon's they saw that, they'd kna' ye're on to them. Need to be a bit more subtle, like. Here, pick the lock an' let's see the engine."

So while Harry kept a lookout and Aunt Bridget stood

ready to create a diversion should anyone appear in the doorway, Fingers unlocked the driver's door and Nutty threw up the bonnet.

"Easy-peasy wi' diesels," he said, loosening the union coupling that connected the fuel pipe to the engine. "All ye've got to do's let a bit run out. Let's have the torch over here." For a few seconds the bright diesel splashed to the gravel. The pipe emptied. Nutty wiped off the drips and reconnected it. "There y'are. That's an air lock in the system. Rev it from now till doomsday, it'll never start. Need somebody that kna's what they're doin'." He checked the joint, rubbed it round with a handful of waste and slipped the spanner back into his pocket. Softly he shut the bonnet. Fingers locked the door and they crept away. From start to finish, the operation had taken less than three minutes.

"When we get back," Aunt Bridget said as they walked through the quiet village, "I am going to buy you a cigar and the biggest single malt you ever saw."

Nutty shook his head. "Thanks, but there's highlights from a Newcastle–Arsenal match. I'll make a cup o' tea in me room. Keep us from worryin' what ye're all gettin' up to down at that lake."

"Loch," Harry said again.

"Whatever. An' mind ye dinna gan in that speedboat, there's summat not right. She's frisky."

They hid the Land Rover in a disused and overgrown quarry and walked the last half mile to the landing stage. There were four of them: Auntie Florrie, Aunt Bridget, Fingers and Harry. On this expedition the talents of Max and Angel were less likely to be needed, and there had to be room for Dot and

Huggy on the way back, not to mention the piles of loot they hoped to be carrying.

Clouds had covered the sky in the early evening but now they were parting. As the little group descended, all carrying tools, a full moon appeared and cast a dagger of light across the loch. The waves sparkled. Harry stopped to look. The soft, incessant roar of the river rose on the air. Apart from this all seemed silent. But as he listened closely, he realized that all about him, scarcely audible, tiny rustles came from the heather as the night creatures went about their business.

We're night creatures going about our business too, Harry thought, and ran to catch up with the others.

There were four boats at the landing stage, all securely chained and padlocked. Fingers released the nearest while Harry picked the lock of the boathouse and returned with a pair of oars. Aunt Bridget, meanwhile, stepped aboard and Auntie Florrie passed down the pickaxe, mallet and chisel, handpick, crowbar, spade, saw, paraffin lamp, canvas bags, torches and everything else they might possibly need, which they had purchased at the hardware store. Iron chinked against iron.

"Careful!" Fingers said.

The boat began to drift out. Harry held it alongside and was the last to climb aboard.

Aunt Bridget rowed. It was magical out on the moonlit loch. Harry trailed his fingers in the water. This, he thought, was what even the violent Eddie Carver had loved, though he had been out there for a very different reason. As they were themselves. He had been taking the proceeds of crime to its hiding place on the island. They planned to bring it away.

They drew close. A heron, the second he had seen that day, rose from the shallows and flapped away on ghostly, silent wings. They rounded the dog's nose, and all too soon were approaching the crumbling jetty.

Huggy and Dot were there to meet them.

"No luck," Dot whispered at once. "We pulled all the bits of floor out, searched everywhere."

"Didn't get into that part under the fireplace though?" Aunt Bridget said.

"Tried but we couldn't."

"Fingers crossed then. If it's not there, I don't know where to start digging."

Dot caught the mooring rope, tied a bowline and dropped it over the rotting post.

"You bring the tools?" Huggy said.

Harry passed them up.

"And food? I ravishing!" She bared her tombstone teeth in the moonlight. "You vatch out, Harry. I so hungry I eat you."

"Keep him for afters." Auntie Florrie handed up the packed suppers. "Chef made them specially. Smell good."

"Oh, ja!" Huggy retreated to the tree which covered the summer house and tore open the wrapping. "You right. Is *very* good."

They mounted the steps and Aunt Bridget distributed the torches.

"Right then," she said. "Let the dog see the rabbit. Harry, bring the crowbar. Never mind the other stuff for now." Carrying the handpick, she gripped a branch with her lean hand and climbed into the tree.

"I've got the lantern." Auntie Florrie, also, was being

businesslike. "Fingers, can I borrow your matches?" She followed her sister into the branches.

"I come in five minute." Huggy brandished the bushman saw. "Vhen I get my strength back."

Harry joined his aunts on what remained of the summer house and looked down into the space beneath his feet. Dot and Huggy had smashed the slabs of floor into smaller pieces and dragged them aside. A rough and ready clearance had been made round the box-shaped column that supported the fireplace, and the stove, and the fallen tree above it.

Aunt Bridget climbed down and shone her torch on the dirty stones. She raked the handpick along the mortar. The surface crumbled. It was harder within, but the lime and sand they used in the old days was not as hard as cement.

"Well, here goes." She balanced the torch on a ledge, spat on her palms like a labourer, and crouched to the task.

Scrape-scrape! Pick-pick! Aunt Bridget worked with her customary energy. Drifts of mortar fell about her shoes and filled the space with lime dust.

The torch did not give enough light, shadows got in the way, so Auntie Florrie busied herself with the lamp. A stink of paraffin filled the enclosed space. A match flared. She touched it to the wick and replaced the glass funnel. After a little adjustment, the light shone clear and golden. In its glow the rubble and debris, plunging branches and earnest figures, took on the dramatic appearance of a film set.

"That's better," Aunt Bridget said.

"See all right if I stand it here under the overhang?" Auntie Florrie straightened some worm-eaten timbers and set the lamp on top.

"That's fine."

"Don't want to advertise we're here."

Harry said, "Can't see us from the landing stage. It faces the far side of the island."

"You're quite right." Aunt Bridget chipped and raked away at the mortar. "But there's no point taking *chances*." She tugged at a pebble. "The less anybody knows the *better*."

The groove deepened. She tackled a single, irregular stone: along the bottom, up the side and along the top.

Fingers stood above them. "My turn, let me 'ave a go," he said after a while. "No point wearin' yourself out."

"Right, thanks." Aunt Bridget looked up. Her face shone with sweat. She rubbed her eyes with a wrist.

Fingers took her place.

At their backs, Huggy had commenced cutting a passage through the tree. The razor-sharp teeth of the bushman saw sliced through twenty and thirty-centimetre branches like butter. One after another, she hauled them aside.

Soon the stone they were working on stood clear of its neighbours. A black cavity, more than half a hand deep, ran all the way round.

Fingers stood back. "Give it a go wi' the ol' crowbar now? What d'you think? Who wants the honours?"

"Why don't you?" Aunt Bridget passed it down.

Fingers jammed the tip between the stones and pulled. An edge crumbled. He set his feet and *heaved*. The heavy stone seemed immovable.

"Mebbe it's solid right through," he said.

"Or maybe you von veak man." Huggy squeezed through the gap she was making. "Come on up." She flapped a hand the size of a tennis racket.

As Fingers started to climb, she caught him by a wrist and

lifted him the way a mother lifts a toddler. "Right." She jumped down, making the earth shake. "This stone here, ja?"

The crowbar, which had been a heavy tool in Fingers' hands, seemed suddenly half the size. Wielding it as lightly as a cook wields a ladle, she inserted the angled tip and tugged. The mortar cracked. The stone shifted. She put the crowbar in the other side. The stone scraped back and slid out half a centimetre.

Harry's heart was in his mouth.

Huggy worked the stone to and fro. Little by little it protruded from those which surrounded it until at last she was able to lay the crowbar aside and grasp it with her powerful fingers.

"Ready?"

"Soon as you like, Huggy."

Her forearms knotted, her shoulders bulged, she frowned with effort. With a scratch and a scrape the heavy stone slid out. A black hole appeared in the trunking. Huggy threw the stone aside.

She looked round for the torch. "You vant I explore?"

"Of course," Aunt Bridget said. Then, "No, let Harry."

"Oh, ja! He discover."

She made room and Harry climbed down. But after his earlier fright about snakes, he wasn't putting his hand into that hole straight away. He shone the torch and peered.

All was dark. Then he saw something at an angle – a stick. And something smooth and oval, several of them – water-worn stones. His heart sank. Where were the mounds of gold and diamond necklaces he had dreamed about?

"Nothing." He shook his head.

"Empty?"

"Just some stones and bits of stick."

At least it was nothing to be frightened about. He reached through, first to the elbow, then to the shoulder, and felt around. A stone lay beneath his hand, flattish and cold. He gripped an end and drew it out.

"Let me see that." Aunt Bridget reached down.

"It's just a stone off the shore."

"All the same."

He passed it up.

Aunt Bridget examined it. "Are there many of them?"

"Yeah, it's quite full up."

"I wonder." Her glasses reflected the lamplight. "Why would anyone bother to carry stones from the loch and dump them in there?"

Harry shrugged. "To make it stronger."

"Not necessarily. And you said sticks."

"And bits of branch."

"Let's see."

He raked around and pulled one out. It was twice as thick as his finger and about fifty centimetres long. The bark had gone and it was smooth to the touch. Years of sun had bleached it so white that it gleamed in the light. Like the stones, it had come from the shore.

"Well, this certainly doesn't make it any stronger." Thoughtfully, Aunt Bridget ran her thumb over the stub of a broken-off twig. "Let's look a bit further."

"Do you still think it might be –" Harry let the words hang.

"Who knows. OK, Huggy?"

"If that vhat you vant."

She took the handpick and began scraping round the next

stone in line. Now they had made a start it was easier. The crumbling mortar fell to the ground. Harry took a turn. And when the time came to use the crowbar, he heaved until he thought his bones would crack. The stone did not stir.

"You getting von strong boy." Huggy took the crowbar and gave it a little push and pull. The stone broke loose. She threw it down beside the first.

The third was a corner stone. Then Aunt Bridget said, "Go down a bit. Take out one in the next layer."

Harry had the pick. He was tired. Two of his fingers were blistered. Lack of sleep was catching up with him. "It's just stones," he said. "What's the point?"

"The point's on the end of the pick," she said. "That sharp bit. Just do it."

He began to scrape. After a few minutes Huggy took over. She inserted the crowbar beneath the stone and leaned hard. The stone resisted – then suddenly broke free with a *crack* and leaped into the space beyond. The hole was quite big now.

Aunt Bridget said, "Have another look, Harry. Burrow down a bit if you can. Get rid of some of those stones."

Weariness made him clumsy. Harry pulled out stone after water-worn stone, and sticks, and bits of branch. As he did so, he scratched the back of his hand on the hole. Then the heavier stone, which had fallen inside, slipped and jammed his fingers. And not a minute later, groping in the dark, he ran a splinter up his nail. It burned like fire. Turning to the lamp, he drew it out with his teeth.

Harry shone the torch into the hole. There lay the offending timber. He flung it to the ground. Once that was gone, the stones and scraps of wood seemed little different from when he had started. Then, over at the back, he caught a glint of metal – gold and red, bright gold and redder than the blood that streaked his finger.

"What is it?"

"There's something there."

Harry reached across, pressing his cheek to the mortared stones, stretching until his shoulder nearly dislocated. He touched it. Shore stones were in the way. He pushed them aside. The thing slid away from him. He raked it back with a stick. At last he was able to grasp it: round, light, cold.

A rusty beer can!

Harry was about to throw it away in disgust when Aunt Bridget stopped him. "Let me see that." Her voice was urgent, excited.

He passed it up.

"This I do know," she turned the can in her long hands as if it were a priceless artefact. "The Victorians never drank *McEwan's Export* out of cans. Somebody has been here. Somebody within the past few years has thrown down a beer can and a lot of stones from the shore. And pulled the stove back on top. What I want to know is who – and why?"

Harry tingled from the roots of his hair to the soles of his feet. The figures above him crowded round the hole.

"Go on, 'Arry," Fingers shouted. "Keep diggin'!"

Heedless of his sore hands, he threw down a dozen more stones and pushed others out of the way. All at once his fingers encountered something different, a level board of wood. He felt around it – broader than a plank. Harry shone the torch but couldn't see. He groped for an edge, splintery like chipboard. He gripped it with his fingertips. It wouldn't lift, the stones were too heavy. Muttering words his aunt would not have approved, he struggled in the dark.

"You vant me to try?"

"No, I'll do it."

He changed arms; and changed again. At last he managed to lift the awkward board a few centimetres. It slipped sideways. A stone fell through. Harry thrust his fingers into the gap and felt –

He jerked his hand away. What was it? Tentatively he explored again. Ice-cold beneath his fingers. Smooth. Regular. Rock-hard yet with a silky feel.

"What is it?"

"I dunno." Eyes wide, tiredness forgotten, he stared up.

Whatever it was, there were several of them. All the same size. Stacked neatly. And cloth. A bag of some sort. He squeezed it, living through his fingertips. Something small inside. Lots of them. Beads, slithering around each other like a bean bag. He returned to the smooth surface, forcing his hand beneath the chipboard.

"I think I've—"

"You've got it, boy!" Fingers was shouting. "You've got it!"

Aunt Bridget said again, "What is it, Harry?"

The edge was cutting into his wrist. "It's like a—"

The fallen tree, right overhead, gave a lurch. He snatched back his hand and ducked. A loud CRACK! came from the fireplace. The hole they had made crunched shut with a violence that would have crushed Harry's arm and crippled him for life. The whole structure was collapsing.

For no one had realized that when the great tree fell, smashing the summer house to matchwood, its whole weight had come to rest on the fork that lay in the hearth and held the pot-bellied stove in its grip. Since the great storm it had sat there. Now the old pillar that supported it was being cut away.

The tree weighed many tons. As it shifted, bits of floor broke off and fell into the hole. The hearth split. The top stones popped. The pressure was too great. With a sudden BANG, the whole pillar exploded.

Harry was struck aside. In that split second he had an image of flying rocks and bright beads and shining yellow bricks. Then something hit him on the head and the world went black.

Chapter 34

Full Moon

Something kept hitting him in the face. He heard his name, over and over, coming closer: *Harry! Harry!*

"He's coming round."

He opened his eyes and saw leaping flames. Panicked. Tried to struggle back.

"All right! Is all right!" Huggy held him round the shoulders. Her big hand rested against his cheek.

His head ached. He looked up wildly.

"The tree fell," she said gently. "Knock you on back of the head."

Black legs surrounded him. Yellow flames sprang up before his face. "What's—"

"Sshhh! It break the lamp, sqvash flat. The paraffin, it run down the rotten vood. Ve accidental have fire. Is nice, ja?"

Harry struggled to a sitting position. They had carried him up from the hollow. He put a shaky hand to his head and discovered a bump. It made him feel sick. "What about the treasure?"

"Never mind the treasure. It's you we care about, darling." This was Auntie Florrie. "Do you feel awful?"

"A bit." He blinked to clear his eyes.

"Just stay there a few minutes," she said. "Then we'll take you home."

He made an effort. "But people will see the flames. It'll all have been a waste of time."

Gripping Huggy's shoulder, he clambered to his feet. The world swam: darkness, flame, tangled branches.

"Easy, 'Arry." This was Fingers.

He gritted his teeth and in a while his head stopped spinning. "I'm all right."

"No you're not."

"I'm all right!" he said savagely and caught hold of a branch.

Beneath him the hollow was lit by flames. Harry looked down – and blinked again. The earthy space, criss-crossed by branches and strewn with rocks, shone like an Aladdin's cave. A hundred bricks of gold littered the ground like a child's building blocks, in places heaped together, elsewhere gleaming from dark corners. There were jewels too. The bag he had felt, and other bags, had rotted and been ripped apart. Diamonds were strewn from wall to wall and winked from crevices where they had come to rest. It was like looking down into a night sky. Not all were diamonds, there were rubies, too, and emeralds. Nor were all single stones. A buckled tiara lay among rocks. Necklaces hung from crusted roots. A pretty casket disgorged its contents on to the churned ground.

Harry raised his head. Speechlessly he looked from one to the other.

"What d'you think?" Fingers grinned in the firelight. "Worth comin' for?"

"It's fantastic!"

"Better'n a poke in the eye with a sharp stick, that's for sure."

Auntie Florrie said, "How do you really feel, darling? Do you think you're going to be all right?"

"My head's sore but yeah, in a minute."

"We'll take you to the hospital as soon as we get back."

The flames leaped head high. Harry said, "Can't you put water on it or something."

"Well we would, now you're back with the living. There's a whole loch there but nothing to carry it in."

Harry tried to think. Thinking hurt but he'd seen something. "There's some old pots in the graveyard. Used to have flowers in them."

Aunt Bridget stood silent, stricken with guilt. Harry might have been killed – her grand-nephew, whom she loved more than she could ever say. She was so shocked by what she had allowed to happen that she could not even bring herself to hug him. Instead she said, "Brilliant! Come on, everybody," and set off through the gap Huggy had made in the branches.

The moon was so bright they hardly needed torches. There, among seeding grasses, stood the little gravestones. The pots were cracked or had drainage holes in the base, but Dot found an old plastic bucket, and there was a glass dome covered by weeds. It took just minutes to fill them at the jetty and carry the water to the bonfire. The timbers sizzled, clouds of steam billowed into the air, white in the moonlight.

Now that Harry was safe they were re-energized, and as soon as that part of the blaze closest to the treasure was extinguished, Huggy jumped down into the hole. The gold ingots were the shape of bricks only much smaller. Even so, they were heavy, twenty kilos each. Huggy grabbed two, one in each hand, and threw them up.

"Watch out." Fingers climbed down to give her a hand. But when he took hold of a yellow brick and tried to straighten, nothing happened. Startled, he took a firmer grip and got it as high as his knees. The ingot slipped and landed on his toes. He gave a howl of anguish: "Me foot! Me foot! I've broke me foot! Aahhh!"

"Shut up! You vant vake up the whole castle?"

"Me foot!"

"All right, you break your foot. Vhat you vant me to do, kiss it better?"

He took off his shoe and examined his foot by torchlight. No bones seemed to be broken. In fact there wasn't a mark. "It'll be black by breakfast time," he said gloomily.

"Ja, ja. I sure you show me. Look, ve vant no more injury. Leave the gold to me. You collect the sparklers."

He nodded. "Bob's your uncle." With quick fingers, neat as a pecking bird, he gathered up the diamonds and rubies and dropped them into his shoe. Jewelled rings went in as well, and earrings, and studs, all the small items. Slowly his shoe filled. It was, Fingers thought, a bit like picking blackberries.

The others, meanwhile, had developed a system. Dot and Auntie Florrie threw water on the fire, while Aunt Bridget carried the gold to the jetty and stacked it near the steps. Hers was the hardest job, carrying the twenty-kilo bricks, one at a time, through the branches, clambering down, and picking a path through the weeds and thorns. As soon as the most visible flames had been extinguished, Auntie Florrie left Dot to douse the fire completely and gave her sister a hand.

Harry sat watching. Slowly his head stopped throbbing. When he touched the bump he no longer felt sick.

Stiffly he rose. "Can I help?"

"If you're ready, yeah." Fingers straightened. His shoe was full. "Fetch us one o' them canvas bags over at the boat."

Harry did so. Fingers tipped the glittering, moonlit stream from his shoe and pulled it back on. "Ow!" A couple of diamonds had got stuck in the lining. He knocked them out.

A number of larger items had been laid aside: the buckled tiara and other headbands, jewelled collars, a heap of necklaces, flashing bracelets, handfuls of brooches. Fingers added them to the bag.

Harry tested the weight. Several kilos, and all precious stones.

"I bet that's worth a bit."

"You don't know the 'alf of it." Fingers leaned on his elbows and picked through the contents. "You're talkin' seven figures 'ere, boy. An' the first of 'em's not one."

Harry shone his torch. The inside of the cheap black holdall blazed and flared, a light so intense it seemed it must melt.

"See this?" Fingers pulled out a bracelet and shook off a clinging necklace and a couple of loose stones. "Beautiful, yeah?" He turned it to catch the light. "Belonged to the Duchess of Ludlow. The *Calcutta Bracelet* that is. Worth two hundred grand of anybody's money." He poked deeper, plunging his hand into the white fire, rattling the jewellery like dice, and produced a ring with a blood-red stone the size of a grape. "Tsar of Russia gave that to his wife just before the revolution. She gave it to Rasputin. Known as the *Rasputin Ruby*. Went missing when he was murdered. Worth a fortune."

"How much?"

"Depends what collectors'll pay. A lot more than the bracelet anyway. History, see." He threw it back. "I wouldn't thank you for it mysel'. Brings bad luck."

He returned to his work.

Auntie Florrie, meanwhile, stepped aboard the rocking boat and Aunt Bridget passed down the ingots on the jetty. "Watch you don't drop any," she said. "Go straight through the bottom. We'd be marooned."

Auntie Florrie placed them around the boards to spread the load. There were twenty – four hundred kilos. The boat settled lower in the water.

They resumed carrying the gold from the summer house. A second stack of ingots built up on the jetty.

A few last wisps of smoke rose from the fire.

Fingers searched the hollow, turning over rocks, winkling among roots for the last of the jewels.

"Sshhh! Everybody!" Aunt Bridget raised a hand.

She had no need for they had all heard it. The sudden roar of an engine.

"The speedboat," Dot said.

Harry put a name to it, "*Red Sky*."

"I knew it was too good to last." Auntie Florrie sighed. "Here it comes."

"What?" Harry said.

"Trouble."

"Yes, but who?"

"Well not Priestly and that crowd," she said. "They'd hardly come in the speedboat, wake up the whole countryside."

"The fuzz then?" he said.

"Wouldn't call the fuzz all the way out here just for a bonfire on the island."

"Nah, it'll be them keepers Lord Goole was talkin' about," Fingers said.

"I think you're right. Leave the talking to me." Aunt Bridget led the way to the jetty.

"Better cover things up a bit," Auntie Florrie said.

Harry looked around. "Those branches Huggy sawed off. Stack them over the gold."

"Good boy," she said. "That knock on the head hasn't affected your brains anyway."

For a minute there was a mad scramble.

Red Sky should have sped to the island in no time but the occupants were having trouble. As Nutty had said, there was something not right: the acceleration was too sudden, the throttle too delicate. It needed careful handling and they were clumsy. The boat proceeded by a series of swooping starts and stops. Three times water boiled at the stern, the bows leaped forward, curving a wild moonlit track across the loch, then it glided to a halt. Once it careered astern, so violently that Harry thought it must go under.

But it didn't, and at length the speedboat drew close to the jetty. It stopped short and someone on board paddled the last few metres with a boathook.

Nutty and Lord Goole had washed the boat down, the paintwork shone.

There were three people on board, half hidden by the cockpit. Until they came close it was hard to make them out. One was short and dark. A second was blonde, hair bright in the moonlight. An awful suspicion made Harry's skin crawl. He took a step backwards. His aunts had been wrong. There was no mistaking the immaculate figure who sprang to the steps, nor the Beretta sub-machine gun in her hands, nor the ice-cold voice which had whipped and bullied Harry for the first ten years of his life.

"Well, well, well! A reception committee. Do you see that, Percy? They've come down specially to welcome us."

Dot made to slip away.

"Don't even think about it!" Gestapo Lil's voice would have splintered glass. She brandished the machine gun. "Chop your legs off with this and you'd not be much good for all your cat-burgling and acrobatics, would you? Come back here where I can see you."

Dot did as she was told.

Priestly threw a mooring line. At his third attempt it landed on the jetty. Without taking her eyes off the group, Gestapo Lil looped it round the mooring post. Priestly and Mad Ruby scrambled ashore.

"This is nice," he said. "Haven't seen some of you for a long time." He drew a fat, half-smoked cigar from his shirt pocket.

"Cony Hill, that's where," Auntie Florrie said. "In jail, where you should be this minute."

"And where you'll be again, very soon," Aunt Bridget added. "I can promise you that."

"Ah, promises, promises." He blew smoke at the moon.

"Felon Grange, that's where I seen you," Fingers said. "Last New Year when you done a runner."

"And the Old Bailey," Huggy said, "vhere they put you away for five years. It should have been tventy!"

"Yeah, yeah." Priestly flapped a hand. "Ancient history. But I'm here now, and *we've* got the machine gun."

"And the sawn-off, I have no doubt," said Aunt Bridget.

Mad Ruby twitched her skirt to reveal the weapon strapped to her thigh on its Velcro fastening.

"And a snubby for a full house." Priestly drew it from a shiny new holster.

"Well look at you, John Wayne," Aunt Bridget said contemptuously. "What a lot of nasty toys. And GBH has got the Exocet, I suppose. Where is he, by the way? Not like you to travel this far without your minder."

"He watch'a the car, guard the prisoner," Mad Ruby said.

"What prisoner?"

"You fix the Range Rover, no? I donno how, but you fix. You think that stop us? We flag down a car coming into the village."

"And took the driver prisoner?" Auntie Florrie said.

"So what?" She shrugged. "Who care?"

"Didn't hear the car."

"What you expect'a, loudspeakers on the roof? Is long freewheel, all the way down river to the landing stage."

"Boats all chained up but they left the shed unlocked. So we took the speedboat." Priestly was pleased with himself. He tried to twirl his little automatic and dropped it on the stones. "GBH will take care of any snoopy keepers that come poking their noses in."

"You talk too much," Gestapo Lil snapped. "The pair of you – talk, talk, talk! Just do what we came to do and let's get out of this God-forsaken place. You," she jerked the machine gun. "Harry Barton. Come here."

Harry stepped forward, his headache forgotten.

"If you know what's good for you, you'll tell the truth for once in your miserable life. We've read what's in the computer. We know what you're doing here. What have you found?"

He stared at the wicked weapon.

"What, eh?"

Still he did not speak.

"Keep them covered," she said to Priestly and grabbed Harry by the collar. "What?"

He struggled.

"Tell me, or do you want us to mow this disgusting lot down and tow their remains out to the middle of the loch where no one will ever find them?"

His eyes rolled. In the panic of the moment he looked from the branches on the jetty to the branches in the rowing boat.

"Ah!" She threw him aside and raised the machine gun again. "Percy, have a look under that lot."

There was nothing they could do. The leafy branches were dragged aside. The carpet of gold gleamed in the moonlight.

"Aahhh!" It was almost a hiss.

Mad Ruby snatched a torch.

Priestly fell to his knees, stroking the yellow bricks with podgy hands. "Beautiful! Beautiful!" He struggled to lift one and failed, then spread his arms across the pile as if to keep other people away. "At last! Rich again!" Finding the gold so close, he leaned forward and kissed it with fat lips.

Harry was disgusted.

"Yes, well don'a get too excited," Mad Ruby said coldly. "Half belong'a your mamma."

Gestapo Lil said, "Look in the boat, Percy."

Clumsily he climbed aboard and threw the branches over the side. Ruby descended the crumbling steps. More gold shone in the moonlight.

"Seems we got here just at the right time." Gestapo Lil swung back. "Right, where's the rest of it?"

No one answered.

"That the summer house?" She nodded towards the ruined building. Wisps of smoke rose through the branches.

Silently they stared back at her.

"What a bunch! Think keeping your traps shut will make any difference?"

A path had been trampled through the weeds. The sawn-off ends of branches were white in the moonlight.

"That's it all right. Just like it says in the laptop. Been a bit of a storm, that's all." She turned to Harry. "You, rat-face. You lead the way."

Aunt Bridget had stepped forward. Harry looked at her.

"Never mind the old bat." Gestapo Lil dragged him by the jersey. "Just get over there and pull those branches out the way."

He resisted. She gave him a yank, as she had done a hundred times in the past. Harry stumbled. His sudden weight pulled her off balance. The machine gun swung aside. Though it was only for a second it was enough. Aunt Bridget leaped forward and grabbed the weapon with both hands, forcing it away from Harry and her friends. Gestapo Lil's finger tightened on the trigger. TAT-TAT-TAT-TAT-TAT-TAT-TAT! The chatter of the Beretta shattered the peace of the night. A stream of bullets whipped the surface of the loch. The stink of cordite filled the air. Gestapo Lil fought back. She had no chance. Aunt Bridget's muscles were like iron. The barrel grew hot but she did not let go. Exerting all her strength, she wrenched the machine gun from Gestapo Lil's grasp and flung it away into deep water. Briefly Harry saw it silhouetted against the stars, then it landed with a splash and was gone.

Gestapo Lil gave a scream and rushed at Aunt Bridget, nails hooked to claw her face. It was unwise. She had seen Aunt Bridget in action before and should have remembered. For during her years at Oxford Aunt Bridget had two sports, rowing and boxing, and had represented the university at both. Now she stepped neatly aside, feinted with her right, hit her opponent in the ribs with a short left jab, and finished the job with a right overarm cross that would have felled an elephant.

In under ten seconds it was all over. Gestapo Lil lay motionless. Priestly, in the rocking boat, struggled to pull his automatic from its holster and nearly went over the side. Mad Ruby fell on the treacherous steps and scraped her knees. By the time she reached the top and snatched the sawn-off from its fastening, Aunt Bridget stood with her hands above her head in an attitude of surrender.

With satisfaction Ruby surveyed the prostrate figure of her son's fiancée. It was what she deserved, the two-faced bitch. All the same, it had been a dangerous moment.

"Percy!" she snapped. "Get yourself up here. Stop dithering. We need'a get these geriatrics organized."

He clambered from the gold-laden boat.

"Right." Ruby gestured with her gun. "All together where I see you. That better. Now, unlike that person there," she glanced at Gestapo Lil who was beginning to stir, "I have some experience with these things." She patted the sawn-off. "I keep record, see?" She held it out and Harry saw a little row of notches. "Eight'a, so far." She counted down with a reflective thumb: "One-leg Louis, Joey the Contender, Mamma di Maggio, Bull Bastinado. . . Plenty room for more. I don'a mind a bit."

Priestly bent above his beloved. Her tights were ripped, her hair trailed in the weeds, her lips were swollen like a boxer. "Poor Lavvy-poo!" He repressed a grimace. "You wait there."

"Stupid woman," Mad Ruby said. "The whole castle will be down here."

"How many's that?" he sneered. "One decrepit old lord and a couple o' haggis-bashers. GBH'll handle them, no problem."

"So you say." She looked at the gold on the jetty. "We use the speedboat, it carry more. Tow the other one."

"Good thinking," he said. "You take care of that. I'll see what's left in the summer house."

"Watch'a your back," she said. "They're slippery as eels."

"Dead eels, they give us any more hassle." He checked his automatic. "Right, you," he bundled Harry ahead of him. "Show us the summer house."

Harry had no option. He led the way to the fallen tree and pulled aside the sawn-off branches.

Priestly hauled himself over the trunk. "No tricks," he wheezed and jabbed Harry in the back with his pistol.

A score of gold bricks stood on the edge where Huggy had stacked them. A few more and one or two winking diamonds lay in the hollow.

Priestly's thick lips parted in a smile. "Worth breaking out for after all." He called to his mother, "Loads more yet. Let's have some of that lot over here."

"One thing at a time." Her voice came back. "Finish the loading first. We need Lavinia, keep an eye on things. She sitting up now."

Priestly shone his torch around. "What's that?"

413

In the rush of trying to hide everything, Fingers had pushed the canvas bag of jewels into a hollow beneath the tree-trunk. The manufacturer's label hung from a handle and caught the light.

Harry pretended to see nothing.

"Over there." Priestly directed the beam. "A bag of some sort."

"No idea." Harry climbed down among the earth and stones and gold. "Do you want me to start collecting the stuff in here?"

"No, I don't." Priestly's voice took on an edge. "I want you to start collecting that bag under the tree. Is that plain enough?"

Harry looked at the automatic. Reluctantly he did as he was told.

"Open it."

He pulled back the zip.

Priestly shone his torch inside. The jewellery blazed back. His mouth fell open. "Oh, my God!" Hustling Harry ahead of him, he grabbed the bag and scrambled back through the branches.

Gestapo Lil had recovered enough to join Mad Ruby on the jetty.

"Look at this!" He directed his torch into the holdall.

Moonlight shone on the top of their heads. The glow of the gems illuminated their faces.

"Take what we have and let's get out of here," Mad Ruby said.

"Are you crazy? There's a fortune back there."

"I don'a care. We got a fortune here. This enough. No sense we take chances."

"What chances?"

"Machine gun chances. GBH chances. Working with idiots like you chances. The sooner we get out of here now, the better I feel."

"Have a nice swim. If you think I'm going to leave all that gold behind, you're off your head. There's diamonds back there as well. One hour and we'll have the lot. One hour, the world's our oyster – for ever."

"Oh, Fercifofs!" said Gestapo Lil, her lips so swollen she could not say 'p'. She fell to her hands and knees, rooting among the jewels. "See how they're all sfarkling! Look at that. And that!" She pulled out the Rasputin ring with its huge, blood-red stone. "The same colour as my lifstick. That is mine!" She slipped it on and spread her fingers like a newly-engaged girl.

"Come on, we got to go," said Mad Ruby.

Gestapo Lil turned on her. "We're staying!"

Priestly thought for a moment. "With the Beretta gone, that's only two guns. We'll have one each end. I'll take the summer house. You," he told his mother, "take charge of the loading. Lavvy," he handed her a heavy stick, "stand by the tree. Anyone tries any funny stuff, give 'em a clout."

She swung it and grinned lopsidedly. "My fleasure. Sfecially if it's that little toad or his frecious aunts."

They were divided up: Huggy back in the hollow, Auntie Florrie aboard the speedboat, Aunt Bridget handing down the ingots. The rest – Harry, Dot and Fingers – were put to carrying the gold from the summer house to the jetty. It was hard work. None was strong and every brick seemed heavier than the last. Fingers was limping. Harry's head was sore and his ribs bruised from when the tree fell on top of him. Time and again the gold slipped from their hands and had to be recovered from among the branches and weeds.

Steadily the summer house emptied. The speedboat settled lower in the water.

Half an hour passed. Harry looked for ways of escape but could not forget those ripping bullets from the machine gun. Gestapo Lil watched every step. When he reached the summer house, there stood Priestly, his vicious automatic gleaming in the moonlight. And when he reached the jetty, there stood Ruby Palazzo, nursing her sawn-off shotgun with eight notches in the stock.

Time was running out. What would happen when all the gold had been transferred?

Then unexpectedly, as he returned through the branches for the eighth time, Harry saw his opportunity. Priestly was pointing at a jewel lodged in a crevice.

"There, for God's sake!" he said to Huggy. "Up a bit. No, *up*! And to the left. The *left*, dumbo!"

Harry stood right behind him. It would have been so easy to give him a shove, straight down into Huggy's vice-like grip. But the automatic was pointing at her chest. Any sudden violence –

He backed away. Silently he climbed to a branch and squeezed between two others. Huggy saw him, almost straight in her line of vision. She kept her eyes averted.

"Who you call dumbo, you fat palooka!" she said angrily to the man with the pistol. "You vant this diamond, you tell me vhere, precisely. Left, right, up, down, make up your mind."

"Listen, you ugly great troll. Who d'you think you're talking to?"

"To somevon who mad for gold," she said. "Who on the run from prison. Somevon who not know his ankle from his elbow!"

Harry swung to the next branch, lowered himself to a tree-trunk, tiptoed along and slid through foliage. Priestly's torch was ten metres distant. Softly he crept away through the undergrowth.

The moon stood high. At Harry's back lay danger. Ahead lay the tangled ruin of the island.

Chapter 35

Red Sky at Night

"Fercy, is that little wretch with you?"

"What?"

"That fain in the fackside, Harry Barton. Is he with you?"

"No."

"But he went through for another load three or four minutes ago."

"I haven't seen him."

"Well where is he?"

There was panic. Harry was missing.

"Out, out of there." Huggy was driven at gunpoint from the summer house and made to stand with the rest a short distance from the jetty.

"Where is he?"

They shook their heads. Only Huggy had seen him go.

"Come on."

"It's no good threatening us if we don't know," Aunt Bridget said shortly. "And will you stop waving that shotgun around, it might go off."

Mad Ruby turned on her son. "Happy now? Got what you want? A fortune not enough for you, oh no! Had to have every last penny. Now he's gone."

"Good swimmer too," Gestapo Lil said. "Frofer little water rat. Wouldn't fut it fast him to try to swim ashore."

"What, right across?"

"And raise the alarm. He's swum the mile. Got medals for it, that fosh school he went to before his farents snuffed it."

"Perhaps he'll drown," Priestly said. "Get caught in weeds."

"Let's hofe so."

"Or perhaps he won't," said Mad Ruby. "Perhaps he never even thought about it'a. Perhaps he hiding behind that tree right now, listening to every word we're saying. He never ran off this end, that for sure. You let him go, you get after him. The pair of you."

Priestly and Gestapo Lil looked at each other.

"Go on! Take two torches. He only a boy. You got the piece, you got a stick." She glanced up. "Full moon like that, what more you want?"

They ran off.

Mad Ruby was right. Though by this time Harry was fifty metres away, her furious words reached him in the silence. He had not thought of swimming, not seriously. The idea of all that black water beneath him, alone in the moonlight, was too scary. All he was doing was trying to get away. Beyond that his mind was a blank. And now he heard footsteps in the undergrowth, and swearing, and Priestly and Gestapo Lil talking to each other. He saw the flash of their torches.

On hands and knees he crawled behind a bramble thicket to the shelter of another fallen tree. The roots rose high overhead. He slipped into the moon shadow behind. Rain water had gathered in the earthy hollow. He waded through it, trying not to splash.

Where now? A patch of bracken offered shelter but the tossing heads would attract attention. The torches were heading his way. He set off in the opposite direction, ducking beneath branches, wriggling on his belly like a snake.

"He's been here, look, the grass is flattened." Gestapo Lil's voice was clear. "Try over there."

Harry redoubled his efforts, crouching along a small gully, crawling through weeds. By night the thorns were doubly treacherous: brambles coiled round the legs of his jeans; wild briar clawed him across the chest. A dozen fiery scratches were added to those of the afternoon. Harry hardly felt them.

He rested behind a boulder. Without intending it, he saw that he was heading for the shore. Bushes that had survived the hurricane stood above a rocky bluff. A short distance beyond them, the edge of the loch was steeped in shadow. He peered back into the wilderness and saw the torches still heading in his direction. Harry thought for a moment and slithered down the slope.

The shore was narrow, a couple of metres, and shelved steeply into deep water. Away from the jetty, the obvious way to run, it broadened. In the other direction, back the way he had come, it vanished completely. Black ripples lapped a cliff. Harry hesitated. Voices reached him. Torchlight swept the bushes overhead. Which way should he go? Heads or tails? He lowered himself into the water and swam back towards the jetty.

It was difficult to swim without making a splash. His trainers dragged his feet down; his jeans clung tight; his jersey sagged heavily. But Harry had learned lifesaving, which involved swimming fully dressed. By a combination of breast stroke and dog-paddle, he made his way round the cliff and into a small bay hidden from his pursuers. Legs trailing, he clung to a rock and caught his breath.

Priestly and Gestapo Lil were behind him, but now he heard other voices, Auntie Florrie and the harsh tones of Ruby Palazzo. The water here was too shallow to swim but the shore had reappeared. Harry circled the bay and climbed a low headland. A rocky knoll rose above it. He crawled to the top and peered through long grasses. One way lay the jetty where the two boats rocked gently at their mooring. The other way lay the interior of the island. Right before him, only twenty metres distant, Mad Ruby levelled the sawn-off at his aunts and their friends. She had made them sit on the ground, hands in front where she could see them.

For the moment no one was speaking then Ruby called loudly to her son, "Any sign yet, Percy?"

A distant, "No, nothing," drifted back. "We thought we had him but he's disappeared. We'll get him though."

Gestapo Lil added her voice: "You hear that, Harry Barton! My word, when we get our hands on you!" There was a cracking sound as she smacked her stick against a branch.

Harry was already so frightened that another threat made little difference.

Mad Ruby stood with her back to the jetty. He looked from the group to the boats and back again. Might it be possible, he wondered, if he was *very* quiet, to take the rowboat and paddle away? *Red Sky*, of course, would be better, but starting the engine, even if he could manage it, would be much too slow and noisy. Mad Ruby would be above him with the shotgun before he had gone five metres. In the rowing boat, however, especially if Aunt Bridget and the others provided a diversion, it might *just* be possible to steal away unnoticed.

But he would have to swim again. The only way to reach the jetty without being seen, was to cross thirty metres of deep water. A small patch of reeds grew midway; apart from that it was completely open. Mad Ruby had only to turn and he would be in full view.

Harry tightened his lips and descended to the shore at the far side of the headland. His jersey had been clumsy. He tugged it off. His T-shirt was red but in the moonlight it merely looked dark. The night breeze chilled his wet arms. Quietly he slipped into the water and began to swim. After a few strokes Mad Ruby's back came into view. And then the others. They saw him at once. He raised a hand and sank from view behind the reeds. It was well that he did so for Auntie Florrie was startled and turned her head. So did Fingers.

Ruby swung round. "What you looking at?"

"Nothin'," Fingers said.

"A fish jumped, that's all," said Auntie Florrie.

"Salmon, prob'ly."

"Salmon?" Ruby said angrily. "What you talk about?"

"Din't you know? People drive 'undreds o' miles to come fishin' 'ere. Costs a bomb."

"Wasn't big enough for a salmon." Auntie Florrie shook her head. "Trout more likely. What do you think, Bridget?"

"I think it's no good asking the opinion of Mad Ruby Palazzo," said Aunt Bridget, joining in to distract Ruby's attention from the loch where Harry had surfaced again. "All they've got where she comes from is scampi and sardines."

"You watch'a your mouth," she said.

"And famous old ruins, of course," Aunt Bridget went on. "A bit like her, really, only bigger."

"You're right with the last bit," Auntie Florrie agreed. "But I wouldn't say she's famous. Not like Eddie Carver. Now he was famous. And some of us, of course. She's very small cheese."

"What sort of cheese?" Dot said.

"Smelly Gorgonzola, vhat you think?"

"Well said, Huggy."

"Always seemed more like a black widder spider to me," Fingers said. "Eatin' up all the men in her life. Imagine them skinny arms around yer. Cor! Turns yer tripes to water."

"I warn you!" Mad Ruby took a threatening step. "One more word!"

Harry swam out from behind the reeds, heading for the old stone jetty. So softly that he hardly heard the ripples as they flowed past his ears, he crossed the intervening metres. If Mad Ruby had turned he was in plain view. The rest saw him clearly, black as a bear in the silver streak of the moon.

He reached the jetty and swam round the end, hidden from those on shore. *Red Sky* and the rowboat were touching. He pushed them apart. Three strokes took him to the broken steps. His hair was sleek. Water streamed from his clothes.

The mooring line for the rowboat dipped past his shoulder. It was spliced into a ringbolt at the prow. Dot had tied the shoreward end in a loop and dropped it over the rotted post on the jetty. The only way to release it was to come right out into the open. Hardly daring to breathe, he crept to the top of the steps.

Auntie Florrie and the rest saw him behind Mad Ruby. One rattle of a pebble and she must have heard him.

"What about that pathetic son of yours?" Aunt Bridget commanded her attention. "Percy Pig and his nasty girlfriend. What do you think of them *really*? Sending you to Bolivia. And that night you spent with Baba Yawkins! Can you forgive them for. . ."

Red Sky had come in later. Her mooring line lay on top. Harry unwound it and lifted the rope for the rowing boat from underneath. Holding it firmly lest it should slip back with a splash, he descended the steps and pulled the boat alongside. The cargo of gold bricks, spread over the bottom boards, gave it stability. Careful to avoid scraping the jetty, he stepped aboard.

Leaving the oars for the moment, Harry caught *Red Sky* by the gunwale and pulled the rowboat along. The bag of jewels had been placed in the cockpit. He leaned far over and caught it by the handles. The rowboat began to slip away. Water gaped beneath him. With a supreme effort, he hooked his feet over the side and pulled it back. The boats bumped lightly. For a moment he clung tight. As soon as he had recovered and regained his balance, Harry settled himself on the central thwart and set the bag at his feet. It was open. A ray of moonlight glittered on the precious stones. He zipped the bag shut and pushed out into open water.

It was quieter to paddle than to row – oars creaked in the wooden rowlocks. Harry sat facing forward and took a single oar. Gripping it halfway, he dug the blade into the water as he had done a score of times at Lagg Hall, pretending to be an American Indian – or when he had lost an oar. The boat slid forward, heavier and more sluggish than the boat he was used to. It swung to port. He dipped on the other side.

424

Wood clunked against wood. He froze and looked back. The Wrinklies held Mad Ruby's attention. Tingling to the roots of his hair, Harry paddled on.

Priestly and Gestapo Lil, meanwhile, were getting crosser by the minute. The sticks and nettles and thornbushes did not reserve their stabs for Harry. Their legs stung. Midges and mosquitoes were in their hair, up their sleeves and down their necks.

"What a useless article you are, Fercy Friestly!" she snapped. "Can't even keef an eye on a frimary schoolboy."

"Oh, shut up, you nagging old crow," he said. "Fatlips!"

She whacked him, none too gently, with her stick.

"Do that again," he said, "and I'll black your eye."

"Just try it," she spat. "Hitting women! That's just about your level, isn't it."

Where was the wretched boy? They had climbed to the highest point of the island where the night breeze gave a little relief. Together they looked down on the wilderness of branches.

"Who's that?" Gestapo Lil pointed past the jetty.

The rowing boat, a black silhouette on the silver water and paddled by a single figure, headed out into the loch.

"My mother! She's gone off with the gold!"

"No it's not, it's him! I know it. He's doubled back. Ruby!" she screamed. "What's the old hagwitch think she's doing? Ruby! He's getting away!"

Down by the jetty they heard her screams. Aunt Bridget and the rest turned round.

"Stay where you are! Don'a move."

On the rocks by the tall pine tree, two figures were dancing.

"What?" Ruby yelled back. "I can'a make out what you're saying."

"The boy!" Priestly roared, if a voice as high-pitched as his could be called a roar. "Look! He's getting away!"

"Are you blind!" shrieked Gestapo Lil. "Turn round and look, you shrivelled old frune."

The words were unclear but plainly something was amiss. Ruby shook the shotgun. "Move, I blow a hole you drive a truck through," she warned savagely and looked all round.

What was the fuss about? All was in order her end. Then she saw that the rowing boat was missing, and in the same glance saw Harry, fifty metres out and heading away from the island.

In one movement she swung up the shotgun and fired.

The spread of pellets from a sawn-off is wide. Vicious little spurts of water leaped up around the boat. A few rattled off the planks. Three hit Harry. Luckily he was too far off for them to do serious damage. The one on his back he hardly felt. The one on his hand stung. The one in his scalp burned like fire.

Instantly he ducked, wrapping arms around his head, waiting for the next shot.

It never came. Mad Ruby needed her second barrel to keep the Wrinklies at bay. And at that distance Priestly's automatic was no use at all. Besides, he and Gestapo Lil had already left their vantage point and were heading back to the jetty as fast as their legs and the fallen trees would allow.

After half a minute, still guarding his face, Harry glanced back. There stood Mad Ruby. There sat the hunched figures of his aunts and their friends. There was nothing he could do, not personally. His one aim must be to get ashore and go for help.

Briefly he explored the hurt in his hair. Something was lodged in his scalp. Small and hard. He picked at it with a fingernail and it fell out at once. A lead pellet. He peered at it in the moonlight and threw it aside then examined his scalp again. It felt better. His fingertips were slippery with blood.

For a few moments longer he waited. Still no shot came. Greatly frightened, Harry resumed his seat, facing astern this time, and took up the second oar. He felt vulnerable, a real sitting duck, and wanted to guard his eyes. It was impossible. Careless how much noise he made now, he rattled the oars into the rowlocks, braced his feet, and pulled with all his strength.

The boat had been drifting. Harry turned its head towards the nearest point of land. Slowly it gathered momentum.

Meanwhile, as Priestly and Gestapo Lil descended from the crown of the island, they were hot, uncomfortable and in a foul mood. Their fear of Harry's escape and the loss of the treasure was as great as *his* fear of being shot. Headlong they crawled through branches and fell over hidden stones.

"How the hell did you let him get away like that?" Priestly shouted at his mother as they approached the summer house.

"She's fast it, I've told you," Gestapo Lil panted. "Mafia queen, ha! I bet the Nafles mob gave a big cheer the day she flew out."

"Aaahhh!" Mad Ruby's voice was a hiss. "Who lose the Beretta? Who leave me with that piano player? One day I *fix* you, Lavinia McScrew. But why you talk'a? The boy escape, get after him. Go on! Hurry! Hurry!"

Priestly's fat knees were buckling. Followed by Gestapo Lil, he ran to the steps and tumbled aboard the speedboat.

"Don'a worry about these." Too fast even for Aunt Bridget, Ruby ejected the spent cartridge and slipped another into the breech. "I take extra good care of them."

They had forgotten the mooring line. It was attached to the bow by a spring clip. Gestapo Lil crawled forward to release it while Priestly examined the controls. All seemed in order. He pressed the starter.

The engine was in gear. The speedboat leaped forward and crashed into the jetty wall. Gestapo Lil, still at the bow, shot backwards, shot forwards, rebounded off the jetty, crashed over the windshield, and landed on Colonel Priestly in the cockpit. The engine stalled.

In a tangle of arms and legs, a very angry tangle, they lay on the deck. Painfully they unravelled.

"I couldn't see properly. Gimme a torch." Priestly clutched his nose, which felt as if his fiancée had given him a headbutt."

"It's not a torch you'll be getting if you don't buck your ideas uf." She grasped the boathook. "Switch on the lights, you fool."

By a stroke of luck he found the light switch. A minute later, more out of control than in it, the temperamental speedboat cannoned off the end of the jetty and roared out into the moonlit loch.

Halfway to shore by this time, Harry heaved on the oars. The events on the island had been hidden by darkness and fallen trees, but he heard the speedboat. He planned to land well clear of the landing stage because GBH was there and, like the rest of them, he had a gun. Time and again Harry scanned the shore but saw no sign of the waiting thug. Where was he?

Then *Red Sky* appeared round the end of the island. The white paint gleamed. Water foamed at the stern.

Two hundred metres to go. Harry pulled till he thought his back would break.

The speedboat streaked towards him. The roar of its engine shattered the calm of the loch. Harry could not see who was aboard but as it flashed past he made out two figures in the cockpit. One screamed at him. Her words were lost but he saw the blonde head. It was Gestapo Lil.

His boat tossed in the wash as *Red Sky* turned ahead of him, heeling far over, screamed past on the opposite side and turned again. Priestly tried to slow the speedboat to come alongside but the speed and bouncing made him clumsy with the throttle. The engine cut out. Fifty metres astern of Harry, *Red Sky* drifted to a halt.

He gripped his boat's side as the wash subsided and wondered why they had not come closer.

"You've got no chance." Gestapo Lil's threat rang across the water. "Give yourself uf before we have to come and get you."

Harry hesitated then dug in the oars and resumed rowing.

He heard muttered words. Priestly straightened, then there was a little flash and almost instantaneous bang. Where the bullet went he had no idea, but they were *shooting* at him! Instantly he ducked below the gunwale. The gold bars were beneath him. He pressed his face into the bag of jewels.

A second shot. The bullet clipped the boat's side and whined away.

A third shot.

Silence.

He risked a peep. Their heads were together. Priestly ducked from sight. The engine coughed . . . coughed again . . . then roared into life. But Priestly was as bad at starting the engine as he was at stopping it. The speedboat leaped forward. They were thrown backwards. *Red Sky* cut a wild S-shaped curve, heading away down the loch in the wrong direction.

What were they doing? Harry resumed his seat and took the oars. Barely a hundred metres to go now. The boat had drifted off-course. He turned his bows towards the shore.

But the murderous pair aboard the speedboat had taken some sort of control. From far out on the loch it came racing towards him.

Whether it was Priestly's intention to try again to come alongside, or cut close ahead and frighten Harry into submission, or even give the rowboat a nudge, it is hard to say. But what happened was that Gestapo Lil snapped, "You're going too fast."

"I know what I'm doing," he retorted.

"And too close," she cried.

"No I'm not."

"Keep out a bit." She grabbed the wheel.

"Get off!" He pushed her back. "Let go!"

In the brief tussle, *Red Sky* swung to port, then to starboard, and leaped on a little wave of its own making. Priestly lost his footing and clung to the wheel for balance. The throttle was knocked full open. The powerful boat surged forward, curving flat out towards the rowing boat. He struggled to regain control.

Harry was only thirty metres from land. Frantically he tried to row out of the way. It was too late. The howling speedboat bore down upon him. He let go of the oars. With a crash like a runaway lorry, *Red Sky* smashed the bow of the rowboat to splinters, bounced off, and sped headlong towards the shore.

Seconds later, with a noise of burst plastic, rending metal and destruction, it met the stones, leaped upwards, bounced from a grassy bank and took off. A dozen metres further on, a clump of hawthorn and rowan trees grew right in its path. Neat as the glove of a wicket keeper, the branches plucked it out of the air. The propeller was stripped. For several seconds the engine screamed. Then it seized up. A herd of Highland cattle, gentle creatures which had been lying near the trees, ran off in panic. Silence returned. Three metres above the hillside, the ruined speedboat hung in a nest of leaves and berries.

Out on the loch, meanwhile, weighed down by its golden cargo, the rowboat went down like a stone. In the second that was left to him, Harry hurled the holdall towards the rocks. Then he was struggling in the cold water.

Chapter 36

The Oak Wood

It was not deep. After a couple of strokes Harry's feet touched bottom, the water to his chest. A metre or two ahead of him the black bag was still afloat. He plunged towards it and caught the handles just before it sank.

In the wake of *Red Sky* the water was agitated. He gazed up the hillside. No movement came from the speedboat – then a moonlit hand appeared. Harry ploughed towards the shore. A second hand appeared. Uncertainly, like strange plants in time-lapse photography, the two hands waved in the air then fastened on the boat's side. Harry reached the stony beach. Twenty metres away, Gestapo Lil hauled herself upright in the cockpit. Her sleeve hung in rags. Long, moon-white hair straggled about her shoulders. If Harry had been closer and had a torch, he might have seen that she had a dazed look and – *without* being socked by her fiancé – one eye was rapidly closing.

"Fercy?" she whispered. "Fercy, are you there?"

A grunt issued from somewhere beneath her.

"If you could stand uf a minute." She looked slowly to left and right. "We affear to be in a tree."

As far as they were concerned, Harry thought, he was safe

for the next few minutes, though somewhere in that cockpit there was a pistol. But where was GBH? There was no way anyone within a mile could have missed the catastrophe of the past few minutes. He ducked into the shadow of a rock and looked all round.

A minute passed. Nothing moved on the moonlit shore. That meant GBH was still at the landing stage. If Harry wanted to reach Lord Goole and the safety of the castle, there was only one way to go. He must climb up into the oak wood beneath King's Crag and circle round, giving the landing stage a wide berth.

The holdall was impossibly heavy. He looked inside. Tiaras and necklaces lay in a swamp of loch water. Taking care to lose no diamonds in the process, Harry poured out as much as he could and zipped the bag shut. Then he tugged his jeans more comfortable, wriggled his feet in his squelchy trainers, and set off diagonally up the hillside towards the wood.

The cattle scampered aside as he passed. But they were inquisitive creatures and returned to gaze at the strange object which had nested in their tree. Gestapo Lil was frightened of cows. She had been frightened of the white cattle in the long meadow at Felon Grange, and was doubly frightened of these Highland beasts with their shaggy coats and tremendous horns. They gathered round, ready to run again, munching, burping, staring, lifting their tails to spray the ground.

"Fercy," she whispered again, and gripped the boat's side as if to hold it firm against attack. "We're traffed!"

With an effort he dragged himself from the deck. "It's only a few cows."

"But see how they're looking at us!"

"Pull yourself together." He had been shaken by the crash but the sight of Harry, only fifty metres away, with a bag in his hand worth several million pounds, the pick of Eddie Carver's treasure, was enough to rouse even him from a wallow of self-pity.

"Hey! You!"

The cattle started and fled a few metres then turned back. Harry halted.

"Come here."

"You must be joking."

"I said come here, you little oik!"

"Get stuffed," said Harry, who had never spoken like that to an adult in his life.

"We'll get you yet." Priestly ducked below the edge of the cockpit.

Guessing he might be searching for the automatic, Harry started running.

He was right. The sharp crack of a shot rang out, echoed instantly from the cliff which blocked out the sky above the wood. A rustle in the heather a few metres away might have been the bullet.

Harry flinched and ran on, or did his best to. The heavy bag made proper running impossible. And though his determination burned as fiercely as ever, his strength was ebbing. He shifted the bag from one hand to the other. Sometimes he carried it in both hands, bumping against his knees.

By this time he was halfway to the wood. In a couple of minutes he would be among the trees.

Two more shots rang out.

He began zig-zagging. It was asking for trouble. On such a broken hillside, particularly at night, carrying an awkward bag and staggering with fatigue, Harry should have been wearing boots, not slithering wet trainers, and taken the greatest of care where he set his feet. A hundred metres from shelter, as he dodged left and then right again, he failed to pay attention to a shadowy peat bog and ran straight into it. Instantly his leg sank to the knee and he pitched sideways into the ooze.

Behind him, meanwhile, the cattle had scattered and Gestapo Lil was recovering her nasty manner. "Come on, Fercy," she said impatiently. "Get after him."

"How?" he snapped back. "Parachute? Are you planning to jump?"

It was too far. The hawthorn was spiky. They looked down the other side. And over the stern. And came back again. The movement made the speedboat shift. It slumped sideways. For a moment it seemed it was going to roll right over and tip them out head first. Gestapo Lil screamed. Priestly yelled. Then it came to rest against a berried rowan tree. There were strong branches, good footholds. Clumsily they clambered to the ground.

Two hundred metres ahead of them, Harry disappeared into the trees. Priestly pulled the automatic from his pocket. Gestapo Lil grasped her stick. Ruthless and determined, they set off in pursuit.

Harry was covered in muck. His leg had sunk to the top of his thigh. Sprawling half in the ooze and half on the heather, he had managed to drag it free, almost losing his trainer in the process. His leg stank. So did his hands. His face was streaked.

The wood had withstood the hurricane better than the exposed island. Harry grabbed branches to haul himself up the slope. Without the bag his progress would have been better. Lungs on fire and knees close to buckling, he wished he had never even heard of Eddie Carver, never discovered Whitewater Castle, never seen the wretched treasure. The only thing he wanted in the whole world, at that moment, was to be at home with Tangle and Mrs Good.

His ankle turned and he gave a little cry, but he was not hurt.

He paused to listen. Crashing footsteps came from the wood below him. Priestly and Gestapo Lil were catching up.

There was no way he could escape carrying the bag. He must hide it. But where? A stream tumbled through the trees. Moss-covered branches, decades and centuries old, lay across it. Torrents of winter had carved caverns into the bank. Clinging to stems of ivy, Harry skidded down into the water and pushed the bag into an earthy hollow.

He had to remember the spot. A short distance above him the stream splashed over a low waterfall; foxgloves grew by a rectangular stone; the air smelled of something dead. Harry fixed them in his memory.

The cold water soothed his feet. For a minute he thought about staying there and taking his chances. But if they found him they would find the treasure: and if they found the treasure, what use would they have for him? He dragged himself back up the bank and pushed on.

His pursuers were climbing. Harry did the same, scrambling up slopes so steep that sometimes he balanced with his fingertips. The moonlight and black trees, many hung with rags of moss, gave the wood a spooky feel. But ghosts and the scary creatures he had seen in horror films were the least of Harry's worries. What he was frightened of was a little fat man with ginger hair who carried a gun, and the normally elegant blonde woman who had once been his nurse and now hunted him down with a heavy stick.

Increasingly, as he approached the foot of King's Crag, the hillside was littered with boulders. Not a hundred metres above him the moonlit wall, higher than Wreckers Crag, soared above the treetops.

Harry turned parallel and for five minutes he made better progress. Sweat ran from his hair. It was hard to tell how far he had come, for not just the landing stage but the whole near end of the loch was hidden by trees.

Then unexpectedly the wood opened out. From a cleft in the crag a long scree tumbled down through the trees like a river. He leaned against a trunk, listening for his pursuers, reluctant to venture out into the open. For a minute he waited, legs trembling with fatigue, then launched himself at the slope. Avalanches of small stones slid away beneath his feet. In normal circumstances Harry would have jumped to make the avalanches bigger. Now, with the moon upon him, every rush of stones seemed like a roll of drums, a clash of cymbals to announce his presence. And he was right in the middle, twenty metres from the wood on either side, when there was a shout from below:

"There he is!"

"We see you!" came Gestapo Lil's clear cry.

"Bloody boy! Don't think you're going to get away."

"Give me the fistol."

Thousands of times she had been vile. Hundreds of times she had hit him. Now she took careful aim. A loud CRACK!

split the silence. The bullet ripped the leg of his jeans, hit a pebble and whined away into the night.

Harry plunged on.

She fired again. A second bullet smashed into the scree. Then Harry was back among the trees.

Below him, Priestly and Gestapo Lil ploughed across the river of stones. Greed gave them strength.

Fear did the same for Harry. He hurried on, almost running now.

Surely, he guessed after ten more minutes, he was past the landing stage by this time. If he turned downhill, he would emerge by the river and the track that led to the castle. He longed to do so. The rest were counting on him. But where were his pursuers?

The thought of those whipping bullets kept him high. What would it feel like to be shot, he wondered. Would it be a burning agony, or a blow like the kick of a horse and numbness until – just nothing? He halted to listen. All was silent. Then behind him and a little below, he heard a crash and an oath as if someone had fallen. They were higher than before, climbing towards him, but he had increased his lead. In five more minutes, he thought, if all went well, he could begin his descent.

But all did not go well. No sooner had Harry set off again than he heard the snap of a branch a short distance ahead. He froze. What was it – a badger? a stag? Lord Goole had told him they fed in the wood. Or was it GBH – big, ruthless GBH with a rifle – who had seen them from the jetty and climbed up to cut him off?

Which way should he go? There was only one answer – up. Up to the foot of King's Crag and find a place to hide among the rocks. Then out of the blue he remembered Mike's cave: the cave Lord Goole had told him about and he had seen from Lady Island. If he could reach it and hide, that would be the perfect spot. But where was it? Not far away – he recalled seeing the run of scree. If only he'd paid more attention! He peered up at the crag but the bottom half was obscured by nearby trees. Wherever it might be, he had to move on. Harry set his face to the cliff and began to scramble straight uphill.

Luck was with him. As he left the trees behind and found himself among car and truck-sized boulders at the foot of the rock face, he came upon something unexpected, a hanging white cloth just a stone's throw away. He hurried across. It was a tattered flag made out of a tablecloth and nailed to a pole jammed at an angle between the rocks. Something was painted on it though he couldn't tell what. Another painting, on the foot of the crag itself, shone in the moonlight. A metre-high skull and crossbones.

Harry looked up. For the first few metres the bottom of the cliff was broken by a series of heathery sills. Hastily he scanned them and saw nothing. Then seven or eight metres higher up, there it was – the black entrance to Mike's cave. It would not, he saw, be difficult to reach, not compared with Wreckers Crag and the other climbs Dot had taken him – although now he had no rope. At once he tore down the flag and threw the flagpole aside, then started up a crack in the rock face.

Soon he reached a slanting ledge, high above the sills. It was quite broad, at least thirty centimetres, and there were plenty of handholds. The only danger was his slithering wet trainers.

A much greater danger lurked beneath. Harry wore dark clothes. The peat bog had given him added camouflage and dappled his face like a soldier. Had he remained motionless, they might never have noticed him. But as Gestapo Lil glanced up at the moonlit crag she spotted the movement, saw him spreadeagled like a spider against the rock face.

"There he is!" She pointed. "We see you, Harry Barton. You'll not get away this time."

Harry climbed on. The cave came close.

"He hasn't got the bag," she cried.

"Where's the loot?" Priestly had reloaded. "Tell us or I'll kill you. I mean it."

Harry trembled so much he almost fell. Face to the rock he shouted, "I don't know. I dropped it."

"You're lying. This is your last chance."

"I don't, honestly."

Holding the pistol in two hands, Priestly took aim.

"All right!" Harry shouted. "All right, I'll take you to it. Don't shoot."

"That's more like it," Priestly sneered. "Sense at last. Come on down." He lowered the automatic.

Harry counted to five, then scrambled on along the ledge as fast as his legs would carry him. There was a shout and a bang. And then another bang. Chips of rock stung him on the ear. Seconds later he reached the mouth of the cave and ducked through into safety.

But what safety! A colony of bats took off from the roof, fluttering around his head, hitting his face with their wings as they escaped into the night. A third bullet shot through the opening and ricocheted about the cave like a demented wasp. Power spent, it hit him on the sleeve and dropped to the floor.

Harry slid down the wall until he was sitting, and hid his head in his arms.

Chapter 37
The Bean is Mightier Than the Bullet

His eyes adjusted to the darkness.

The cave was rugged and uneven, roughly four metres deep, three at its widest, and two metres high. Mike had made himself a bed of dry bracken. Some comics or magazines lay on top. Whatever else there might be was hidden in black shadow.

Harry needed a weapon of some sort, rocks to throw down if Priestly and Gestapo Lil attempted to climb up – or GBH when he joined them. He felt around him and found nothing, then crawled from end to end, groping with both hands.

Mike had made the cave his summer camp. It was well equipped. Harry found an oil lamp, matches, a Primus stove, a saucepan, eggshells, cans of beans. Great for Mike but not much protection against a pistol, or whatever firearm GBH was carrying.

A rock overhung the entrance, keeping it in shadow. Harry scraped some peat from his jeans, spat in it and blacked his already dirty face. Cautiously he looked down.

They were talking. Gestapo Lil stepped back.

"Harry?" she called. "Harry?"

"What?"

"You know you can't get away." The moon caught her raised face. "Tell us where the diamonds are, take us to them, and we'll not touch a hair of your head, I fromise."

"No," he said.

"Give yourself up, boy." This was Priestly. "You've got no option."

"No," he said again. "Jailbird! Bastard!"

"Oh, very folite," she said. "Well if you don't, we'll have to come uf there and get you. What might haffen then – I wouldn't like to be in your shoes."

Harry threw the oil lamp. It missed Gestapo Lil by a whisker and shattered at her feet.

"Oh, if that's the way you want to flay it!" She snatched the automatic and loosed off three shots at the cave mouth. "We'll find the bag anyway, it'll just take a bit longer. There's no one else going to be searching these woods, is there, not with those old aunts of yours out the way."

Harry had retreated.

Gestapo Lil thrust the pistol back at Priestly. "Right, Fercy. Uf you go and get him."

He looked up at the cliff. "Me? I'm not going up there."

"Of course you are. How else do you frofose to get him out? Wait till he dies of old age?"

"Not me! I can't stand heights. Along that ledge? Not on your life."

"What kind of man are you?"

"A live one."

"You're not going to leave it to a woman, I hope."

"Why not?"

"Oh, for goodness sake!" She grabbed back the pistol and

442

thrust it into her belt. "You can throw stones, I hofe. That won't strain your fragile ferson?"

"No need to be sarcastic."

"You could have fooled me. Well chuck some rocks, big sharf ones. Keef him traffed in there till I arrive."

"Good thinking," he said.

She rolled her eyes. "And try not to hit me."

She scrambled up the heathery sills and began to climb.

Inside the cave, meanwhile, Harry marshalled his ammunition: three full cans of beans, three empties, the saucepan and the primus. It wasn't much. The box of matches scrunched under his knee. It gave him an idea. He could send a signal. Somebody might see. Hastily he bundled the dry bracken and comics to the mouth of the cave. A couple of metres away a stone cracked against the cliff. Why were they throwing stones when they had a gun? Had they run out of ammunition? He unscrewed the cap of the primus and splashed the paraffin over the heaped-up bedding.

A second stone bounced off the cave mouth. Cautiously he peered down. Priestly was hunting for more rocks. But where was Gestapo Lil? He looked sideways along the crag and saw her seven or eight metres away, edging towards him on the ledge. She saw him at the same instant. Her free arm came up. As he ducked back into the cave, Harry saw the flash and heard the crack of the pistol. The bullet hit the entrance and sang away into space.

If he did nothing she would be in the cave with him, like a nightmare. He picked up a can of beans and prepared to throw it. She was just along the ledge. He judged the angle. Keeping out of sight, he stretched out his arm to throw blind.

443

Gestapo Lil was waiting for him, the pistol raised. There was another deafening bang. A blow like the kick of a horse hit him in the hand. He had been shot! Cold blood sprayed his face. With a cry Harry sprang back, nursing his ruined hand. The blood ran past his nose and reached his lips. He tasted tomato sauce. His blood tasted of tomato sauce? He tried to move his hand, held it towards the moonlight. It was numb, tingling, but all his fingers seemed to be there. He hadn't been shot at all, she had hit the can. It had exploded. He scraped beans from his eyes.

Where was she now? Harry picked up another can, gripping it with difficulty.

Out of nowhere he had an idea. For a moment he thought about it. It might work. He began wailing as if he had been shot:

"Aahhh! My hand! Aahhh! Aaaahhhh!"

He took up a position just inside the cave mouth. As he did so, his feet became tangled in the pile of bracken. It gave him a further idea. He jammed the can into his jeans pocket and scrabbled for the matches. Roughly he kicked the bracken to the side where Gestapo Lil would appear.

"All right!" he cried. "Don't shoot! I'll show you where it is. Aahhh! My hand!"

For a moment he was still. Match at the ready, he listened for the scrape of her shoes along the ledge.

Another rock bounced off the cliff.

He cried out again with the pain. And whimpered. And listened.

Then there it was, a faint scratch of leather, a brush of cloth against the cliff. He counted – one, two, three – then struck his match and threw it down.

Instantly the dry bracken caught fire. Blue flames ran over the paraffin. In seconds it was a blaze. Seconds later it was a bonfire. Gestapo Lil drew back. Then, beyond the fire, Harry leaned out, saw her through the flames, and flung the can of beans with all his strength.

It hit his murderous nanny on the collarbone. There was a loud crack. An electric jolt ran down her arm. The pistol fell. She lost her grip on the crag. With a loud cry, clawing for another hold, she toppled into space.

The heathery sills broke her fall. Gestapo Lil bounced once, bounced again, and landed smack on top of her fat companion.

Harry kicked the blazing bracken over the edge. A ball of fire that could be seen for miles, tumbled down the crag. As it broke up, some of the bracken caught on snags. Some stuck on the sills and set fire to the heather. Most fell on Priestly and Gestapo Lil. They shouted with fright. Frantically they knocked it aside and scrambled clear.

A few wisps remained at Harry's feet. He scraped together the last of Mike's bed and threw it on top. It blazed up. Savagely he kicked the fire down, aiming for the two below.

From far away, in the direction of Lady Island, there came a single gunshot. He froze. It was followed by a hubbub of shouting, faint as a gnat at that distance. What was happening? So many guns! Mad Ruby! Had one of his aunts been shot? Fingers? Huggy? He could not bear it.

Beneath him, Gestapo Lil sat clutching her shoulder amid the wilderness of stones. She was hurt. Her honey-coloured hair straggled over her face. With one hand she held together her blouse which had snagged on a rock and been torn open to the waist. Priestly, too, was injured. When she crashed on to his head, knocking him to the ground, he had twisted his knee badly. Side by side, hoarding up spiteful things to say to each other, they sat nursing their pain.

Then out of the trees behind them stepped GBH. Harry closed his eyes in despair. His weapons were gone. Nothing remained but the saucepan, the empty primus and the last can of beans. It was the end of the line.

The tall, moonlit figure climbed through the rocks. He carried a walking stick. "What in God's name's going on here?"

Harry's head jerked up.

"Guns, fire, speedboats. You!" the man addressed Percy Priestly. "Who are you? Who's this person with you? What are you doing here this time of night trying to set my woods on fire?"

A second man, and then a third, emerged from the trees at his back. They had dogs with them.

"Eh?" said the tall man. "Couple of scoundrels! What have you got to say for yourselves?"

He stamped on the flames.

"Lord Goole!" Harry shouted down.

He looked up. "Who's that?"

"It's me. Harry Barton."

"Harry? Good God! What are you doing up there?"

It was too much. Harry's knees gave way and he sank to the floor of the cave. He began to tremble. A horrible, sick feeling like a balloon swelled up in his chest. He tried to stop it but was quite unable. The balloon rose up and up. It reached his throat. He was choking. Then the balloon burst.

Helplessly, for the first time in years, Harry began to cry.

"You're sure they didn't just mean to frighten you?" Auntie Florrie said. "Get you to give yourself up? Tell them where you'd hidden the diamonds and stuff?"

"No, they were firing *at* me," Harry said. "I told you. She nearly shot my hand off."

"Oh, my vord. The vicked bitch!"

"I hate guns," Aunt Bridget said, not for the first time.

"Me too." Lord Goole nodded. "And goodness knows, I've seen enough of the things."

"Cowardly weapons," she said. "Never know where you're going to end up once guns come into the equation."

They sat in the big castle kitchen: all the Wrinklies, Lord and Lady Goole, Jamie and Calum. Like the kitchen at Lagg Hall, tea was at every hand and whisky at quite a few. The black holdall had been recovered. Rubies and emeralds, diamond tiaras and priceless necklaces, lay on the table in pools of watery mud. A small stack of gold bricks stood against the wall.

The keepers' dogs and Lord Goole's two Labradors snoozed on a scrap of carpet at the end of the room. Harry crossed to make friends.

Auntie Florrie had taught Lord Goole the secrets of a Bosun Blinder. He blinked with shock then smiled benignly. "Absolutely delicious. I think this is going to become a speciality of the castle." He passed it to his keeper. "Here, Jamie. Have a taste of that."

Distant shouts came from the dungeons where Gestapo Lil, Percy Priestly and Mad Ruby Palazzo were safely under lock and key. Harry had been taken down to see them, following Lady Goole along cold corridors and down dripping steps to their ancient, underground prison.

Gestapo Lil, always so beautifully groomed, was scarcely recognizable, her eye purple and bloodshot, her mouth swollen, her hair scraped back, one arm in a sling. In place of a smart jacket, she wore a sack with a hole for the head and two for the arms, which Lady Goole had provided to cover her torn blouse. The *Rasputin Ruby*, which had brought her the same bad luck as its previous wearers, had been pulled from her finger and lay with the other jewels on the kitchen table.

Colonel Priestly had pulled up a trouser leg and sat nursing his knee in gloomy silence. Before the day was out, he well knew, he would be back in Cony Hill Prison and facing a string of fresh charges.

Mad Ruby clawed through the bars like a malevolent witch. "When I get out'a here," she threatened Harry, "I hunt you down and I kill you."

"By the time *you* get out of prison," said Lady Goole, "if that's what we decide to do with you, he'll be six foot tall and you'll have to chase him on your zimmer."

Ruby spat at her. Harry was glad she was behind bars.

Back in the kitchen he said to Huggy, "What happened out there on the island, after I left?"

"Bridget already tell you."

"I know."

"You vant the story again?" She smiled. "You von dirty boy. I never see dirtier boy, not even in the back streets of old Vladivostok."

Harry scratched his head. Flakes of dried peat fell on the table.

"Vell," Huggy said, "that *evil* little voman — you know, Mafia Ruby vith the sawn-off — she keep us sitting on the ground—"

"'Avin' all our blood sucked out by the mozzies," said Fingers, whose face was a mass of lumps.

"Ja, they vere terrible. You react badly."

"I'm all right wi' the English lot, it's these Scotch ones." He took a cube of ice from his drink to cool his bites, sucked it clean and popped it back in the glass.

"Anyvay," Huggy went on, "ve sit there vhile you row avay and nasty Priestly and Lily Gestapo go after you in the fastboat. Then ve hear crash, but no vay ve can see because it over far side of the island. Is up in a *tree*, no?"

"Yeah."

"I vish I see. So ve vait. Ve hear shooting. Ve all go crazy. But nothing happen. After long time Mad Ruby she say, 'Come on, ve vaste time. Bring the rest of the gold to the vater.' Ja? And she make Dot sit right there in front of her. She hate her, you know, after vhat happen vith the toasting fork. 'Von of you play trick,' she say, 'I blow her head avay like coconut in fairground.' She sound she mean it too. So ve carrying the gold vhen ve hear *more* shooting and suddenly this big fire appear, high up the mountain above the vood. Mafia Ruby, like the rest of us, she look up. Von moment only – and Dot attack her like a tiger. She strong, you know! Von barrel fire into the ground. Then Fingers run up and hit her on the head vith a gold brick. I not know vhere he get the strength. She go down *plonk!* like puppet vhen you cut the string."

"Beautiful," said Auntie Florrie.

"Like when 'Uggy gives someone the ol' forearm smash in the ring," said Fingers, who was her number-one fan.

She shrugged. "So there ve all are, marooned, until you come out vith the boats to rescue us."

Harry nibbled a shortbread and thought about it.

"Tell us again about GBH," Auntie Florrie said to Lord Goole.

"Better ask Calum," he said. "He was there from the start."

They turned to the blond, powerfully-built young keeper who sat in the background with his nip of whisky. He was a man of few words.

"Och, there's not that much to tell," he said in a precise Highland voice. "Me and Jamie, we hear the speedboat and come down to the landing stage. Here's this big Volvo saloon pulled back into the shadows, and this chap steps out with a two-two. He tells us to lie down, so we do. Keep the dogs back, don't want them to get shot. Then we hear the shooting on the island, and a wee while later Davie's boat comes out in a hurry. They can't control it very well, hit the laddie, there, and go scooting up on the rocks." He looked at Lord Goole.

"Yes, well." His lordship took up the story. "All this damned noise woke us up. Machine guns, for God's sake! Not used to it these days, you know. Couple o' poachers is more the usual thing, and Calum and Jamie take care o' them. Thought I'd better go down and have a look-see. And here's this fellow with a damned rifle. Pointing it at these good chaps. Can't have that, you know. Well, I could have taken it from him, I suppose—"

"His lordship was a colonel in the SAS," Jamie explained with some pride.

"Yes, well they teach you that sort of thing. But I couldn't see the point. So I just told him, What the hell d'you think you're doing? The police are on their way. Only one road out of here. If I were in your shoes I'd get my skates on – unless you want to end your days in a shoot-out."

"Like *Butch Cassidy*," said Harry.

"*Bonnie and Clyde*," Auntie Florrie said enthusiastically.

Lord Goole was startled. "Something like that, yes. Didn't take him long. Showed a bit of sense. Got some other fellow in the boot of the car. Mystery to me. Said he'd drop him off in the village an' drove away up the road." He looked around. "That's about all there was to it really."

"Except we heard shooting from along by the speedboat," Jamie said. "Saw those two set off up the hillside. So we climbed up through the wood to cut them off."

"So we did," said Lord Goole. "Bloody great fireball droppin' out the sky. And there's Harry, here, up in the cave." He rumpled Harry's spiky hair and more peat crumbled to the table. "Damned good show."

Aunt Bridget's eyes brimmed over. Huggy put a comforting arm round her shoulders.

"And what happens now?" said Auntie Florrie.

Lord Goole gave his horsy smile. "Well, as a JP, and a friend of certain people, and all the rest of it, I know nothing about any of this, of course. Evie and I were tucked up in bed, never heard a thing. But I suppose we've got to get all this gold and everything out of here." He flipped the jewels with his fingernails. "Better not waste too much time. So I gave Gunther a tinkle a short while ago. Got him out of his pit. Gave him the gist. Says he'll fly up later this morning. Got a few arrangements to make first. Arrive round midday. Mike heard about it, so he's coming too."

"Where will he land?" Fingers said. 'Is there an airfield nearby?"

"Doesn't need one. Helicopter or seaplane, land on the loch. Take it straight off the estate. God knows where to.

Some place offshore, I expect. Overseas. Bit of a financial wizard. Unlike me, as you can see. He knows about money markets and banks and all the rest of it." He looked at Aunt Bridget. "Still happy with the arrangement, I hope."

"Absolutely." Her eyes were red. "Couldn't be better. I'd trust Gunther with my life."

"Then he'll cash it in, I suppose. Shift the money about, launder it a bit: Switzerland, Cayman Islands, I don't know. Give it a few months. Then whenever you want your dosh, there it is. Ready and waiting to start building that hospital of yours. Sinking the wells. Marvellous idea."

Calum nodded.

"We were out there for the Red Cross, weren't we, Sandy," Lady Goole said. "Visiting some of those African bush villages. All that suffering and disease, dirty water, cross-infection. You'll save hundreds of lives. I'd like to go out there myself and help set it up."

"My wife was a doctor," Lord Goole explained.

"I know," Aunt Bridget said.

"I have no idea of the legal position," said Lady Goole, "but if anyone knows a better use for money, I've yet to hear it. I think it's the kindest, most encouraging thing I've heard in years." The diamonds, emeralds and priceless jewellery winked from brown pools. She heaped them into a plastic washing-up bowl and wiped the table with a dishcloth. "Incidentally, don't worry about those three down there in the dungeons. I've patched them up, they don't need a hospital. The blonde woman, a nice clean break to the clavicle. I've put her arm in a sling, that's all anyone can do. Be right as rain till you all decide what to do with them."

"Will you hand them over to the fuzz?" Harry said.

"Oh, don't!" Auntie Florrie clutched the neck of her jumper. "Always the fuzz."

Aunt Bridget sighed. "The word is police, Harry. The *police*. But I don't know." She looked at Lord Goole. "What do you think?"

"Don't ask me. I know nothing about it, remember. But I must say, my instinct would be to keep as far away from the law as possible."

There was a chorus of: "Hear, hear! Absolutely! Took the words right out o' my mouth."

"Well, that's how I feel too, keep the police out of it, although if we had to, I'm sure we could do a deal with the three down there. If we were to report everything that's happened – kidnapping a schoolboy, use of firearms, attempted *murder*, for goodness sake, and all the rest of it – they'd never see the light of day again. But if they kept their mouths buttoned about the treasure, and we only turned them in as jailbreakers, they'd get what – seven years, out in five?"

"Sounds about right," Fingers said.

"I mean, they're never going to sniff the money now, so they've got nothing to gain by blowing the whistle, and a terrible lot to lose. It's too high a price to pay for revenge. I'm sure they'd play ball, be fools not to."

"We'd have to take them back to Felon Grange," Dot said. "Couldn't hand them over here."

"I don't see that as a problem."

"And most important of all," said Auntie Florrie, "with the three of them back behind bars, Harry would be safe."

"Of course," Aunt Bridget agreed. "That's our first consideration."

"But I thought you said you didn't want to bring in the cops," Fingers said.

"Indeed I don't," she said. "This was just *if*. I think Huggy's got a much better idea."

All eyes turned.

"Ja." Huggy pushed back her teacup. Keenly she looked at the four from the castle. "I need promise you not speak to nobody, never!"

Lord Goole glanced at Calum and Jamie. "You don't need to worry about that."

"Good, because it not a game, you know." She set her massive forearms on the table. "The rest of us, you remember nasty Priestly and Lily Gestapo vant send Ruby to South America?"

"Yeah, to the copper mines," Fingers said. "Not a very nice fing to do to yer mum."

"Vell, Black Boris, a friend of mine, he run a similar operation. People other people vant rid of. He load them aboard a fishing boat in Hull and drop them at a town called Nordvik on the north coast of Russia. It long journey, rough seas. They gut fish to earn their food. Then two thousand mile by cattle truck to people Boris know in Siberia who look after them good. They vork in forest cutting down trees. Herd the reindeer. From there they never escape. There is novhere to escape to."

"Sounds good to me," Fingers said.

Auntie Florrie agreed. "It's what they deserve."

"Better than bringing in the rozzers," Dot said.

"Rozzers?" Harry said. "Don't you mean the police, Dot. The word is *po-lice*."

Aunt Bridget laughed. "Cheeky brat."

"You vant I contact Boris? Ve need act qvickly. Snow come in September. The sea freeze nine month of the year."

"Sounds lovely," Fingers said. "Who'd want to go to the Riviera?"

"Well, I think that's decided," Aunt Bridget said. "Off they go to Siberia. But we'll have a powwow after breakfast. Hear what Angel and Max have to—"

The telephone rang. Lady Goole glanced at the clock. "Who on earth's calling at five o'clock in the morning?"

It was for Aunt Bridget. She listened briefly. "Good . . . good . . . oh, excellent! Yes, we'll tell you all about it when we get back. . . . Well, I'm not sure. Probably the day after tomorrow, we all need a good sleep. How did the recording go? . . . Oh, good for you! . . . Yes. . . Bye."

She returned to the table. "I phoned home when we came in. Mr Tolly's just been over to Felon Grange and got the laptop. So that's a relief."

Lady Goole rattled a couple of frying pans on to the Aga and went to the fridge. "I heard you mention breakfast. What about a good fry-up?"

"Oh, no," Auntie Florrie said. "You've been kindness itself, we couldn't possibly—"

"Nonsense, no trouble at all. I'll get busy this end. Maybe one of you could set the table." Her eyes went round the room. "Ten places. Sandy will show you where everything is."

"No sooner said." He went to the dresser. "I don't know when these friends of yours will be turning up, but straight after breakfast we'd better make a start getting the rest of this gold up from the bottom of the loch. Not too deep, Harry says. Should be simple enough."

455

"And bring the last over from Lady Island." Dot shook out the tablecloth. "See what's left in the summer house. Come on, Harry, off the table."

He was trailing a necklace like a ruby snake.

"Everything ready for when Gunther arrives," Lord Goole said. "That's the idea. All boxed and bagged up. No loose ends."

"As far as possible anyway." Aunt Bridget massaged her knuckles; she had bruised them when she relieved Gestapo Lil of the machine gun. "Incidentally, one thing I haven't mentioned yet. Once we get the money sorted out – depends what Gunther gets for it, of course – we want a million or so to come to you here at the castle."

"What!" Lord Goole was startled. "Absolutely not, wouldn't dream of—"

Aunt Bridget raised a hand. "It's no good protesting. We've discussed it among ourselves and it's all decided. If you really don't want it, Harry's going to stand on the bridge out there and make a hundred thousand Bank of England aeroplanes, and fly them away down the waterfalls."

Harry crossed to a window that faced down the loch. It was half an hour to sunrise. Looking out on the blue mountains, the pearl-grey loch and quiet sky, he thought he had never seen a landscape so peaceful. There stood Lady Island, mirrored in the water. He angled his head to see the oak wood and King's Crag. Tangle would love it here, he thought, and Morgan, and the geese. Perhaps he could bring Tangle if Mike invited him for a holiday.

He yawned and looked down at his filthy jeans and T-shirt. They had dried on him. How nice it was that nobody made a fuss and shoved him away to the bathroom. At his back the frying pans hissed. He smelled bacon.

A hare lolloped from behind a wall and crouched to nibble the sweet, dewed lawn. He watched. It hopped forward and nibbled some more.

Then abruptly the hare sat bolt upright, ears erect. Like a spring released, it shot away across the grass. It was too late. A tremendous bird crashed down from overhead, talons outstretched. The hare squealed, bowled along the ground. The eagle pursued it, wings flapping. A claw caught the hare by a hind leg. It wriggled free. The eagle lunged again – and missed. The hare took to its heels.

Deprived of its meal, the eagle stood looking around then gave a hop, a lazy flap of its wings, and landed on a crumbling peak of wall.

Harry beckoned the others. "Come here, quick!"

The eagle saw him, stared at the window with wild yellow eyes, then looked away and began preening.

"I'd have come all the way up here just for that." Aunt Bridget leaned past Harry's shoulder. "Isn't he *marvellous*!"

"That's Attila." Jamie joined them. "Never seen him this close. You're honoured."

One smallish person was very well, a window full was too many. Attila shook his golden head then gave a powerful sweep of his wings and lifted away over the river.

Harry ran outside. Already the eagle was a hundred metres distant, high above the loch. For minutes he watched as Attila grew smaller and smaller, climbing and circling until he was a dot against the brightening sky.

"Harry, you vant von egg or two? Lady Goole is asking."

"One," he said.

"And fried bread?"

"Thanks."

Attila was gone. Nothing remained to mark that brief, life-or-death struggle but a dark patch on the silver lawn.

Harry took a deep breath of the sweet morning air and went indoors.